THE THIRD REVOLUTION III:

THE BLACK FLAG

By Gregory Kay

Books by Gregory Kay

Fiction

THE THIRD REVOLUTION
THE THIRD REVOLUTION II: THE LONG KNIVES
THE THIRD REVOLUTION III: THE BLACK FLAG
DARK PATHS

Non-Fiction

THE CODE OF HONOR (Historical reprint, edited by Gregory Kay)

Coming Soon! The _final_ volume in
The Third Revolution Saga:
THE THIRD REVOLUTION IV: THE WARLORD

gregmkay@yahoo.com.

About THE THIRD REVOLUTION Series

THE THIRD REVOLUTION saga is a four-book series set in the near future South, and centered around the experiences of Franklin Gore and Samantha Norris during the outbreak of a second War for Southern Independence. It is unique in its unabashed Southern point of view, its unashamed political incorrectness, and it's technical accuracy in the realm of guerrilla warfare.

It is highly recommended that you read the first two books in the series before beginning this one. Most of the character development and seminal events of the conflict take place there, and this book will be a lot easier to understand if you've been through that first.

DEDICATION

To Jerry Baxley

As much crap as you've put up with, you deserve a little something!

A NOTE OF THANKS

Thanks first to God, and his Son, Jesus Christ. Thanks to Eric, the fulltime public school teacher and part-time mercenary who taught me Popeye's neck break. Also, thanks to Jerry and Sam, and the usual cast of misfits and malcontents selflessly willing to devote their time and effort to assist me.

"The troops of your command in this section of the country are committing outrages known only to barbarians. And if, like the other Federals, you undertake to justify such conduct, I will not only hoist the black flag, but fight under it, and show no quarter to any claiming protection under the Stars and Stripes!"

~ Major Cockerill, CSA

AUTHOR'S NOTE:

This book is about war; in fact, it's about the most brutal kind of war, that of guerrilla forces fighting in their own land. The story reflects this in a realistic manner, and its content may be disturbing to some. This is not a book for young children, although well-adjusted teenagers should have no problem with it.

Some readers will be put off by the unflinching realism, particularly with my depiction of the treatment of guerrillas in United States captivity. To those people, I can only say that this is accurate, and it is the way things are done. Everything described concerning that subject is not only truthful, but is as timely as today's newspaper. This is the real world hell of many people, from Abu Grahaib to Guantanimo to a hundred other secret detention facilities around the world. It's what US forces do *now*, and there is no reason to presume those tactics would mellow in the face of a guerrilla war here.

On the contrary...

~ Gregory Kay

DUTY ROSTER

CONFEDERATE ARMY PROVISIONAL

SUPREME COMMANDER: Field Marshal Jonathon Edge
EXECUTIVE OFFICER: General Franklin Gore

SOUTH CAROLINA THEATER

HEADQUARTERS STAFF

CAP INFORMATION OFFICER: Colonel Samantha Gore
COMMANDING OFFICER: Captain Charles Carnes
SERGEANTS: William Sprouse
James Reynolds
PRIVATES: Kerrie O'Brien
Cynthia Dover

1ST COLUMBIA IRREGULARS

COMMANDING OFFICER: Captain Robert Johnson
FIRST SERGEANT: Basil Caffary

ALPHA SQUAD
SERGEANT: Ronald Hodges
CORPORAL: Mitchell Stanley
PRIVATES: Casey Graham
Jerry Smith
Doug Long

BRAVO SQUAD
SERGEANT: Andy Buchanan
CORPORAL: Wayland Fowler
PRIVATES: Henry Toland
David Worley

Daniel Worley

CHARLIE SQUAD
SERGEANT: Marion Stock
CORPORAL: Jack Lewis
PRIVATES: Bill McGuire
           Frank Godwin
           David Snipes
           Arnold Kessler

DELTA SQUAD
SERGEANT: John Thompson
CORPORAL: William Wilson
PRIVATES: Tim Matthews
           Dean Yates
           George Cox

ECHO SQUAD
SERGEANT: James Kowalski
CORPORAL: Jay Knott
PRIVATES: Daniel Drucci
           Jack Davidson
           Hubert Moore

COLUMBIA HEADQUARTERS

INTELLIGENCE OFFICER: Colonel Michael Dayton
EXECUTIVE OFFICER: Captain Thomas Richardson*
PRIVATE: Donna Waddell

DOJO SQUAD

COMMANDING OFFICER: Captain Thomas Richardson*
(*dual command)
EXECUTIVE OFFICER: Lieutenant Joel Harrison

SERGEANT: Ralph Steiner
PRIVATES: Archie Baker
Randy Collins
Tim Handley
John Sergeant

PROLOGUE

A few months can be a long time during a war, and that's what it truly was now. Try as they might, no one could deny it; America was in the grip of a full-scale revolution. The Confederate Army Provisional was going to see the South independent or die trying, and the United States was determined to keep Dixie in the Union, even if it meant killing everyone there in order to accomplish it. History began to repeat itself once again, only this time it was even worse than the 1860s.

Using the techniques of subduing the civilian populace it had learned during its post-war occupations of other nations like Germany, Japan, Serbia, Afghanistan, and Iraq, the United States military unleashed an unheard of state of barbarity not seen in North America since the Indian Wars, and they did it with full presidential approval. Little nuances of law like habeas corpus and the Bill of Rights were long in the past, consigned to the dustbin of history. Beatings, torture, indefinite imprisonment without trial, confiscation, and even looting, rape and murder were ignored or often even sanctioned by the administration, and excused by the right and left alike, since it was being done, depending on the side doing the talking, either to preserve America or to fight racism.

Dixie did not take it lying down, however; this time the Union didn't find a Southern leadership determined to fight like gentlemen and not respond in kind to the excesses of the enemy. Led by hard men like Field Marshal Jonathon Edge, whose ruthless pragmatism was infamous even among his own men, and his second in command, General Franklin Gore, who had a personal debt to pay to the ones who had tortured and nearly killed his wife, the Confederate guerrillas gave it right back to them with equally determined force and fury. Most of their guerrillas had been part of the enemy's own forces at one time themselves, and the United States was surprised to find its own methods used against it. Add to the mix the independent gangs and individuals from all sides or no side at all, who took orders from no one and were driven by political, religious or racial

13

zealotry, a chance for loot, or simple bloodlust, and the South turned into something very close to hell on earth. Its only consolation was that it wasn't by itself.

Edge's bloody brainchild, Operation Long Knives, had targeted far more than simply Federal resources. Its destruction of the National Association of Black Persons leadership during the Columbia bombing led directly to major rioting in Northern and Western cities with large Negro populations like New York, Detroit, Cincinnati, Chicago, and Los Angeles. Much of the unrest caused was caused by the Confederate Army Provisional's immediate and well-planned disinformation campaign accusing the Federal Government of a false flag operation: taking advantage of the confusion and planting the bomb themselves in an effort to destroy all Black leadership. Even though the government did its best to suppress the actual figures, hundreds of Blacks were known to have died in pitched battles with other ethnic groups as well as the police and National Guard, and large sections of those cities were now under martial law just as was the South. President Plants declared a full, nationwide state of emergency, assumed dictatorial powers, and, just as Edge had counted on, informed the public that, under the circumstances, it would be impossible to hold the elections scheduled only months away. As he was a Republican, this set off another, even worse wave of Black rioting; in Cincinnati and Los Angeles, as well as Houston and Atlanta, and this second wave was put down by Marines and regular Army troops. Even though they were under orders to handle the demonstrators with kid gloves, no plan ever survives contact with the battlefield. Soldiers are soldiers, not riot cops, and the resulting bloodbath left several hundred more dead, a second enemy for the Feds in the form of the Colored population, and a great deal of racial tension within the heavily diverse ranks of the Army itself.

The CAP, of course, exacerbated those tensions at every opportunity, and promptly expanded them to include a religious element as well. On the advice of Senior Councilman, noted Calvinist and Southern fire-eater, Dr. Andrew MacFie, the Confederate Council issued an order banning all abortion in Dixie except in the cases of rape or the mother's life being in danger, under penalty of death. This caused a rift in the Christian community, both Protestant and Catholic, causing several people to openly ask the previously unthinkable question about which side God was really on.

More properly put, they tried to ask it. Under the President's self-assumed emergency powers, the right of free speech, once called the first freedom, no longer existed. Those who printed or said the wrong things or asked uncomfortable questions frequently found themselves the subjects of investigations, intimidating warnings, Homeland Security gag orders, or else they simply disappeared into secret detention facilities. Those who pressed too hard to determine where they went often suffered the same fate. Others never got to that point, but were brutally attacked and often killed, either by pro-US right-wing "patriots" or by left-wing "anti-racists," depending on which point they made or on which question they asked. This last was mostly in the Northern states, though; in the South, the Confederate guerrillas tracked down and executed anyone harming their supporters with neither mercy nor exception, and after a double handful of bloody examples were made, most "do-gooders" quickly realized that informing against or attacking Southerners was not at all conducive to longevity.

Meanwhile, outside the borders of the United States and the occupied Confederate States, others were circling like vultures. It has been said that the Chinese word for catastrophe is the same as the term for opportunity, and they scented opportunity big-time. Along with China, the European Union, Latin America, the Middle East, Russia, and even Japan kept an ever-closer eye on the Third Revolution, because no matter who won, everyone knew the world would never be the same in its aftermath.

Of course, neither would the people who fought it...

DAY 209

CHAPTER 1

Homeland Security Phone Conversation

"What're Edge and Gore worth to you?"

"You've seen the reward posters: 100 million apiece."

"I can give them to you."

"When?"

"When I can – one at a time, or maybe both of them together, depending on the circumstances."

"Why would you do this?"

"I don't like either of them, and I do like money. I just need insurance to make sure you're really willing to pay. I want 50% up front."

"Fat chance. Try again."

"You don't seem to understand the risk I'm taking..."

"Tough. Here's the way it will work. I'm going to give you a contact number, which will be your personal code. You'll call me – me, and no one else, understand? – with their location, and I'll arrange a good-faith payment of ten percent into whatever account you provide. If your information turns out to be accurate, resulting in them being killed or captured, the balance will be paid into that same account.

"Fair warning – don't try to screw me. If I can't reach you, I'll see your name is leaked to the Confederates."

"You're not the one I plan on screwing. I'll be in touch"

Russian News Service (English Edition)

The following excerpt was taken directly from a public letter from the head of the Confederate Forces, Field Marshal Jonathon

Edge, to the President of the United States, Jack Plants, via the United Nations:

"The forces of the Confederate States of America demand that the torture and mistreatment of the Confederate military and civilian personnel currently in United States custody cease at once. We demand that they be treated as prisoners of war in accordance with the provisions of the Geneva Convention, to which the United States is a signatory, and to which it is bound by international law, and by the laws of God, common decency, and civilized behavior.

"If the current violations of human rights, including torture, rape, property confiscation, and murder continue, the Confederate States of America will have no choice but to retaliate. Further, any captured United States military or civilian personnel who have taken part in the above illegal activities will be subject to trial for war crimes, and crimes against humanity, and subsequent punishment up to and including execution..."

The letter provoked the following response from the American President in a special press conference at Camp David:

"The terrorists of the Confederate Army Provisional are in no position to make demands of the United States Government, nor are they entitled to the considerations due to prisoners of war. These people are violent, racist criminals, nothing more, and if taking them out requires extraordinary measures, rest assured that those measures will be taken.

"Having said that, you may also rest assured that the United States does not and has never participated in torture, even against terrorists..."

When pressed on the subject in a later press conference, the President's Press Secretary, Mary Feldstein, insisted that the United States still follows the "no-torture" protocols laid down during the second Bush Administration, an administration internationally notorious for its use of torture...

NETWORK NEWS BROADCAST, USA

In other news tonight, the Neo-Confederate Terrorists have threatened to begin torturing and killing US military POWs if their demands to be treated as prisoners of war instead of international criminals are not met. The Administration has rejected these demands out of hand, and has threatened retaliation for any mistreatment of American armed forces personnel at the hands of violent, racist thugs...

"Oh say, does that star spangled banner yet wave..."
Yes, it did, at least for the moment. The voice of the Republican rally crowd grew louder by the minute, amplified by beer and patriotism, and intensified by the veritable sea of US flags flying all around and seemingly in every hand. The banners had competition, however, in the form of a nearly equal number of ribbons demanding that people *"Support our troops!"* and Republican buttons and signs touting sound-byte benefits of President Jack Plants and his policies. Red, white and blue bunting was everywhere, decorating the tables groaning under the weight of boiled crawfish, corn and potatoes, still steaming in the mild Louisiana autumn. The only ones not partaking were the small army of Secret Servicemen, and the full battalion of Marine infantry who formed the outer ring of security.
"...and the home of the brave."
The crowd whooped, hollered and cheered, and when the noise finally wound down a little, a tall, slim, dark-haired man stepped up to the podium and blew a single quick breath into the microphone to make certain it was working. When he spoke, his deep bayou accent was clear in his voice, even if it was toned down somewhat by extended periods away.
"Now, was that fun or what?"

The cheering began all over again, and his tanned, clean-shaven cheeks spread in a smile that threatened to reach is high, angular cheekbones. Finally, he raised his hands.

"You all had better save your breath; we've got plenty more coming after I get through bumping my gums" This led to still more cheers and laughter, both at the speaker's folksy, self-depreciating manner, and at the very thought that those expensive pearly white teeth he seemed to be constantly flashing could be anything but his own. "Alright, first, I'd like to thank you all for coming out today, to support our president, our troops and the United States of America." He paused, waiting out another barrage of cheers. "As you know, I served our country myself, and I know just what your support means to the soldiers, sailors, airmen, and marines who risk their lives and often give them in defense of our freedom."

More cheers.

"I also want to thank you for supporting President Plants as he courageously does what is necessary to hold this great nation of ours together in the face of terrorist attacks by the traitors and racists in the so-called Confederate forces. I'm the great great grandson of a Confederate veteran, and named after a Confederate general, and I can tell you today that, as much as I may revere my ancestor, their cause was wrong then and it is even more wrong now. America is one nation, under God, indivisible forever!"

"You damned traitor! You scalawag son of a bitch!"

The crowd gasped at the unexpected yells as an angry, twenty-something white man in their midst yanked a Confederate Battle Flag out of his sleeve and held it overhead in both hands as he shouted his defiance. He was bold, but he didn't shout long.

In an instant, the Plants supporters grabbed him, ripping and clawing at his flag and clothes, and the only thing that prevented him from falling was that he was being pulled in so many directions at once. Fists hammered on him, some of his attackers beating each other in a berserk effort to reach the target of their rage. Finally enough of the attackers happened to drag him in the same direction to override the tugging of the rest. He went down, and was kicked and stomped for several seconds before the Secret Service could intervene. Shoving the crowd back, three of the agents knee-dropped the troublemaker in various places while others waved Uzi submachine guns and Glock pistols, looking for targets. In less than a minute he was "cuffed and stuffed," dragged away, bloody and half-conscious in a rain of spittle and thrown objects from the angry mob.

"Looks like another terrorist bites the dust," the man at the microphone quipped to the laughter and cheers of the crowd. Someone yelled, "Go TJ!" and he smiled broadly as he winked and delivered his trademark double thumps-up to the man. "Now then, while the Secret Service takes out the trash, without further ado I'd like to introduce our guest speaker, the Secretary of State Irving Lieberman!"

He gestured broadly with his left hand at the cabinet member approaching the microphone. Relinquishing the podium, the host stepped down, clapping as he went, and returned to his seat as the last few claps of introductory applause petered out.

Turner Jonathon Ashby – or TJ as he preferred to be called – kept the proper and expected expression on his handsome face: a mixture of controlled excitement and just a little deference. Just a little, because, after all, he was a very important man himself: the rich Cajun who was the single most important behind-the-scenes driving force in support of the Republican Party in Louisiana. He was, quite literally, a kingmaker for the GOP, a major contributor, hosting this latest of a continuous string of fundraisers. Only forty-five, an Annapolis Academy graduate, Navy veteran, and a billionaire several times over due to his inheritance and savvy management of major interests in oil and gas, and in river and coastal transportation, he was a very influential man. He was also one of the few left in the South whose loyalty to the United States Government was never questioned, and who escaped overly close scrutiny because he never ran for office himself, only assisted others in doing so. As far as the press and Democrats were concerned, he was just one more rich big businessman trying to help his ideological cronies stay on top (Of course, if he had been supporting them, of course, he would have been a wealthy, socially-conscious benefactor.). Still, he wasn't really of much interest since he stayed in the background, so his opponents were generally content to leave him there.

Which, he often reflected, was a damned good thing. After all, there was no better cover for the chief of operations for the Confederate Army Provisional in the Louisiana Theater and the primary link in the CAP supply chain nationwide.

Named for the famous Confederate commander from the War of 1861, TJ's family had always been Southern in outlook and identity. It had been only natural for him to gravitate to the heritage organizations commemorating the past, and the innocuous contacts he made there eventually led him to the head of a small but militant Southern Nationalist element: Jonathon Edge. Edge had suggested that, due to TJ's power and influence, he could best serve the Cause by standing against it in the public eye.

"Consider the chameleon," the Field Marshal had told him. "When his enemies – either his predators or his prey – look at him, he looks like everything around him: a limb, a leaf or a stone. He never changes, though; in reality, he remains exactly what he is. Because of his subtlety, he can do that right under the nose of the enemy with no one ever guessing he's anything but what he appears to be."

TJ had taken those words to heart, but it was hard at times. His own people – Southerners, like the protester who was hauled off today – considered him a turncoat and a scalawag, and there had been more than one attempt on his life by independently-acting Confederate guerrillas who, like the US Government, could only think he was what he appeared to be. Even though their attacks reinforced his cover, his heart went out to them. Still, he had a job to do that was bigger than they were, and he couldn't do it if he were out in the open, or worse, dead.

Besides, he had to admit there was nothing like the adrenaline rush of being a secret agent, and there was a certain satisfaction to be had in smiling at your enemy across the dinner table even as you scooped another shovel full of dirt out of the grave you were digging for him.

Even while the Secretary of State was busily lauding TJ's unimpeachable loyalty, his company's tankers and barges were hauling far more cargo than was listed on the manifest. His handpicked captains smuggled aboard assault rifles, mortars, anti-tank weapons, and explosives. He had picked them for their dishonesty; they thought they were making the deals with guerrillas on their own and lining their own pockets, and didn't have any more of a clue than the shadowy men who paid them to smuggle the goods that both were dancing on TJ Ashby's strings.

Right at this very moment, one of his towboats was pushing a line of fuel barges up the Mississippi, and carrying an auxiliary cargo of Russian-made SAM's: surface to air missiles with a more recent point of origin in the Middle East. He knew that Field Marshal Edge and General Frank Gore had made some sort of a deal for them, although he didn't know exactly what. That was because he had no need to know, although he had a general idea from some off-the-record conversations with assorted bureaucrats and government functionaries. The scuttlebutt had it that General Gore had captured a handful of Mossad agents who had been sent to kill him at the behest of Uncle Sam, and they had been swapped to some of the more radical Islamic Republics in exchange for the anti-aircraft weapons. Considering the intelligence that the Muslims could squeeze from them, as well as their usefulness as bargaining chips with Israel, they were worth quite a bit, and it showed in the number of missiles, explosives, and other weapons that had recently been passing into his supply chain

If it did nothing else, the boldness and innovation of that particular deal gave TJ a lot of confidence in their leadership.

Thinking of the pair, he allowed himself a broad smile that everyone watching thought was in approval of the Secretary of State's droning rhetoric on battling terrorism. That wasn't quite it; he just found the thought amusing as to how Lieberman would react if he realized that the two top leaders of the Confederate Army Provisional were less than a hundred yards away. In fact, they were currently holding a meeting in TJ Ashby's media room, right there in his mansion on whose grounds the rally was being held.

Preening under the sunny smile of his Republican host, Lieberman deigned to nod sagely toward him from the podium, and TJ happily nodded back.

Mama was right; the best place to hide something is right out in plain sight, where no one would think to look for it.

"I have a plan."

Jonathon Edge looked expectantly at his second in command, Frank Gore. When the younger man asked for him to meet with him as soon as possible, he readily acquiesced, immediately dropping everything else in order to accomplish it. There were few people Edge even remotely trusted in the rebel movement he headed, and an unusually accident-prone sawmill worker could count the number of those he actually considered to be friends on one hand. Frank Gore was one of those carefully chosen few.

Maybe *friend* was too strong a word since the two had nearly shot each other on more than one occasion, generally tended to rub each other the wrong way, and really didn't socialize much unless they had to. Still, when the chips were down, Frank was the one who risked his own life – and very nearly gave it – to save the Field Marshal during a coup attempt, even though it would have been greatly to his own advantage if Edge had been taken out of the way. If that wasn't actually a friend, it was close enough in Jonathon Edge's world. It was also enough to bring him to a meeting at TJ Ashby's mansion. Besides, just as it did to their host, the idea of having the enemy use its resources to insure their privacy was extremely satisfying for both the Confederate commanders. The food went over well too; several plates stacked with oyster and crab shells, crawfish heads, and corncobs testified that they had just finished the same Cajun boiled meal as the Republican dignitaries and supporters outside. They held off on the alcohol though; they were working.

Their workspace was comfortable enough, at least: far more so than what they were used to. The media room reflected their host's wealth in dark, solid mahogany paneling, half a million dollars worth of electronics, including a flat screen TV big enough for a small movie theater, and deep, comfortable chairs upholstered in ox blood leather. They were utilizing a pair of the latter at the moment, facing each other across an original bronze Art Deco coffee table.

"What do you have in mind?"

Frank leaned forward, resting his elbows on his thighs and tenting his fingers between his knees. He kept his eyes fixed on the cold blue orbs of his commander, something most people had trouble doing.

"The total social, political and economic destruction of the enemy in one fell swoop."

Edge would have thought any other man was joking or simply blowing hot air, but not this one. His interest sparked, leaned forward himself, his eyes warming by a degree or two.

"Tell me more."

"In January of 1989, an article was published in *Omni* magazine by former Nixon aide, G. Gordon Liddy. It was fiction, in the form of a letter to the President, and it outlined how a group of only a few hundred terrorists had completely shut down the United States: air travel, trains, electric, gas, the works. It made for some very interesting reading, needless to say, and it got me thinking."

Edge stroked his iron gray moustache in thought. "I seem to recall hearing something about that once, but I never saw it." Even before the current conflict, immediately following the 9-11 attacks on New York and the Pentagon, the government had begun a program of censorship, with anything that might remotely 'aid terrorists' being pulled from the shelves and quietly classified or stuffed down an Orwellian 'memory hole' somewhere. He was surprised to learn the piece still existed in the public venue. "Where in the world did you find it?"

Frank smiled. "Thank Sammie and Mike. She was doing some research for an article and ran across a brief reference to it. Something about it intrigued her, so she put the Intelligence Officer on it. Mike managed to acquire a .pdf of a scanned copy via the Internet from a bit-torrent site based in Russia. As soon as she read it and saw it was everything she had hoped, she gave it to me."

Edge silently reflected, and not for the first time, that his appointment of Frank's lovely wife Samantha as the Confederate Army Provisional's Information Officer was one of the best moves he had ever made, second only to making peace with her husband and making him his second in command. Not only did she put a very pleasant face
on their propaganda machine, but she was also a professional journalist:
motivated, extremely intelligent, and highly competent.

Besides that, she, even more than her husband, had saved his life. She was the one who shot Councilman Neil Larson just as he was getting ready to assassinate the Field Marshal. She had received the information about Larson's plot after it was uncovered by the CAP Intelligence Officer, Mike Dayton, and, even though she had been given good if false reason to believe Edge might be going to kill both her and her husband, she had traveled a long way across occupied South Carolina at enormous personal risk to put an end to the plot. That was also why he promoted both her and Dayton to full colonels, despite his stated reason that the higher rank was more in line with their positions and abilities.

"A lot of the stuff in the article was dated," Frank continued, "but I used it as my inspiration in developing a plan of my own. If it works – and unless it's compromised from within, I see no reason why it won't – it will literally shatter the enemy at his political and economic base and, within twenty-four hours, he'll be on a downhill slide it's unlikely he'll ever pull out of. Further, if their reaction as they fall is what I think it will be, they'll finally drive the majority of the Southern people into our camp by default, and it will be at the time when the enemy can least afford it."

"Give me an overview."

"The attack is multi-prong, and needs to be in the dead of winter, for reasons that I'll outline in a few minutes. To set this up, we're going to have to infiltrate the North with about one hundred to two hundred people, divided into squad-sized cells, but with no cell knowing about the others, or that there are any other missions

26

besides their own. The personnel are going to have to be solid, because their reliability is paramount.

"Twenty-four hours before the attack begins, we intend to sow the seeds of financial panic. Mike's people will begin releasing rumors over the Internet of major moves in the international currency market. People will tend to believe these because they will be coming from legitimate business websites he's hacked his way into over the years. Within an hour or so after these begin to appear, mass e-mailings begin, claiming that the government is trying to force the companies to recant, and say that the reports were never officially issued, that they were only accidents or malicious disinformation from terrorists. Of course that's what the companies will say – after all, it's true – but by releasing the accusations before hand, no one will believe their denials. Through the next nineteen hours, the pressure via cyberspace is continually ratcheted up, including reports that officials from both China and Japan are meeting secretly in an emergency economic session. Finally, three hours before zero, we drop the real bomb; an announcement is made – again, via hacked legitimate websites – that both those countries are completely divesting themselves of the US currency they hold, and selling it off ASAP."

Edge whistled. Although not a stockbroker, he had been a businessman with market holdings of his own in his earlier life, and he knew very well that a currency sell-off by those two Pacific rim nations would utterly destroy what little was left of the US economy. It would make the stock market crash of '29 look like a game of tiddlywinks.

"That's just the start?"

"Oh yeah, that's the warm up. Then, after giving them two hours to go into total chaos, we spread the rumor, supposedly from an anonymous high-level cabinet source, that the President is going to create an emergency that will take their minds off it. Then, when everyone is glued to his computer, Mike will release a computer virus into the corporate and military web. After giving it a final hour to spread, we shut everything down."

"Everything?"

"Everything; that's where our infiltrators come in; they can work in most of the North because their security is much more relaxed than it is down here. They're going to go after the energy and transportation infrastructure.

"Liddy's fictional terrorists targeted major gas lines, railways, and electrical substations, and we're going to do all of that and more. Besides the transmission infrastructure, we're going to actively target the generation end of things: the power plants themselves. Practically all the generating turbine assemblies and substation transformers are made overseas – primarily in Switzerland, by Brown-Boveri. They're manufactured on demand, and if we damage them, it will be months before replacements can be shipped over – assuming the Swiss are even willing to do so – and at least a week or two after that to get them reinstalled.

Edge instantly grasped the implications. "The middle of winter – January, early February, the coldest times – no heat, no light, no power to pump gas..."

"And no gas to pump; I want to target at least a few fuel barges and tankers in the locks and port facilities themselves." He gestured with a nod of his head towards the curtained window. "TJ will be our key to that end. If we can blow up two or three, they will hesitate to send any more unless their safety can be guaranteed.

"The important thing is that all these attacks occur in the north; their infrastructure is functionally wiped out, and when it comes to the turbines and transformers, it'll take a long, long time to fix...unless they take the parts from somewhere else."

Edges eyes lit up in realization. "They'll have to take them from the South!"

"Exactly," Frank said with a nod. "They already take over half of the electricity we produce, leaving us with continuous rolling blackouts. That's a major source of friction *now*; what do you think will be the public reaction when Southerners see them shutting down plants down here entirely, laying off the people, disassembling the main components, and shipping them north?"

"The people will go off the deep end. The Feds don't even have the option of rerouting the power either, because they have to know they can't guard thousands of miles of overhead lines that run from here to there. We can sever them faster than they can repair them."

"Bingo. They'll have to take the parts from here, and these are big parts, weighing several tons apiece. I suppose you could take a big Sikorsky helicopter and fly them out or load them in C-130s, but with those surface-to-air missiles, we can put a stop to that; air-freighting them out will get damned expensive real quick. That leaves road, river or rail transportation, all of which are vulnerable to easy ambushes. We'll cost them money, manpower and equipment, and look good to our fellow Southerners doing it. After all, we'll be fighting to keep the power on down here."

"You mentioned rails; I take it nothing will be coming into the North that way either. Do you think our people can get past the guards they've got on the bridges now?" Since CAP guerrillas had killed hundreds of Yankee National Guardsmen by blowing trestles and dropping their troop trains into the Potomac, Ohio and other rivers, the enemy tended to take that particular arena of security pretty seriously. The average trestle along the main lines looked like an armed camp.

"I don't intend to target the bridges, at least not primarily. Instead I want to target the trains themselves, causing derailments in various places. If we target chemical trains in particular, it'll take a long time to clean up the mess. There are only a few trestles but tens of thousands of miles of track, much of it isolated; like with the power lines, they can't guard it all.

The two spent the next twelve and a half hours huddled together over a laptop computer screen after Frank inserted the finger joint-sized flash drive – a *stink stick* in guerrilla slang, due to the way their couriers often carried them in a tied-off condom and inserted into their rectums to avoid detection during casual searches – that he had brought with him. Edge commented, occasionally suggested changes, and once they got in a fairly heated debate, but they finally reached an agreement. In a very rare emotional gesture for him, the Field Marshal reached out and put a hand on his subordinate's shoulder.

"Frank," he said finally, "you may have just won this war for us!"

"No, sir. One man doesn't win a war. This depends as much on the men carrying it out as it does having a good plan, and like Hamlet said, there's the rub. Even if only a fraction of this operation is successful, it'll still have a devastating impact; that's the good news. The bad news is that it's going to take a lot of men, and that's going to require the cooperation of every state. Every theater commander has to get on board, without exception and without knowing anything about what's up, beyond his own small part. That's not going to set too well with most of them, but that's the way it has to be, because we can't risk the enemy getting wind of this. It's the single most powerful weapon in our arsenal, and we'll only have the chance to use it once. We can't take the risk of *anyone* outside our immediate staffs and the people already involved – Sammie and Mike – being captured or otherwise compromised. We really can't even explain it to the commanders that way, because the risk of the Feds finding out something big is up would be almost as bad as them knowing exactly what, at least in the results department."

Edge knew Frank was exactly right. He had once heard the expression, *"as independent as a hog on ice,"* and that pretty much described the attitudes of many of those in the Southern Liberation Movement in general, and the Confederate Army Provisional in particular. All too many of them failed to grasp the most basic difference between an army and a government: a government protected rights, while the army secured them. There was one thing required of all successful armies: that, except under the most extreme circumstances, those beneath obeyed the orders from those above, even when they didn't agree with them, didn't understand their purpose, or simply didn't like them or the person giving them. Ideals of states' rights and personal sovereignty were what they were fighting for, but they could only have them *after* the victory, and not before. The widespread failure to recognize that had been a drag on Southern Nationalism long, long before this war ever started. In fact, it was one of the root causes for the failure of the first War for Southern Independence a century and a half before, and now it was a millstone around the neck of this latest rebellion. There was a small but fanatically determined and fairly influential faction as part of the movement in every state, who referred to themselves as the SN: *"Sovereignty Now!"* Late one evening after a few beers, Frank himself had coined what had become the more widely-used term, YABOM, in referring to them: the *"'You ain't the boss of me's !"* He knew they meant well, but, they had taken things to the point that they, just like the enemy, were yet another strategic obstacle that CAP had to deal with anytime it planned strategy or tactics.

Needless to say, they were not on Field Marshal Edge's Christmas list.

"They'll cooperate, or they'll be replaced," he said icily. "Any man that won't will be considered a traitor and will be treated as such. If I have to set an example, I will."

Frank pursed his lips for a moment before speaking. "Just be sure your *examples* don't have the opposite effect. I think YABOM is as big a pain in the butt as you do, but we can't afford a war within our own ranks right now."

Edge's temper began to flare, but he instantly dampened it. He knew Frank was looking after the best interests of the movement, because he had proven it time and time again. He also knew when his subordinate spoke, he was usually worth listening to.

"Don't worry. I can be subtle."

Frank considered this, but kept silent. Like he said before, concerning the state commanders and his plan; this was something he didn't need to know, and more, it was something he didn't really *want* to know. He looked up when Edge added something.

"I'm glad you're the one who thought this up, because it's going to be your baby. You're going to be running CAP during the time of the actual operation."

"What?"

"Most of the Councilmen are not going to be around. Jim Boggess already has an issue up in West Virginia; you already know about that one." Indeed he did; in fact, Frank had provided resources to assist his jug-eared Mountaineer buddy in an upcoming operation that would put the working class of one of the strongest labor states solidly in their pocket. "Sam has finally set up a series of meetings with two of the most powerful figures amongst the American Indians; there's a very real chance we might finally bring those nations on board as allies. Not only are there a lot of them, but they're strategically placed fairly close to the southwestern oil fields."

"Also, I have some news of my own. You know how we've been trying to get foreign recognition and assistance? Well, we've finally got a chance at it, but the timing on it is just as critical as it is on your project. I'm going to be in Europe then, talking to some people in government."

Frank raised his brows, impressed.

I should have figured he wouldn't be sitting around on his butt waiting for things to happen.

"What about Doctor MacFie?"

Edge pursed his lips. MacFie was *definitely* not part of his small circle of friends, but the two had reached an accommodation, due in large part to MacFie changing his mind about a coup at the last minute and shouting the warning that helped keep Edge alive, and, in larger part, to Frank threatening to kill them both if they failed to make peace. Still, what he had to say irked him to no end.

"MacFie is in reserve. You're going to be directing this operation and the remainder of the Council will be moving around; we can't afford to bunch up, not now. We're all vulnerable, and God forbid something happens to any or all of us, we need someone in authority ready to take the reins immediately, someone that the people will follow. I've asked him to go to ground and tell no one where he is; not even me."

Edge hoped and prayed that situation never came about. MacFie was a highly intelligent man, a politician and speaker and philosopher, but Edge doubted he could general his way out of a wet paper bag. Still, in the ultimate extremity, he would be the only chance they had left, and Edge would just have to take it...not that it would matter to him, because he'd be dead in such an eventuality anyway.

Frank was stunned, not only at how far they had advanced on the political front as indicated by Edge's revelations, but much more at the scope of the responsibility that had just been dropped directly on his broad shoulders.

"That's great, but...we can postpone this action – "

"No we can't. This will be perfect – better than perfect. If this happens right in the middle of the negotiations, it'll drop a bomb and demonstrate our full capabilities to the world in a manner that they can't ignore. Best of all, it'll happen during, not before, so they won't have time to think about it. They'll be off-balance, and we'll have the advantage in the deal."

Frank couldn't fault Edge's logic on that score; in fact, he admired it. Approaching a strategy of what was essentially a business negotiation exactly as one would plan a campaign for fighting a war made perfect sense. He grinned inside; he had first approached the winning of the beautiful reporter who was now his wife in exactly the same fashion...of course, that plan was modified by force only hours later when the enemy threw them together.

At the though of Sammie, he swallowed hard.

Baby, I miss you so much! I wish I could be with you now!

Of course, he knew that was an impossibility. He had things to do, and a duty to make a better world for her, and for their unborn child in her womb to be born into. He would have to wait, and steal his chances when he could. He suddenly realized Edge was still speaking.

"Besides, you're going to be doing a little diplomacy of your own well before then. I understand you speak Japanese."

"Yes," Frank cautiously admitted. He did speak passable Japanese, due largely to his years in the martial arts, along with the fluent Spanish, French and German he had taken in college, but he found the question odd, and anything odd these days was a red flag.

"Good. I need you in Georgia tomorrow afternoon..."

DAY 211

CHAPTER 2

Leaning back against the tan cloth upholstery of the Toyota Camry's back seat, Nobuo Hiro did his best to remain calm. Outwardly the young Japanese diplomat appeared to be exactly that, but inwardly he was shaking like a leaf. He was a person of no real importance and he knew the guerrillas would have nothing to gain by kidnapping or killing him, but he sincerely hoped they knew it too.

Even if the Confederate Army Provisional intended that, they wouldn't have to lure me all the way to Georgia to do that...I don't think. Westerners think we're all stoic and inscrutable; they don't know I'm about to piss my pants right now!

He realized the lines on his sharp, angular face must have tightened, because an unseen voice full of concern came from the front seat, "Are you okay, Mr. Hiro?"

Turning his head blindly in the direction of the source of concern, unable to see because of the wraparound sunglasses he wore, their lenses painted opaque black on the inside to act as a blindfold, he nodded.

"Yes, thank you. I am fine," and was instantly irritated at himself when he heard his voice betray him by tightening, raising the pitch a couple of octaves above normal.

If his companions recognized his tension, their voices gave no sign. "Good. We'll be there in just a few more minutes, sir, and then you'll be able to take off the glasses. Again, I'm very sorry for the inconvenience, but I'm sure you understand. If you need anything in the meantime, please don't hesitate to let us know."

"Yes, of course. Thank you."

Hiro understood some things, but certainly not all. What he understood was that the two men with him were scrupulously polite and, obviously, someone had taken the time to drill them in Japanese customs and mannerisms; they were the most polite Americans he had ever met outside of diplomatic circles, and they actually had better manners than most of those. He suspected that even their choice of vehicle, the product of a Japanese car company, was intended as a mark of respect to him and the country he represented. He knew that no one would have gone to all that trouble unless they wanted something from him, and it bothered him not a little that he didn't know what.

The not knowing bothered his superiors in the Japanese embassy too, which was why they sent him when they received the rather enigmatic contact from the Confederate Army Provisional requesting a meeting. If the United States discovered that a high-ranking diplomat had met with what they considered to be a terrorist organization, particularly if such a meeting had taken place in the embassy itself, there would be hell to pay and much loss of face. Senior diplomats didn't get where they were by taking such risks, so they sent Hiro instead. As an ambitious lower-mid-level embassy employee – little more than a paper-shuffler – his meeting with the rebels entailed little risk, at least as far as his superiors were concerned. If he was found out, they would simply throw him to the wolves, make all the proper noises, and send him home in disgrace, his career finished. That was the unspoken rule.

The coin had another side, however. If he could pull off a major success, and do it in secret so that the United States spy agencies never found out about it, it would put his career on a fast track, with all the accompanying economic benefits and perks that went with it, so it was well worth the risk.

Suddenly thinking of Asami, his lovely wife of only eight months, he amended his thoughts. *Maybe it's worth the risk. I guess it depends on how it all ends.*

His train of thought was broken when the car slowed and turned right, bumping over what was apparently the entrance to a driveway. The vehicle came to a stop, he heard a garage door opening, and the driver pulled forward once more before killing the engine, and the voice needlessly informed him, "We're here, sir."

Over the words, Hiro could hear the garage door closing behind them, and there was a lessening of the light filtering in around the edges of his blackout glasses.

As he heard the car doors opening and felt the chassis' weight shifting as the men got out, he had no idea where 'here' was, other than somewhere in North Georgia...at least, he assumed they were still in the Peach Tree State, as the natives referred to it. They had been driving for quite a while, so he supposed they could be anywhere bordering it.

They helped him out, then one of his anonymous companions gently took his elbow and began leading him around the vehicle. He heard the car door slam behind him, and then the turning of a knob and another door open ahead of them.

"There's a step coming up, sir, about twelve inches in front of you. There are three stairs total. Please take your time; there's no hurry."

As the other man steadied him, he lifted his foot and awkwardly felt for the higher surface, and quickly found it. With the man at his side still guiding him, he felt the softness of carpet under the soles of his shoes as he was led into a house and heard the door close behind him. After taking him a few paces farther, he was brought to a halt.

"You can take your glasses off now, Mr. Hiro. We'll be in the other room, and we'll take you back to your car as soon as you're through."

Hiro removed the opaque glasses to find himself in what looked like an ordinary American middle class home. That wasn't particularly surprising; what was surprising was that none other than the infamous General Frank Gore, complete with freshly starched gray fatigues with a silver star on each shoulder, was there to welcome him. The Japanese was so startled at unexpectedly meeting the living legend himself, he was at a momentary loss for words.

If he is here, then this is big! I can hear opportunity in the distance like a train rolling up a track!

Frank stood at attention, bowed formally at the waist in Japanese fashion and respectfully addressed him.

"*Konichi wa, Hiro-san.*"

37

The bow was correct and the enunciation was almost exact: obviously *gaijin* with the faintest hint of a Southern drawl showing through, but certainly among the best he had ever heard from a Westerner. His host had obviously put great effort into getting it exactly right.

Recovering his equilibrium at the unexpected but familiar greeting, he bowed in return. *"Konichi wa, Gore-san,"* adding in nearly flawless English as he straightened up and offered his hand. "Your Japanese is very good."

Frank grinned and switched languages. "You're too kind, Mr. Hiro." Waving a hand at a chair beside the table, he asked, "Would you care to sit down, sir?"

Once he was seated, Frank offered whiskey, which his guest accepted. Sipping at his glass and swirling the amber liquid around in his mouth without seeming to, Hiro reflected that it was very good bourbon; apparently they hadn't spared any expense. Over his own glass, the guerrilla general thanked him for coming.

"You're welcome; it's an honor to meet such a famous man." He was telling the truth; normally, such a contact would only be through a much higher-level diplomat. This meeting alone would be a *'feather in his cap'* as the Americans were fond of putting it, and if it was productive, it would end up being so much more.

"Or infamous," Frank said with a grin, "depending on who you ask."

Hiro offered a polite smile in return, relaxed enough to manage a quip on the obvious.

"Most things in the world are that way; what they are depends on who you ask."

As they chatted amicably about the weather and Hiro's trip there, the kind of small talk that preceded the main thrust of any meeting, something about Frank's respectful yet easy manner tended to make the nervous diplomat feel relaxed, and that bothered the Japanese a little, because he knew the guerrilla general wanted something from him.

"I'm sure you're wondering why I invited you here."

"Yes." Hiro said simply, toying with his glass and intentionally keeping both his face and his voice neutrally friendly while his mind raced, searching.

"I wanted to offer you reassurances. Japan has several businesses in the Confederate States, particularly automobile factories. I've heard rumors that they're considering pulling out."

Hiro considered for a moment before answering, noticing that the General simply sipped his whiskey, looking at his glass rather than staring expectantly at his guest, all the while maintaining his relaxed attitude. He seemed to be neither surprised nor impatient at the diplomat's hesitation; that was an unusual and welcome change from most Westerners he had dealt with, who were always in a hurry. Mulling it over, he decided that, since the subject had made some of the minor newswires, it would be proper to admit to it.

"I believe that has been discussed. Due to the unstable situation, you understand."

"On behalf of the Provisional Confederate Government, I'd like to officially request that you reconsider."

The diplomat pursed his lips.

Now that's a surprise!

"Pardon me, General, but I would think you would want the US economy damaged."

"Not if it's going to damage our own in the long run too." Frank leaned forward. "May I be straight-up with you?"

"Please do."

"We intend to win this war, Mr. Hiro, and when we do, we will need infrastructure already in place: manufacturing infrastructure. There is no question that the US companies will pull out of Dixie – many will be thrown out because of their active opposition to us – and we want to be something more than a banana republic. We're not fighting for the freedom to become a third world nation, and we have to be more than that if we're to survive. Motor vehicle manufacturing is a basic necessary industry, particularly for defense, which is a priority in any new country. You're the only ones who will be likely to keep their factories here, and we'd like to invite you to stay. Following victory, most of your competition will be gone for some time, giving you a golden opportunity to secure your own position under what will be, for all practical purposes, a temporary monopoly."

That makes good sense, Hiro reflected, but it would not do to appear eager. Besides, there were other issues involved.

"I appreciate your offer, but you must understand that for our companies to remain here is also a major risk. Even with the best of intentions, post-revolutionary conditions are often dangerously... unstable."

"I do understand; that's why I asked you to come, and why I'm meeting with you personally. We want to make some promises to you, and we'll give them to you in writing.

"First, we will not interfere with you, your citizens, your places of business, or your employees, provided they remain neutral in the current conflict. Any man or any unit who does so will answer directly to me. Secondly, when we win, you can continue to operate, and almost certainly under a less restrictive regulatory system than you do now. You have my word that we will not nationalize your equipment and facilities in the South as long as they remain here and in operation."

An experienced if relatively minor diplomat, Hiro could easily read between the lines. *Those companies, US, Japanese or otherwise, who do leave will have their factories and equipment remaining on Southern soil seized, nationalized and, considering the Confederates' leading political philosophy, probably sold at auction. In any event, it will be months or even years before they can return to full production, giving our companies a solid foothold. No doubt the Confederate military would have to be letting out defense contracts at that time as well...*He realized Frank was speaking again.

"Further, we'll need friends in this world, and we would especially value the friendship of another nation that understands the concept of nationalism, believes in tradition and knows who they are. The Confederacy will need friends like Japan. You're a First-world nation: a civilized, industrialized, and technologically advanced country, and a respected and vital player on the international stage. Once this war is over, with the combination of depression and destruction, we're going to need investors and trading partners, and we're going to need them very badly. We'll have infrastructure to rebuild, and currently we have very little steel manufacturing: certainly not enough to meet our needs. I'm prepared to offer you a free trade agreement between our two countries for a term of seven years, to begin at the war's end. You'll risk nothing by staying here now, remaining ostensibly neutral, and continuing to make money, but you'll also have the chance to gain much greater profits, influence and good will in the future."

Frank knew full well that this action – approved by Jonathon Edge and the Confederate Council – was not going to be popular with a lot of the rank-and-file Confederates; he also knew it was something that had to be done anyway.

What I'm offering is going to upset a lot of people; I also know it's something we have to have if our new country is to survive...assuming we make it that far.

He paused in his thoughts, shrugging mentally. *Besides, as long as the factory and its equipment is on Southern soil and staffed by Southern workers, it doesn't matter whose name is on the paperwork.*

Meanwhile, Hiro pursed his thin lips as he read the white areas between the words once more. The Confederacy would need friends, of course: *friends* that went beyond the causal and diplomatic senses of the word. A country torn apart all the way to its core, first by depression, then by war, would need investors with a big influx of cash, most likely along with high-tech military gear. The word, *OPPORTUNITY* flashed in great big glowing red neon letters, but he had one more question.

"General, please forgive me for being blunt, but what makes you so certain you will win?"

Frank's gaze was unwavering and his voice had the sharp, hard edge of truth to it.

"We'll either win or we'll die; there are no other choices for us, for the people involved."

An image suddenly flashed in Hiro's mind, of the tales of his own country's past, of the Samurai heroes who faced the prospect of violent death as calmly as the man he was looking at now. Those were the legends he had grown up with, the stuff of heroes, and it dawned on him that he was seeing that very thing in the flesh, if in an alien race and a different culture in a faraway land. Rising, he bowed formally and then extended his hand.

"Officially, I'll need to relay your offer to my superiors, of course." His face split in a broad smile. "Personally, I look forward to doing business with you, General."

Hiro's smile was not only sincere; it was triumphant. Even as he accepted the envelope containing the proposed agreement, he had no doubt his country's government would agree to the Confederate offer, as they would be fools not to do so. Besides profit and influence, there was also the matter of satisfaction. As much as the Americans like to pretend otherwise – and as much as Japan had been forced to pretend along with them – no one likes to have their face rubbed in their defeat. That Japan had already sued for peace well before the end of World War II, beginning all the way back in 1943, only to become unique in world history to have hundreds of thousands fall victim to nuclear weapons in order to force an unconditional instead of honorable surrender, was a permanent sore on the Japanese soul. That the Southerners had been part of their defeat was of little consequence; they had been victims of United States occupation just as surely as his own country had, and if they were to be the ones to collect some measure of justice, then the least Japan could do was help them recover once they broke the superpower. Besides, with economies tied as tightly as those of the two countries were likely to become, Japan would have a powerful ally with good reason to support them in the face of their giant, increasingly expansive, and all-too-near neighbor, China.

The diplomat was unable to suppress his joy. Just as importantly, on a personal level, his own future was almost certainly secured. If the Confederates won – and, being privy to diplomatic information not generally available, and especially after meeting Frank Gore, he believed they had a reasonably good chance of doing so – he would very likely be appointed the Japan's first Ambassador to the Confederate States of America. Asami would be proud!

He and his wife would be rich too, he reflected as the polite men reentered the room and apologetically handed him to blindfold. As soon as he was returned to his car, he determined to use the driving time back to the embassy in Washington to give his broker a call. He suddenly felt the pressing to buy stock in his country's car companies with factories in Dixie. No doubt the senior diplomats would do the same after seeing the agreement, but Hiro intended to avoid the rush.

DAY 212

CHAPTER 3

Wall Street News Wire

Moods were uplifted both on Wall Street and in Washington today, courtesy of the Japanese Government. Tokyo has assured the US that it has no plans to close its American factories at the present time. The Prime Minister told reporters in a press conference today that, "there is absolutely no substance to the rumors," and that Japan "would always consider the friendship shown us by the United States in any economic decision we make." The Minister added that there, "might be some reshuffling" of some of their less profitable factories, but promised no wholesale closings or transfers to other countries.

US Secretary of Commerce, Morris Seligman, touted this as just one more example of the success of President Jack Plants' foreign policy stance...

To all appearances, the building was nothing more than a big, red, sheet metal pole barn, built to house tractors and livestock: no different from a thousand others just like it on the farms scattered across rural western South Carolina. This one served that purpose; its owner's tractor came and went in and out of it everyday, and his horses and a dozen dairy cows returned to it at night, along with several dozen free ranging chickens and turkeys. The machinery and animals, though, only occupied the center section that ran like a tunnel through the building from the roll up door on one end to the identical one on the other. The rest of the space was separated by two plywood and waferboard walls stretching from end to end on either side of the rollup doors. Behind those sheets of wood, concealed from casual view, were partitioned training areas and

45

classrooms, barracks and latrines, all belonging to the Confederate Army Provisional. It was the single largest guerrilla base in the State, and their main headquarters.

I wonder why they call it morning sickness? It's ten o'clock at night!

Colonel Samantha Gore raised her head from its position over the toilet. She had been nauseous longer than most during her pregnancy, but it had finally tapered off to the rare occasion, like tonight. Even though this particular bout that had brought her nude, wet and dripping from the shower had thankfully been a false alarm, albeit accompanied by a lot of retching and gagging, her mouth still felt foul. Straightening up, she went to the sink and opened the cold water valve; the cool liquid felt good spilling over her hands, and even better when she brought cupped handfuls to her mouth and rinsed. As she picked up her towel from the rack, she caught her reflection in the full-length mirror that someone – *no doubt a dedicated sadist* – had thoughtfully hung on the inside of the plain plywood door.

Samantha had never considered herself a vain woman, but now, at last, she was honest enough to admit it to herself. It went with the territory of her former job as a TV personality: a basic survival skill of the profession, she supposed. Still, she'd never pictured herself looking like this.

Logically, she knew the differences in her appearance since her abrupt and violent change of career were subtle, if, in fact, they existed at all. *No*, she assured herself, *they existed all right, and in more ways than one.* She could see it in the tiny lines at the corners of her eyes that weren't there even six months ago, and stranger's frightening stare she sometimes caught looking back at her from the mirror.

She had made an almost complete physical recovery from her ordeal in Federal custody, although the beatings had left her with some chronic joint pains and prone to kidney infections – all inside and out of sight, at least. Now, though, without her makeup, she could see the tiny scars on her full lips where the blows had split them by driving them against her teeth, and she didn't care what

Frank said; she could tell the difference in her nose where it had been broken.

At the thought of her husband, Samantha sighed and turned sideways, regarding her body's altered profile. She didn't know what he saw in her, especially now that her belly had begun to swell. At almost five months along, she had only gained a grand total of five pounds – one a month – and she exercised religiously in order to keep it at that rate. Despite all that, she felt fat and misshapen...and if Frank were here, he'd take her in his arms and love her, just like always.

She sighed again before dropping the towel in the hamper and slipping into her nightgown and housecoat, and slinging the belt with the holstered .357 magnum that never left her side over one shoulder. She opened the door and was making her way down the narrow plywood hall when the calendar caught her eye. It was one that Billy had hung up, from some tool company or another, complete with an overly endowed model in a too-small flannel shirt and a pair of cutoff 'Daisy Dukes' that left little to the imagination. Samantha casually hated her, despite having never met her in the flesh.

She stumbled, missing a step when the realization abruptly dropped on her head like a falling cinderblock. The calendar with the empty-eyed and full-bloused model suddenly brought home to her that it was the 28th of September. Today was her birthday; she was twenty-eight.

Twenty-eight on the twenty-eighth, and I didn't even notice it...until now, when the day's almost over with.

She was really depressed now: pregnant, another year older, Frank gone for over three weeks this time, and nobody here giving a damn...

No! That wasn't true; it was only self-pity talking. They'd care if they knew; they'd throw a party, and Billy would probably bake me a cake!

They didn't know, though, because she hadn't mentioned it, since she'd forgotten about it herself. She could feel another mood swing coming on; they were a regular thing due to her Post-

Traumatic Stress Disorder, but the pregnancy exacerbated it by an order of magnitude. Of course, the stress of being an officer in a guerrilla army in the middle of a war zone didn't help either.

Just before she reached her door, she felt something against her hand and looked down to see Thumper. With the unerring instinct of animals for human emotion, the hundred-plus pound bulldog comfortingly nuzzled her hand.

She smiled sadly as she leaned over to pet him.

"You understand, don't you, boy?"

She managed a single stroke on the white fur of his huge head when a coyote howled somewhere outside. In an instant, the big dog was moving again even as his ears pricked at the sound. Trained as a stock dog as well as a watchdog, Thumper had an almost pathological hatred for coyotes. They were his private obsession; he would hunt them, kill them, and sometimes even eat them. In a moment his big hindquarters disappeared around a corner on his way out, and she was alone once more, sighing heavily.

"Happy birthday to me!" she muttered sarcastically to herself as she opened the unpainted plywood panel that served as the door to her room.

"That's my line, only it's happy birthday to *you*, not *me*. Mine's not until July."

Samantha spun at the sound of the familiar voice. "Frank!"

Instantly she was in his arms, pressing her face against his chest and reveling in the feel, and even the familiar smell of him.

"I've missed you," she heard him say in a voice muffled by his mouth pressed into her blonde hair.

"Oh, God, I've missed you, honey! I've missed you so much!" She was crying now, so hard she was shaking, only this time it was from joy.

She felt him move, then to her surprise, she found herself picked up in his arms like a child and carried to bed. As he laid her down, she asked him, "How did you manage to get here?"

Her husband shrugged nonchalantly, but she could see from the fatigue redness in his eyes and the residual tension in his face that there had been nothing casual about it. There couldn't have been;

48

Dixie was crawling with Federal occupation troops, with Frank right at the top of their most wanted list. Add to that all the crime and crazies and vigilantes that the poverty and the climate of violence had spawned, and you took your life in your hands just stepping out your front door. She had heard that Frank had been in Louisiana only three days ago; that he was here now, in the rural farm country of western South Carolina, meant that he had almost certainly taken some serious risks to get back in time for her birthday – unacceptable risks, in fact. She promised herself she would take him to task for it – *after all, seeing to my husband's welfare is my duty as a wife* – but later, much later, maybe tomorrow or the next day. For right now, there was only joy, and she wasn't about to spoil that.

Reaching into his jacket pocket – he was dressed in a dark sport coat and jeans, she suddenly realized: casual chic except for the old 1911 .45 automatic Mary had given him resting in its shoulder holster, it's butt peeking out at her – he produced a tiny black velvet box wrapped in a red ribbon and placed it in her hands.

"Happy birthday, Sammie."

She heard him playfully snickering at her efforts to remove the ribbon without breaking it, but she ignored his gentle teasing and took her time. Finally she set the strip of satin aside and opened the box, and her eyes widened.

"Frank...oh, honey..."

"I never got around to getting you an engagement ring," he told her as he removed the gold band with the diamond solitaire and held it up. "I thought maybe your birthday would be a good occasion to rectify that situation."

As he lifted her hand and slipped it on her finger, he added, "It's pretty appropriate too, because I'd marry you all over again."

"Thank you, Frank. I love you."

He told her he loved her too, and then proceeded to show her just how much.

DAY 213

CHAPTER 4

The next morning Samantha awoke lying naked on her side, spooned against her husband, cuddled in his arms while her bottom pressed against him. By his deep, regular breathing, she knew Frank was still asleep, so she settled for snuggling in tighter and relishing the sensation of his skin against hers.

I think I've missed this most of all.

The new life in her belly was insistently pushing on her bladder, but she determined to hold out as long as she could before going to the bathroom. These precious moments came far too seldom, and she fully intended to make the most of them.

Finally she couldn't hold it anymore; it was either get up or wet the bed. Trying her best not to wake him, she slipped out of his arms, put on her robe, and headed for the latrine. She was not surprised but still a little disappointed upon her return to find him awake, leaning on one elbow and waiting for her.

"I'm sorry I woke you, honey, but – "

"Nature calls," he finished for her. "Sammie, don't try to hold it on my account; that's not good for your kidneys."

"Okay," she said sheepishly at his gentle chiding as she climbed back into bed.

He doesn't miss much; one thing about it, I can never accuse him of not paying attention to me.

"I just...missed you so much," she added by way of explanation.

"I missed you too."

Samantha grinned and slipped back into his arms, facing him this time. "That's obvious; I didn't know if I'd still be able to walk this morning!"

Frank kissed her. "Flattery will get you everywhere."

"I hope so."

Unfortunately, before it got him anywhere this time, there was a knock at the door, and they recognized Kerrie O'Brien's voice.

"Sammie, is Frank awake? I have a call patched through from Colonel Boggess in West Virginia."

Frank muttered under his breath even as he got out of bed. "On my way."

"No rest for the wicked?" Samantha ventured mischievously, re-belting her robe around her as he pulled on his jeans.

Her face fell when she heard him say, "Not for long, honey; duty calls." She instinctively knew from his tone that their time together would probably not last long this time either. Not that she had expected it to, of course, but she always hoped.

As she watched him dress quickly and efficiently, she was becoming more than a little jealous of his ever-more demanding mistress who went by the name of "Duty." After slipping his shoulder holster over his plain black tee shirt, he brightened her mood just a little by turning to give her a quick kiss before heading out the door. It didn't quite close when Kerrie entered, pushing it shut behind her.

"Here." She offered her a steaming mug with a wedge of lemon on the side. "It's some herbal tea one of the locals gave us." Looking at her superior officer critically, she kept a straight face as she added, "You'd better suck the lemon first."

"Why? Is it that bad?" Samantha asked, looking into the cup in askance.

"No, but maybe it'll wipe that silly, satisfied grin off your face before anybody else sees it."

Kerrie's freckled nose wrinkled as she burst out laughing at her own joke, and after a moment, a somewhat shocked Samantha joined her. Not because it was funny, but because it felt so good to see this abused girl opening up and becoming more alive by the day.

And, besides, it *was* a little funny, not to mention true.

"Jack?"

"Frank! You're a hard man to get a'hold of!"

"I know; that's all that keeps me alive."

The Mountaineer laughed out loud.

"Well, keep it up; we need you." He paused for a moment. "Have you got anything else for me on this project of ours up here?"

Even though their conversations were heavily encrypted – as evidenced by the weird electronic sound of their voices – and were sent as background static behind an innocuous, pre-recorded conversations between elderly ladies discussing unappreciative children, philandering neighbors, and cancerous relatives, they still made a point of not going into unnecessary details as a basic security precaution. Still, both of them were well aware of what they were talking about.

Essentially, Jack Boggess' theater of operations – West Virginia – had been turned into an internment camp. Over than thirty thousand people were currently being held prisoner in more than a dozen detention facilities in various parts of the state. The inmates were not guerrillas – those went directly to the Army's interrogation centers – but instead were their families, and other suspected sympathizers from all over the Southeastern States, in particular people who had said or written the wrong things, or who were known to hold views in opposition to those of the United States Government. More than a few dissidents, uncooperative journalists and labor activists from the Northern States had involuntarily joined them as well. Jack had been wanting to launch a mission to break at least some of the people out, not only to recover some of his men's families, but to get some new recruits on board, in the form of the freed prisoners, who would have no other choice but to join.

Frank knew it was a good plan, and a big one, and because of the latter, both he and Jonathon Edge had been holding off on giving their approval, despite Jack's constant badgering. They knew such an act would put other such camps in other states on high alert, and make difficult or impossible any similar effort on the part of those state units: efforts which, just like West Virginia's, were already planned but put on hold for the same reason. The Confederate Army Provisional Command wanted it done, but they wanted it done at the time and place of their choosing, where it would have the most impact on the enemy while doing the least damage to their own and everyone else's efforts.

Frank grinned; at last this time, he had something to give his friend and comrade.

"It's a go. You finalize the plans and we'll pick the date, sometime around late winter."

"That long?"

"Yes. Also, you're going to have to set aside two squads of reliable people ASAP. They'll be under my command until after your project is over."

Boggess' irritation was plain in his voice. "Two squads? Hell's fire, Frank! Why don't you just tie my hands behind my back while you're at it?"

"Sorry," Frank said patiently, "but I need them."

"Can you at least tell me what for?"

"Again, sorry: need to know only, and I'll have to ask that you don't discuss this with anyone else outside of your XO, Putney, and tell him to do the same. I can tell you that not all of them have to be men, or even physically fit – in fact, it would be best if some of them weren't – although at least half of each group needs to be in good shape."

Frank distinctly heard the sound of breath blowing out in exasperation, just as he himself had done many times.

"Alright, I reckon; it's not like I have a hell of a lot of choice."

"None of us have had that for a long time now," Frank responded in sympathy. "Get them selected and put them on standby, ready to go on twenty four hours notice."

After Frank hung up the phone, he realized he was going to have to have some version of same conversation with ever other state theater commander...

Like hell I am! I'm either in command or I'm not!

Dropping his fingers to his keyboard, he began typing a form letter.

Sir:

You are ordered to immediately select two squads of reliable people of either sex, at least half of whom to be physically fit males. They are to be put on standby, and be ready for call-up and transfer to my command on 24 hours notice. Notify headquarters immediately when you have done so. You are not to discuss this with anyone other than your executive officer, Field Marshal Edge, or me.

By order of General Franklin Gore
Confederate Army Provisional

Finished, he called out over his shoulder. "Kerrie!"

Cynthia Dover came in on the run, her sneakers slapping the floor in time with the rattle of her equipment. Only seventeen, the blond-haired girl was a very petite, but extremely hard-eyed, with a Charter .44 special Bulldog revolver and a long Randal Mark II combat dagger balancing one another on either side of her slender hips, an MP5 submachine gun slung behind her back, and Heaven only knew what else hidden from view. The girl had been the victim of a vicious racial gang rape once, and had been infected with HIV in the process. She had determined not only would she never be a victim again, but nobody around her would either. Although she was technically part of the information department, primarily as a graphic designer, she was also Samantha's self-appointed bodyguard. Samantha had long ago given up attempts to discourage her as futile, and had accepted her as a permanent shadow who felt comfortable enough to leave her alone only when Frank was around.

"Sir?" she inquired crisply.

Her commander smiled. She was all business, as usual.

"Hey, Cynthia; I didn't know you were pulling communications duty this morning."

She relaxed and managed a slight, tight smile of her own at his softened tone, something she did all too seldom. "Kerrie's eating breakfast, so I'm filling in until she finishes. What do you need?"

"Well, for starters," he said, gesturing at the screen, "I need this encrypted and sent to each State Theater Commander, without the others knowing that anybody else is getting one. That means each is to be sent individually, with no *UNDISCLOSED RECIPIENTS* in the address. Then, I need to get Mike up here ASAP – today if possible."

Her smile briefly grew. "Kerrie will be thrilled!"

The corners of Frank's mouth turned up as well at Cynthia's sheer joy for her friend's good fortune.

"I know, and so will he. When he shows up, would you mind trading duties with her, so she can spend a little time with him?"

"You'd have to order me not to."

He nodded his thanks before speaking again. This next thing was going to be a little harder.

"Now, I'm going to ask you a personal favor."

"Of course."

"Sit down here and talk to me."

Puzzled, she took the indicated chair facing his, and was startled when Frank reached out and took both her hands. Her appendages were tiny compared to his, but she trained so hard and continuously that they were almost as calloused as his own. The feeling was unnerving, but it was the other calluses he was worried about: the kind that didn't show on the outside. He looked directly into her eyes and made sure she was looking at him before he spoke again.

"Are *you* doing alright?"

"Why...yeah, of course. Why wouldn't I be? I've still got plenty of medicine."

Frank grimaced inwardly at the mention of the HIV drug cocktail that was all that kept this young girl alive. That he didn't know – couldn't have known – what the consequences of giving her journalism club an interview would be did little to soften his guilt, but he refused to let it show on his face.

"That's not what I'm talking about. I try not to get into other people's business, but at the same time, as a commander, it's my duty to keep an eye on my people, especially the ones I depend on the most." He paused. "Most especially the ones I care about personally. I'm worried about you."

Her eyes widened.

"Me?"

"You. Everybody here at headquarters seems to have some kind of a social life, at least as much as the war will allow...everybody except you."

Cynthia blinked in surprise.

He really does keep track of what's going on!

"Frank, with the disease and all – "

"Don't try to bull-sh...er, pull that on me." He paused, gathering his control. The stress of the war had been getting to him; he had been using a lot more profanity lately, and there was no point in it. Besides, he hadn't been brought up that way. "There's a hell of a lot more to you than just your disease. You're not a germ; you're a living, breathing human being, and a very beautiful young lady with so much to offer. I'm not asking you to jump in the sack with somebody; in fact, I'd just as soon you didn't. I'm just asking you to loosen up and have a little fun once in awhile, whenever you get the chance. This war is hard enough, and God knows it's taken enough away from you. I guess what I'm asking is that you don't let it take your humanity away. Please don't let it do that, Cynthia. Please; for me if not for yourself."

Overcome with emotion, she surprised them both by suddenly jumping forward and hugging him tightly.

"I'll try," he heard her whisper from against his neck. "I-I don't know if I can do that, but I promise; I'll try!"

She pulled away just as quickly, bounced to her feet, and left the room, never letting him see her face.

Frank sighed and went back to work. Most of it was routine; requests for men, money and equipment he didn't have to give, ideas for big operations with no chance of success, and the death reports that were all too common. There were guerrilla casualties every day, but they made up for it in enemy soldier deaths, and more than made up for it with those of civilian collaborators. Of course, the enemy killed or captured similar numbers of the CAP's sympathizers as each side played a deadly game of one-upmanship.

Mostly, he simply reviewed what was before him, as he largely trusted the state-level commanders' judgments, but occasionally he got involved. He dispatched orders for some extra antibiotics for Kentucky, one hundred pounds of C4 and/or Semtex, whichever was currently available, for Missouri, two extra SAM's to New Mexico, and strongly *"suggested"* to the head of the Texas Theater that he needed to make certain of the guilt of the collaborators in his State before he executed them; a few of their units were getting somewhat trigger happy down there on even the flimsiest of evidence, and it was handing propaganda to the enemy. He also reminded them to consider the intelligence value of their chosen targets, as they might want to black-bag some of them instead of simply killing them out of hand.

Then he began issuing some death warrants of his own. Most such things were taken care of by the various state and local forces, but occasionally the Confederate Army Provisional Command took a hand, especially when rewards were being offered. Put four or five figures on someone's head in an economy gone straight to Hell in a handcart, and many on the shady side of the civilian populace would be tempted to collect. Money is always green, regardless of race or politics, and as a result, more than half of such payments ended up being issued to Black and Latino gangsters, normally mortal enemies of the Confederacy, but still anxious to make a buck from whomever was willing to pay it. The use of these resources served a dual purpose; besides carrying out the mission, their involvement opened up a second front against the Federal forces, forcing them to divide their attentions that would normally be solely aimed at the White faces of ethnic Southerners.

Still, these top level warrants were seldom issued, and were reserved for special cases, usually those that involved undue risk to CAP personnel. Today there were three Marines in Alabama who had gang raped a civilian woman, a squad of six soldiers stationed in Georgia who had murdered the family of a guerrilla, and a Colonel in Virginia who was notorious for encouraging his men to torture information out of captured guerrillas. He carefully budgeted out the money for each killing; the Confederates had developed the reputation of scrupulously paying promised rewards regardless of who carried out the hit, and thus their targets tended to have a low life expectancy.

The message was a simple one: harm our civilians, go outside the bounds of civilized behavior with our prisoners, and you *will* die. Each time he signed his name, he executed a man – perhaps not literally, but just as surely as if he had placed the muzzle of his .45 against the target's head and pulled the trigger himself. In fact, each time he gave his approval, he forced himself to visualize doing exactly that, to keep things in perspective for fear that he might someday become casual about it.

The process was cold and methodical, and despite the necessity, it bothered the ex-cop a little...just not very much. As he realized that, he carefully looked inward, searching his own soul as he wondered if he was doing the same thing he had feared concerning Cynthia: losing his humanity.

To be honest, I don't know!

He hoped not, but he was still determined to do what he had to do, regardless. If he lost it, he could only hope that, somewhere along the line, he might find it once more. For now, it, just like his life, was the price of a dream.

"Yeah, Mike? What do you need?"

Colonel Michael Dayton grinned up at Donna Waddell from his wheelchair. As soon as he'd called for them, she'd immediately come to his basement command center.

The Chief Intelligence Officer for the Confederate Army Provisional was a paraplegic computer geek who lived in his parents' basement...which made the perfect cover. His parents had died several years before, so the house was his. His computer was a homemade supercomputer he had designed and assembled himself, compiled from dozens of PCs and using a large chest freezer for housing and cooling it. He himself was not exactly a run of the mill nerd either; despite the stereotypical pale complexion, thick glasses, and withered legs, he also sported the thick chest and 18" arms of a bodybuilder, thanks to the weight machine in the corner. He was a Confederate soldier, and was more valuable to the Cause than almost any of his comrades with two good legs.

"Frank's back at headquarters, and he wants me to come up today. You and Tommy up for a road trip?" Mike's car was equipped with hand controls and he could have easily driven himself, but he knew the couple would enjoy going as well. All of them had close friends at "command central," and they got to see them far too seldom.

Her eyes lit up. "Hell, yeah! Anything to get away from this Columbia bull-shit for awhile!"

Mike cocked an eyebrow at her in friendly warning.

"Well, your Uncle Sam's up there, so you might want to start watching your language."

Donna blushed and looked down for a moment. She might be nineteen, but that didn't matter to her Godfather, who was still more than willing to take her to task for what he was fond of referring to as 'unladylike behavior.'

That made her sigh inwardly. She was grown up, living with Tommy, and was a soldier in the middle of a war. She had been shot at and had killed people herself, so she didn't see what the big deal was about a little cussing, but the man who had been a second father to her for as long as she could remember definitely did. She knew better than to buck him on it, too, because Sam had a temper, and the consequences of arousing it unnecessarily would certainly end up being embarrassing, at the very least.

Still, the opportunity to get out of war-torn Columbia for a while was golden, and she wasn't about to miss it. Besides, she would have a chance to see her friends and catch up a little. She was already looking forward to exchanging the latest gossip with Kerrie and Cynthia, and seeing how Sammie was getting along with the baby...and for sure, she wanted to see Frank.

Frank was like a sore tooth; she couldn't keep from going there, no matter how much it always hurt. She was head over heels in love with him, and had been from the very beginning. He had never encouraged it – *I wonder if he even knows it?* – and she knew nothing would ever, or even *could* ever, come of it, because he loved his wife, and was as faithful to her as Rin-Tin-Tin. Even if he wasn't, she still couldn't let it show, because she couldn't do that to Sammie, the woman she loved like a sister.

On an intellectual level, she hoped she couldn't do that to Tommy either, even though, if the opportunity ever presented itself, her heart wasn't quite as sure of that as her head. There was no question that her boyfriend loved her – he had even asked her to marry him once – and she knew she loved him...just not quite as much as she adored the man she could never have.

And despite all of that – knowing exactly what it would do to Sammie, and Tommy – if Frank ever made the offer, I'd do it in a heartbeat. Damn it! Why does life have to be so complicated?

"I'll go upstairs and tell Tommy; I'm sure he'll want to go too."

And it would probably be the best thing if he does, so I don't end up doing something stupid!

CHAPTER 5

The trio rolled in at one o'clock that afternoon in Tommy's old S15 pickup. In order to travel openly out of the city, they were unarmed; one roadblock from the South Carolina Law Enforcement Division and three from the US military that they had to pass through in order to reach their destination made sure of that. They could have slipped out of Columbia, of course, but the Feds weren't stupid; they checked IDs and logged them to keep track of who entered and left, and the reasons they gave for it, and frequently compared the lists for suspicious behavior. That meant, if the guerrillas didn't follow the approved procedure, they would have to slip back in again, doubling the risk. For this mission, it was unnecessary, and it didn't pay to take the chance unless it was. Simply staying alive was risk enough.

It had been over a month since their last visit, and their welcome was effusive. Before anyone at headquarters could speak more than half a dozen words to Mike, Kerrie had corralled him and disappeared with him, unwilling to waste any of the precious time they had together. Billy homed in on Tommy, good-naturedly mauled the hell out of him, then tossed a laughing, squealing Donna up in the air, catching her on the way down. Without giving her a chance to touch the ground, he turned and handed her to a startled Sam, plunking her into his arms. She immediately kissed her Godfather on the weathered cheek.

"I missed you, Uncle Sam."

"The Lord knows, I've missed you, honey. Are you doing okay?"

"Fit as a fiddle!"

"I know, but I'd feel a lot better if you were up here at our main headquarters."

The *"and not living in sin with Tommy"* went unspoken, but was plainly understood just the same. Sam and the biker/ paramedic/ Confederate officer were friends, yes, but the fact that he was

63

sleeping with the Councilman's Goddaughter still rubbed him the wrong way.

"Look, we've already been over this..."

"Alright, the old man will shut up now." Dropping her lower half to allow her to set her feet on the ground, he glanced over to see Tommy letting go of Samantha and grabbing Frank's hand. Pointing Donna in the Information Officer's direction, he affectionately gave her a light swat on the tight seat of her jeans and said, "Now go see Sammie."

Donna was happy to do that, and was comforted more than she would have thought by the older woman enfolding her in her arms and holding her tight. She couldn't help but feel Samantha's swollen abdomen pressing against her, and she let go to run one hand gently over the rounded surface, making the mother-to-be grin ruefully.

"I must look like one of those little fat Buddhas; everybody wants to rub my belly for good luck."

"I'm sorry! I was just..."

"Oh, it's alright!" Samantha told her, laughing. "I was teasing you!"

"So, is everything going okay?"

"Sure, other than being fat and in the middle of a war, everything's just peachy-keen."

"Sammie! You're not fat! You're – "

"Pregnant," she finished for her, "yes, I know."

She laughed again, and Donna laughed with her.

"So, do you know what it's going to be yet?"

Samantha shook her head.

"Ultrasound machines are sort of scarce around here, so I guess we'll have to do it the old fashioned way and just wait and see." Considering it for a moment, she added, "You know, I think I like it better this way."

"Really?"

Samantha shrugged. "It'll be a surprise."

"But I'd like to get something for your baby shower; how can I do that if I don't know what it's going to be?"

"Get diapers," Frank said, catching the tail end of their conversation, "I figure that's one thing we'll definitely need."

"Spoken like a man," Donna said sarcastically, then softened the remark by throwing her arms around him and snuggling tightly against his chest. It felt so good to be held by him, and she abruptly forced herself to let go when she realized she was holding on a bit longer than mere friendship called for.

"It's good to see you," Frank told her sincerely, and Donna thought, *if you only knew!*

"It's good to see you too."

Looking over at Tommy, he nodded towards her and asked, "Are you making this little rascal behave?"

Tommy opened his mouth to speak, but Donna beat him to it.

"I make him walk the chalk," she declared, giving her boyfriend a broad wink while trying to ignore the sting of being called "little" by Frank. At least, it helped distract her from her feelings; now that the first flush of the reunion was over, she was back on familiar ground, and rapidly dropped back into her normal outgoing persona. "I figure I'll have him doing the dishes before long."

"Fat chance of that!" Tommy grumbled loudly, clearly offended by the very idea.

An hour later, Mike paused a moment by Frank's open office door to say something to someone unseen on the other side. From the broad smile on the Intelligence Officer's face, Frank had no doubt it was Kerrie. When Mike finally turned back to the room, he saw the General waiting, and shoved the door closed even as Frank walked up to him and extended his hand.

Mike took it immediately.

"It's really good to see you again, Frank."

"You too, my friend." Glancing at the closed door, he added, "I'll let you visit some more with Kerrie as soon as I can, but I'm afraid this is going to take awhile."

Mike half-grinned even as she shrugged the broad shoulders that sharply contrasted with his atrophied, paralyzed legs.

"That bastard Sherman was right about one thing; war really *is* hell."

A hard look flickered briefly across Frank's face and he couldn't help saying, "Tell me about it!" even though his voice was so low as to be almost inaudible. Snapping out of his darkening mood, he gestured towards the table. "Grab a plate; we've got fried chicken, mashed potatoes, biscuits, and gravy. We can eat while we talk."

Looking at the table, Mike replied, "Maybe I should request a transfer; it looks like you all eat pretty good out here."

"Usually it's greens, beans and cornbread, unless somebody poaches a deer, traps a possum, or hijacks an enemy supply truck. This is a special occasion; Kerrie, Sammie, and Cynthia jumped in with the regular kitchen duty and worked their butts off once they knew company was coming."

As Frank scooted his chair in and helped himself to a drumstick, Mike shook his head in embarrassment. He had been a nerd, an outcast virtually his entire life, even before his back was broken. Other than his family and Tommy – and later Billy – he wasn't used to being well treated. Most people didn't intentionally try to mistreat him, of course, but, especially after he was crippled, they did even worse; they ignored him.

"They didn't have to do that."

"No, they didn't," Frank told him, crunching a mouthful of the poultry's crisp brown coating even as he poured them each a glass of iced tea from the frosty pitcher on the table, "but they wanted to; they thought you deserved it." He paused. "For that matter, so do I."

"Tell them thanks." He paused. "Why aren't they joining us?"

"Because they don't have a need to know the details of what we're discussing."

There was a lot wrapped up in that one sentence. Not only did it exemplify a basic security paradigm that all too many of the Confederate Army Provisional's own officers couldn't seem to grasp, but Frank remembered what his wife had told him sometime after her rescue.

'I never want to know any more than I need to again, Frank. You can't imagine what it's like when they have you so close to the

66

breaking point that you're ready to betray the ones you're loyal to, and...even the ones you love. That was the real torture; I'd rather suffer for having nothing to give them than risk that again.'

"But what about Sam? He's South Carolina's Councilman."

"He eating in the other room with them. He doesn't need to know either; besides, it's too big of a risk. He's going to be traveling some, and that always potentially dangerous. We can't take the chance of this falling into enemy hands if, God forbid, something should happen to him.

"Anyway," he went on, after shaking the persistently intruding black thoughts out of his head, "I'll let everyone know what they need to in order to hold up their end of the job. That's all I intend to give to anybody involved: only their part of it. There's too much at stake; other than Edge, you and me, *no one* is to know more than he has to."

Mike paused in his chewing. "What are you up to, Frank?"

"That idea you and Sammie came up with, the one based on the Liddy article? I've taken it to Edge, and it's a go. We move in early February."

Mike almost spit out a mouthful of mashed potatoes onto the table in surprise. He choked, and it was several seconds before he could speak again.

"February? Damn it, that's only...*four months away!* That's *impossible!*"

Frank was unperturbed by his outburst. "Then make it possible; we have to hit them when it'll hurt the most. If we do that, we'll have them on the ropes."

"Yeah, but..." The meal forgotten, the intelligence officer began absently tapping his plate with his fork as he ran the calculations in his mind, trying to put them in some sort of logical order. "If we pick the best targets only, the weakest points of the critical infrastructure, the choke points...we're still going to need a butt-load of men!"

"Each state will contribute units to this project, with the numbers from each one not enough to adversely affect what's going on within their borders. The rest of the war can't be put on hold while we do this." He paused, thinking carefully, particularly about what Jim

Boggess had told him earlier that morning. "Although there are some projects that might be best held off on so they can take advantage of it.

"Right now – as soon as you get back to Columbia, I mean – I need you to use your resources and start the preliminary selection of the targets. You know the goal – total disruption of their infrastructure – and we want to be sure we hit the key points that will do the most towards accomplishing that.

"First, have you got your preliminary cyber-strike ready to go?"

"Pretty much; I can have it in its final form within a week." Mike didn't bother adding that the week in question would no doubt be a hundred hours or more of hard work, because that didn't matter. All that mattered was that it had to be done, and he was the only one who could do it.

"Do it then; get on it first thing when you get back.

"During the strike itself, once you've gotten them sufficiently stirred up, the first priority is power. It's vital that we drop the entire grid, and keep it down for an extended period of time."

"I can have those targets for you within a couple of hours, probably. I've already analyzed the grid for potential weak points."

"I figured as much," Frank said, pointing at him with the half-eaten drumstick. "If you ever feel like you're taken for granted, that's because you are; I don't have to worry about you. You know your job, and you're damned good at it."

Mike smiled at the compliment. It was true, of course, but it was still nice to hear someone say so anyway, especially someone he respected.

"I take it you know where the gas lines are too? I don't want any natural gas getting through for a long, long time."

The intelligence officer had another mouthful of food, so he just chewed and nodded affirmatively.

"Rails?"

Nod.

"Ports?"

Nod.

"Air traffic?"

68

Mike set his fork down and paused, wondering exactly how to phrase the question he wanted to ask. Finally, he decided just to lay his concerns on the table.

"Yes, and that's something that's been bothering me. Do you intend to start bringing down civilian airliners?"

Frank shook his head. "No, at least not loaded ones. We could do it, of course; we have the SAM's after all, but I don't want to intentionally kill a bunch of innocent civilians unless I have no other choice. Enough of them are going to die as a result of this operation without targeting them directly."

From the changed tone of Frank's voice, Mike could guess that this had been a sticking point between him and Edge. He knew both men well enough now to know that Edge would do it a hundred times over and never flinch at it, while Frank...He looked in the other man's eyes and came to a realization.

Frank would do it too, but only if absolutely necessary, as a last resort, not simply as the most efficient way to accomplish that part of the mission.

"So, what do you propose?"

"We attack a few of the airports themselves, with mortars or rockets, and ambush a military craft or two with the SAM's when they're leaving a civilian airport. Of course, any craft carrying military personnel or equipment, or Washington officials is a legitimate target of opportunity. That should do it, I would think."

"It should," Mike said with a nod, before reluctantly adding, "although you might want to keep the other option open."

"I am." Frank's voice was grim. "It's got to be shut down, one way or the other, but I want to try the means with less collateral damage first. Besides, from a purely practical point of view, we have a finite supply of those missiles.

"How's the reverse-engineering going on those, by the way?"

"Alright so far; I've got a couple of engineers in Texas and up in the Piedmont Triad working on it. I think – *tentatively* – that we might be able to test our own in about six months or so."

"Good; keep me posted. Back to the mission itself, then; what kind of resources do you need?"

Mike thought about it for a few minutes, and Frank continued eating in silence, enjoying the all-too-rare treat of good food and plenty of it while giving the Intelligence Officer time to consider.

"I need scouts. I need a few people on the ground to evaluate these targets and their possibilities and report back."

"Makes sense. Whenever possible, I think these scouts should also be part of the teams going up to do the job."

"Agreed, although fit men of military age might attract attention."

Frank grinned. "What makes you think I'm going to send only fit young men? Think about the way we did Operation Long Knives; the less-fit went on the support teams, lookouts, backup, and the like. These people are perfect scouts because, like you told me once, folks tend not to pay attention to people in wheelchairs; in fact, you make them uncomfortable, and they want to look away. The disabled or teenagers or the elderly or the homeless, can go places without raising eyebrows that would set off alarms if anyone else tried it. Besides, sometimes they're the most anxious to do it."

"I know what you mean," Mike told him sincerely. It bothered him quite a bit that he was out of the action, and was spending the war running computers and intelligence. Even though he knew on an intellectual level that Frank was right when he had told him – more than once – that he was technically the most valuable member of the revolution, on a more basic level, he felt like he was shirking by not getting his hands dirty. He knew he'd jump at the chance to do something like this, but he also knew better than to ask.

"I do have another possibility for expanding the attack, but it's internationally-based."

Frank looked at him curiously. "What do you mean?"

"There is a small group of fugitive hackers in Europe that include some of the best in the world: two Brits, a Frenchman, and a couple of Russians. They're living legends in the hacker community. They've been wanted by Interpol since they managed to take temporary control of both a military and a civilian communications satellite a few years ago. They're on the run, and if they were approached right..."

Mike's voice trailed off at Frank's expression; the General's face was lit up with pure excitement.

"Approach them. You have my authorization to offer them commissions in the CAP Intelligence Department under your command, as well as full citizenship following the war, provided they can perform what we need them to do during this mission. What do they need to get here?"

"Air travel is pretty much out of the question, considering who they are; they'll need a boat I suppose."

An idea popped into Frank's head. "Get Davy Jones in the Florida theater."

Mike grinned.

"The crazy Hawaiian shirt guy?"

"That's him, down in the Keys. He owns a big trimaran he uses for charters when he's not running guns for us, and as of now, he and his boat are part of the Confederate Navy. Set it up, please, and then notify me."

Mike's smile grew. He would enjoy this part, not only because he would get to work with some hackers he greatly admired on a professional level, but because he knew how much Davy Jones, the unlikely combination of Confederate and 'Parrothead,' would love the assignment. His concentration was broken when Frank added something to it.

"Oh, and tell Davy he'll have an outbound passenger as well."

"Who?"

Frank grinned. "Jonathon Edge."

Mike's jaw dropped.

"What? Why?"

"Need to know, Mike," Frank chided. "Need to know."

Mike laughed out loud before grabbing another piece of chicken.

They finished their meal and made plans for several hours afterwards; then Frank pushed back his chair.

"I hate to do this to you, but you're going to have to get back to Columbia soon."

"I know," Mike replied with a sad nod, thinking about Kerrie. He was hoping to spend more time with her, but he had too much work to come up here often, and she was wanted, so she couldn't go to him.

"For now, though, I think I'd better keep you here until morning; the roads aren't safe at night, and I may need you for something." He winked, showing Mike what he already knew; that this was merely Frank's excuse to let him be with Kerrie. "Go spend a little time with her. She's known, so I can't send you all out to dinner, but I'm having a nice meal for two brought in this evening from the best restaurant around here, such as it is, I mean." He looked around at the inside of the barn that was their headquarters. "I'm afraid I can't do much about the surroundings, but maybe some wine and candlelight in her quarters will give it that ambiance."

Mike's eyes widened at the thought of a fancy dinner with Kerrie, and how much she would enjoy it, and how much they'd both enjoy each other afterwards.

"Damn, Frank...thanks. I don't know what to say..."

"You just said all that was necessary. I told you once to treat her right, and you've more than held up your end of the bargain. I've never seen anybody as head-over-heels in love as she is with you."

"Yeah, you have; you're looking at him right now."

Frank clapped him on the shoulder.

"I know that, partner."

When Frank told Mike he had ordered supper for him and Kerrie, it was only a half-truth; he had ordered one for himself and Samantha as well. He had put on his sport coat and a borrowed tie, and Samantha was wearing the best dress she could find that would fit as they sat together in their quarters, having ginger ale with chicken Alfredo. Due to her pregnancy, wine was out of the question, so they settled for putting the sparkling soda in the stemmed glasses instead.

"The candlelight brings out your eyes," he said, looking at her across the flickering tapers.

"I think it brings out your silver tongue," she replied with a smile before leaning her elbows on the table and propping her chin on the palms of her hands, "but please; tell me more. Like I said this morning, 'flattery will get you everywhere.'"

"What else can I say? You're beautiful and I love you."

"I'm fat and I don't know why you love me, but I love you too."

"You're not fat!" he protested. "You're pregnant, and, to be honest, it suits you. You've just got this – "

"So help me, if you say I've got this 'glow' about me, you're liable to wear this chicken Alfredo."

He chuckled. "You must be psychic."

"No, I just know you pretty well. You don't want to make me waste good food."

"If you don't want to waste it, you'd better eat it then."

She looked at him mischievously. "Are you hinting that you have something else planned for me?"

"Could be..." His voice trailed off into a lecherous wink. "Actually, I've got a couple of things in mind."

"Mmm. If that's the case, I think I'm full anyway." She paused to empty her glass. "What exactly *do* you have in mind?"

As if I didn't know!

"Well, aside from the obvious, I realized that there's one thing we haven't done...yet."

For the life of her, Samantha couldn't think of what that might be, so she was surprised when Frank stood, crossed the room to her CD player, and slipped in a disk. As the melodious strains of a waltz began coming from the speakers, he turned back to her and extended his hand.

"May I have this dance?"

Taking it, she felt the warmth of his palm as she rose to her feet.

"For the rest of my life," She told him, her blue eyes glittering in the candlelight.

DAY 214

CHAPTER 6

"I'm going to miss you."

Mike looked at Kerrie lying beside him and snuggled tightly in his arms, and nodded his agreement.

"I'll miss you too. I'll try to get back up here as soon as I can."

"I know, but it's just so hard. Everyone here is nice, but you're the only one who really understands."

He nodded his agreement. "I could say the same thing about you."

They did understand something of one another's plight, at least enough to feel secure enough to undress in front of each other, with his atrophied lower body and the scars that striped her back from her thighs to her shoulder blades. Both of them had been victims of violence, and both felt like freaks because of the traumatic results. The same attack that broke his back and paralyzed his legs had left his sexual functions less than predictable, seeming to have a mind of their own, but they made the most of it. Even though Kerrie was fully functional physically, it had taken her a long time to get over the fear and disgust over the abuse from her parents, and over the things she had had to do to survive on the streets of Columbia, but with his help, she had. Even though their times together were far fewer now than when she had been at CAP's Columbia headquarters, they remained unselfconscious with each other, probably because they were so deeply in love. Modern logic might have insisted that a relationship between a traumatized girl barely eighteen and a crippled man of thirty was doomed to failure from the start, but theirs showed no signs of fading, despite their age differences and long separations; if anything, it grew stronger by the day.

"I've got another few minutes before I have to leave," he told her.

"Good," she said, and kissed him deeply. He returned it, running his hands over her pale skin, doing his best to absorb and retain the feel, the smell and the taste of her to sustain him until he could see her again.

"We're getting ready to head back, Frank," Mike paused at his commander's desk. "Is there anything else you need before I take off?"

Pushing himself away from his keyboard, Frank turned his swivel chair to face him.

"Just this; I want those hackers. More, we *need* them. I've been thinking..."

Mike grinned. "Is this the part where I say uh-oh?"

"Maybe, because it's the part where I make a lot more work for you. I want you to recruit every good hacker, cracker and cyber-geek you can – covertly, of course. I'm going to sweeten the offer a bit. You're a geek; you all live for this computer stuff, don't you?"

Mike told him he couldn't deny that, in good conscience. He was somewhat surprised at the direction the General was heading in, but knew he shouldn't have been; Frank had a habit of taking the germ of an idea and growing it into something much bigger.

If I handed him a bolt, he wouldn't see a simple fastener; he'd see the machine he could build with it!

"Alright, here's the deal. *Anyone* who signs on and actively assists us in cyber-war *now*, during the Revolution, will have a full-time job doing what they love once we win."

"You have the authority to guarantee that already?"

Frank nodded.

"Assuming we all live through this, Edge has told me he's determined to make me the Secretary of Defense for the renewed Confederacy."

"I don't think they'd find a better man for the job. The truth is, I think you'd make an even better President."

Frank shook his head emphatically even as he held out both hands as if to physically push the suggestion away.

"No! Having to take the Secretary's job is bad enough; I don't even want that one. Still, it looks like I'll be in charge of that end of things, and in this day and age, we'll need a powerful cyber-war department if we're to survive, let alone prosper. This is the 21st Century, and the Confederacy is going to have a 21st Century war machine, designed for modern defensive realities, starting from day one. Anyone who comes on board now will have a guaranteed spot there...under *you*. You'll be maintaining your position as Chief of Intelligence for national government, just as you have for the CAP."

Mike's eyes widened along with his mouth, and it took him a minute to recover his voice.

"What? Don't I get a say in this thing?"

"Sure; if there's someone you don't like, you don't have to hire or keep them."

"That's not what I'm talking about and you know it! I don't want to be in charge anymore, once this is over! Don't I have a choice?"

Frank cocked his eyebrow at him.

"Did I?"

Despite Frank's grin, the finality of his tone plainly supplied the answer to his own rhetorical question, and all Mike could think of to do was to swear futilely, but with great feeling.

DAY 225

CHAPTER 7

Edge had forgotten how noisy mangrove swamps could be at night, and just how pleasant that noise really was, or would be if not for the damned mosquitoes that seemed bound and determined to suck him dry. Still, despite their vampiric attentions that the repellant only moderated to the slightest degree, he had to admit that he was enjoying himself immensely. The canoe paddles rhythmically dipping their blades in the salty water, with the insects singing in the background, was a soothing mantra in the deep, womb-like darkness among the trees.

He and the two men from CAP's Florida forces had been winding their way through the twisting labyrinth of brackish channels for hours, sticking to the almost impenetrable forest of oyster-encrusted prop roots rather than risk being spotted in the open water of Florida Bay. Since there was a hundred million dollars riding on Edge's head, discretion was definitely the better part of valor. The two swamp rats guiding him felt much the same, and fortunately, the pair of fulltime fishing guides, sometime poachers, and occasional smugglers knew the maze of backwaters like the backs of their hands. Added to their advantage were the night vision goggles they wore. Just in case of problems, two M4s, an AK47, and half a dozen fragmentation and incendiary grenades lay ready in the bottom of the boat.

Edge, although he didn't have one of the two available pairs of starlight goggles (wisely preferring to reserve their use to the men who were actually steering their craft), did have his own armament, consisting of two Para Ordnance .45s: a P13 in a shoulder holster, and a compact P10 in a belly band that concealed the second pistol's outline under his shirt. Unfortunately, no matter how he adjusted it, it always seemed to be in exactly the right place to rub a raw spot as his body twisted back and forth while paddling, but the former SEAL had learned to ignore such petty concerns long, long ago.

As they rounded another bend, what looked like a giant, deep blue-on-black gash appeared in front of them, marking the end of the swamp and the beginning of the sea.

"Stop," the man behind him whispered, and Edge immediately complied, leaving his paddle in the water rather than lifting it out, which would result in the falling droplets making the tell-tale dripping that could be heard a surprisingly long way. The bowman did the same.

The one in the stern continued stroking, but slowly and gently, twisting his paddle in a light J stroke that barely moved the canoe any faster than the ebbing tide. The man in front stowed his own paddle and used his hands to push them away from any prop roots that came too near, and finally, before they could break into open water, he grabbed one and brought them to a halt. Raising his free hand, he gestured towards his ear.

His buddy pulled a parabolic microphone from the floor of the canoe, inserted his earpiece, and pointed it ahead. After a moment, he laid one hand on Edge's shoulder and whispered again.

"Coast Guard."

Edge's hand instinctively reached for his pistol, but the guerrilla stalled him.

"No," came the whisper again, "it's planned."

Edge cocked his eyebrow, but the man just said, "Shh," then, "Here."

Edge felt the earpiece being pressed into his hand, so he slipped it on, and instantly heard voices.

"Hey! How're you all doing?"

"Sir, what are you doing here?"

"Well, to be honest, I'm anchored, relaxing with ol' Captain Morgan and hoping to catch a snapper or two for my supper."

"Please put out fenders to port. We're going to board your boat for inspection."

"Sure thing, man; just a second."

There was a pair of dull thumps as the rubber fenders went over, followed by a squeak when they were rubbed between the two hulls as they were secured together.

"Do you have any weapons on board?"

"Yeah, there's a shotgun in the cockpit locker, but I've got a permit for it. It's with my license and log book."

"I'll need to see them, please."

"Sure; right this way.

There were several minutes of muffled conversation, apparently from inside the boat's cabin, along with footsteps and the sound of objects being moved.

"Well, Mr. Jones, it looks like your boat's clean."

The return voice sounded slightly frustrated.

"Told ya, man, I'm just doing a little fishing and enjoying the myself."

"We're sorry to bother you, but these waters are a hotbed for smugglers, some of them guerrillas."

Edge heard the man behind him stifling a snicker.

"Tell me about it!" the voice came through the earpiece again. "I can't get any peace for those bastards. I'm always afraid one of 'em will shoot me for my boat."

"That has happened, I'm sorry to say. That's why it's dangerous for you to be out here alone."

"That's why I got the permit for the shotgun. Don't worry; I'll be out of here first thing in the morning. I'm picking up a charter and heading to the Bahamas. To be honest, I'll be glad to get away from all this crazy shit for a while."

"I can't say that I blame you for that, sir." There was a brief laugh. "I swear I'd go with you if I could."

"Hell, maybe you can sometime. Here's my card, man. I'm headquartered in Largo; when you two are off duty, come on down and look me up. We'll go do some fishing, sailing, whatever you want; I'll give you a twenty percent law enforcement discount."

"You know, I might just take you up on that. Well, you have a good evening, sir."

Edge heard more squeaking as a boat fenders rubbed again.

"I plan to. You all be safe now, you hear? I might need you to come and save my ass if I get into trouble."

"We'll be there."

Edge heard a loud, thumping roar as a pair of huge engines fired up, and a moment later, a black, shark-like shape shot across their narrow view of the ocean and out of sight again with astonishing speed, leaving a visible V of white foam behind. The engine noise faded rapidly into the distance, and all that was left was the gentle slapping of the boat's wake against the roots.

"That was the local Coast Guard's new boat," the stern man said in a slightly louder, more relaxed voice, taking back his earpiece. "The damned thing's a thirty-six foot cigarette boat with a Kevlar hull, dual 454 motors in the back, a 20mm automatic cannon on the front, and a pintle-mounted fifty caliber machinegun amidships. That son of a bitch will top out at better than sixty five knots; I ain't never seen the like. Trust me; you don't want them after you."

Edge thoughtfully filed the information away in his mind, and asked, "What did you mean when you said, it was planned?"

"We had to wait for the Coasties to come and go. They check most of the boats down here these days anyway, so whenever we need to do something, we call and report the boat as suspicious ourselves, before we start. They come over and check it out, and then we do whatever after they've seen it's clean and left. The boat's description and number are logged, and if they don't feel suspicious, the rest of 'em will see it and not stop us again, at least for a few days. Come on; they're out of sight now, so let's get to paddling."

As they put their paddles in the water once more and slipped out of the estuarine forest, the sea opened before them. It was a clear night, and the pinpricks of millions of stars were reflected as wavering light on the water, matched by tiny spots of phosphorescent plankton swirling in their wake. There was no swell tonight, just the gentle lapping of the waves against their hull. A long white object plain against the darkness rode on the quiet sea about three hundred yards ahead of them, a single light gleaming from its cockpit, and the canoe turned towards it. As they drew closer, they heard someone clear his throat.

Instantly the bowman cleared his own three times.

"Ahoy!" the voice from the boat called.

"Ahoy your own self, hippie!" the bowman called back.

As they drew nearer, Edge could make out a pair of upright masts – a ketch rig – on the deck of a white, forty-foot trimaran, it's three hulls seeming to drift like a leaf on the water. Closer still, he saw Davy Jones standing in the cockpit, revealed by its light, and his heart sank.

Davy Jones was a local character in the Keys. He looked a lot like the singer, Jimmy Buffet, and had been mistaken for him more than once, even though he was generally more unkept than the much more famous Floridian. He always wore bright Hawaiian shirts above the waist and shorts, usually cutoffs, below, and unless he was going ashore, he seldom bothered with shoes. The shaggy, sun-bleached blonde hair framing his weathered forty-something face completed the picture. Right now he was grinning, showing a glint from a gold tooth that matched that from his earrings.

Standing on one of the carbon fiber/S-glass composite outriggers, he extended a hand.

"Welcome aboard the *Green Eyed Lady!*"

"Thanks," Edge responded, taking the assistance while stepping from the canoe to the boat. Turning back, he accepted the duffel bag that contained his belongings from the men in the canoe, who promptly pushed off.

"See ya, Davy!" they chorused, and began paddling back towards the mangroves, leaving Edge behind.

Meanwhile, after they crossed to the main hull, Davy stopped and looked Jonathon Edge over.

"You know anything about boats?"

Edge stiffened. "I was a Lieutenant Commander in SEALs."

"Don't worry," Davy said, shrugging, "I won't hold that against you. I suppose you'll at least know port from starboard."

The Field Marshal glared at him, and Davy laughed, expelling a cloud of rum-scented breath, before slapping him on the shoulder. "Hey, man, lighten up!" He retrieved a bottle of *Captain Morgan Tattoo*, the spiced rum so dark it looked like cola, and took a big slug himself before extending it to Edge. "Drink up; hell, we won't be sailing for another few hours yet."

So saying, Davy propped one foot up on the cockpit seat, assuming the exact posture of the iconic picture of the buccaneer captain on the bottle and gave his best piratical "Arrrh!"

Edge took the bottle, wiped off the neck, and took a long swallow. He had the feeling he was going to need it.

DAY 250

CHAPTER 8

"Ladies and gentlemen, I know you've been wondering why I called you here."

Frank knew he needn't have said that; the curiosity in the eyes of the ten men and two women gathered behind the locked door of the Myrtle Beach nightclub's offices were plain to see. Outside those doors, in the main bar area, the place operated as a drinking establishment cum dance club catering to beach music aficionados; even now, the mellow tones of the classic *Drifters* recording, *Under the Boardwalk* drifted through the walls, and customers danced on, blithely unaware that the future of the War was being decided only a few feet away. The club was managed by one of CAP's sympathizers, and it occasionally served the Confederate Army Provisional cell as a meeting place...like tonight, and for the past several nights.

The Grand Strand Confederate Militia, as they called themselves, were low key, having stayed that way on Frank's direct orders. They had provided backup and reinforcements for other South Carolina units, and committed a handful of assassinations and kidnappings of Dixie's enemies, but had done so quietly, carefully, and out of the immediate area. Frank wanted nothing to disrupt the tourist trade in this particular spot, or to attract undue Federal attention. The crowds, although reduced by half or more, still thronged the streets despite the depression, giving the perfect cover for moving people and weapons in and out. The nearby Atlantic and its maze of coastal salt marshes meant that CAP had a lot of traffic coming and going through there.

Even in the environment of the club that reeked of stale smoke, spilled booze, and over-used cologne and cheap perfume, Frank's sensitive nose could still pick up the salty tang of the Atlantic only a few hundred yards away, and even though he knew it was his

85

imagination, he could swear he heard the faint eternal throbbing of the breakers rolling on the sand.

He couldn't help but sigh, just thinking about it. He loved the ocean; he always had, and before the war had made the trip from Columbia every weekend he could get free. In fact, the beach had been his regular stomping grounds since he first got his driver's license, so much so that he could surf, shuck oysters, and dance the shag with the best of them. He had a reoccurring fantasy of being here with Sammie, swimming in the ocean and lying in the sun all day, and dancing and clubbing all night, without a care in the world beyond keeping the sand out of his shorts and being sure to put on sunscreen. No guns, no bombs, no multi-million dollar rewards on his life; just peace and a family with the woman he loved more than life itself.

Setting his lips, he pushed the waking dream away. If that was the world he wanted, he was going to have to make it happen. From behind the manager's desk, he surveyed the crowded room, and the people who sat facing him.

This was the Arkansas contingent; over the past week in this same spot, he had already briefed equal-sized groups from Texas, Arizona, Kentucky, West Virginia, and both North and South Carolina, and he still had Virginia, New Mexico, Alabama, Georgia, Mississippi, and Missouri to go. Even though the briefings were virtually the same, with only the difference in targets, each one had to be given separately for the sake of security. Each team was to know only about its own mission, and not that there was any other project even being considered. That way, if they were captured, the most the enemy could torture out of them was what they themselves were up to; the others could go ahead as planned.

Through sheer force of will, Frank managed to keep the worry off his face as he looked at them, but it wasn't easy. These were not only living, breathing human beings, but they were Southerners: his people, not just comrades, but, in a nationalistic sense, blood relatives. As their commander, he was responsible for them. He knew very well that, in all likelihood, he was sending at least some of them to their deaths; the probability that each and every team would achieve their goals and return alive and safe was remote. All he could do was to give them the best chance of success he could.

"I hope you said goodbye to your families, because as of now, you are out of communication until your mission is over." He noticed several of them looking sad at that, but that was expected; he knew how they felt. "That's a direct order, and it's as crucial for your own safety and that of your families as it is for the success of your mission. You are going to be operating in the North, hundreds of miles behind enemy lines, right on his home turf. Once you're in the field, the *only* contact you will have is with your controller, who will call you with instructions as necessary. You will not contact him, *unless* it's an emergency, as in you are under attack or you have been compromised.

"From now on, secrecy is your watchword, because neither you nor your controller nor your mission will survive if you are found out. To be brutally honest, if you are in danger of being captured, it might be better if you don't survive."

Several heads nodded in solemn agreement; they knew the score, or at least thought they did. He doubted that anyone who hadn't seen it firsthand was capable of grasping the brutal reality of it.

"Because of that, you must blend in. As a Southerner, you will be immediately suspect; therefore, we're going to make you seem like something else. You'll be undergoing two weeks of intensive classes designed to 'scrub' your accents, and teach you the mannerisms and manners – or lack thereof – that will let you operate undetected in your assigned area of the North."

There was a rumbling of discontent, and one tall, thin man raised his hand, and then stood when Frank gestured at him.

"Sir, with all due respect...I don't want to lose my accent! I don't want to sound like one of those people."

"You're not going to lose your Southern drawl; you won't be up there that long, and I give you my word that, if need be, I'll send you through some 'de-programming' when you get back in order to get it back to normal. This is a temporary sacrifice you're going to have to make for your country."

The man sat back down again, looking far from convinced and more than a little dissatisfied, and Frank decided he couldn't really blame him.

"You'll be given a target, including all the information we have about it. You will study it and learn it upside-down and inside out, because, for security reasons, you will not be carrying anything outside your own memory with you. You will infiltrate the area, rent rooms, and begin covertly scouting, learning everything about your assigned objective you can; part of your classes will deal with this. You'll be supplied with identities, cover stories, and money. You'll take no contraband, nothing illegal, and *absolutely* no arms with you; those will be smuggled into you later, by your contact, along with whatever explosives or other supplies you need to do the job.

"Please understand that what you are doing is vital to the war effort, even though you won't understand why at the time; rest assured, everything will be made very clear later.

"I hope and pray to see everyone of you at the debriefing when you get back."

He snapped to attention and saluted them, and they instantly rose to their feet and returned the gesture.

"God save the South!"

DAY 263

CHAPTER 9

Edge stood in the cockpit as they passed through the Straits of Gibraltar, watching the iconic rock going by to port, marking their entrance into the Mediterranean. The sea looked different here, and even smelled different, carrying with it the scent of history and the exotic. As he watched other craft passing – freighters and fishermen, tugs and yachts, he reflected that he had enjoyed the past weeks on the *Green Eyed Lady* more than any period in his life since the tragic deaths of his wife and son so many years ago.

Sailing aboard the *Lady* was nothing like being on a naval ship; duties weren't scheduled and regimented, but simply obvious. With two of them on board, when one wasn't on watch, the other was. When a sheet frayed or a sail tore, you repaired it; when there was a gale blowing, you worked the boat until it blew itself out. When you were hungry, you ate, and when nothing else was going on, you sat there and enjoyed it. With a fast, strong, well-designed trimaran as a boat and Davy Jones as her captain, the latter was usually the case.

Edge had developed a strong respect for the eccentric Key West 'Conch.' Davy knew what he was doing, and loved every minute of it. Even though his personal weirdness and outgoing *bonhomie* was unnerving to the staid, tight-lipped former SEAL at first, it grew on him as he relaxed...maybe *because* he relaxed. After all, for the first time in months, the war had been pushed to the back of his mind by necessity. He was out of communication, other than what news they could pick up on the short wave, and he had learned long ago that it didn't help to think too much about something he couldn't affect. Once or twice, he surprised himself by realizing that he hadn't thought about the conflict for hours, something utterly unprecedented.

He knew he could thank Frank for that, as much as Davy. This trip needed to be made, and, in fact, was long overdue, but had been impossible up until this point. To put it simply, he couldn't trust anyone else to attempt what he was about to try, and there'd been no one trustworthy enough to leave behind in charge during his absence. His friend, Councilman Sam Wirtz, was too soft-hearted, as was the Council head, Russell Nash. Even though he had buried the hatchet with his old rival, Councilman Andrew MacFie, Edge still didn't trust him as far as he could throw him. Jack Boggess, the West Virginia Councilman, was solid but not nearly experienced enough; besides which, the YABOMB faction in the deep South wouldn't cooperate with him since he was not only from the upper South, but even worse, being from *West* Virginia, he wasn't a *real* Southerner in their books. As for the rest of the Council, he knew them to have all the faults of the others, often as not rolled into one. Now, though, he had Frank. For the first time, he could delegate something to someone he could trust to do it, and not stab him in the back in the process. Getting a break in the action without having to worry unduly was a novel feeling to the paranoid Field Marshal.

Of course, it wasn't like he was loafing, either. What Edge had set out to do was just as important as what Frank was doing back in Dixie, and, in the long run, maybe even more so. Certainly it was *at least* as risky, but if this worked out...

And if it doesn't work out, I'll die, just as surely as I would if I messed up back home. I'm taking the same risks...so why do I feel a little guilty about it?

Eying the gleaming white gulls soar high above while the wind blew through his gray hair and the deck rocked under his feet, he smiled broadly, showing his teeth.

Probably because I'm enjoying this trip so damned much!

Watching him from the helm without appearing to, Davy grinned at the pleasant expression on Edge's face...from what he could see through the Field Marshal's beard, anyway. The CAP leader had grown it on the trip to make himself harder to recognize, and the *Lady's* captain had to admit the idea had worked. Tanned by sun and wind and spray, with the bush of silvery bristle covering his face, Edge had taken on a striking similarity to the cartoon Popeye's sire, Poop-deck Pappy. He knew Edge never noticed the fancied resemblance, and even though Davy found it privately hilarious, he decided not to point it out.

I don't want him to get all tight-assed again.

Of course, even before he had met him, he knew from what he had heard that the Confederate leader was 'tight-assed' by nature, and he had no doubt that Edge would revert back to it once he got his feet back on land. Still, for now at least, the voyage had mellowed him considerably until he was reasonably pleasant to be around. Of course, vacations – even working ones like this – tended to do that to most people.

Edge worked, no question about that; he pulled his weight. He knew little about the actual mechanics of sailing, but he learned quickly, and when Davy gave an order, Edge obeyed it instantly, asking why after completing the task if he wanted to know. His strength and endurance were surprising for a man his age; despite Davy's being twenty years younger than the CAP chief, he knew Edge was a good deal fitter than he was. More important still was his passenger's careful, calculating nature; it wasn't long before the Captain clearly understood why this guy was their leader. Through the relaxing rhythm of the sea, the camaraderie engendered by two lone men living in close quarters and pulling together, and the bottles of Captain Morgan rum and Jamaican Red Stripe beer, Davy had gradually drawn him out – or Edge had opened up a bit, whichever – and he had heard some of the Field Marshal's vision for their country. The vision was grand, but Edge had stressed that it wouldn't be easy to achieve. They had a century and a half of brainwashing, corruption and inertia standing in their way, and Edge was determined to root it out.

It was that last part that worried Davy Jones – not getting rid of the past, for that was a necessity, but the process it would entail. It would be hard, and there would be bloodshed, without question. Davy also realized that this was the only man he had met in the movement that made him confident that he could pull it off.

That was the only reason Edge was still alive.

A lot of people in Davy's State of Florida didn't like Jonathon Edge. They didn't like his command style, they didn't like his personality, and they really didn't like it that he had apparently executed an influential movement politician from Jacksonville. Herbert Saunders, one of the leaders of the YABOM faction, had been covertly urging the Sunshine State's forces to refuse to recognize the Field Marshal's authority, or that of the Confederate Council. Three days after defiantly refusing a warning to cease and desist immediately and get with the program, his body was found attracting flies in the thick underbrush of an abandoned tangerine grove, with a bullet hole in the back of his head big enough to put a thumb into. No one knew exactly who pulled the trigger, but the object lesson was abundantly clear. Most of the people in the leadership of CAP's Florida Theater forces who suspected the ultimate source of the fatal bullet, including their Councilman, shrugged, said something to the tune of, "That's what you get," and went on about their business of trying to secure Southern independence for themselves and the rest of the Confederacy; they figured they could sort out whatever needed sorting after they won. For a minority, however, the death didn't go over well at all. Even though Davy told them nothing of his mission (He had ran guns and the occasional load of weed enough times to know the value of tight lips.), they were informed that he was going to be attached to the CAP Central Command for an extended period. The word was passed to him by a particularly important man within that faction that, if the opportunity ever arose, it would be advantageous, both monetarily and for his rank in that state's forces, for the *Lady's* captain to rid them of the source of their irritation, and gave him a long list of reasons why.

Davy Jones had merely nodded, noncommittally. The smuggler hadn't stayed alive and free this long by accepting anyone's word on anything, or by taking things at face value. He would wait and see.

Of course, he automatically discounted nothing either. Davy had heard quite a bit about Edge, both before that meeting and during it, and was glad for the chance to see for himself. He knew a lot of people in the CAP thought the Field Marshal was a dictator, an autocratic menace, and from what he had heard, he tended to agree. Still, the Floridian had also met General Gore, the one who started

92

this whole thing, and was more than a little impressed with him. He knew Frank was not only content to follow Edge, but was one of his strongest supporters, so Davy thought he owed him a chance. Once he got to know the man...

Granted, he grates on you sometimes, but he definitely knows what he's doing.

Once he had gotten Edge's measure, and was satisfied with Frank Gore's assessment, he decided not to blow the Field Marshal's brains out while he slept: an idea he had been considering, and would have carried out if he had thought it would've been best for the movement.

What really changed his mind was a conversation they had, only a few days out. It was sunset, and the sailing was easy enough that they had been drinking a little, just enough to relax in the hot Caribbean sun. Still, it was Davy's watch, so maybe Edge had been drinking a little more. They were running almost directly before the wind in a fresh breeze of eighteen knots, rounding the Dry Tortugas, when he noticed Edge, a rum bottle dangling from one hand, standing and staring hard into the distance. Following the line of his gaze, Davy could make out the silhouette of Fort Jefferson against the sky.

Davy remembered frowning in consternation when he saw Edge's expression, particularly when he saw that the older man's eyes seemed to be glistening.

"That's wild looking, ain't it?" Davy had offered, not knowing exactly what else to say.

"Jefferson: the same first name as President Davis," Edge replied, not seeming to have heard him. "Since he was the Secretary of War before that, I guess you could say he was responsible for the place for a period of time."

"Secretary of War for the US? Really? I didn't know that."

"Do you have any idea how much that man suffered for his country?"

"A lot, I know..."

Edge didn't let him finish. "He suffered more than any soldier on the battlefield. You know why?"

Davy had simply shaken his head, interested in drawing the man out to find out where his head was at.

"He suffered more because he was the one who had to send them." Edge's voice was deadpan, and he never once looked at the *Lady's* captain while he spoke. Davy wasn't even sure if he was actually speaking to him, so much as talking to himself, or to the ghosts only he could see. "For the good of his country, he sent over two and half million men to their deaths. That they went willingly was beside the point; he was their commander and chief, and he bore the ultimate responsibility. My God, they must have hung around his neck like millstones! The weight of that would have been heavier than any of the shackles the Yankees put on him. If the Cause had been won, that would have been bad enough, but to have sacrificed them only to see it fall...He saw them all at night, every last one of them. They haunted his dreams; when I looked at his picture, I could see it in his eyes! I *know! Damn it!*"

Davy watched Edge viciously fling the nearly empty bottle far out into the sea. Then, straightening to attention, he turned and walked to the cabin, and went below without another word.

Neither man mentioned the incident again, and Edge never drank quite as much as he had that day. That was the only time during their voyage the Field Marshal's mask had cracked enough to show any weakness, but Davy gave up any thought of killing him then and there. Not only did he understand that Edge fully realized the price of leadership, but he also knew it wasn't President Davis he was talking about, but himself.

It was obvious that their leader was human after all, and did penance in his own soul, not only for the hundreds who had already died, but for the thousands – maybe millions – more who would die before this thing was over. Edge suffered, but he was determined not to suffer as Davis did, and Lee, for the lives sacrificed for a cause lost. General Lee had told Governor Stockdale after the war, *"If I had only known..."* Edge knew, and, perhaps as much for himself as for the Confederacy, he intended to win...he *had* to win.

Davy Jones didn't blame him for that.

DAY 284

CHAPTER 10

Frank sat at his desk, going through the regular daily routine, paradoxically chafing at his own inaction while at the same time thankful for the time spent with his wife.

Nothing too far out of the way was happening yet; in the South, the low-grade guerrilla war ground on its bloody way, seemingly going nowhere for either side. In the North, his people were fitting in well on the whole, becoming just another part of the local society until they were needed. There had been only one real problem there; one man of the Virginia contingent assigned to target an electrical substation in New Jersey had taken to drinking a little too much, and tended to shoot off his mouth much more than his comrades were comfortable with. They'd approached their area controller for instructions, and the controller passed the question up the chain of command, wanting to know if he should send him back, kill him, or what.

Rubbing his hand over his short beard, Frank sighed in frustration. Killing him would be the smart thing to do, the secure thing to do, and certainly what Edge would do, but it was the last thing he wanted to do. He knew these men and women missed their families, and he could imagine the kind of pressure they must be under. Hell, it was no wonder they drank a bit.

His first thought was to have the man sent home, but that presented problems in itself. Crossing into the occupied South entailed numerous checkpoints and questionings, and if the man was a security risk now, could he risk him arousing suspicions and possibly even being captured with the knowledge of the mission yet to come inside his head?

No. The enemy cannot be allowed to learn even a tiny part of what we're up to. The mission aside, I've also got the lives of the other eleven people in the contingent and their controller to think about.

From the information the controller had sent, it would be just as big a security risk to leave him where he was. According to message, his comrades had warned him several times, and one of them had actually knocked him out inside a bar when he was in the middle of saying something that would have definitely aroused suspicion if anyone had been listening. If the quick-thinking guerrilla hadn't been present, and had the presence of mind to take action, the whole thing could easily have been compromised.

Since his own comrades had been having enough of a problem to take it to their controller, Frank knew just how serious it must be, but he also knew the deleterious affect it would have on their morale if he was eliminated...if they knew. Oh, they'd know, even if he just disappeared, but if that happened, they could pretend not to.

I'm the one who can't pretend.

Setting his lips in a thin line, Frank typed a brief return message.

If you think it advisable, do it, but be subtle. ~ F

His finger hesitated just a moment over the SEND button. Once he pressed it and sent the email on its way, he knew exactly what would happen. He could see it in his mind's eye; the controller would call the man in alone, away from the others, probably under the excuse of sending him with a message back to the South. That's what his team would be told as well, and they'd believe it, even though they knew better, because it was easier that way. It was doubtful that the body would ever be found, and if it were, it would be put down just another unsolved murder in a country increasingly full of them.

One man dying versus eleven – twelve, including the controller – living, and the success of the mission: the answer was a no-brainer. That still didn't stop him from hating himself or thinking of just how cheap life had become when he mashed the button.

Leaning back in his chair, he stretched and rubbed his eyes before hearing the office door open and his wife's footsteps coming through it.

Sensing her husband's tension, Samantha came up behind him and put her hands on his shoulders, digging her fingers deeply into his muscles, forcing them to relax by the sheer effort of her will.

"Thanks."

"My pleasure," she told him before kissing him on the back of the head. She didn't know the specifics of what he had just done; she didn't have a need to know, and, frankly, she didn't want to know. She was aware of some of the grimmer things his job entailed, and, even though she felt selfish by doing so, she couldn't bring herself to try to share that particular burden, even assuming he would have let her. The most she could do was to try and make him feel better, and she did, every time she got the chance.

"I've got some good news for you."

"I could use some."

"I know, honey." Kissing him on the cheek this time, she moved around him and took the chair beside him before gesturing at his computer. "Bring up your inbox."

He used the mouse to move the cursor, and left-clicked to find a message from her.

"It's the Red Cross thing," she told him before he could open it. "It's working like a charm!"

The "Red Cross thing" was a propaganda brainchild of Samantha, designed to make the enemy look bad, something really not all that hard, while at the same time, maximizing the confusion caused the impending operation. The United States had maintained, since the beginning of the war, that Confederate prisoners were criminals, terrorists, or unlawful enemy combatants, and had steadfastly refused to allow the Red Cross visits mandated for prisoners of war. In doing so, they had woven the rope that the CAP Information Office would use to hang them in the public eye.

The Confederates had invited the neutral Swiss Red Cross in to visit the US prisoners under their control. President Plants had flatly refused via his Press Secretary, on the grounds that "The

Confederates were not prisoners of war but unlawful combatants," and, "The United States could not guarantee their safety from the Confederate terrorists." Then the head of the Republican Party, in an interview with a popular neo-conservative talk show host, made a remark that might best be described as undiplomatic:

"You can't trust the Swiss; they stood there and did nothing while we were fighting to save Europe from Hitler!"

Obviously, Samantha and her people had had a field day with that refusal, angering many people in the North as well as the South, most particularly those families who had military members in guerrilla captivity. The situation also royally pissed off the Swiss – the source of much of the electrical generation equipment that was amongst the guerrillas' main targets – who felt their centuries-old record of scrupulous neutrality was being called into question, and took it as a personal insult. In fact, they took it so personally that they instructed a pair of low-level bureaucrats attached to their embassy and covered by their diplomatic immunity to join the Red Cross and accept the Confederate invitation.

Frank's lips turned up in a smile, and then broke open into a full-scale grin as he read the article on the screen before him.

International News Wire

The Swiss branch of the International Red Cross reported today that they had been allowed to visit several United States military prisoners being held by the Confederate Army Provisional insurgents.

"We were allowed unrestricted interviews with prisoners in several locations, and they were permitted to send letters to their families through our auspices, as well as to receive aid packages from us" Red Cross official Heinrich Gustav told INW today. "The individuals we examined appeared to be in good health with no untreated medical problems. There were no complaints of ill treatment, although there were concerns about close confinement and the lack of opportunities for exercise. We expressed these

concerns to Confederate Army Provisional officials, and they assured us that they wished to give their prisoners that opportunity, but their options were limited due to the nature of the guerrilla conflict. Still, they promised to do what they could to alleviate the situation, and gave us the names, ranks and serial numbers of all the prisoners in their possession, to pass on to their families, as well as the US military."

Mr. Gustav has filed another request for access to Confederate prisoners being held by the United States, but once again, it has been rejected...

Internet Blog

Once more, we see the United States for exactly what it is: a rogue nation that refuses to recognize international law or the standards of common decency and humanity. The Confederates – the ones called 'terrorists' – allowed International Red Cross representatives from a neutral county access to their prisoners, who were found to be in good condition. Yet the United States – you know, the ones who claim to be the "land of the free" – refuses to do that, or even release the identities of the prisoners they hold, which number at least in the tens of thousands. What are they hiding?

Torture, perhaps?

US News

President Plants has condemned the holding of American POWs in inhumanly close confinement by Confederate terrorists, as determined by the International Red Cross, and has called for their immediate release.

In related news, a scandal has rocked the diplomatic world today. The embassy of supposedly neutral Switzerland has been accused of spying on the United States, and directly aiding and abetting Confederate Army Provisional terrorists. The State

Department has ordered the expulsion of two Swiss diplomats involved in the scandal. Zurich has denied the accusations and vowed diplomatic retaliation...

"That's beautiful, Sammie; that is just beautiful! Good job!" Still grinning, Frank pushed back from the desk. "I think that deserves a big hug."

He didn't have to ask twice; in less than a handful of seconds, she was ensconced on his lap while he held her in his arms. With neither bothering to consider whether her efforts deserved a kiss too, their lips met, and stayed together for a long time, until someone cleared her throat behind them.

"Excuse me," Cynthia said wryly from the open door. "I knocked, but no one answered. Would you like me to come back later?"

"No, not at all," Frank lied as a slightly embarrassed Samantha quickly stood. "What's up?"

"You've got a post card."

Before she could approach, he rose and stepped towards her, meeting her halfway. Taking it from her hand, he studied the picture on the front: arid mountains and tile roofed stucco houses running down a slope to an impossibly blue sea. Flipping it over, he saw that the wording and postmark indicated it originated in Italy. His own code name and the address of the farm where they made their current headquarters were penned in a neat hand beneath the printing. Below that, in equally tidy letters, were the words, *"I made it; I'm here!"* It was signed simply, *"Jonathon."*

Looking at Samantha, Frank was unable to fully contain his excitement when he said, "He's done it!"

Four men walked with Jonathon Edge: one in front, one to either side, and another behind. They were coldly polite but grimly efficient, and the way they automatically kept in step with one another spoke as clearly as their unconscious grace of movement and the almost indiscernible bulges under their expensive dark suits as to just what they were. Edge knew their type and respected it, because he was the same type himself.

The building was artistically rich almost beyond belief, but the corridors they traversed were plain and utilitarian. Oh, their floors were polished hardwood and the occasional painting broke the unfurnished monotony of regularly spaced mahogany doors in white plaster walls, but they were functional for all that. Servant's halls, where armies of personnel behind the scenes could carry out their errands unseen, and often unguessed by those who walked the grander ways.

Unseen by those not meant to see, Edge mentally corrected himself, but under constant observation by those whose purpose it was to see everything. The tiny cameras were nearly invisible, and would have gone completely unnoticed if the Guerrilla chief hadn't been trained to breech similar installations, and thus knew where to look for them.

They didn't have any distractions at the moment; the halls that would normally have been filled with a constant stream of people at any hour of the day or night were empty now, save for this deadly party of five. Obviously they had been cleared for a purpose; some things it didn't do for anyone to see who didn't have to, and a secret that could turn the balance of power of the entire world on its head definitely fell into that category.

After weeks of sneaking and hiding in safe houses and back alleys, and negotiations carried out through the cut-outs of other cut-outs, now, at *last*...

Finally, the Field Marshal and his entourage stopped before an unmarked door that, to his eyes, looked no different from any of the others. The lead man glanced back at him. When it came, the faint Swiss accent in his carefully enunciated voice was deceptively soothing.

"Wait here, please."

Edge waited, not that he had much choice. Outside the door the first man had closed behind him, those on either side and behind appeared totally relaxed, with their hands folded over one another at their waists, but ready in an instant to spring into action to restrain, draw weapons, or kill without hesitation.

A moment later, his escort returned and held the door open to allow him to enter.

"You may come in."

As the door closed behind him, between him and the guards, he reminded himself to make no sudden moves. No doubt electronic eyes and ears were glued to him with single-minded concentration, and he was sure at least some of the room's panels held much more dangerous things than empty space behind them. He knew the crawly feeling of unseen weapons trained between his shoulder blades was not his imagination; all it would take was a wrong move on his part, or the merest gesture on that of the only other occupant, and it would all be over but the burying. Still, that wasn't what bothered the former SEAL the most; unlike what he faced now, being shot at – and a couple of times actually being shot – was not a novel experience.

Edge did his best not to be awed by the man who sat before him in the leather-upholstered chair, but it was hard not to be. Nothing about him physically seemed remarkable; he was an old man, with soft features and kind eyes, and gentle, steady hands that bespoke serenity and personal peace. Even the room he occupied wasn't ostentatious; merely a high quality gentleman's study with fine dark wood paneling and an unusually rich collection of books on the shelves: expensive, certainly, but not showy. Still, the place, like the man, fairly radiated power.

"Please sit down," his heavily accented voice crooned as a wrinkled, parchment-skinned hand gracefully indicated another identical chair across the round Chippendale table from his own. When Edge eased himself into it, the creaking of the leather seemed remarkably loud.

"Thank you for seeing me, sir," Edge told him, and the old man smiled and nodded pleasantly, but the expression in his eyes said something else entirely when he leaned forward in a graceful, practiced motion. Edge realized, despite his first impression, those eyes were not so soft after all, but were sharp and calculating, the eyes of a man who had done much to gain power, and who fully understood its use and retention; in fact, the eyes were much like Edge's own.

"Would you care for a cognac?"

"Thank you, sir."

The old man's smile never wavered as he reached for a bottle to pour a measure into each of the two snifters on the table. Edge had invested in vintage wines and liquors at one time, and immediately recognized the vintage as being a rarity, well over a hundred-fifty years old; something he had seen only in pictures. Accordingly, he cupped the proffered snifter in his palm with its stem between his fingers and held it up, swirling the liquid in the light to admire its golden clarity, while allowing the warmth of his hand to transfer through the glass, activating the bouquet and sending the delightful aroma to his nose. Taking a sip, he sighed in appreciation; he had never tasted anything like this.

"You have a fine cellar, sir; this is excellent."

Instead of accepting the compliment by either word or gesture, the old man took a sip himself, carefully watching Edge over the rim of his glass. Apparently satisfied with what he saw, he sat his snifter on the table between them. The Field Marshal held onto his; it removed any temptation to fidget, and its presence in his gun hand might help forestall any potentially unpleasant...*misunderstandings* with the unseen guards he knew were watching.

"I understand you are seeking diplomatic recognition, Field Marshal. Edge."

Good, Edge thought to himself, *at least he's direct.*

"Yes sir, we are. That's why I've come to you first; a predecessor in your office graciously offered that same recognition to the first Confederacy a century and a half ago."

His host tented his fingers before his lips and rested his wrinkled chin on his thumbs."

"I'm telling you nothing you don't already know when I say your cause is not popular with many people. Can you tell me why we should risk recognizing you?"

Edge took a deep breath. He had studied what his answer would be for months, but he still didn't know if it would work. He hoped so; the future of the war might ultimately ride on the response it drew.

Well, here goes.

"Sir, we intend to build a Christian country."

The old man cocked his head the merest fraction to one side. "Do you mean a country or a nation?"

"Our nation is already Christian for all practical purposes, sir; we're probably the last nation in the world that takes Christianity seriously as a whole. What we want to do is to build a country to enable that nation – and that faith – to survive. We've already outlawed abortion except in case of rape or to save the mother's life, which is a step farther than any other First World country."

The man leaned forward and fixed Edge's eyes with a hard, direct gaze, although his voice remained calm and soothing.

"Just what sort of Christianity do you mean, Mr. Edge?"

Edge didn't expect the potential sticking point to come quite that early in the conversation, but he rose to it without hesitation.

"All kinds, sir. We intend to declare Christianity the official religion of the resurrected Confederacy, with no discrimination between its various branches."

The old man looked thoughtfully at him for long enough to make him uncomfortable.

"And how is this a good deal for us?"

"Because your church will have the same chance as everybody else to grow as you will in a Christian-friendly environment. The love and respect for Christ will literally be built in, giving it a leg up on heathenism. We'll outlaw no religion – we're not setting up a theocracy – but Christianity will definitely come first, both officially and otherwise. In fact, we intend to require that the poles for the display of our national flag on all central government offices be topped with a cross to show our nation's submission to Christ in all things and that our country relies on Him for support. I don't think you'll find that anywhere else."

The man leaned back in his chair and pursed his lips. "So you are not offering us anything...*extra*?"

"Only the chance to get in on the ground floor, and acquire the good feeling and *very* sincere gratitude of a new country by the prestige your recognition would bring us: gratitude that I've no doubt you can turn into growth." His host was a highly intelligent man, so Edge didn't bother pointing out that the growth he'd mentioned would be in a first world country, whose Christians had far more money to fill collection plates than those in any third world nation; he knew the man would figure that out on his own, and undoubtedly already had.

"There is that," he said, chuckling. "But how do I know *you* are sincere, Mr. Edge? Your own branch of Christianity has been, oh, how should I put this...*less than friendly* towards my own for many years. How do I know you really respect us, and are not simply using us as a means to an end – as a tool to be used and then cast aside when no longer needed?"

Careful to keep his movements slow and deliberate, Edge set the cognac aside, rose and came to the man. Kneeling before him, he reached out, and for probably the first time in history, a Southern Baptist kissed the hand of the Pope of Rome. The CAP commander's expression never altered, but inwardly he was shaking his head.

The things I do for my country!

The old man with the kind face and sharp eyes placed his hand on Edge's head in benediction and triumphantly said, "Bless you, my son. Go in peace."

Newscast, European Union

In a shocking move by the Vatican today, the Pope has given the Holy See's diplomatic recognition to the Confederate States of America. He stated that it is the Church's duty to support openly Christian governments wherever they may be and whatever form they may take, and that he was following the precedent laid down by

Pope Pius IX in his recognition of the original Confederacy in the 19th Century.

The US State Department immediately condemned the statement as, "an interference of religion in politics," and in opposition to the American doctrine of the "separation of church and state," and it was also condemned as anti-Semitic by the spokesman for the Defenders of the Jewish People. The situation has led to massive outbreaks of rioting in the EU, primarily among the Muslim population. Thousands have taken to the streets in Paris, London, Rome, Brussels, Barcelona, and Munich, and violent confrontations with the police as well as the Catholic population are ongoing.

In related news, the Italian Parliament is meeting in special session today, to determine if Italy should also extend its recognition...

DAY 300

CHAPTER 11

There were few words needed, and those few were whispers, soft as the breath of a gentle wind. They carried death with them just the same.

Through hooded eyes set in a leathery face, Captain Rob Johnson watched with approval as the 1st Columbia Irregulars filtered through the piney woods of central South Carolina, moving like ghosts whose footsteps barely rustled the rust-brown fallen needles. They knew the value of silence, and through constant hard training, they had become masters of it.

The path was just that: a path, two ruts worn in the forest floor by the occasional four wheeler transporting hunters and fishermen during better times. Lately, the local occupation unit had taken to using it frequently during their regular patrols, which, if Rob had his way, would be their last mistake.

The former black-ops soldier turned guerrilla officer needed little more than the occasional brief hand gesture, and his experienced men took care of the rest. Sergeants Buchanan and Stock spread Bravo and Charlie Squads along the path, in a parallel line about fifty yards back into the woods. Sergeant Thompson took Delta across the trail and formed a short line directly across from the end of Bravo's, running perpendicular to the path. Between then, they formed a classic L ambush, allowing Bravo and Charlie to put out a wall of fire the length of their line, while Delta raked the target at an angle. Rob could see First Sergeant Caffary moving through the men, checking their positions.

He couldn't see either Alpha or Echo Squads, which was good; it meant Sergeants Hodges and Kowalski were doing their jobs, not that he had any doubts on that score. The ex-Marine Kowalski was further back along the trail and back deeper into the woods; once the fight started, his men would move to the path and sweep forward across it, cutting off any retreat in that direction. Alpha, under the command of the big skinhead Hodges, was a hundred meters into the woods opposite Bravo and Charlie, ready and eager to take on anyone trying to get away in that direction.

He didn't bother looking for Private Godwin, the company sniper, because he knew he'd never see him. He was somewhere up the trail, waiting with his infinite woodsman's patience in case the enemy's point man passed the corner of their manmade L before the bulk of their patrol entered its killing zone. The only thing they would hear from Godwin was his rifle fire when he had a target to engage, and since he could shoot better than quarter minute of angle, whatever that target was, it would be dead.

Once everyone was in position, Rob took his place in the line with Bravo and Charlie, while Caffary joined Delta, taking cover at the base of a large tree by developed instinct, rather than thought. After that, it was simply a matter of laying and waiting. The men were well camouflaged, and they faded into the landscape as if they had never been. Within a few minutes, birds began fluttering through the thin underbrush, squirrels came down to forage in the fallen pine needles, and a doe, still accompanied by that year's practically grown fawn, wandered out on the trail, browsing at the low plants growing there, all blissfully unaware that violent death lay only a few feet away.

Most of the Irregulars were hunters, and they enjoyed watching the wildlife, even when they were hunting bigger, much more dangerous game. It kept them from getting bored, but more importantly, it was their early warning system. When the doe suddenly popped her head up to gaze back down the trail, swiveling both large ears forward and nervously twitching her tail, they knew something was coming. The pair of deer stepped off the path and faded into the woods opposite their line, and the squirrels began returning to their trees. It was time.

Rob felt the pager silently vibrating on his belt, and clicked it off. That would be Kowalski, farther down, warning them that the enemy was on their way.

Their point man appeared first, and Rob noted with professional respect that he was alert, carefully scanning the woods to either side as he moved quietly, feeling for potentially snapping twigs each time he set his boot down.

The enemy soldier's comrades were about fifty yards behind him, and Rob saw that their intelligence had been right; they numbered thirty, two men stronger than the Irregulars. The men were in varied states of alertness, but even the tired ones who were obviously just going through the motions were still disciplined enough to keep their rifle muzzles pointing outwards, in the direction any attack would come from. They had a pair of flankers out as well, one on either side of the trail twenty-five yards out...not quite far enough.

The main body of the enemy kept enough spacing to make it impossible for a single grenade blast to take out more than one or two. A good idea, but the guerrillas weren't going to be using grenades from fifty yards away; instead, they had something bigger.

Just as Rob had suspected might happen, they were forced to let the point man pass through in order to insure the main body was inside the long leg of their L. As soon as they were in place, he pressed the button on the detonator.

Only a few yards back from the trail, a pair of Claymore mines went off with a roar, sending hundreds of steel balls the size of buckshot into the enemy. The hail of shrapnel shredded flesh and equipment alike, and painted the trees opposite with a spray of blood and meat.

The flanker on their side happened to be passing behind one of the mines unaware, and, though he missed the shrapnel, the back blast slammed into him, stunning him and knocking him to the ground.

A split second before the first shot was fired by the ambush party, Rob heard the crack of a rifle from up the trail. Godwin had taken care of the point man.

When the firing began, it was a continuous roar, with single shots nearly unable to be picked out, even though most of the men were intentionally shooting in semi-automatic mode, more interested in hitting what they aimed at than in how many rounds they could throw at it. The exception was the venerable M60 machine gun on the short leg of the L, which was chug-chug-chugging away short bursts in its slow, deliberate, almost dignified manner, raking the enemy patrol's flank with 7.62mm bullets. Even over the noise of his own M4 and those on either side of him, he heard the distinct sound of Godwin firing methodically, shooting over the heads of his own men, choosing any target that came into sight. Still more shots came from down the trail, as Kowalski's squad moved in and sealed the back door.

A few of the tattered remainder of the enemy platoon tried to charge into the ambush in an effort to break free, but they were too little and too late; none of their lifeless bodies came to rest more than ten yards from the trail. A few more tried to cover, but they couldn't cover themselves from all directions at once. A couple tried to run, but only the opposite flanker made it, as he had a twenty-five meter head start. Crashing through a bush, he ran headlong into a surprised Sergeant Hodges, who was in the process of moving Alpha forward. They collided chest to chest, and the big skinhead, promptly dropped his rifle, grabbed the flanker in a bear hug, leaped off his feet, and body slammed the man into the ground with all of his two hundred-fifty pounds on top of him. Breath and consciousness both left the soldier's body at once, and by the time he recovered them a few seconds later, his wrists were already being secured behind his back.

Back at the ambush site, the firing had tapered off, and moans and cries could be heard, along with someone yelling, "I surrender! I surrender!" over and over.

"Hold your fire!" Rob called out, to be echoed by First Sergeant Caffary on the opposite side of the trail. "You on the trail; drop you weapons and facedown on the ground! Do it now!" Two men cast their rifles away like they were hot, and one more did so more reluctantly, but that was it. The only other movement was that of the seriously wounded, and there were few enough of those.

Rising, the Irregulars cautiously moved forward. The flanker who had been too close to the rear of the Claymore was still alive; the back blast had stunned him, and he lay quivering and whimpering with his face pressed tightly against the ground, both hands clenched in panic against the back of his head. Two of the men from Charlie squad forcibly straightened him out and secured him before tending his wounds.

The trio who had surrendered all had relatively minor wounds; one private had a small piece of his cheekbone shot away, a second had somehow managed to catch a single ball of Claymore shrapnel in each bicep, and the sergeant who was the last to give up had a 5.56mm round through his right thigh that had just missed the bone. Five more were still alive, but in much worse shape, and none of them were mobile.

Rob opened his mouth to give the orders, but Caffary beat him to it.

"Sergeants, check your squads and report! Delta and Echo: form a perimeter! The rest of you, check out the prisoners, triage, and secure! Move it, people! We don't have all day!" Glancing at Rob, he added, "With your permission, sir," almost as an afterthought, and Rob nodded his satisfaction.

Even as Sergeant Hodges came up and dumped his prisoner with the rest, three guerrillas were already stripping their captives prior to scanning them. The electronic wand confirmed that all of them were carrying a *legionnaire* – a tiny, implanted RDF chip just beneath the skin – and Casey Graham produced some alcohol pads and a Leatherman combination tool. Opening the razor-sharp blade, he told them, "Hold still, because this may hurt."

Even though he was neither wantonly brutal nor intentionally gentle, it did, but he still had the chips out in less than thirty seconds each, and then slapped some antibiotic ointment and a Band-Aid over the tiny slits he had made to get to them.

Meanwhile, the non-mobile wounded were dragged to the middle of the trail. They were in bad shape; their body armor had protected their torsos for the most part, but they had head and neck wounds, or arms and legs shattered and, in one case, severed by the Claymore and subsequent gunfire. Their fighting days were over, assuming they survived at all.

In a impersonal, business-like manner, the guerrillas dressed the wounds with the soldier's own pressure bandages, used their belts for tourniquets where needed, and propped their feet up on their helmets to prevent shock, all the while being recorded by a video camera in the hands of Corporal Fowler of Bravo Squad. Not only was it the decent thing to do, but it made for great propaganda.

"All right, people!" Caffary yelled again, "Get the prisoners lined up and let's get this show on the road."

"What are you going to do with them?" the enemy sergeant asked as he leaned on the private with the face wound, who was supporting his weight. He was happy that the guerrillas had given them their uniforms back, but he was more than a little concerned for his wounded men.

"We can't take them with us," Rob told him, "and I frankly don't want to shoot them. Their war's over, and they're no longer a threat to us. We'll leave them here for whoever comes looking for you all to find."

"But they're badly wounded! Some of them will die by then!"

"I expect they will. If it'll make you feel any better, as soon as we're clear of the area, I'll put in a call to have one of our contacts call the Army and give them their GPS coordinates."

The sergeant looked at him in disbelief for a moment, then nodded.

"Thank you, sir."

"You're welcome. Now, get moving."

Rob had killed so much in his life that it didn't bother him much anymore, but he had never killed wantonly or unnecessarily. Besides, he was being practical. It would cost the enemy an enormous amount to mount an operation to recover the wounded, and then give them the months of care they would require afterwards. In addition, their sparing, just like the care the Confederates had given them earlier, was of great propaganda value, particularly when the US did not respond in kind. Mercy, granted in the right time and place, could be very profitable.

Even though Rob wouldn't admit it to himself, or perhaps couldn't admit it, he had another reason. The man many people referred to as "the stone killer" behind his back could feel nothing for those whose existence he had abruptly put an end to over the course of his life, first as a United States soldier and now as a Confederate guerrilla. That didn't bother him at all, but the fact that it didn't bother him did. He knew there was something badly wrong with him, and if there was such a thing as *karma*, he had built up a full stock of the negative variety over the years. The subconscious instinct to try to do something about it had been growing stronger of late, and something deep inside him felt better whenever he listened to it, like today.

Rob rubbed his eyes, thankful that the day was finally over. They had made it back to the rendezvous point with their prisoners, and he had kept his word and given one of their civilian operatives a call with instructions to give the coordinates of the enemy wounded to a local police department. The cops – the smart ones who wanted to live, anyway – kept an undercover but nevertheless sincere neutrality in regards to the guerrillas; not hard, since not a few of them had become outright sympathizers. It would do no good to contact the Army; they'd suspect an ambush and not come, but the cops would, bringing emergency personnel with them to try and stabilize any of the wounded who were still alive.

Following that brief chore, the Irregulars had turned their prisoners over to some of their civilian auxiliaries who spirited them away to various hiding places around the state. Only then came the debriefing and stand down for the worn-out men. They would be sleeping inside tonight, at least, in the large, century-old house of a retired couple who were sympathetic to the Cause. With beds, couches, and air mattresses on the floor, and fresh auxiliaries standing guard throughout the night, they could relax at last, at least if the owners could ever stop their well-meaning harassment of endless offers of food and drink.

He'd let the men worry about that; feeling his age, he had slipped off into a spare bedroom and had just stripped down to his shorts when his cell phone rang. Ignoring the temptation to pretend he didn't hear it, he picked it up and mashed the button.

"Hello?"

"Rob?"

He grinned as he recognized the voice of Cynthia Dover. He had been her rescuer, mentor, and more; now the petite girl was like the daughter he had never gotten around to having. Both of them knew it, but neither one would have mentioned it, of course; they both pretended their relationship was purely professional. Maybe it was easier that way, but the mutual filial affection was there, just the same. She was a quasi-adopted daughter to be proud of too; in the few months she had been with the CAP, she had become an excellent soldier, and expert shot, and had developed an outstanding hand to hand fighting ability, all through total dedication and sheer hard work.

"Hey, Cynthia!" he said tiredly. "How's it going?"

"Everything's fine. I'm still carrying your present, by the way."

Rob had sent her the vintage Gerber MKII combat dagger she carried; he had taken off the body of an enemy officer who no longer needed it. The wasp-waisted blade was in good shape but old, probably dating back to the Viet Nam period.

"You're welcome, for about the tenth time. Does it fit your hand alright?"

"It does now. I did a little file work on the handle, flattening the sides a little to make it easier to orient the edges, and it fits great."

He told her he heartily approved of the modifications.

"You need to bring the family and come and visit as soon as you can. Dad needs some help with a project they've got going on up here."

Rob mentally translated the code she had used just in case their encryption had been broken: *Frank has a mission for you and the Irregulars.*

"Can it wait till morning?"

He heard her dry chuckle, and realized he must have sounded as tired as he felt. He was pushing fifty, after all, and he was suddenly terrified of the thought of what he would do when he could no longer be a soldier. The warrior's path was the only one he knew.

"Yes, by all means. Get some sleep, and tomorrow..." She paused, and he heard her voice break ever so slightly. "Please, Rob, be careful."

"I didn't get this old by being careless. Tell them we'll pull out in the morning."

Sheriff's Department Report

Following an anonymous tip, Deputies Carson, Devlin and myself discovered the site of what appears to have been a battle in the woods about two miles west of Sprinkle Road. Twenty-three men in US Army uniforms were dead, and four were wounded but still alive, their wounds, and those of one of the deceased, had been bandaged by person or persons unknown. No arms or ammunition (other than spent brass) were in evidence, having apparently been removed from the scene...

US News Report

Twenty-three soldiers died today in a brutal ambush by Confederate terrorists in South Carolina, and three are reported missing. Surrounded, the four survivors, despite their massive wounds, managed to drive off the vastly superior enemy numbers, killing nearly two hundred terrorists in an hour-long battle that involved hand to hand combat at one point...

Internet Forum

NAKED TRUTH: I saw the evening news, and it was a crock of horse manure. I invite everyone to go to the link below to check out this video. It shows Confederate guerrillas treating the US wounded following the ambush. It's amazing that they give a damn, after what we've done to them when they've been taken prisoner...

*SUPER PATRIOT: That's all make-believe shot in somebody's basement, you stupid ****tard! Those CAP racists are nothing but a bunch of terrorists! So what if our interrogators get rough with them? If it saves just one American life, it's worth it...*

NAKED TRUTH: SP, I thought terrorists were the people who abuse, rape and torture helpless civilians and prisoners. Looks to me like you're confused about who the terrorists really are...

WEB HOST: By order of Homeland Security, this forum is now closed...

DAY 309

CHAPTER 12

US News

Secretary of State, Irving Lieberman, issued a warning today to any country considering harboring, aiding, or meeting with Confederate Army Provisional terrorists, or recognizing them as a diplomatic entity.

"You may rest assured that there will be serious consequences; nothing will be off the table when we consider the United States' response to any such action!" he said.

Secretary Lieberman's strong words come on the heels of President Plants canceling an already scheduled meeting with the Pope, and with the United States severing its diplomatic ties with Switzerland due to their assistance to terrorists...

It was a day of parting. The 1st Columbia Irregulars milled about inside the barn, waiting and ready to go. Rob and Caffary moved amongst the sergeants, the sergeants moved amongst the men, and Frank moved amongst them all. The Captain and First Sergeant ordered, the sergeants made the last minute checks, and Frank patted the odd shoulder, told the slightly off-color joke, and spoke the occasional quiet encouragement...and the men loved it.

Samantha could see it clearly; Rob might be in command, but these men were Frank's men. They didn't belong to the Confederate Army Provisional or to South Carolina; they belonged to Frank Gore, and would charge straight into the mouth of Hell with a squirt gun if he asked them to, because they knew he'd do the same for any of them without hesitation. He had proven that when he saved their lives along with his own from a traitor in their midst, and had saved their families at the same time.

She knew exactly what kind of man her husband was, but even if she hadn't, the almost worshipful regard the men he commanded held him in would have told her. Just seeing the open admiration in the eyes of Sergeants Hodges and Buchanan as they laughed at something he said was ample indication of how they felt.

I am so proud that this is my husband, and the father of my child! And I am so damned sad he's leaving!

Samantha desperately wanted to cry, but she wasn't about to make things any harder on Frank. She knew, deep down inside, he felt the same way.

He wouldn't show it in front of the men, of course, no more than they would in front of him. To all appearances, all of them were rip-roaring and ready to go and do something that, to her mind, was incredibly dangerous.

Frank was getting ready to launch his big operation within a month, but he, backed up by the Irregulars, was going over a hundred miles away into North Carolina to do it.

"Why North Carolina?" she had asked him. "Why not here?"

"To begin with, it's better for morale if I'm seen directing it from another spot rather than bunkered up in my own headquarters and my own state. It's also safer for you all here, as well for the Confederate Army Provisional as a whole."

She had felt a chill go running down her spine.

"What do you mean by 'safer?'"

He had looked as though he devoutly wished he had kept that part to himself, because now he had no choice but to answer.

"Remember what you learned about patrolling in our little impromptu Special Warfare School? You don't bunch up; not only does that make you easier to kill, but it also attracts more attention, making you easier to spot in the first place. Tactically, it applies just as much in the broad, large-scale sense as it does to small units."

"Fine, I understand that." Actually, she understood it all to well, and the implications frightened the hell out of her, even though she couldn't argue with his logic. "But why North Carolina? They've got so many...problems up there."

Indeed they did; of all the states, there was more internal friction amongst the Tarheels, due to an unusually powerful YABOM faction that was pitted against an equally strong conventional one. The hostility had gone well beyond verbal barrages; several people on both sides had been wounded and a few were missing and presumed dead, or had been found definitely dead from the vigorous internal squabble. To Samantha's way of thinking, that would be the last place Frank should be. He saw things differently.

"That's part of why I'm going. I don't hate the YABOM'ers; I actually agree with a lot of their points, but their sense of timing sucks. Right now, in the middle of a war for our survival, they want to fiddle-fart around with politics and philosophy, and this just isn't the time. We need to be pulling together, and all this division is killing us. If I set up operational headquarters in North Carolina for the single biggest mission of the war to date, it will put the practical-minded faction ahead, maybe enough that we can cut this friction until after the war's over."

She remembered the mischievous grin that had spread across his face.

"Besides, it just might be a Queen Elizabeth lesson."

"Queen Elizabeth?"

"Yes. Elizabeth the First had a lot of factions in her kingdom too, and some pretty powerful people were plotting against her. Whenever she got wind of it, she would pay them the 'honor' of moving in with them, along with her entire court: a 'keep your friends close and your enemies closer' kind of thing. They didn't dare plot against her right under her nose, and the logistics presented by the presence of so many people loyal to her right in their midst kept them too busy to get into too much."

"You're not Queen Elizabeth," she had said, and he'd laughed out loud before turning to shout yet another joking comment to one of the Irregulars. Turning back to her for a moment, he added, "I hope not!" and then went to consult with Rob and Caffary.

Still, at least as far as the Irregulars were concerned, he was royalty.

Samantha's thoughts were interrupted by a hand on her shoulder.

"How you holding up, Sammie?"

Reaching up, she grasped Sam Wirtz's fingers. "As well as can be expected, I guess."

"I know." He gave her a little squeeze for reassurance. "Just keep doing it. Frank's got to be strong for everybody else in this movement, but I think he needs someone to be strong for him."

She turned and smiled at the shorter, older man.

"Did anyone ever tell you you're a very wise man?"

"Not bad for a pig farmer, huh?" Smiling, he said, "It's good to be appreciated."

"You're more than appreciated. I'm going to miss you too; you know that, don't you?"

Sam was leaving along with Frank and the Irregulars, but was only going partway. He was going to be riding concealed in a loaded cattle truck bound for Texas. They actually had a hollow mockup of a large, white-faced steer lying down that a taxidermist-turned-guerrilla had covered with skin. Sam wouldn't be riding inside what he referred to as the "Trojan cow" all the way of course, but he could squeeze into it whenever they stopped...or were stopped.

He also had half a dozen fragmentation and concussion grenades, his old .357 magnum, and a Buck General Bowie knife, just in case things went sour. Not that he was likely to survive if discovered, of course, but if it was his turn to walk that lonesome valley, he didn't intend to make the trip alone.

"You just be careful while we're gone; you hear?"

"I hear," she said with a sigh, and was rewarded with a hug that she gratefully returned. In the few months of the Third Revolution, Sam had become practically a substitute father to her, as well as to every other woman and girl at the base younger than his own half-century or so, and she had come care for him more deeply than for anyone save her husband.

"Stay safe, Sam. I mean it; you stay safe."

"I intend to."

Over his shoulder, she saw Frank giving some final order, and the men began hoisting packs and weapons as he turned back towards her. Seeing her in his friend's embrace, he grinned.

"Hey there, Old Timer," he teased in his best John Wayne imitation, "you'd just better put my wife down right now."

"Old timer?" Sam shot back at his friend with mock offence. "Did I ever tell you the story about the young bull and the old bull?"

"Only about half a dozen times. If you're going to tell it again, though, we probably better wait until we're out of mixed company."

Sam reddened. "You know I wouldn't tell that one in front of her..."

Their banter was interrupted by a cry of, "Uncle Sam! Uncle Sam!" and they turned to see Kerrie coming on the run, auburn hair flying behind her and a small cooler in her hand. Sam immediately let go and turned his attention to the teenager, who threw herself into his arms and hugged him unselfconsciously. "You were going to leave without saying goodbye!"

"No I wasn't. I knew my pretty little niece wouldn't let that happen."

"Oh, you! Here, I packed you a lunch."

Leaving them to it, Frank and Samantha slipped their arms around each other.

"I miss you already," she whispered, and her husband nodded.

"I know what you mean." Glancing down at her swollen abdomen, he added, "I'll worry the whole time I'm gone."

"I'll be alright," she assured him with much more confidence than she felt. "You just concentrate on your mission, not on me. I want her father to stay alive."

"I intend to...wait a minute: *her* father?"

It was Samantha's turn to shrug.

"That's what Mrs. Simpson says: you know, the older lady who helps out here?" The term "older" was being charitable; Mrs. Simpson was a volunteer who must have been at least eighty-five if she was a day, but she was dedicated and could work most of the younger women into the ground doing the thousand and one things required to keep even a small base of operations running. "She said, if it was a boy, I'd 'be carrying it in the butt.'"

His brow wrinkled in puzzlement.

"Wouldn't that be a physical impossibility?"

"Silly! She meant I'd be gaining a lot of weight back there, rather than all in front...not that my rear end's not getting bigger anyway."

Frank reached down and patted the object in question.

"You're imagining things; your bottom is just as cute as it always has been."

"Flatterer! I love you."

"And I love you too. I'll be back as soon as I can." He gently touched her stomach. "Sooner than that, anyway."

"Promise?"

"The good Lord willing."

She managed not to cry until they were out of sight; then she retired to her room, and spent a solid hour bawling into his pillow as she held it to her, wishing it was him.

Despite the dangerous circumstances, despite even what was at stake, Jonathon Edge was elated. He was among men of true power, and he was one of them, accepted by them. He had to defer to them a little, of course, since he had come seeking favors, but the fact that they accepted him at all was a huge ego boost, not to mention a boost for his Cause.

There is so much potential here...both good and bad.

He was not in Europe anymore, at least technically, but in Asia, in an isolated country estate deep in the frozen heart of central Russia. Originally a palatial home of one of the Tsar's powerful supporters, the centuries-old building had changed hands during the Revolution, becoming a retreat for the Communist Party faithful. Afterwards, once the walls came down, it was owned for a short period by one of the oil oligarchs, a Russian Jew who had made the mistake of believing his money would protect him while he squeezed the Russian people. He found out differently during President Putin's Administration; he was arrested and his holdings were seized and sold, this estate ending up in the hands of the Russian Government once more, compete with the original priceless antique furnishings, and coupled with all the modern conveniences. Miles from the nearest dwelling and with a landing strip cut out of the birch forest in the back, they had seen its potential value for meetings just like this one.

Edge covertly studied the other men even as they did the same to him. There were two officers – a general and an admiral – each with a singularly silent lieutenant for an aide. Both commanders were cut from the same cloth; if most Americans had been asked to draw a picture of a Russian, theirs would have been the portraits produced. Broad and stocky, square-faced and heavy-jowled, they had astonishingly bushy brows that seemed to be reaching for their hairlines, and their deep-set eyes were as narrow and suspicious as their wide smiling mouths were welcoming. Their aides were opposite; young, expressionless, trim and athletic, with bulges under their uniform jackets that couldn't be accounted for by mere muscle.

If they're not Spetsnaz commandos, I'll eat my hat.

Earlier, under the guise of going to the bathroom, Edge had casually glanced out the window. The number of soldiers his experienced eye picked up in a few brief seconds told him that there had to be more, *many* more of the same scattered around the snow-covered grounds outside. That he saw that many so quickly led him to estimate that there must be at least a battalion surrounding the place to insure their protection and privacy. The general and admiral, however, weren't the reason.

Neither were the two senior members of the Russian Parliament, one of whom, save for his shining bald head, could have been a brother to either of the pair of senior officers. The other, with light hair and cold blue eyes, looked much more like the last man in the room, and the most important.

Even though he was around sixty, about Edge's own age, he was every bit as athletically built as the former SEAL-turned-guerrilla-leader. Once a young *Spetsnaz* officer during the changeover from Communism, he had graduated to bigger and better things following *Perestroika*. Even if Edge hadn't known who he was from pictures and television, he would have recognized the Russian President simply from the deference shown him by the others, and by the aura of power the man exuded himself.

Stepping up the Confederate, he stuck out his right hand.

"Welcome to Russia, Field Marshal Edge."

"Thank you for having me, Mr. President," Edge told him as he shook the offered hand. "It's truly a pleasure to meet you."

"The pleasure is ours," he returned, and Edge wasn't sure if he was referring to the men in the room, to Russia in general, or speaking of himself in the royal plural. He had heard rumors that he might be as reluctant to relinquish power as some of his predecessors had been...Still, that was Russia's business he quickly decided as his host genially took him by the arm. "Come, sit with me; we have a lot to talk about."

The Confederate Army Provisional Commander couldn't argue that point. They had one hell of a lot to talk about, but he couldn't shake the feeling that there still might be more than he expected.

DAY 310

CHAPTER 13

Edge felt like he was dying, and he was fairly certain some unknown creature had already expired inside his mouth; something furry that had given up the ghost weeks ago, if the taste was any indication. He blinked hard for a moment, forcibly loosening his gummy eyes as the slits of morning light through the blinds slashed across them like a handful of razorblades.

He moved slightly, and the soft, finely woven sheets felt like sandpaper on his skin; even his hair hurt, right down to the very last individual follicle.

The worst part of it was that he had known this was going to happen, but he went through with it anyway. He had no choice, not if he wanted to save face with the Russians. Edge had studied their culture like he did every one he expected to come in contact with, and he knew the Russians placed a certain value on a man who could handle his liquor; a small value, true, but when a man came with his hat in his hand looking for the help he needed in order to insure the survival of his people and the freedom of his country, if he was smart, he took every advantage available.

He rubbed his pounding head. *Some advantages cost more than others, I suppose.*

"*Dobraye ootra*" – Good morning.

Edge's eyes popped wide open at the unexpectedly deep but very definitely feminine voice speaking Russian beside him, close enough for him to feel the warm breath that accompanied it swirling around his left ear. Turning his head, he blinked again, trying to focus as he looked into a beautiful set of blue eyes set in a milk-pale face, incongruously topped with thick hair as black as a raven's wing. The mattress shifted and the covers moved as she snuggled closer to his side, and he could feel her naked skin against his beneath the sheets.

What the hell is she doing here? What am I doing?

Swiftly he ran through the events of the evening before in his damnably fogged brain. Besides the Russian President and the original group, more officials had appeared at seemingly random intervals throughout the day, presumably from departments associated with whatever subject was being discussed at the time, and nobody seemed to leave. After about eighteen straight hours of negotiations with a room full of bureaucrats, intelligence agents, generals, politicians, power brokers, and God only knew what else, the results had been productive beyond Edge's hopes. The Russians had not only promised to recognize the Confederacy on the floor of the United Nations, but had also assured them that Serbia, along with several other countries who either owed the Russian Government a favor or owed the United States a hard slap in the face, would do the same. China, and the rest of the SCO – the Shanghai Cooperation Organization – it was predicted, could be convinced to follow suit. There was also the strong hint that additional covert military aide in the form of weapons, training, advisors, and most importantly, information, would be forthcoming in the near future...in return for certain *favors* of course: favors that were as yet to be specified, but would be collected upon once the Confederates won. These favors wouldn't be onerous, they assured him, just one friend returning a back scratching to another. That last worried Edge more than a little, but better an independent country owing a "friend" a favor than no country at all.

At this point, it's not like we have a choice. Without a great deal of outside help, the overwhelming power of the enemy will eventually prevail again, just like it did in 1865.

Following that marathon session, another one had started: a celebration involving mountains of food and oceans of vodka. Russians prided themselves on their abilities as hosts, and they favored guests who took full advantage of what they offered. Edge knew that politeness required he try at least a bite of every course, which turned out to be at least couple dozen dishes, as his host country's culture measured the worth of a meal by how little of the table cloth could be seen under the piles of food. He also knew to empty his glass to every toast offered, but he never, not in his younger days as a naval officer, not aboard the *Green Eyed Lady* with Davy Jones, not even in his wildest dreams, expected there to be that many. Elbows were raised, sometimes linked through his, at such a furious rate that the clear vodka soon had no more taste on his alcohol-numbed tongue than the water it resembled, and he slugged it down glass for glass with his hosts, to the accompanying cheers that grew ever louder.

For the first time, Edge was thankful he had been drinking a bit more since the death of his wife, as he could never have kept up otherwise. He supposed he had done well enough, since a couple of bureaucrats and one of the intelligence officers were already comatose by the time the music and dancing started.

Now he remembered; that's where he met the woman. She was the undersecretary to something or other, and she had been introduced as...Victoria; Victoria Slastyonoff; yes, that was it. She was beautiful, no doubt of that, and, although Edge hadn't been able to muster any real interest in women since the death of his wife, she still didn't fail to attract his attention. She gave her age as forty, but she was certainly well preserved, and she looked almost a decade younger. Elegant, long-legged and graceful, with arched brows and fine, slightly elongated features, he had spoken to her in passing, and she seemed to hang on his every word. Later, she had asked him if he danced, and within an hour he was calling her Vika, her chosen pet name.

The rest of the evening was a blur, but now that he thought about it, it all came back, including how they had adjourned to this bedroom, arm and arm, and what followed.

"Good morning," he replied in the same language. It was all he could think of to say, although it wasn't good from his point of view, not good at all; as anyone who knew him could attest, Edge was notably, almost pathologically, un-fond of surprises.

"Bad head?"

"Yeah."

With studied idleness, she traced the polished, carefully manicured tip of her index finger through his graying chest hair. "I was afraid perhaps...you were regretting something."

127

He thought about that for a moment. On one hand he couldn't honestly say he regretted it, other than the hangover, but on the other, he felt emotionally torn, and the foggy thumping-pounding of his head didn't help either.

"It's not you, Vika," he sighed, "it's me. Since my wife died, I haven't been with anyone...until last night."

Resting her hand on his chest, she propped her slightly pointed chin on the back of it and regarded him calmly.

"I am Russian, Jonathan; that means I understand pain, and I can see yours in your eyes. It was a terrible thing, what happened to your wife and son, and I have no doubt you loved them deeply. But must you love the pain of their passing even more, so that you carry it around on your back like a cross?"

That made sense – far too much sense, particularly as he had never mentioned his late family, and Edge's antennas instantly went up, although he kept his voice carefully neutral.

"You seem to know quite a bit about me."

"I've made it my business to know. Your country – the United States, I mean – and mine have not always been friends. Well, let's be honest; we've *never* been friends. Because of that, we made it a point to learn all we could about your military, especially those in the elite forces: the ones our own soldiers would be most likely to confront in the low intensity conflicts of the Cold War. Early-on, in the very first days of my intelligence career, when you were still a SEAL, I was assigned to study you. As events advanced, you became an enigma to us; an elite soldier who resigned his commission, turned his back on the service and threw away his medals on principle. Somewhere along the line, I became fascinated, and continued to watch you, even after my assignment changed. Some of my colleagues suggested I was obsessed, and perhaps I was. I know I've spent hours staring at your photos, trying to fathom what was behind those cold blue eyes of yours. Of course, after you assumed leadership of the Southern Rebellion, you were even more interesting. Once I heard the rumor you were coming here, I pulled in every favor that was owed me in order to get a chance to meet you in person." She looked down, toying with his chest hair again. "I guess I had what you Americans call a crush."

Edge frowned. "Are you telling me you're...a groupie?"

She clamped her hand over her mouth in a failed attempt to stifle her laugh.

"You're an attractive man, Jonathan, but you're not exactly a rock star. As for me, I'm a bit old to be a groupie."

Without thinking about it, he reached out and caressed the side of her face, brushing aside the strand of ebony hair that was hanging over it.

"You're not too old."

Her grin turned mischievous. "And if last night is any indication, neither are you. At least, not when you...how do you say it, 'loosen up' a little."

He sighed again, only inwardly this time, as it came to him just how much he had sacrificed for the movement over the years, and how much more it would surely require.

"I can't afford to loosen up."

Her finger moved again, tracing the long white line on his left pectoral, one of several scars that dotted his body, and each one of which had carved his soul just as surely as it had carved his flesh.

"Relaxing is the way you loosen scar tissue. You have so many scars, Jonathan, but most of them, and certainly the worst, I think, are on the inside. Your war will not last forever, and if you live, the time will come when you need to be human again."

Without knowing why, Edge pulled her close and held her, but his mind was elsewhere. Although he would never admit it to anyone, the thought she had just expressed scared the hell out of him. He didn't know if that time would ever come again, and, if it did, if he would be able to do it. He wasn't sure he even remembered how.

DAY 330

CHAPTER 13

Homeland Security Phone Conversation

"Hello?"

"My reporting code number is 394-A46. We've spoken before on the subject of Edge and Gore."

"What have you got?"

"The current location of Frank Gore: the exact GPS coordinates."

"Son of a bitch! Are you bullshitting me?"

"No; he's there right now, even as we speak."

"Give me the location!"

"Not so fast; that wasn't the deal. I need the good faith payment we discussed transferred to my account first."

"Damn it! He may get away!"

"That's your problem, but they're there right now. Every minute you waste trying to get out of paying me increases the chances you'll miss him all together."

"Give me the account number and I'll get the authorization. Warning: this had better be real!"

"Oh, it's real alright..."

It was late winter in central North Carolina, and the trees were bare where the red clay of the Piedmont stretched down to meet the coastal plain. At any other time, even now in bleak February, the woods would have been beautiful, but a storm had finally moved in. As the men looked out through the cracked-open doors of a massive metal building that was once a trucking company garage, the wind was picking up, and the falling rain was right on the verge of freezing. It was cold, wet and miserable.

Still, the Confederate Army Provisional's North Carolina Theater Commander, Watis Suggs, was in a good mood, despite himself.

Forty-eight years old, Suggs was a Tarheel born and bred, and as tough as they came. He were those of one of the common White genetic types of that state: stocky and round faced with a small, wide-nostriled, slightly pug nose, but in his case, the resemblance to most other men stopped there. A natural mesomorph in the extreme, at five foot ten, he carried almost three hundred pounds of hard-earned muscle on his powerful, big boned frame. He was so broad that his shaved head and bristling, shiny black beard looked somehow too small and out of place on his thick, sloping shoulders. Unlike many big men, Watis Suggs had never touched a weight in his life; only timber, shrimp nets, and motor blocks. Although hard as stone, he looked less like a sculpture and more like a gnarled rock thrust out of the ground by sheer geologic force, its shape hammered into being by the storms of life.

Growing up in a poor, hardscrabble life in the mountains, he had run off for the coast at fourteen and gone to work as a commercial fisherman. Since then, save for a stint in the Marine Corps, he had traveled with the seasons, pulling nets in the Atlantic when the fish and shrimp were running, and cutting timber and doing mechanical work in the hills when they were not. His dark, hard, calculating eyes told even more than the scars on his knuckles and his face that he had seen it all, done it all, and wasn't the least impressed by a damned bit of it.

He was impressed, however, with Frank Gore, who stood beside him now, looking out through the doorway of the hilltop garage.

At first, Watis was fully ready to despise Gore, the rising star Johnny-come-lately in a movement notorious for its personality cults, but after working with him at a distance over the months, he couldn't help but like him. In person, his rough good looks didn't cut any ice with the Tarheel commander, but his quiet confidence and outstanding abilities forced his respect, and his humble good humor was impossible to resist. It still galled Suggs somewhat that Gore had blasted to the forefront of the movement and been placed over everyone – including him – that was south in the chain of command from Field Marshal Edge himself. Still, he couldn't deny Frank's competence, which, he was honest enough to admit after what he had seen, exceeded his own, and he actually felt comfortable following him: much more comfortable than he felt with Edge himself, who was always cold and distant with everybody.

He was real distant now, if the rumors were to be believed. He heard it through the grapevine that right now Jonathon Edge was somewhere overseas, probably Europe or the Middle East, cutting a deal with somebody for weapons and political recognition. Frank was now in charge, however, and he had chosen North Carolina for his mission command center for the current operation. That suited Watis just fine, although the honor the General was doing his State did nothing to satisfy his curiosity.

"Can you tell me yet what you're up to yet?"

"Nope," Frank said with a tight grin, sipping at a bottle of Dr. Pepper, "not yet. You won't have to wait long, though; I figure about two or three days, give or take. Trust me; you'll *know* when it happens. I am going to have to ask that you don't tell Tarbox even that, though. He has no need to know."

"Harrumph!" Suggs snorted. "I ain't gonna tell that son of a bitch shit about nothin' I don't have to!"

He didn't elaborate, and he didn't have to. Frank had his sources, and he knew the internal situation in North Carolina was about as screwed up as it came.

Rather than simply having a Councilman represent their interests to the provisional government and a military commander run things in their area for the duration of the war as the other states were doing, a few of the most influential members of their branch of the movement – all from the Sovereignty Now faction – had insisted on having a politician in charge of their internal workings, one Lawrence Carter – 'LC' – Tarbox, an attorney and once a prominent member of Dr. MacFie's original peacetime faction. The problem with him was that he was both militarily ignorant and such a constant pain in the ass that Edge refused to deal with him at all, or even recognize him, bypassing him entirely and giving his orders directly to Tarbox's increasingly nominal underling, Suggs. There was no love lost between North Carolina's military and political arms in the first place; theirs was a constant internal power struggle. Tarbox tried to exert his authority over Suggs on a regular basis, which didn't go over well. Suggs respected no man who wasn't willing to fight for what he believed in, and had gone as far as calling Tarbox a pussy to his face in the middle of a state meeting, in front of supporters from both sides.

"I'm a soldier," he had said, "and I take my orders from my superior officer, not from some pecker head who doesn't know his ass from a hole in the ground about what I do!"

One of Tarbox's friends had leapt to his feet and called the military commander a unionist, a centralist and a traitor to his State. Suggs response was to break his nose and several of the surrounding facial bones with one well-placed punch. The man nearly died as a result of his skull fracturing when his head bounced of the concrete floor as he fell.

The meeting had gone pretty much down hill from there. North Carolina's Councilman, Paul McDonald, with post-war political aspirations of his own, lacked the courage to deal decisively one way or another with the situation. Regardless of who was wrong or right, he tried his best not to take sides in the affair in an effort to keep peace amongst the two factions, and as a result was largely so disliked by both for his inaction that he was left with no real power at all. Both groups pretty much ignored him, other than to give him conflicting instructions on how to vote on Council matters. Ultimately, though, Suggs had support of his men – the ones with the guns – and, perhaps more importantly, the support of Edge and the rest of the Council. Tarbox and his clique of followers knew better than to buck them openly, particularly Edge; more than one overly-independent-minded person had caught lead and died from attempting that very thing. Tarbox was forced to settle for spending his time consolidating his own power base and nibbling at the edges of Suggs' sphere of influence at every opportunity.

Frank disliked Tarbox, but, much more importantly in his book, there was something about the man he simply did not trust. It was that gut feeling that cinched things for the ex-cop...that, and the fact that he felt pretty much like Suggs did about a man who wouldn't raise a hand to fight for his own people. This was not a war for power; it was a war for the South's very survival. He knew that in every theater there were many operatives of both sexes in the field – *soldiers, by God!* – who were too young to raise a full crop of pubic hair, too old to stand up straight, or too crippled to walk, yet they took the risks and did their assigned jobs, putting their lives on the line every single day, and all to often giving them. That any healthy man claiming to be a leader of Southerners who lacked the guts to do the same, but preferred to hide behind the lines and undermine the effort itself, was something beyond his ken.

As far as dealing with Suggs was concerned, in addition to Frank's own feelings about Tarbox, Edge's plain orders on the subject, and Suggs' inherent, instinctive capabilities, the General simply liked the irascible man, because he was so bluntly and openly honest, you never had any doubts where you stood with him. What he said was exactly what he thought. In a movement long notorious for more pitched battles, shifting alliances and casual backstabbing within its own ranks than against the enemy, that was a commodity to be valued.

That was part of the reason Frank picked North Carolina for his base the Confederate Army Provisional's climatic operation, and was now standing beside the Colonel inside the garage-turned-Tarheel guerrilla supply dump. He trusted Suggs, and his presence with him would enhance the North Carolina commander's status and power within his state's forces, helping to pull the fragmented organization together.

Although he would never have admitted it to anyone, there was a second reason as well. His current position was just over a hundred miles from his South Carolina Headquarters and Samantha, making it easier to get back to her once everything blew up, or if something went wrong beforehand. Her time was getting close and, war or no war, he intended to be with her when their child was born.

The chopper came in fast and low, almost brushing the treetops. It was the only one in the vicinity, and it shouldn't have been in the air; the wind was howling, freezing rain was falling, visibility was almost non-existent, the satellite was useless...in fact, the weather sucked. Worse, there was no backup, and wouldn't be for at least half an hour.

The pilot, seated above and behind the copilot in the craft's angular tandem cockpit, grunted as he thought about it. *More like two hours, or maybe three!* Money was short and maintenance was way behind, in addition to the brass having their heads firmly up their collective asses as usual when it came to the real world, off the big, secure bases. Apache helicopters generally attacked in a swarm, and this solo run with no backup was breaking every rule in the book, but despite all that, they had been ordered to do it in no uncertain terms. "Get to the target, blow the hell out of everything that moves, and keep doing it; this chopper stays as long as it has ammunition and fuel."

"Whoever's down there," the pilot muttered to himself, "they must want them pretty bad!"

"You say something?"

Glancing down at his co-pilot's helmet, he shook his head.

"Just talking to myself."

"Bad habit, dude; people will think you're crazy."

The pilot laughed. "Good; right now, I can think of a lot worse things than a Section 8 discharge."

"Yeah, me too; they could send us to the South." the co-pilot replied dryly.

"On target in two."

"Ready to rock and roll."

The pilot wasn't overly concerned, at least not about the guerrillas. The AH-64 he was flying might not have been primarily intended as an anti-personnel weapon, but it would kill people just as well as the armored vehicles it was designed for use against. The pods of Hydra-70 rockets slung under its stubby wings and M230 30mm chain gun beneath the nose would make hash out of personnel, buildings and cars just as easily as they could armored vehicles. Shooting a man with a 30mm anti-armor weapon loaded with M789 High Explosive Dual Purpose – HEDP – rounds was a lot like was like plinking rats with a .458 elephant gun; it would definitely kill them, but it left a lot to be desired in the efficiency department. At the moment, he was actually more worried about the violent wind gusts and freezing rain; the Army designation of "all-weather" didn't necessarily mean *all* weather, and it was taking everything he had just to keep the helicopter on a steady course. Contrary to the government propaganda parroted in the news media, the guerrillas pretty much owned the countryside, and if you had to set down – or crashed – out here, in all likelihood, you were truly and righteously screwed.

"On target in one."

"Look out Rebels! I've got something for you!"

Over the noise of the wind and rain, the men huddled beneath trees while on guard outside didn't hear the chopper until it was practically on top of them, closing at its attack speed of over a hundred-sixty miles per hour. Even as they recognized the threat and shouted a warning into their radios, the firing began. Three rockets blasted out of their pods, one after another, their telltale trails of smoke pointing like accusing fingers directly at the metal truck garage.

Before the men inside could react, the left half of their shelter shattered in a one-two-three blast of rolling fire that took everyone off their feet and turned furniture and supplies into flying shrapnel.

Frank raised his head even as he spat out a mouthful of blood after being hit across the face with a flying chair; the fact that the padded seat had caught him instead of one of the harder parts was all that kept him alive, let alone conscious. His MP5 hadn't faired so well; it was nowhere in sight.

There was no time to look for it, or to take inventory of who might be injured, if he wanted them to live. Even as he scrambled to his feet, the room was already filling with smoke as their supplies started to burn.

"Outside!" he roared over the noise of the chopper, the thumping of falling debris, and the screams of the wounded. "Everybody, outside! Now, damn it! Move it people! Move!"

His hand brushed someone and he turned to see Watis Suggs rising as well, the right side of his face a mask of blood, running from the sliced open skin of his forehead. The big man glanced at shattered stock of the M14 he carried, and cast it aside with a curse.

"Get 'em out of here, Watis, and put fire on that chopper!" The way out was obvious; most of the damaged side was now open air, apart from the flaming debris and pieces of the collapsed roof in front of it. Turning even as he moved toward it, he shouted back into the ruined building. "Irregulars! To me! This way!"

He heard Rob and Caffary simultaneously yell, "Coming!" followed by the First Sergeant's practiced bellow echoing the command, and he sensed as much as saw other figures heading his way, even as another rocket hit the right rear corner, peeling the metal back and detonating a small propane tank beside it. The resulting ball of fire shot inside through the gap like a flamethrower. Several of the wounded's cries cut off abruptly, only to be replaced by new ones.

With a mixed group of Irregulars and Tarheels following in his wake, Frank rushed at the opening and jumped over a smoking pile of rubble. Landing outside, his feet sliding in the mud as he came to a halt, he immediately saw the enemy, circling all too close overhead, hovering and darting like a dragonfly, and spitting fire like a real dragon from a fairytale. The only weapon he had left was the old .45, but Frank's instinct was to take the fight to the enemy. His sights were lined up on the machine and his finger was squeezing the trigger in less than a heartbeat.

The co-pilot grinned as he looked at the armed men spilling form every exit of the burning ruin. A couple were on fire, and began rolling on the ground as soon as they were outside.

"Must be the right place; looks like somebody kicked over an ant hill."

138

"Let's not give 'em a chance to go too far."

Pivoting the chopper hard to port, they lined up on the row of cars and trucks parked outside, the vehicles that had transported the guerrillas there. All the copilot had to do to aim was look; the 30mm was slaved to his helmet display, and pointed where ever he wanted, questing like a hound sniffing for its quarry. Touching the triggers, he walked his fire down the row, the explosive shells ripping the vehicles apart and sending metal and glass flying. A pair of rockets followed, gas tanks ignited with loud whooshes, and pools of liquid fire began crawling across the ground, hissing like fiery snakes as they went.

Whether they hailed from North or South Carolina, the first-line Confederate guerrillas were well trained, and knew what to so. Everyone who made it out joined Frank in the counter fire, and the pilot involuntarily flinched as bullets began spattering against the hull, and immediately began taking evasive action even as his copilot pivoted his head to return fire. Apaches were a hard craft to kill with small arms, but not impossible; they were still a helicopter, after all, with thin skin and more than a few complicated parts that didn't stand up well to multiple impacts.

Shouldn't be a problem; we'll just kill them all, and then let those douche bags in maintenance worry about the rest when we get back.

Watis Suggs had the same instinct as Frank, although his weapon of choice was a Smith and Wesson Model 29 .44 Magnum. Cursing as he blinked blood out of his shooting eye, he began firing, flinging 240 grain copper-jacketed bullets at the chopper, the big revolver's recoil barely moving his huge hands.

A rock thrown by a 30mm explosion struck a man standing to his left in the head, crushing his skull. He fell dying, his finger still locked on the trigger of his M4 set on full-auto. As his body convulsed, a line of his unknowingly fired bullets, their impacts marked by regularly spaced splashes in the mud, swept past Watis, and the Colonel's left leg folded inward with a new, unnatural joint halfway between his knee and ankle. Barely slowed by the bones and flesh, the tumbling projectile continued its course, plowing its way through his right calf, kicking that leg out to the side and dropping him instantly to the ground. The impact drove the splintered ends of his left tibia and fibia, broken by the bullet's passage, through his flesh in a compound fracture, pushing their bloody tips into the mud.

No one had ever heard the big man scream before, and the sound was like that of a wounded fighting bull: angry fury as much as pain.

Blood was spurting from his severed arteries in time to his heartbeat as he furiously emptied his remaining rounds at the chopper, and a Tarheel Corporal named Johnny Biscoe, who was standing nearby, stopped firing long enough to tie a pair of hasty tourniquets around his commander's torn legs, heedless of the flying bullets and shrapnel buzzing around him, or of Suggs cursing and groggily struggling to line up his speedloader through his fading consciousness.

It was chaos; between the helicopter's engines and it's 30mm cannon, and the small arms answering it from the ground, backed up the roar of flames, the yells of the healthy, the screams of the wounded, and the occasional blast of a rocket, the din was literally earsplitting. Something – shrapnel made of metal, earth or flesh – clanged off the burning garage loud enough to be noticed even over the noise, turning Captain Rob Johnson's attention that way. Everyone who could get out of the building's growing inferno had done so; a few kept on running, but most – including all the Irregulars Rob Johnson could see – stood their ground and were giving the Apache hell. As he saw two of guerrillas – one a Tarheel and the other one of his men – spin and fall, he also knew that, barring a miracle, it wouldn't be enough. The Apache AH-64 meant death to everyone on the ground unless it was stopped and stopped quickly. The only one way that was likely to happen was with one of North Carolina's Surface to Air Missiles, and he knew the only ones in the vicinity were still boxed up inside the garage. Staring at the leaping flames and billowing smoke for just a second, he cleared his mind. Then, heedless of the ammunition already cooking off in the heat, he sucked in a huge, final breath of fresh air, and charged back into the inferno, dodging falling debris, groping blindly through the acrid smoke as he sought the SAMs. He prayed they hadn't been destroyed in the blast.

Some part of him heard Watis yell and saw him fall, but Frank kept firing, the .45 brass flying through the air like a blizzard. Even as he held the empty clip between the left little and ring fingers and slammed in yet another full one with the same hand, he knew it was useless – with a handgun against the airborne killing machine, he might as well have been throwing rocks – but he had to rally the men and keep them focused on the target if they were to have any chance at all. Besides, if he had to die, he determined to go down facing the enemy.

There was a loud explosion and a swelling ball of fire when another rocket crashed into one of the pickups. A seventeen year-old Tarheel guerrilla nearby was momentarily engulfed in the resulting fireball and blown off his feet. Bruised by the impact and singed by the flames, the shock of the experience threw him into a panic. His only thought was to get away from the heat and noise, and he scrambled to his feet and ran blindly, his rifle forgotten in hand. Frank saw him coming and yelled out to him.

"Stand and fight! Put fire on that chopper!"

If the young man heard the order, he gave no sign, but continued fleeing on a path that would take him just to Frank's right. At the last minute, Frank slammed his right arm up and clothes lined him under the chin as he went by. Suddenly the private's feet were higher than his head, which slammed into the ground with a sickening thud. The boy's body lay limply in the mud; Frank didn't know if he had killed him or not. He hoped not, but right now he didn't have time to worry about it. He needed what was in the fallen man's hands.

Snatching up the old M1 Garand, Frank seated it against his shoulder, centered the Apache, and began squeezing the trigger. The heavy weapon's recoil against his shoulder was satisfying, as was the knowledge that the copper jacketed 7.62mm bullets would do one hell of a lot more damage than the .45. Of course, the realistic part of his brain told him it still probably wouldn't be enough, but right now, he'd take whatever he could get.

As he and everyone else still there and on their feet concentrated on the helicopter, he was unaware that the young guerrilla whose rifle he had abruptly appropriated had recovered enough to begin crawling desperately away.

In the meantime, the chopper rained a hail of death in the form of 30mm rounds, pouring down like hail. With so many, more than a few hit things besides the ground. Another rocket flashed just over Frank's head, so close he felt the wind of its passage, and hit somewhere behind him. It exploded, and he was startled when something smacked him hard between the shoulder blades, staggering him. For an instant, he thought he had been wounded, but some part of his brain recognized the wet, soft object as a large piece of flesh that had to have been bigger than his fist. He had no way of knowing whose it was, and no time to think about, so he kept firing.

The clip was almost empty when line of craters forming on the ground from the gunship's 30mm cannon swept past him, so closely the mud and pebbles snapped at his clothes and peppered him painfully. Immediately after the M1's action kicked out its last round, he looked down to find that the teenaged guerrilla was gone, and he had taken his ammunition with him. Then he saw something from the corner of his eye that got his undivided attention.

Sergeant Caffary's left leg was abruptly knocked out from under him. Falling hard, he rolled over and attempted to get up, but for some reason he couldn't manage it; he could feel his leg moving, but he couldn't seem to get any traction. Looking down to see what the problem was, he stopped and stared for several seconds, not believing what he saw. His left leg was simply gone; it had been torn off, leaving a bloody stump less than six inches below his knee. Through his shock, he realized he was looking at his boot, with his foot and what was left above it still in it, several feet away. It had landed upright, standing there like it was waiting for him to catch up.

It took a moment for what had been done to him to sink in, and his shock turned to fury. With a roar of rage, he turned on his attacker, and held the trigger back as he sent a long burst at the helicopter from his seat on the ground.

"Son of a bitch!" he screamed. "Shoot my leg off, you damned son of a bitch! Take that!"

The rain was sizzling on his rifle barrel as he quickly exhausted the clip, and he was reaching for another when a pair of strong hands grabbed his arms and yanked him upright. An instant later, he was even more shocked to find himself bouncing along on General Gore's back. Frank had tried for a fireman's carry, but when the amputated stump of the First Sergeant's leg slipped from his grip, Frank grabbed the other arm and pulled one to either side of his neck. He went running, trying to get the wounded man to cover. Caffary's legs dangled behind, the toe of his remaining boot leaving a single track with a patterned spray of blood beside it.

"Let me go and get the hell out of here, sir!" the older man shouted in his ear, suddenly afraid for the first time: not for himself, but for his commander. "Damn it! Get out of here!"

Frank ignored him, saving his breath for the effort, and sprinted for the dubious cover of a nearby ditch. He would drop Caffary into its shelter, and then take up the fight again as soon as he could find another weapon. For some reason, a prayer he had heard once from an Orthodox-practicing guerrilla he had met in Florida began unconsciously sounding in his head like the backbeat to a song.

Lord Jesus Christ, son of the Living God, have mercy on me, a sinner.

Although he never let it slow him down or loosen his grip on Caffary in the slightest, Frank had a sudden burst of intuition, a realization that something very bad was about to happen to him.

Just a few more feet! Just a few more feet! Just a few more...

They were nearly to cover when the rocket struck the ground only a few yards behind them, and in his last split-second of consciousness, Frank felt as though he had been hit by a truck when the blast engulfed him. His joints stretched impossibly and his flesh rippled and flattened as the rushing air pressure caught him up and flying objects slammed into him like a storm of hammers. He never heard Hodges shouting, "No!" or saw the sheer horror on the big skinhead's face.

Sergeant Hodges could only watch helplessly as his commander, Sergeant Caffary still on his back and dirt, blood and meat flying, was hurled forward across the ditch and driven face down into the opposite bank. No sooner had he slammed into the ground than a second rocket hit the top of that same bank with a roar and a ball of fire, and the earth collapsed, burying them together.

Rob staggered back out through the door of the burning building, smoke trailing from charred spots on the legs of his fatigues, and from the crewcut that had been singed off the right side of his head. His left hand had a tattered flap of melted skin hanging from its palm where he had jerked away a flaming piece of wood blocking the crate, and the cold, biting wind and rain brought new agony to the burns. Hacking and choking as he began prepping the Russian-made Igla-1 launching system, he tried to block out the pain; there simply wasn't time for it.

Finally ready, Rob shouldered the long launching tube. Squinting his watering eyes, still stinging and half-blind from the smoke, he closed out everything else, so there would be no distractions; all he could see was the helicopter, not the men firing and flailing and falling, not the line of craters in the mud rapidly advancing across the ground towards him, not even the sudden realization that he was going to die here on this North Carolina hillside; none of that mattered now. He was a professional, and that meant he concentrated on his job to the exclusion of all else. He squeezed and the solid fuel rocket left its tube and blasted skyward at Mach 2. Less than a tenth of a second later, the 30mm shells reached him.

It was strange, he thought almost idly as he was knocked off his feet, the round jack-hammering him at the waist, slamming him to the ground on his back. He had been stomped by a mob one time, and this was a lot like that: brief, heavy, hard pummeling, but this time there was no real pain. The shock to his nervous system as the 30mm explosive shell tore him in half was far too great for his nervous system to register.

Fortunately, the 9K38 missile from the Igla – the *needle* in Russian – didn't need him anymore. The infrared guidance system locked on to the Apache and, at such close range and at the speed the missile was moving, neither the pilot nor copilot had time to realize what was happening before the slender projectile slammed into them and exploded. Lying face up in the freezing, bloody mud, his rapidly dimming eyes watched the chopper turn into a fireball. Satisfied with a job well done, he tried to smile, although he no longer had the muscular control to pull it off.

Gotcha!

For some reason, he couldn't hear the sounds of battle anymore, or feel the cold rain, or see anything but the crowd of people approaching him through the gathering darkness filling his vision. His smile grew bigger; they were friends and family and comrades he hadn't seen for a long, long time. His parents were there, and the members of his old squad from the Balkans, and...*yes! By God, there's Chucky, nerdy glasses and all!* The logical part of him knew they were all dead, but that part of him was going fast, and such trivialities were no longer relevant. The rest of him stood up, whole once more and with no pain at all, and went to them. They welcomed him and embraced him, and he walked away with them, towards the light.

The chopper and its crew made a light of their own as they crashed into the nearby trees, blossoming into a series of secondary explosions as the ammunition inside began to cook off at the touch of the burning fuel.

North Carolina Captain McEvoy was sickened as he looked at the carnage around him. The gunship was no more than a pyre behind the trees whose flames rose almost to their tops, and the barn was so completely engulfed that the falling precipitation evaporated long before it could reach it; he could feel the heat from where he stood fifty feet away. Worse, he could smell the human flesh cooking inside. Anyone still in either place was a goner, and most of those outside weren't much better off. Bodies, whole or reduced to parts, were scattered all around, and the rain spread the blood until it ran like rivers across the ground. Someone, he didn't know who, was screaming continuously, seemingly without taking the time to draw breath. The man's wounds must have been mortal, because his cries were abruptly cut off by the sound of a single gunshot as one of his comrades put him out of his misery. Glancing around, he saw a dozen of his men left alive out of the forty he'd started with, and two of them were loading the semi-conscious Colonel Suggs onto a stretcher, both legs splinted and bound with field-expedient bandages.

McEvoy frowned. If it were up to him, he'd leave the son of a bitch here for the Feds; then maybe North Carolina would have a real State Army, not taking orders from anybody outside. A devoted follower of LC Tarbox – part of the same CAP internal dissident faction as the late Herbert Saunders of Florida – he knew his patron would be overjoyed to have Suggs taken permanently out of the way, but he also knew that most of the men liked their bearded colonel well enough to shoot the Captain if he made any overt attempt to make that happen. He supposed they were going to have to pack him along, and right quick, too. Bad weather or not, more of the enemy would be showing up soon, and it was time to get out of Dodge.

Maybe I'll get lucky, and the bastard will die on the way!

"Alright, boys! Fall in and get ready to move out on the double! We'll be having company before long!" As the Tarheels began scrambling, gathering their wounded who couldn't walk and scavenging the weapons belonging to the dead, he turned to Hodges, one of the fifteen Irregulars still up and moving. "Get your people out of here, Sergeant! Fall in with us!"

"No!" Hodges roared in return as he and the men of first squad who remained alive clawed at the collapsed pile of earth with their hands, ripping away their fingernails unnoticing while the ragged remnants of their company secured the perimeter, checked for wounded, and gathered ammunition from the fallen. The big skinhead's teeth were bared in a snarl and his eyes were wild. "General Gore is in here somewhere!"

"Damn it, he's *dead*!"

"No he's not! He's not dead until I see it! *He's not dead!*"

"I gave you an order!" McEvoy snapped, only to see Casey Graham jerk the muzzle of the M203 grenade launcher mounted below the barrel of his M4 in his direction. Seen head-on, the bore looked impossibly wide, but no wider and no scarier than the eyes of the guerrilla who held it with his finger on the trigger.

From the foothills of western South Carolina, Graham was almost entirely Irish and Scottish by blood, and it showed in his sharp features and reddish brown hair, along with his strange eyes that matched his hair color almost perfectly. More than that, it showed in his temper; although not particularly large, he was powerfully built and would fight anyone over anything if they chose to force the issue. He had spent several years involved with various radical Aryan splinter groups, and even amongst them and his fellow Irregulars, he was known for his fearlessness, tenacity and utter ferocity when aroused. A few of them suspected he might be more than a little psychotic...like now.

"We're the 1st Columbia Irregulars, by God!" he shouted back as the blood from a head wound soaked his face and neck, "and we take our orders from General Gore! You want to run, then you tuck your tail and freaking run! We stay with Frank Gore!"

The North Carolina Captain came to the abrupt realization that Graham was ready, able and perfectly willing to kill him. He shook his head, and began getting his own people moving. "It's on your head, then!" he said over his shoulder. "Come on, lets get the hell out of here!"

Hodges ignored them all and kept digging until he heard Corporal Stanley's voice.

"I've got something!"

The dark haired soldier, arm buried to the elbow, pulled for a moment, something gave, and he withdrew his hand from the dirt and stared at it in abject horror. It contained a chunk of torn flesh, and a broken piece of jewelry chain with a locket they all recognized adhering to it.

"No! Oh God, *no!*"

CHAPTER 14

Samantha shifted in her chair again for the third time in five minutes, desperately trying to get comfortable and failing miserably. She glared down at her swollen belly. At almost nine months worth of pregnant, it always seemed to be in the way anymore. As if to emphasize it's defiance, her belly button protruded, making a little peak in the cloth of her shirt.

That made her smile in spite of herself, because it made her think of her husband.

She felt ugly, cranky, and miserable – and as big as a house – but Frank didn't seem to mind a bit, and constantly told her she was more beautiful than ever. In fact, he seemed fascinated with her belly's new shape, and most particularly with her navel, now that it had become an 'outie.' Samantha was extremely ticklish at the best of times, but lately, Frank had taken to catching her unawares, and then he would make her squeal by gently flicking her new protrusion or rolling it between his fingers. Once, when he had been rubbing some lotion on her stomach for her to help reduce the chance of stretch marks, he had suddenly grinned with inspiration before dropping his head and gently nibbling on it. She had almost peed herself that time, and, much to their embarrassment, her screams had caused those on guard duty to sound the alarm, thinking a raid was in progress. Oh, she had been so angry!

God, how she missed him!

He was gone more than he was with her, often being absent for weeks at a time. He had no choice; the war demanded it, and Frank was a man who understood his duty. It seemed like he was always off somewhere, first one place and then another, keeping their army together while trying to stay one jump ahead of the enemy. He got home whenever he could, of course, and when he did they both tried their best to make up for their time apart. Pregnant or not, the very real possibility – more like a *probability* – that their time would run out at the end of a gun lent a sense of desperation to their lovemaking, driving their passion until it almost became obsession whenever they came together. Neither of them knew even *if* there would be a next time, let alone when, so they made the most of what they had, and spent every spare minute they could beg, borrow or steal behind the closed door of their quarters. They knew their activity was noticeable enough to be scandalous and the favorite subject for jokes and gossip in what Frank referred to as their "own little Peyton Place," but neither one cared. It was far, far more than simple libido; it was a serious case of love.

Samantha tried not to worry, but there was no way to keep from it. She trusted in her husband's abilities, but she prayed a lot too.

Shifting once again, she spread her legs a bit more, bumping the stainless steel Smith & Wesson strapped to her thigh – no wide gun belts around her expanded waist right now – against the drawer, and got as close to the desk as her altered anatomy would allow her. Finally, she decided she was about as comfortable as she was going to get for the moment, and had just began tapping in her latest project on the keyboard, when someone knocked at the door.

"Come in."

The door opened to reveal her bodyguard, complete with her usual armament.

"Hi, Cynthia."

"Sammie," she said, "don't forget your class."

"I won't. When does it start?"

Cynthia hid a tight smile as she glanced at her watch. "About five minutes ago."

"Oh, no!" Disgustedly, the Confederate Army Provisional Communications Officer slammed both palms against the edge of the desk in frustration before awkwardly grabbing the armrests and heaving herself to her feet. It aggravated her to see Cynthia standing braced, ready to catch her if she lost her balance; she was quite capable of getting around by herself, thank you very much, but she bit off the outburst she felt like making. The girl meant well – *and she's probably right* – and anyway, Cynthia had been through more than enough already in her short life.

All of us have.

Before she was all the way out the door, Jim Reynolds and Billy Sprouse rose from their chairs on either side with weapons in hand, ready to escort her. Jim was tall and quiet, and as pale and gaunt as a corpse, still suffering from being shot through the lung months ago, leaving a wound that still refused to properly heal. Billy, wounded and captured by the Federal forces along with Samantha in the same battle, was just the opposite. He was a literal giant. At six and a half feet tall and over three hundred pounds in weight, the formidable biker was as strong as an ox and had a loud, boisterous, irrepressible personality that fit his form to a tee. Frank had asked them to provide for his wife's security when he wasn't around, and they had been honored by his trust. Both men literally owed him their lives, and either one of them would die to preserve hers without giving it a second thought.

"Are you alright, Sammie?" It was Billy who spoke. Jim seldom did, but they both fussed over her like mother hens, and worried constantly that something might happen to her, especially *'in her condition.'*

"I'm fine, thanks. Don't worry, Billy, I'm not the first woman to get pregnant."

"No, but you're the first one of 'em I've been responsible for looking after," he declared, somewhat miffed, "and I'm not going to let either you or Frank down."

She treated him to a smile. "I've never had to worry about that from either one of you," she said as she patted him on his huge, tattooed bicep before looking at Jim. "I'm in good hands." Jim seemed to straighten up his slightly stooped shoulders another notch, and Billy, always tenderhearted despite his rough, crude exterior, appeared to suddenly discover he had something in his eye.

Cynthia moved up beside her and the men fell in behind as she walked – *Who am I kidding? I'm waddling!* – down the hall of the large barn converted into one of their underground headquarters. There was a narrow tunnel through the building for the tractors and other equipment of the farmer who owned it to go in and out, but the space to either side had been walled off and divided: barracks on one side, offices and classrooms on the other. This was the South

Carolina Command's latest training center, where recruits of every age and sex were turned into soldiers for the Cause.

Following operation Long Knives that had decimated their enemies' presence in Columbia, and the full scale U.S. military occupation that had resulted, all the wanted personnel had been moved out, and their former headquarters there had been abandoned to a skeleton crew. Mike Dayton now shared his house with only Tommy and Donna. Although they had individuals and small cells scattered across the city, the only organized force at the Capital was the squad formed by Tommy and run by him and Lieutenant Joel Harrison, that operated out of the front of a Karate dojo. Since none of them were known to the enemy, they stayed on, occasionally giving the occupation forces a violent reminder that the city wasn't theirs, and that they weren't welcome. Usually these reminders came in the form of remotely detonated roadside bombs and sniping or mortar attacks. Even though the Columbia Rebel forces there were small and their efforts scattered, they still accounted for an average of a dozen enemy dead and four times that many wounded every month, and a lot of lost sleep in Washington DC.

Of course, it wasn't only the South Carolina capital; there was a war going on now with those casualties being duplicated and, in some cases, exceeded in every Southern state, as well as the border states of West Virginia and Kentucky. Most major Southern cities could be called nothing else but war zones, and the countryside was even worse.

"How do you reach the masses of people? How many believe you do it with logic and reason?"

From her position in front of the white board showing a variety of charts and graphs, Samantha watched the majority of the hands in the room go up and hid a smile; she had believed that once herself.

"I'm sorry to say, you're wrong. Oh, the leadership has to rely on reason – at least they'd *better* rely on it – but the bulk of our people, of *any* people, are either unwilling or incapable of doing that."

She looked around at the furrowing brows that clearly indicated the doubts they were too polite to mention.

They're thinking 'elitist' but don't want to say it.

"I see some of you are skeptical. Ask yourself this question then; why did the majority of the people believe what the United States Government told them time and time again, even after they were lied to by that government every time?" She paused as if waiting for an answer she knew wasn't coming, and then looked toward the other side of the room. "Why did the majority, liberal and conservative alike, actually believe there were real, substantive differences between the Democratic and Republican Parties, even when both took exactly same stance on every issue of real importance, over and over again?"

"Because they're *sheeple*, Ma'am; they're incapable of doing anything else besides going where they're led."

She knew the owner of the gravely voice before she looked at him; thankfully, he was one of the few who wasn't in awe of her. Captain "Lucky Charlie" Carnes respected her, but didn't put her on an uncomfortable pedestal either, and she liked him for that reason. Of course, Lucky Charlie wasn't too much in awe of anything, not that she could blame him.

Captain Charles Wayne Carnes, originally from Conway, had earned his nickname as a black-humored play on the old joke about a dog with one eye, one ear, three legs, and a broken tail, and went by the name of 'Lucky.' While serving in the US Army in the misnamed Operation Iraqi Freedom, his armored personnel carrier had run afoul of a powerful Improvised Explosive Device: an IED, a roadside bomb, leaving him the only survivor. He didn't have a tail to break, but he did lose both his legs halfway to his hips, his left hand and a third of the forearm it was attached to, his left testicle, and most of the left side of his face, including his eye and ear to the blast and subsequent fire. The substandard care he got in the overcrowded and under-funded military hospital didn't help either; between the slip-shod surgery and subsequent infections, he came out looking like Hell on Sunday morning, with artificial metal legs, an articulated hook for a hand, an eye patch, and a face divided almost exactly down the middle, with the right side roguishly handsome and the left looking like a patchwork quilt of mismatched and mangled flesh. His pretty young wife of two years had taken one look at him and promptly left for greener pastures. When a nurse tried to cheer him up by telling him how lucky he was just to be alive, he loudly informed her, in a voice that had echoed across the hospital ward, "Yeah, baby; I reckon I'm lucky as hell!" and the name stuck.

Discharged, disillusioned, and disgusted with the United States, when the Confederate Army Provisional had asked for volunteers, Lucky Charlie stepped up – well, bounced up on his artificial legs with his leaf-spring feet that made him look like a robot from Star Wars – and they not only took him, scars, assorted missing parts and all, but did so at his previous rank. He was the base commander of their current headquarters, but he liked to sit in on the classes whenever possible.

"You're right in one way, but wrong in another. That does describe most people, but a propagandist can't allow himself or herself to think of them quite that way, or it'll come through in their work. Nobody likes to be talked down to, so you have to do it in such a way that it's not obvious. As much as I hate to say it – as a professional journalist, it disgusts me to say it – but to the vast majority of people, presentation is much more important than content. As a matter of personal principle, I only work with the truth; some of my colleagues do not, specializing in disinformation. Regardless, there's no difference in the way either one is put across.

"The purpose of propaganda is not so much to *inform* the people as to *reach* them. What we present has to appeal to something inside them, beyond logic; it has to contact them on a spiritual level. It has to touch their hearts before they'll be willing to believe it in their minds." She smiled at Lucky Charlie. "Hearts first, Captain, isn't that what they say? Hearts and minds?"

The mutilated officer grinned back, and the effect was more than a little disturbing.

"Yes, ma'am, that's what they say. Sometimes, though, there's another way to reach them. If you've got 'em by the balls, their hearts and minds will follow."

A few of the people gasped, both at his use of the vulgar phrase in mixed company and at his casual attitude towards Samantha, but she only laughed.

"As long as you can get hold of them, I suppose that would motivate most people too, although I can't speak from personal experience, of course."

The tension broke and there was general laughter from everyone in the room.

"Now," she said, "if you can't reach their personal parts, you have to reach their hearts some other way..."

A voice suddenly sounded, not in her ears but inside her head: a familiar, loving voice that cried out her name in agony.

She abruptly stopped in mid-sentence. A wave of pain swept over, nauseating pain, and she stumbled and doubled over, grabbing her stomach with her left hand and the desk with her right to keep from collapsing in the floor. In that moment she somehow *knew*...

Frank! Oh please God, no!

Her face went deathly pale and she felt the baby violently kicking inside her, as if equally aware of her distress. By that time, half class was already on their feet, concern in their eyes.

"Ma'am? Colonel Gore?" Lucky Charlie's voice rose and octave or two and his mechanical hook accidentally plowed a deep scratch across the desktop as he heaved himself erect. "Are you alright?"

Cynthia was already beside her, holding her elbow and partly-helping, partly forcing her back into her seat.

"Is the baby coming?" she whispered, and Samantha shook her head as the first tears began. Instantly assessing the situation, Captain Carnes addressed to the shocked class.

"File out right now! Go to your next class. Wait there for your instructor."

They hesitated, and Lucky Charlie barked, "Move your asses, damn it!" slamming his hook down on the desk hard enough to knock a chunk out this time, and adding a few more expletives just to make certain they got the message.

They moved, and the Captain followed, stopping on his way out to pat her shoulder with his remaining hand.

"I'll get them settled and get your people in here ASAP. Do you need a medic?"

She shook her head, unable to speak.

He was as good as his word, and in a moment, Billy and Jim were with her.

"What is it Sammie?" the big man demanded, the worry plain in his voice. "What's wrong?"

When it came, her voice was a banshee wail that rose like a hand-cranked air raid siren from the first word to the last. "Something's happened to Frank!"

The three looked at each other as chills ran down their spines.

"Sammie," Jim began, much more calmly than he felt, "sudden irrational fears like this aren't uncommon during pregnancy…"

"It's not irrational! I just know! I heard him call my name, just now!"

"It's easy enough to find out," Billy said before turning to Cynthia. "Kerrie's on com duty; run in there and get her to put out a call for him." Cynthia looked like she was going to balk at leaving Samantha, but the biker grabbed her by the arm, shoved his hairy face almost against her ear and hissed, "You're the fastest, damn it – now go!" and followed it with a shove that sent her stumbling in the desired direction.

Turning back to the Communications Officer, he took her by the shoulders. "You just calm yourself down now, Sammie. We're callin' Frank right now, but you've got to stay calm, or you're liable to drop that baby right here in the floor!"

She knew the truth of what he was saying, and even though she fought to force herself to get it under control, it was so hard.

"This may take awhile," Billy continued, "by the time we get hold of Mike and he gets the encryption goin', let alone trackin' him down, but we'll find him. It's gonna be alright." He said that last with a lot more confidence than he felt. Billy's own mother had said the exact same thing about his father only hours before the police brought her the news about the industrial accident that took his life…*No, damn it! No, I won't believe it…*

I can't believe it!

By the time they got her to the communications room, Kerrie O'Brien was already speaking urgently into the computer's microphone, and spared them little more than a glance; that one look at Samantha's shattered expression was more than she could cope with and still do her job. She had come to consider her and Frank as sort of surrogate parents; certainly she loved them and was loved by them in a way unlike any affection she had experienced at home. She tried not to let the concern show in her voice as she finally turned to Samantha, but inside, she felt like screaming.

"Mike's working on it, Sammie. He should be able to raise him within the hour."

Samantha was no longer listening. Instead, her attention was riveted to one of several TV screens that the guerrillas used to constantly monitor what was going on. The reporter's voice sounded satisfied, almost gleeful.

"United States forces from the 101st Airborne Division ambushed a large Confederate terrorist force in North Carolina today, and are currently engaging them in heavy combat. Early reports indicate that dozens of the terrorists have been killed or wounded, and it is believed by sources in the military that Confederate Army Provisional leader Frank Gore may be among them. Even as we speak, American ground forces are moving into the area in a mopping up operation…"

Samantha refused to leave. Instead, as Kerrie and Mike repeatedly tried to raise Frank, she sat for hours, watching the embedded reporters gloating while the soldiers moved through the cold rain, gathering weapons and kicking the torn, mutilated bodies looking for signs of life, before dragging them into rubber sacks. The camera panned the corpses like it was exhibiting a trophy case, and suddenly there was the mangled, partially dismembered body and cold, dead face of Lieutenant Rob Johnson, Frank's XO and her friend. Cynthia looked up in time to recognize him too, and for the first time since she had joined the Confederate Army Provisional, they heard her cry out loud. Samantha didn't consciously hear her, but instinctively opened her arms and pulled her close, holding her while she shook, her body wracked with sobs. She offered what comfort she could, but her mind was elsewhere; she was staring at the picture, looking desperately for Frank, all the while hoping and praying she wouldn't see him.

OhGodohGodohGod!

CHAPTER 15

Even after hours of negotiations, Sam still found the pair of faces across the table in the Albuquerque hotel suite hard to read, but he was finally beginning to figure them out. They were several shades darker than his own, with features that were just as different: larger noses, higher cheekbones, broader foreheads. Both men were Indians, White Mountain Apache and Navajo respectively. The Confederate Councilman was a great student of human nature – he had to be, just to survive – and while he saw the faint flickering of suppressed hope in their dark eyes, he also saw a much more intense suspicion.

Not that I blame them, considering their history. They're a lot like Southerners; they're so used to getting screwed they've come to expect it.

The Navajo, a big man, much larger than the average *Dine*, in an obviously expensive light blue suit with his long graying hair tied behind his head in the traditional bun of his people, finally got down to the crux of the matter. "Mr. Wirtz, how do we know we can trust you?"

Sam made it a point to look him straight in the eye when he answered, but then again, he did that with most people anyway.

"You don't, Mr. Begay, any more than I know whether I can trust you. The thing is, we're both in desperate straits right now."

"You more than us, I think," the Apache pointed out in a carefully neutral voice. Sam turned his eyes to the heavyset man with the crewcut and deeply lined, craggy face that could have been forty or seventy.

"Depends on how you look at it, I suppose. The worst thing that can happen to us is that we can die. The worst thing that can happen to you is that things can go on with your people exactly as they have for the past century or so: poverty, and continued cultural and ultimately racial destruction. You'll die too; your deaths may be a lot slower, but just as sure. That doesn't have to happen; you've got a chance to stop it.

"By risking everything we have?" Begay asked.

"Mr. Begay, I'm familiar with your social and economic situation. To be blunt, it was smack-dab in the toilet before the depression, and now it's practically non-existent. The reservations are screwed even worse than the general population. What the hell do you have to lose, really?"

Begay blinked behind his stylish, wire-framed glasses, instinctively lapsing into his calm, courtroom persona.

"Oh, lets see; our lives, maybe, and the lives of our people."

"Those are already lost, sir; we're all dying as soon as we're born. You all are about my age; what have you and I got? Another thirty, forty years tops, the last few of which we'll probably spend drooling in our laps in a nursing home somewhere? And your people are just like mine: another three or four generations, what will they be?" Sam tapped the tabletop with his finger for emphasis. "I've been up to Page and down to Flagstaff, and even to your capital at Tuba City. I've seen what's become of your people. It's the same thing that's become of my own: drunks, dopers, whores, thinking of nothing but themselves while they run around with their rap music blaring, their hair in dreadlocks and their pants down around their asses. They're lost! They're being homogenized into the least common denominator; they have no structure, no culture, no identity of their own. Their own elders – *us* – are dead to them; they just haven't gotten around to burying us yet.

"And look at what's being done to your people; even now, the damned government say it, not you, has the right to say who's an Indian and who's not. They set the blood requirements, not you, just like they did to the Cherokee, by making them accept full-blooded Africans as full-blooded Indians! Hell, if nothing else, they'll eventually define you out of existence."

His hosts looked at one another; obviously, he had struck a sore spot with that one.

"Let me ask you this, then," the Navajo finally continued. "What can you offer us that the United States can't?"

Sam took a deep breath. It was the moment of truth.

"It's your choice; either a home-ruled autonomous territorial protectorate or else statehood with full representation just like any other state. I recommend the latter. I know you're aware of the states' rights stance of the Confederate Government; once the dust from this Revolution finally settles, each state will be largely autonomous. No Bureau of Indian Affairs, no Department of the Interior, nothing different from that of any other state."

The two Indians looked at one another, just a single flickering glance, but Sam had played poker enough to know what it meant. This was what they had hoped for; they hadn't expected it, but they had hoped for it. Sam was a decent poker player and more than a little savvy when it came to making deals. Now, unless he missed his guess, they were going to try for a little bit more.

Hell, in their place, I would too.

"You do know the Indians in the South are of several different nations..."

"One state, Mr. Begay, Mr. Chato: one state, or if you prefer, one territory, is all I'm authorized to offer. It may be spread out and a little fragmented, depending on how many tribes want to join you as opposed to remaining part of the current state where they reside, but at least it will be Indian land under Indian rule, part of a larger Confederation for the mutual benefit of all." Sam smiled pointedly. "Hell, it could even be a Confederation within a Confederation for that matter, if that's what you want to make it. If I'm not mistaken in my history, a Confederacy is something at least some of your eastern brethren have had experience in."

"The Six Nations of the Iroquois Confederacy, yes," Chato confirmed, "but those peoples were much more similar to one another than ours and yours."

"That's true, but what was it that held it together? Common interest in a common area, that's what. Your people and mine both live here, and neither one of us has any intention of going anywhere. We live here, but if we don't pull together, we'll both end up dying here."

Begay and Chato looked at one another.

"Well," the attorney sighed, "there is that."

The mellow sound of Indian flute music suddenly sounded from Chato's belt, and he unclipped his cell phone and placed it to his ear.

"Yes?" A long pause, then, "I see. Thank you."

Turning back to Sam, he asked the question, "Just how important is Frank Gore to this Revolution of yours?"

"Very."

"Um. I was just wondering, because the news is reporting that the Army may have just killed him in North Carolina."

Sam had been punched in the kidney once during a bar fight while doing his own stint in the military, and this feeling was a lot like that: instant weakness and nauseating pain. Still, he refused to let it show beyond a slight blinking of his eyes, and seized upon the one key word in the Apache's sentence.

"May?"

"I've just been informed that the news is reporting the 101st Airborne has attacked a Confederate Army Provisional outpost in North Carolina. They're mopping up now, and they claim to have information that your General Gore was there."

Sam knew damned well he was there, and he also knew this was a make or break moment for this proposed alliance, and that his reaction within the next few seconds would do the making or the breaking.

Fully aware of their eyes upon him, Sam did the last thing they expected, and the last thing he felt like doing; he smiled, then chuckled. The two Indians looked at one another and then back at him, as if he had gone mad.

"Sorry," he said, waving a hand as if fighting to get his humor under control, "but Frank Gore isn't easy to kill. I know, because I've seen people try it, and I've helped bury some of them. If they ain't got the body, then he ain't dead."

"But *if* he is," Begay asked, "wouldn't that collapse your effort?"

Sam's face went cold sober. "This army and this war is bigger than any one man, sir. If – and I mean *if* – something has happened to Frank, then he will continue to live on as a martyr and an inspiration to the rest. We can survive the loss of any one person, including him."

162

Inside, though, he wasn't quite so sure.

CHAPTER 16

It began innocently, as most utterly disastrous things usually do. It started when Tommy Richardson bent to pick up a book.

He and Donna were grocery shopping for the Columbia headquarters, otherwise known as Mike Dayton's house. They were in a small strip mall, and he had decided to leave the shopping to Donna while he checked the tiny bookstore tucked away on the end to see if they had anything worth reading. Usually they didn't: just the same old formula characters and regurgitated plots in cheaply-printed and overpriced paperbacks, regardless of the genre. Still, he had a passion for reading, so it was worth a look.

Muriel Parks, a heavy, middle-aged White woman, was working the counter. Nervous at the best of times, she was especially so now. She had been robbed twice in the past six months, and she didn't like the idea of being alone with this scar-faced, scruffy-looking biker one little bit. Something about him fairly screamed *DANGER!* at her in big red letters, and she kept her right hand near the alarm button under the counter.

Tommy was oblivious to her concern, but he wasn't at all oblivious to the book low on the shelves that caught his eye. It was by one of his favorite science fiction authors, and he squatted down to take a look.

Muriel's eyes widened in fear. Tommy's back was to her, and when he bent his knees and leaned forward, the black leather vest he wore over his equally black tee-shirt pulled up. The denim waistband of his jeans was still too high to show the "plumber's crack," but low enough to unknowingly reveal the grips of the 9mm Glock in an inside-the-pants holster at the small of his back.

Muriel pressed the button, and the silent holdup alarm notified the dispatcher at the Columbia Police Department that a robbery was in progress.

Facing away from her, Tommy didn't notice, nor did he see her flinch as he swore under his breath at finding the book to be a reprint of one he had read years before, but now reissued in a new cover.

Probably to fool idiots like me into buying it again!

He stood abruptly and turned, and the clerk bit her lip and stepped backwards. Finally noticing her trepidation, the biker turned CAP guerrilla lieutenant grinned, but his scar made the expression look sinister to her, almost like a particularly sadistic sneer.

Muriel felt like she was going to faint.

Where are the police? Hurry! Oh God, please, hurry!

Tommy wasn't surprised; a lot of people reacted to him that way despite his small size. He just nodded, said, "Nothing today, ma'am" and walked out the front door just as Donna pulled up in the old pickup truck. Tommy got in, kissed her, and they drove away.

Behind them, Muriel Parks rushed to the door to write down the license number.

They had barely gotten out of sight when a police car belatedly slid to a stop in front of the shop in a squeal of rubber. Two cops immediately exited, guns drawn, and Muriel rushed out the front door towards them, only to find herself looking down their pistol barrels.

"Freeze! Police!"

She screamed as she came to such an abrupt halt that she slipped and fell flat on her ample backside on the sidewalk. It took almost five long and uncomfortable minutes before she managed to become coherent enough for the rotund Sergeant Patterson and his skinny colored partner, Officer Starling, to understand what she was trying to tell them, by which time Tommy and Donna were long gone.

"He didn't rob you?" Patterson asked.

"He had a gun!"

"Yes, ma'am, you've already said that. Did he rob you?"

"No, but he had a gun!"

"Yes, ma'am; we've been over that. Did he threaten you in any way?"

"No, but he had a gun!"

Patterson blew out his breath. This was going to be a long damned day. Oh well, that's what rank was all about.

"Starling, get her statement while I investigate the scene."

The other cop rolled his eyes, the effect of the gesture being unusually pronounced by their whites contrasting with his prune-black face.

All the shit falls on me! The only thing Pat's going to investigate is that damned doughnut shop two doors down!

He knew his partner well; the sergeant was already headed in that direction when a pair of Humvees backed up by a Bradley Fighting Vehicle – a rubber tired variant of the older tracked models – pulled into the lot at a high rate of speed. Their drivers either didn't notice of else didn't care about the presence of a speed bump, and the air was instantly filled with curses from the soldiers they were carrying as they were lifted up only to be slammed back down. Coming to a stop beside Patterson, an Army Captain stuck his head out the passenger window of the lead Humvee. When his voice came, it had an unmistakable New England accent.

"What's going on here?"

Patterson kept his bulldog face neutral, but inside he was fuming. He had never been particularly fond of Yankees in the first place, and in the second, the occupation troops were one big pain in the ass. As far as he was concerned, they caused one hell of a lot more trouble than what they were worth. It was getting so a man couldn't fart without them showing up and demanding an explanation.

"Nothing really; just a false alarm." He jerked his thumb over his shoulder in the direction of Starling and the clerk. "The lady there thought she saw a gun under some guy's jacket and pushed the holdup alarm, but all he did was look around and then leave. It looks like he was just shopping. We'll run his plates and see if he's got a concealed carry permit; if not, we'll go round him up."

The door immediately opened the police sergeant had to step back quickly to keep from being hit by it as the captain jumped out. The cop noticed the name *TANGO* one his name tag.

"He had a gun?"

Patterson winced.

Not again!

"It's illegal, but not all that unusual; we deal with it every day."

"What? And you're not reporting it to us?"

"Look, Captain!" Patterson was not overly sweet tempered at the best of times, and he tended to take personal umbrage at anyone who was determined to add complications to his existence, especially if they were trying to tell him how to do his job. "Everybody and his brother owns a gun down here, and half of them pack them around once in a while; they always have. Carrying a concealed weapon without a permit is a crime, and when we catch somebody doing it, he goes downtown; it's as simple as that."

Beneath the shade of his helmet brim, the Captain's face turned so red that he looked as if he would have a stroke, and spit flew from his mouth as he spoke.

"Damn it! Don't you freaking inbred hillbillies get it? If someone has a gun, he's presumed to be a terrorist until we know different!" Finished spraying saliva all over the cop in his self-righteous anger, he spun and shouted at the truck. "Dismount those Hummvees and form a perimeter! Now!"

"You're wasting your time; they're gone."

"No, you're gone; get your stupid hayseed ass the hell out of here! This is a military matter now, and I don't need any help from Andy and Barney!"

Patterson's eyes went wide with anger, and it was right on the tip of his tongue to tell this young punk of a soldier to kiss his ass, but he bit the remark off before it formed. Another of Columbia's cops had done that early in the occupation, and the soldiers had beaten and stomped him nearly to death, and then the military governor ordered Chief Carter to fire him. The PD had no choice but to comply, and now the man was crippled for life and about to lose his home because he had no income and, blacklisted from employment by the Feds as a terrorist sympathizer, he had no chance of getting any.

Damn sons of bitches!

Seething and not trusting himself to speak, the sergeant turned on his heel and stomped back to the cruiser.

"Starling! Get in the car!"

"But Pat, I'm still takin' her statement – "

"You're taking us down the road is what you're taking! This is the Army's case now!"

"But he had a gun!" Muriel shrieked once more while Sergeant Patterson hoisted himself into the passenger seat.

"Yeah, lady, I gathered that!" he muttered as he slammed the door.

As they drove away, Patterson cast one last glare at the soldiers, and Starling wasn't sure, but he thought he heard him muttering something about hoping the Confederate guerrillas would stick a rusty bayonet up somebody's ass. He decided, with the mood his sergeant was in, it would be better not to ask him to repeat it.

Tommy opened the door from the basement steps; Mike had called him down the second they had arrived, and if that wasn't enough evidence that something was very wrong, Donna knew it as soon as she saw her lover's face.

"What's happened?"

He swallowed hard before answering. He knew the Irregulars, every last one of them. He had trained with them, led them, and fought beside them. They were his brothers in arms.

And then there was Frank...poor Sammie!

"You'd better sit down." His voice was hollow and almost metallic, as if he was speaking into an empty bucket.

Whatever it was, she knew it was going to be bad, and the last thing she felt like doing was sitting, but she obeyed anyway, parking her slender rear on the kitchen chair. Tommy did something then that she'd never seen him do; he flopped into the chair beside her. He didn't sit; he simply dropped like his strings had been cut and hit with a thump, and when he reached out to take her hand, she saw something else new: the moisture gathering in his eyes. That by itself frightened her more than anything else.

"Donna, the Irregulars were ambushed in North Carolina earlier today."

"Oh my God..." Her voice was almost a whisper. "How many?"

He had to look away for a minute, his teeth and lips pressed firmly together before he could regain control. "I don't know. Most of them, it looks like. Maybe...maybe all of them."

The faces of the men she had trained and fought with passed before her eyes in a flicker of motion before stopping on one in particular

"Was..." She stopped, then started again, asking the question she had to ask, but fearing the answer more than anything in her life. "Was Frank with them?"

Eyes closed as he fought back the tears for his fallen comrades and for the friend he had come to love like a brother, Tommy's head jerked up and down. "Yeah."

Donna locked up. She couldn't believe it. She was so shocked she made no sound at first, but the tears poured down her face in rivers while she shook her head back and forth in denial.

"No. No. Nonononono!" Once she found her voice, it became a chant that grew increasingly faster, like a motor starting up.

"Keep it together, Donna!" Tommy told her more loudly than he had intended, shaking her hand hard enough to send the motion up her arm to her shoulder and make her body follow suit. "He's one of the few we haven't heard about yet. Maybe he got out."

"You don't believe that, do you?"

"I hope and pray for it!"

"But you don't believe it."

Looking away again, he shook his head. "I'm sorry. He's my friend, and I know how much he means to *you*, but no, I don't believe it."

Something in the way he made that statement cut through the tangled web of her emotions, and she raised her guilty eyes to him.

"So you know; you knew all along."

He shrugged without enthusiasm. "It was pretty obvious to anybody with eyes; you've been head over heels in love with Frank ever since the very first time you saw him, I reckon. Hell, I don't suppose I could blame you: a big, handsome guy, the hero of the Revolution, the avenger of your sister."

Tommy didn't let go of her hand, and she squeezed his tighter, suddenly so very afraid that he would. "But...didn't it bother you?"

"Sometimes...well, to be honest, yeah, it did. But I was the one you came to that night, not him." He didn't state the obvious: that Frank was already taken by a woman whom Donna looked at like a sister, but he didn't have to. She knew very well what he left unsaid.

"I'm so sorry, Tommy; I never meant to hurt you."

"I know that. I reckon love's a lot like the weather; it's one of those things in life we don't have any control over. I'm just glad you loved me too."

"I do love you." She stopped for a second, and even managed a little smile. "I've loved you a lot longer than him too. I've had a crush on you since I was just a skinny little girl, when you gave me a ride on your Harley out at Uncle Sam's farm. I remember squeezing you tight with my face against the back of your leather jacket; I was pretending I was in front of you, and you were hugging me back."

Returning her smile, he said, "I remember that too, but I thought you were hanging on so tight because you were scared." He shook his head. "Life's funny, isn't it, the way things change but always seem to come back around anyway? Of course, you're still a skinny girl, but you're not quite so little anymore."

Lowering her eyes, she blushed. Then, by mutual unspoken consent, they rose, and walked toward their bedroom. There was far too much grief for there to be any real lust this time. Instead, it was just a driving need for comfort, for affirmation that they were still alive, at least for the moment. If Frank was gone, they knew that moment might not last very long.

Below, in the basement, Mike heard their murmuring voices and the direction their footsteps were retreating towards, and sighed. He knew exactly how they felt, and he wished Kerrie was with him right now, because he'd be doing the same thing. He imagined how comforting it would be in her arms right then...

He shook his head, reluctantly clearing the vision from his mind, and put his fingers on his keyboard again. He had work to do, and some desperate prayers of his own to say while he did it.

CHAPTER 17

The late evening wind howled through the trees and the freezing rain was coming down in sheets now, often with sleet mixed with it. As the cold water poured down his face and turned the ground into clinging mud that fought against their every step, Sergeant Hodges thanked God for the storm. The air surveillance, and hopefully the satellites, would be unlikely to penetrate it. They had been running for hours, with no end in sight. The emergency amphetamines – a heady and potentially dangerous homemade speedball of dexedrine, vitamins, ginseng, caffeine, and ginko – they had taken to keep going could only do so much, but despite being able to hear and feel their own blood roaring through their veins, they still had to do more. Their Tarheel guide, Corporal Johnny Biscoe, kept motioning them on, even though he was wheezing for breath himself.

"Faster! Faster! We're almost there!"

It seemed like he had been saying that forever. For the three men left of Alpha Squad, forever might not be very long.

By God, whatever happened now, he was proud to have fought with them, and he had no regrets. They had fought for a good cause and stood like men. Doug Long, with an elongated body and face to match his name, never said much, but kept going like a machine; his muscles shaking with fatigue but his eyes steady. Casey Graham had that fire inside his somewhat shorter form that kept him going as well, a fire that seemed to make his strange brown eyes glow with a fierce light. Biscoe too, who owed them nothing, yet had disobeyed his captain's orders and broken off from his own unit to remain behind to guide them in what was almost certainly a hopeless attempt at escape. "I wasn't brought up to leave men behind," he had said simply, albeit in a voice tight with stress.

Not quite Christian or pagan or agnostic, Hodges still believed in his heart that there had to be a Heaven or a Valhalla or something out there somewhere for the brave, and he had no doubt they had all earned their place in it today. Sparing the energy to turn his head, he let his bloodshot eyes flick over the others to see if he needed to relieve one of them again yet. Casey Graham and Doug Long glanced up from the stretcher they carried, but their faces showed no real expression except weariness and pain. Still, even though their lungs and leg muscles were on fire and their arms felt as if they were being pulled from their sockets, they plunged on, never stopping. Too much was at stake.

They were still on their feet, despite all four of them having minor wounds, mostly from shrapnel, including a chunk that had torn away most of Graham's right ear in passing. Their uniforms would have been soaked with blood if not for the rain constantly washing it away.

Hodges didn't know what happened to the rest of the irregulars. There had been enough survivors left to form a makeshift platoon, under the only other two sergeants still alive, Andy Buchanan and that ugly bastard Kowalski. The three non-coms had drawn straws, and Hodges had lost. Now the others were somewhere back there behind him, fighting a running battle, offering up their own lives as a diversion, a willing sacrifice to block any pursuit, so the skinhead-turned-sergeant and his companions would have at least a snowball's chance in Hell to get the wounded man through. He thought he had heard distant gunfire some time ago, but couldn't tell for sure due to the pounding rain and rolling thunder that followed the unseasonable lightening bolts clawing their way across the black winter sky. He could still hear Kowalski's voice in his ears, and the words he had said when he briefly shook the big man's hand.

"We're depending on you to get him out. See you later, I reckon."

Hodges teeth ground together until they threatened to snap under the pressure. He would never have admitted the water running down his face was anything but rain.

Not that they had had it easy themselves; no, not by a damned sight. Twice they had to cover in the brush and mud while Federal reinforcements passed them, once within ten yards, and all that saved them were the adverse effects of the foul weather on the enemy's visibility and morale, and their own chemically enhanced alertness. One of the units was platoon-sized, and the other looked like company strength. When they had first separated, he had hoped that at least some of his comrades might get away, but now he recognized that for what it was: nothing but a hope in Hell.

Hodges could only assume that other, similar-sized hostile forces were pouring in from other directions as well, and on top of the already vastly superior number pursuing the tattered remnants of the Irregulars, the end result was a foregone conclusion. They would be cut off, and they would be killed to a man.

His mouth set in a grim line. They would have to kill them, because the 1st Columbia Irregulars would never surrender. Even if their honor would allow it, they knew what happened to people who did.

He jerked his head up abruptly when Biscoe's voice cut through the gathering dusk.

"Here it is! Come on!"

They broke through the brush and stepped out onto the shoulder of a narrow asphalt back road, slick and shiny with the first hints of black ice forming in the freezing rain. Looking at the stretcher-bearers, he saw Doug Long was ready to collapse, and he quickly snatched his end from him. Instantly the man bent over gasping, his quivering arms dangling, too weak to even brace his hands on his knees.

The North Carolina militiaman swiveled his head back and forth briefly, trying to get his bearings. Finally he figured it out and had just opened his mouth to speak when they caught the dim glow of headlights from around the nearest bend in the road.

"Back in the brush!" he shouted. "Get down!"

They started manhandling the stretcher back, and when they tilted it, Hodges caught a glimpse of pink water running from the canvas, diluted with blood. Between blood loss, shock and hypothermia, the man wouldn't last much longer; it's a wonder he wasn't dead already. He looked back towards the road, recognizing the headlights as belonging to a pickup.

"The hell with this! Set him down and get your guns ready! We're gonna take this freakin' truck!"

"It could be soldiers," Biscoe warned him in a deadpan voice – not trying to discourage him, but simply stating a fact even as he checked to make certain the muzzle of his Heckler & Koch G3 rifle was clear of mud and debris.

"I don't give a shit! If we're going to keep him alive, we've got to get him out of this damned rain!" He unclipped a flashlight from his belt. "If he doesn't stop, kill the driver first, then whoever's with him. Just try not to hit the radiator or the tires; keep all your rounds in the cab."

With that, he stepped out onto the road and began waving the light in one hand and his M4 in the other, and the truck immediately began slowing. No sooner had the interloper come to a stop than he saw the rest of them step out of the brush, their shouldered rifles pointing directly at him.

Hodges stepped to the driver's door to see the lone occupant, a fat and extremely angry old farmer with a faded tobacco company cap perched cockeyed on his head. The man was furiously cranking the window down.

"What the hell do you want?"

The big skinhead would have grinned at the gravely, irascible voice if circumstances had been different. If the old man was the least bit impressed either by the men or their guns, he didn't show it.

"We need your truck; we've got a wounded man here."

"Well I hope the sumbitch dies, and you along with him! Damn all you bastards to Hell anyway, a'comin' down here and murdering good Southern people! Go ahead and shoot me, you big ugly bastard; I don't give a damn!" He then finished his tirade with a raised middle finger and very graphic suggestion involving both Hodges and the figurative horse he came in on, before leaning his head further out the window to deliberately spit a brown stream of tobacco juice on the big man's boots.

He thinks we're Federal soldiers!

"Sir, we're not US Army; we're Confederate guerrillas."

The old man's eyes widened with shock and something that looked strangely like utter glee.

"Well why the hell didn't you say so then? What are you standing there in the rain for? Get in the truck!"

"Put him in the back," he called out to the others. "Biscoe, you know where we need to go; you're up front with me!"

Fortunately the vehicle had a cap on the bed, so the wounded man would at least be out of the rain and wind. By the time they opened it and dropped the tailgate, the old man was already out of his seat and trying to assist with the stretcher. As they slid their burden into the truck bed, their driver's eyes widened in recognition, despite the hideously battered features of their casualty, and he almost swallowed his cud of tobacco at the sudden realization.

"God Almighty! That's Frank Gore!"

CHAPTER 18

Private Danny Drucci opened his eyes, and the first thing he noticed was that he was in a world of hurt, and couldn't remember how he gotten there.

He was on his back with his lower torso twisted slightly to the side. His head hurt, and it felt like he had a hot spike in his guts. Blinking several times, it finally came back to him.

He and Kowalski had both been wounded during the fleeing Irregulars' first contact with the Federal skirmishers. He still remembered the feeling like a punch in the gut when the round had slammed into him. The sergeant was hit twice, once in the chest and once in the right knee, and another man was killed before the enemy was driven back to regroup.

"Let's get you two out of here," Sergeant Andy Buchanan told them as he motioned the Irregulars to pick them up, but Kowalski shook his head.

"Me and Danny are pretty well done; we're not going anywhere. Hell, neither one of us can even stand up."

"Damn it, Kowalski..."

"No! It's for the best this way. You all pull back, and we'll cover you. We can delay them here for at least a few minutes I reckon, and you can delay them farther along if you need to. It'll make the whole thing last longer, and the longer it lasts, the better chance the others have of getting away with the General. You agree with that, Danny?"

"Hell yeah," he had answered in his out-of-place accent, his voice a grunt from the burning pain in his abdomen. "I'm tired of running anyway. Let's kick their ass."

"But..."

"No buts, Andy!" Kowalski almost shouted, before choking and coughing up a gout of bright, bubbling lung blood from his mouth and spitting it out onto the wet leaves. As soon as he recovered, he continued, "We all know there's only one way this is going to end, and here is as good a place as any, as far as I'm concerned. Ain't no sense in moving around on a blown-out knee just to have the same thing happen someplace else."

His tangled red hair matted to his head by rain and blood, Andy Buchanan nodded and ordered the rest to move out quietly, and they did so at a low crawl, casting more than one backward glance over their shoulders. Buchanan paused, and shook hands with both men. When he pulled his hand away, it was sticky with blood. He didn't bother wiping it off.

"See you soon," he said, and was gone.

Turning his head, Danny looked at Kowalski laying beside him, and the ugly man grinned, showing his bloody teeth as the red spittle ran in a stream from the side of his mouth.

"Looks like it's just you and me, kid."

Despite the growing agony in his gut, Danny managed to bare his own teeth in return. "Kid, your ass!"

Then the enemy came, leapfrogging from tree to tree. There were a lot of them, but the pair of Rebels weren't afraid. When you know you're going to die, what's left to fear?

Kowalski took careful aim and squeezed off a three-round burst, catching one soldier away from cover with two of the rounds: on hammering against his body armor and the other blowing out his hip joint and dropping him to the ground. Suddenly the guerrilla began involuntarily coughing, the blood from his rapidly filling lungs spraying from his mouth and nose as his body convulsed, trying to open his airway.

The soldiers, not seeing Drucci, concentrated their suppressing fire on Kowalski, who was so wrapped up in clearing his lungs so he could breathe that he barely noticed the bullets passing as close as a finger's width from his head. Danny took advantage of the situation as soon as one of them stepped out with the intent of dragging their fallen comrade to safety, and dropped him screaming for help with bullets in both legs. Ignoring him just as he ignored the gunfire shifting in his direction now, the Italian sought a new target.

The guerrillas were being neither cruel nor kind by shooting to cripple; only practical. Every wounded enemy meant even more soldiers taken from the battlefield to care for them, more time wasted, and a better chance for the others to escape. Like the men at the Alamo, they were buying time for the rest, and the price was their lives...and those of the enemy.

Their foe stopped advancing, and it was at a stand off...for the moment.

Then their attackers opened up with grenade launchers, and Hell came raining down.

US Sergeant Dee Grissom felt like throwing up. He had seen dead bodies before, and plenty of them, but these...

Danny Drucci's body, covered with blood, lay half on his side, arms wrapped around his abdomen. Kowalski was on his stomach, his head turned to the left, with a blank look on the left side of his face. The right side, along with that entire side of his head, had been too close to an exploding grenade, and was simply gone as if it had never been.

Oh God, these are my own people! What the hell am I doing?

Grissom was from North Carolina, from right here in this very county; in fact, he had hunted deer and squirrels in these same woods more than once. Like so many Southerners, had joined the army for the usual reasons: an overabundance of patriotism and testosterone combined with an under-abundance of money and good sense. He'd been to Iraq, to Afghanistan, and elsewhere, and even though he'd seen a lot of things that made him question what he was doing, he didn't know just what the hell he could do about it.

Corporal Ortiz pointed at Kowalski and laughed loudly. "This *pendejo's* got what we all want: a little head!"

Several of the men guffawed, only to be interrupted by a shout of "We got one still alive!"

Several rifle muzzles moved to point at Danny, who lay still except for the shallow rising and falling of his chest. His scalp was hanging down over his right ear, and he was conscious enough to recognize the enemy gathered around him, but not enough to move. He became instantly wide-awake when a size twelve combat boot slammed directly into his wounded gut, protected only by his hands.

In shock at the unbelievable pain, it was several seconds before he realized the agonized screaming that filled his ears was his own.

"How you like that, huh?" Private Sharpton, a large black infantryman shouted just prior to kicking him again. "How you like that, bitch?"

Brought back to full consciousness by his agony, Drucci finally recovered enough of his breath to call the infantryman a nigger and ask him how much he liked having sex with his own mother, which earned him another series of kicks that cracked three of his ribs and left him barely able to breathe, let alone speak.

"Get off him, Sharpton!" Grissom barked, shocked beyond measure at their prisoner's thick Brooklyn accent. "Get a medic up here."

"This racist ain't gonna need no medic!" Sharpton said, pulling his bayonet, "I'm gonna nut this mother! Here, help me get his pants down!"

The other four members of the squad began shouting in support of the idea.

"Cut him, Sharp! Yeah, cut that freakin' rebel's balls off! Let's hear him yell some more!"

Sergeant Grissom shifted the muzzle of his M4 rifle in Sharpton's direction.

"I said get the hell off him! That's an order!"

Sharpton sneered at him. "An' what are you gonna do if I don't, huh? You gonna shoot me? Sheeit!" Ignoring the rifle, he began cutting at the fastenings of Drucci's pants.

"Damn you, I said let him alone! *Now*, Sharpton!"

"Hey!" Webb yelled, "I think the sarge is in love with them rebels. After all, he's one of them!"

Grissom started. *By God, he's right.*

It was as if someone had flicked on a light inside Grissom's body, and he felt strange, disconnected. Maybe that's why, as Sharpton bent over Drucci and pressed the knife against the Italian's crotch, he never remembered pulling the trigger the first time and stitching the Negro's head and neck with a short burst that practically decapitated him and dropped him lifeless across the wounded man. The pain of the body falling on him was so intense that Drucci nearly blacked out again.

"What the – " Ortiz yelled, and the sergeant turned and fired at the sound. The first two rounds hit the corporal's body armor, and third entered his upper lip and tunneled its way through his skull to lodge in the lining of his Kevlar helmet.

Webb had the presence of mind to try to grab him, and Grissom drove the hot muzzle brake hard into his left eye socket and squeezed the trigger; in a split second, his own face was covered in his former comrade's blood and brains. As the corpse fell away he turned in time to have three rounds from Corporal Conrad's rifle slam into his own body armor, and a fourth cut a streak of fire across his shoulder as it split both cloth and skin on its way by. The impact against the armor was bruising and stunning, and took his breath; it also saved his life by knocking him staggering out of the path of the fourth round that cut his helmet strap instead of blowing his head apart. Grissom's first return burst broke Conrad's right leg at the knee, and a second did the same thing to his neck when it entered his throat as he fell. The sergeant's loose helmet was tipping over his left eye, and he shook it loose and let it fall as he swung onto the last target. Knowing from experience he had to be out or almost out of ammo, his hand shifted forward to the trigger of the M203A1 grenade launcher attached beneath his rifle's barrel as he swung towards Private Allen. Before approaching the fallen enemy, he had reloaded it with a 40mm buckshot cartridge in case he had to fire up close. Allen knew it very well, because he had one up the pipe of his own identical weapon, and from his point of view, the huge bore protruding from Grissom's hands looked big enough to crawl into.

"No!" Allen screamed, dropping his rifle as if it were hot, and extending both hands, palms-out as if to push the threat away. "Don't shoot me, Sarge! Please God! Don't shoot me!"

Using the M4's depleted magazine for a grip, Grissom's index finger tightened on the trigger, then released only a fraction of an ounce from discharging the anti-personnel round that would have literally turned Allen into hamburger. The sergeant's lungs were working like a bellows as he fought to regain control. Finally he gestured with a twitch of his weapon.

"Run!"

"Sarge, please..." Allen cried, shaking his head, the tears flowing down his face, fully convinced he would be shot.

"Freaking run!" Grissom shouted, gesturing with a stabbing motion of his weapon this time, thrusting the muzzle towards the other man. Allen suddenly turned and did just that, making a beeline away from him at full speed, and quickly disappearing into the surrounding woods, all the while expecting a storm of pellets that would tear him apart. Even over the falling precipitation, the sergeant could hear the fading sound of his passage as he blundered along as fast as his legs could carry him.

Alone now, the enormity of what he had just done began to settle over Grissom, and he felt so weak his legs would no longer hold him up. The joints buckled, and he collapsed to his knees.

Oh shit! What the hell am I going to do now?

"Thanks," Drucci muttered through his agony, and Grissom swiveled his head to look at him. The soldier remembered what his granddaddy had once told him: *'What's done is done, boy; you can't change the past, so just pick up and go on!'*

Dee Grissom set his lips; he had definitely chosen a side now, and it was a choice there would be no going back from.

He rose and went to the wounded man, knelt beside him, and carefully pulled his pants back together. "Can you walk?"

"No."

Reaching for him, Grissom said, "Alright then, I'm going to have to carry you. Brace yourself; this is liable to hurt."

It did hurt, just for a second, before Danny passed out.

CHAPTER 19

The old man abruptly hit his brakes and began slowing rapidly. "There's somebody up there!"

Squinting through the rain-swept windshield, Hodges picked up what looked like the dark silhouette of two men in the middle of the road, one armed with an assault rifle and the other crouched on all fours. The one standing looked to be in uniform, minus his helmet, and, as if to confirm his identity, the figure lifted a hand, waving his rifle at them, demanding that they stop.

"Shit!" Hodges exclaimed as he readied his own M4 for action while they rolled closer. "Get ready, boys!" he yelled through the sliding back glass they had opened to allow them to communicate with the men in the back end, as well as to get some warmth back there for the wounded General. "Casey, when we stop, you bail out and cover the right side and Long, the left. I'll..."

"Hold your fire! Hold your fire!!" The shout came from the throat of Stanley Bauer, and was powered by fear. Startled by the sheer desperation in his cry, the men obeyed despite themselves, although they instantly leapt out and presented a small forest of gun muzzles.

Hodges'eyes widened in shock. They had come close enough for him to recognize the blood-covered face of Private Danny Drucci of 5th Squad in the headlights as he knelt at the man's feet.

Half blinded by the halogen beams, Dee Grissom lowered his assault rifle.

"Dee!" Bauer yelled. "Is that you?"

Grissom shaded his eyes with his left hand against the glare and the pouring rain, and said something that startled the hell out of the rest.

"Granddaddy?"

Hodges ordered him to drop his rifle and he obeyed instantly, following it by raising his hands in surrender. While the other Irregulars and the lone Tarheel covered him, he went forward to check on Danny.

"He's hit," Grissom said needlessly as the big sergeant briefly examined his wounded comrade in the headlights, "just a scalp wound in the head, I think, but he took one hard in the gut. I didn't have time to patch him up."

As he quickly gathered the smaller man into his arms to carry him to the truck, Hodges asked Danny where the others were.

For the first time anyone who knew him could remember, the tough-as-nails Italian suddenly began to cry hysterically and couldn't seem to stop.

The old man walked up to Dee, and the soldier swallowed hard.

"What the hell are you doin' here, boy?"

"I deserted. I just...I just couldn't go on killing my own people!" There were tears in his eyes as he continued. "I broke my oath. I...God help me, but I shot my own men! I couldn't help it. When I saw that man lying there wounded, and him a Yankee fighting for our people like I should be, and they were getting ready to cut him up, I just...I knew then I was on the wrong side."

With tears pooling in the wrinkles around his own eyes, Stanley Bauer threw his arms around his grandson, surprising the hell out of him.

"I'm proud of you, boy! By *God*, I'm proud of you!"

The bullets from the pursuing force only a hundred yards behind the tiny remnant of Irregulars were singing past their ears like angry bees, seeking them as they darted through the trees on the run, shaking even more water down from the saturated limbs to join that falling from the sky. Andy Buchanan turned and shouldered his rifle, sending two quick bursts of automatic fire back at the enemy, and then was running again, following the others along the thickly wooded ridgeline.

Taking a quick moving inventory, he saw there were only eight men still accompanying him.

Good Lord!

Automatic fire from his immediate front brought him to a halt. They had run right into a second enemy unit. He instantly saw there was no way to tear their way through them; from the volume of fire, they sounded even stronger than the ones they were running from. Buchanan knew the Feds were just as surprised as the Irregulars. If they had realized they were coming, they would have set up a proper ambush, and it would all be over by now.

Not that it's going to make a hell of a lot of difference in the end!

Still, the red-haired sergeant wasn't quite ready to give up yet. Just below them on the east side of the hill they were on, a long, narrow hollow stretched downward. He could see its sides were breakneck steep, but it was filled with large, standing trees, along with fallen timber and thick underbrush. If they could get down into it, they had a fair chance of reaching the bottom, and once at the hollow's mouth, they would split up into two groups of four and fan out in different directions, forcing the enemy to split their forces, and then splitting again into pairs a little further on, and then splitting again into individuals. The confusion would increase the chance that at least some of them might get through.

The only other options were to take the west side, which was gently-sloping, mostly open pasture that would put them in a clear field of fire, or to stay and fight it out where they were, caught between two superior forces. Either way would be slaughter.

"Get in that holler! Straight down the hill and out the bottom! Go! Go! Go!"

Pausing only a moment to fire a final burst behind him, Buchanan ran for the hollow and leaped, and the rest of his men followed. Landing on their boots and butts several yards down slope, they began half-sliding, half-running downhill.

David Worley didn't make it that far; he took a round through the skull even as he leapt, and came down in a limp mass, bouncing and rolling down the slope before violently coming to rest against the trunk of a maple tree, folded backwards at an impossible angle around it, his back broken.

Frank Godwin was sliding fast and unable to regain his feet in time, and a jagged fallen limb pointing uphill was driven into the inside of his left thigh. His momentum forced the stick, as big as a woman's wrist, through his jeans and into the flesh all the way to the bone, avulsing the muscle into a roll above the tear and ripping his femoral artery in two. He kicked violently at the protruding object, instinctively trying to knock it loose, but was interrupted when the bullets began throwing wet leaves all over him.

"Damn it!" Godwin shouted while trying to get his sniper rifle to his shoulder, and then repeated himself several times. Finally managing to bring his weapon into play despite the agonizing pain, he began firing uphill as fast as he could work the bolt, failing to understand why his vision seemed to be darkening, and why he felt so sleepy. He was still shooting a minute later when he bled to death from the severed artery in his leg, well before the first enemy round hit him.

The others were just disappearing into the thick brush when Daniel Worley realized his twin brother wasn't with them. Stopping at the edge, he turned to look behind him, but was unable to see his David through the driving rain and failing light.

"Dave!" He shouted in a panic. "Dave! Where are you?"

"Keep moving!" Buchanan shouted from the brush.

"I can't see Dave!"

"Keep going!"

"Where's my broth – "

Three rounds stitched him across the chest from left to right. He spun clockwise, his legs entangled with one another, and he went down on his face.

Andy Buchanan never saw him fall, and wouldn't have had time to do anything about it if he had. His voice was hoarse from shouting, but he had to keep what was left of the unit moving. They had one chance, and only one, if they wanted to live. They had to get to the mouth of the hollow before the enemy got there first and cut them off.

That thought was foremost in his mind when they ran headlong into a wall of fire from yet another force of Federal troops who had been traveling along the bottom of the hill, and were already in place and waiting for them. From their cover behind the trees, the enemy poured shots into them at a furious rate. Huey Long was hit half a dozen times, once squarely between the eyes, and died before he fell to the ground, his big body landing with a dull thump in the wet leaves. Multiple impacts slammed into Buchanan's right hip and lower abdomen, and he collapsed when his leg would no longer support him.

While the pitiful remainder of the Irregulars who remained alive returned covering fire, someone grabbed Buchanan by the collar and dragged him back into the dubious cover of the brush and fallen timber that choked the bottom of the hollow. More shots kicked up the leaves around them, coming not only from the top and bottom, but both sides now.

They were surrounded.

As he lay behind a rotten log, Buchanan realized it was Reverend Jack Lewis, Charlie Squad's corporal and the Irregular's chaplain, that had rescued him. The preacher was still there, lying beside him, trying to stop the bleeding. As the man moved Andy's leg slightly, the ends of his hip's shattered ball and socket joint ground together and his vision exploded in white-hot pain. He screamed before he realized it.

"Sorry."

Buchanan shook his head, hurting too badly to pay attention to roar of gunfire on all sides, and the pattering thumps of the bullets coming down around them.

"Stop," he managed to gasp. "We're surrounded, aren't we?"

Looking surprisingly calm, the chaplain nodded. "Yeah."

"Shit. Well, I don't reckon there's much sense in fooling around with these wounds, is there?"

"No, I reckon not." Suddenly he cocked his ear. "Listen; they're quitting."

Buchanan realized the firing was tapering off, and that commands of "Cease fire!" were echoing through the woods around them.

The Irregular sergeant groaned out his own command. "You all hold up; save your ammunition, but fire 'em up if they start to move. Who's still alive? Sing out!"

"Arnie Kessler."

"Dean Yates."

"Mitch Stanley."

"Jack Davidson."

After a moment of silence, Buchanan groaned, "That's all?"

"Yeah," Reverend Lewis said, nodding grimly, "we're all that made it."

"Damn."

"Yeah. Of course, I reckon we'll be joining the rest soon enough."

"I – *Ahh!* – reckon so."

A voice called out to them from the top of the ridge, but its owner was wise enough to keep under cover.

"Hello down there!"

Buchanan grimaced; the voice had a definite Southern drawl: South Carolina, from the sound of it. Before answering, he hissed, "A scalawag! A damned traitor! You all try to get a fix on his voice. When the shooting starts again, saturate that area first. Yates?"

"Yeah?"

"You got any 'Willie Peter' left for that grenade launcher?"

Yates patted the old M79's breech.

"I got one round I was saving special."

"Well, he's special. As soon as I give the word, I want you to drop it right on that son of a bitch's head!"

The whispered, "Will do," was nearly drowned out by the sound of the guerrilla racking the cavernous chamber of the weapon open to exchange rounds.

"Hello!" the voice echoed again.

"Let me," said Reverend Lewis, patting the sergeant on the arm. "Save your strength."

Cupping his hands to either side of his mouth, he called out, "Yeah?"

"You're surrounded."

"We've already figured that out, thank you very much."

For some reason, that struck Kessler as funny, and he began giggling uncontrollably.

"You don't have to die," came the voice again. Buchanan looked to his left and saw Yates prone behind the bole of a gum tree, his face a mask of concentration as he tried to get a fix on his target.

"Everybody dies, boy, sooner or later."

"Surrender now, and you won't be harmed."

"I reckon you've got some beach front property in Arizona you'd like to sell us too."

"Look, if you make us come and get you, you're all going to die!"

"So come and get us, if you've got the guts!"

Buchanan saw a satisfied smile come over Yates' face as the grenadier began shouldering his weapon and adjusting his sights.

"You don't have a chance!"

"We know that."

The voice was beginning to betray its uncertainty at the preacher's calm tone. "It doesn't have to be this way!"

"You're right, it doesn't; you can always go home and leave us alone. A lot more of you will live to see tomorrow that way."

As his life drained away through his wounds, Buchanan felt intoxicated from shock and blood loss, and he smiled with inspiration and puckered his lips together. A moment later, the enemy was startled to hear him faintly whistling *'Dixie.'*

"Southrons, hear your country call you," Stanley began the lyrics.

"Up, lest worse than death befall you," Kessler and Yates took it up, followed by Davidson and Reverend Lewis.

"To arms! To arms! To fight and die for Dixie!
Advance the flag of Dixie! Hoorah! Hoorah!
For Dixie's land, I'll take my stand,
To fight and die for Dixie!
To arms! To arms! To fight and die for Dixie!"

The men were still singing, their voices echoing out of the holler, but the whistling had stopped. Reverend Lewis glanced at Andy Buchanan, who had just died, his lips still half-open. A tear of pride ran down the Chaplain's face as he reached out the fingers of his right hand to tenderly close his comrade's eyes even as he muttered a prayer for his soul. Then he made sure his rifle was ready.

"Is that your final answer?" came the voice again, insistently.

"No," Lewis told him, motioning to Yates with a chopping movement of his index finger, "*this* is."

Yates squeezed the trigger and jarred under the recoil. The fat shell lifted up in an arc out of the hollow towards its target, but failed to strike the ground. Instead, the round inadvertently hit the overhanging limb of a hickory tree just above the concealed speaker and several other soldiers. Detonating against the wood, the burning white phosphorous spread out in a broad umbrella and, trailing the telltale paths of white smoke behind it, rained down its unquenchable fire on those beneath it. Then the screams began, followed by the shooting.

CHAPTER 20

Bauer flicked off his cell phone and swore once more.

"That was my old woman on my electronic leash there; the army has a roadblock set up between here and home; no way through."

"Mr. Bauer," Hodges said, "if we don't get help soon, General Gore will die, and Danny along with him."

"I know. Look, I've got an idea; how particular are you?"

"Right now, I'm not particular at all!"

"Good," the old man told him, with what looked like a mischievous smile.

"Hey Dee!" he called out to his grandson, in the back with the others, helping them try to stabilize the wounded men, "We're going to go see your daddy!"

Sergeant Grissom's face went white at the thought. His father was a "Red State" Republican and fanatical supporter of the US and the current administration, and he wasn't looking forward to this conversation one little bit.

Ten minutes later, Hodges was looking at the large house set by itself amongst the trees, and at the sign that marked it's driveway.

"You've got to be kidding!"

"Hell no, I ain't kiddin'! He's the closest thing to a doctor we've got, and besides, the scalawag little bastard is family, whether he admits it or not."

With that, they turned into the lot of Doctor Shane Grissom, Veterinarian.

Dr. Grissom looked up from his seat on the living room couch when he heard the pounding on his front door, and frowned at the noise. Tall, thin, gray haired and fifty-two years old, the veterinarian was a creature of comfortable habit, and he hated anything that disturbed the even flow of his universe. Still, he loved animals, and he remained a healer even after hours; an animal emergency was the only thing he could think of that would have one of the locals beating on his door this late.

That's why, when he turned the knob, he was more than a little surprised to see the broad, gnarly face of his father-in-law on the other side. That shock, however, was nothing compared to the sight of his own son, wild-eyed, pale, and soaked with rain and blood.

"Dee! What are you doing here?"

"Dee?" The feminine cry came from upstairs, followed immediately by Jennie Bauer Grissom herself, charging down the steps at a breakneck pace, taking them two at a time after hearing her husband calling their son's name. upon seeing actually seeing him, she squealed with delight and ran for the door to take him in her arms, only to see him shouldered aside by a huge bald man with a rifle in his hand.

"What the hell?" Shane Grissom shouted, but was startled into silence by the arrival of three more men: two manhandling a stretcher between them, and the third carrying yet another casualty.

"I'll tell you what to hell," Stanley Bauer told him. "These are Southern patriots with wounded men that need help." He turned to the stretcher-bearers and pointed toward the back of the house. "Take him that way; his office is in the back."

Casey Graham nodded, the motion sending drops of blood from the amputated top half of his ear spattering on the carpet, then he and Long, carrying the stretcher between them, and Johnny Biscoe with a semi-conscious Drucci over his back in a fireman's carry, promptly left a trail of mud, rainwater and blood across the floor.

"Scrub yourself up! You're gonna have to operate!" the old man barked, but the veterinarian only blinked.

"I don't understand – "

"Here's *all* you've got to understand," Hodges broke in, eyes wild and voice harsh with the effects of stress, emotion, fatigue and speed. "We've got a pair of men who'll die if they don't get help, and you're the closest help we've got."

"You're traitors!" he suddenly shouted, pointing an accusing finger. "Terrorists!"

Hodges began shifting the muzzle of his rifle. "Damn you, I'll show you some terror if you let those men die!"

"Dad," Dee said, stepping between them, putting his body between the weapon and his father, "if they're traitors and terrorists, then so am I. I deserted and joined up with them."

"Oh, Dee," his mother began, but his father cut her off.

"Don't be stupid, son; you're in the United States Army."

"Not anymore, sir."

"Look, I don't care what your crazy grandfather told you, we're Americans!"

His wife immediately rounded on him, her teeth bared in such an angry snarl that she looked as though she might bite. "Don't you call *my* father crazy!"

"It wasn't him," Dee said. "It was the people I served with. I saw them torturing a wounded man, and getting ready to castrate him. I finally understood then, and I stopped them."

Something in his voice made his father hesitate.

"What do you mean, you stopped them?"

"I killed them."

"Oh, Dee," his mother repeated, putting a comforting hand on his arm. Although she seldom voiced her opinion, inside she had always agreed with her father on the subject of the South rather than with her husband, but right now that didn't matter. She was a mother and was on the side of her son, whichever side he chose. Right now, he was in bad trouble, and she would stand by him, come what may.

Her husband, however, was not quite so accepting.

"Damn it, Dee!" He spun and pointed his finger at his father-in-law! "This is *your* fault! You're the one who filled his head with all that bullshit; now look at him!"

"We haven't got time for this!" Hodges shouted, accompanying it with a hard shove that nearly took the animal doctor off his feet as it sent him careening into the closest wall hard enough to shake the house and knock the framed pictures hanging from it askew. Snapping his rifle to his shoulder, he aimed it at the elder Grissom's head even as his thumb flicked the safety to *OFF* and his broad finger slid into the trigger guard, resting on the curved surface of the

195

metal. "Now get your ass in there and help them or you're a dead man!"

Stanley Bauer glared at his son-in-law, but his voice was calm and matter of fact.

"You don't have any choice now, you scalawag little shit. Dee's in it up to his neck, and so am I, and you can't betray them without sacrificing both of us too. If they take these men they'll take me *and* your son along with them, and he's looking at the death penalty if he gets caught." He nodded at Hodges. "Besides all that, I've got the feeling that this big bastard here is going to shoot you if you don't get a move on pretty damned quick!"

Dr. Grissom realized his father-in-law was dead right; he had no choice, not anymore.

"Damn you!" he hissed one final time, then turned on his heel and quickly walked down the hallway.

Dee looked at his mother, and she nodded her approval: tight-lipped and fearful approval, but approval nonetheless. "Go help your father; I'll make some coffee."

DAY 331

CHAPTER 21

The siege of the nameless hollow lasted well into the night.
Despite the disparity in numbers that eventually swelled to more
than thirty to one as more Federal reinforcements arrived, the
dwindling band of Confederates managed to repulse two assaults,
leaving casualties on the steep slopes each time. The cries and moans
of the wounded sounded pitifully through every break in the
desultory firing.

Dean Yates was dead, having taken a bullet through the throat
during the first assault. Jack Davidson was gone too; he had raised
his head to return fire just in time for it to intersect with the
trajectory of a pair of 7.62mm rounds from an M60 machine gun
fired from the top of the ridge.

The rest were still alive, for the moment. Arnold Kessler had
been hit twice through the body, but he was still shooting between
bouts of vomiting dark abdominal blood. A 40mm grenade left
Mitch Stanley's left leg below the knee a twisted, bloody rag held
together by the tattered remains of his pants, but he made a
tourniquet with his belt and still fought on from his position in a
shallow depression behind a log, a depression that was rapidly filling
with blood and water. Chaplain Lewis was coughing blood from his
shrapnel-filled left lung, but still firing at any hostile movement even
as the pink foam dripped from his lips.

Finally, after hours of getting nowhere, the Feds brought up three
mortar crews and set them up at the mouth of the hollow. The dull
thump-thump-thumping of their firing echoed through the wet
darkness, followed by the explosions of their shrapnel bombs raining
down on the Confederates. Every barrage was accompanied by a
gradual enemy advance, tightening their noose. Each time, the return
fire lessened, and finally, after the third round of fire and move,

there were no more shots from the hollow. Moving carefully, leapfrogging from tree to tree, the Federal troops closed in.

Chaplain Lewis never imagined that this much pain could exist in the world. The really surprising thing was that he hurt so much and in so many places that his various agonies seemed to cancel each other out, leaving him with a dull, all over ache that lay upon him like thick, wet blanket, suffocating him under its weight.

He was dying; of that he had no doubt. He felt the blood making crimson spit bubbles on his lips with every breath; bubbles that popped and dribbled down his chin and onto his chest, where their flow joined the scarlet springs draining from several other sources within him. Looking down, he was amazed at how much liquid his flesh contained, but what truly astonished him were the intestines he was cradling in his lap as he leaned back against the tree where he had been thrown by one of the last mortar bombs. It had taken him a moment to come to grips with the fact that they were really his.

I'm so cold!

Managing to tear his eyes away from the sight of his own insides on the outside, he looked towards his comrades. Kessler was draped facedown over the log he had been firing across, his rifle's pistolgrip still clenched in his stiffening right hand. His back was bloody tatters and there was little left below that; an arcing mortar round had landed squarely between his outstretched legs as he engaged the enemy. Stanley was curled in the fetal position, like he was instinctively trying to return to the safety of the womb in death, his body as holed as a Swiss cheese. Other than the faint curls of steaming vapor that rose from their blood, condensing in the chill air, neither were moving.

God have mercy on their souls; Jesus Christ, receive into thy bosom thy warriors.

A sound managed to penetrate the growing fog that filled his head; a whispered order, a subtle shifting of brush, a footstep sliding leaves over mud.

They're coming.

He fumbled at his battered combat harness for a moment, trying with clumsy desperation to find what he was looking for. He thought of Samson, between the pillars.

Lord, give me strength to avenge myself upon my enemies!

Two minutes later, the cautiously approaching soldiers found him still leaning propped up against the tree, his hands holding his guts. The mutilated guerrilla looked unreal in the green glow of his night vision goggles.

"This looks like the last one." He jumped when Reverend Lewis breathed, sounding like he was gargling, and yet more blood poured down his chin. "He's still alive! Yuck, what a freaking mess!"

More soldiers joined him, looking at the mangled man.

"Watch him! He might be armed!"

"Nah, he's got both hands full just trying to hold his guts in. He ain't going nowhere except to Hell. That's what you get for being a traitor to the United States! How about it, Rebel? Was it worth it?"

They couldn't hear the muffled click of metal separating from metal over the sounds of their own jeering voices. A couple of seconds later, Reverend Lewis' right hand emerged from beneath the pile of intestines in his lap, holding the bloody object he had concealed there. He meant to toss it at them underhanded, but he was too weak, his arm rose too slowly and the blood and bodily fluids had made his hand tacky, sticking the thing to his palm, so the motion became almost that of an offering, extending it towards the enemy as if presenting a gift.

Blood sprayed from Reverend Lewis' mouth as he shouted the question, "Who are these uncircumcised Philistines who defy the armies of the Living God?"

The light was so poor and the object so bloody, the soldiers barely had time to register the fact that it was a hand grenade before its blast officially ended the siege, shattering the cold, wet night in a final explosion of blood and fire.

"There were only five?"

"In the bottom of the hollow, yes sir. The others were killed before they reached cover."

"How many men did we lose?"

"We lost nine dead and twenty-six wounded, sir, but the medic doubts that some of the wounded will make it. That's just right here; I don't know how many casualties we had during the pursuit."

"Good Lord! What will General Carmichael say?"

"I don't know, sir."

Two soldiers, both enlisted men, stood quietly in the rainy darkness, listening to their officers' concerns. The pair, one from Georgia and the other from Alabama looked at one another. They had joined the Army long before the outbreak of this Southern Revolution, and since then, what they were doing had bothered them not a little. For months now, they had dared not confide their doubts to anyone but each other. Now, though...

Those were the bravest men I've ever seen.

What the hell are we doing?

Looking at each other through the green glow of their night vision, and the Alabama trooper, Corporal Grant, whispered, "No more. I ain't doing this no more, not to my own people!"

The Georgian, PFC Hill, nodded. "Me neither. I'm not fighting my own, ever again!"

Even through their face covering gear, they came to a silent understanding, and together they casually moved away, fading back in the woods. It would be hours before they were missed, and by that time, they intended to be long gone.

Much to the military's consternation, they would not be the only deserters. Throughout all the units that had engaged the Irregular forces, there would be such a scattering of Southerners going unexpectedly AWOL over the next few days, usually taking their weapons with them, that the military was becoming more than a little alarmed.

CHAPTER 22

"Barring any infection, I think they'll both live," Shane Grissom muttered, falling as much as sitting in one of the chairs pulled out from the table. He had worked on the two men for better than four hours, and he had done so as if his life depended on the results. It had, in fact; Hodges had been very clear on that point, just in case the veterinarian entertained any thoughts about giving the effort anything but his very best.

The big skinhead sat at the same table, looking very out of place in his underwear as Stanley Bauer dug the last piece of shrapnel out of his thigh with a sterilized pocketknife and a pair of tweezers. Three more pieces had come out of his right chest and shoulder; they had failed to penetrate his chest cavity, but lodged in his thick musculature. His heavily tattooed torso was bandaged and bloody, and his face was set but very pale; there had been no numbing agents available beyond a bottle of gin appropriated from the Grissom liquor cabinet. There was little enough of that; although there was plenty in the bottle, they couldn't afford to over-dull their senses or allow the alcohol to thin their blood and promote bleeding; just a single big slug and then suck up the pain.

"Good job, Doc," he mumbled through teeth clenching into a rolled washcloth as the old man grinned and moved aside to allow Mrs. Grissom to step in with her needle and thread to sew him up.

He was the last, at his insistence. They had finally stopped the bleeding from the tattered stump of Casey Graham's ear and taken a piece of shrapnel from just under the skin of his back, and both of Doug Long's forearms were bandaged where they had been sliced by flying metal in the initial rocket attack. Johnny Biscoe had surprised them with the extent of his wounds; a bullet had flayed the flesh open to the bone as it grazed a rib on his right side, but he had quickly stuffed some gauze into it, taped it up to stop the bleeding and said nothing about it until they got to the vet's. He was still favoring Mrs. Grissom's stitch work when he lowered the phone.

"There're some people coming; it'll take them awhile to work their way around the roadblocks, but they should be in the area by morning. That's a good thing, because we can't stay here. I reckon they'll be looking pretty hard for us," he nodded towards Dee, "especially for him, considering.

Shane Grissom glowered at his offspring but said nothing. There was nothing to say, not now and not anymore; what was done was done, and words would have no purpose. Shifting his glare to his father-in-law, he shook his head. The old man was grinning as he patted the big, tattooed guerrilla on the back.

That old bastard is actually enjoying this!

The veterinarian definitely wasn't enjoying it; this whole thing frightened him, more than anything ever had in his life. What scared him the most was what was going to happen to his son.

Shane Grissom had thought long and hard about that as he had x-rayed, probed, cut and stitched together the two men in the operating room. He had said nothing, but instead had covertly studied his son's face whenever he could spare a second to look away. There was a sadness there, and definitely fear, but also a determination, and...pride.

Yes, by God, there had been pride there!

The thought suddenly came to him like a kick in the gut as to how long that pride would sustain Dee when they executed him.

There was no question about that happening; after what he had done, neither the Army nor the United States Government would – or could – allow him to live. There were too many Southerners in the military to allow an idea like that to take hold; an example would have to be made. His son was a dead man as soon as they caught him.

If they caught him...

It surprised the elder Grissom when that particular idea reared its head, and then burrowed into his mind like a particularly industrious worm inside an apple. What he was thinking about was treason, and yet...he looked at the face of the boy he had raised to be a man, a man now with only one small chance at life. That chance was for this ragtag Confederate Revolution to win.

He thought of the country he had served himself, and of the flags and anthems he had stood for, and then compared them to the importance of his own flesh and blood. He came to an abrupt realization.

Compared to that, they don't mean shit!

"You're right," he said suddenly. "Only after what's happened, I suspect they'll get around to searching here long before morning; they have to know he'd come here. We've got to get your men and get out of here now. Dee!" he snapped. "Go get old Bonnie."

The big Amish buggy had been sitting in the Grissom barn for two days. The Miller family's horse had been struck by an Army Humvee within a few hundred yards of the veterinarian's home. The horse had been pulling the buggy at the time, and fortunately it hadn't tipped with the horse, as Joseph's wife and five children were inside. The Humvee's driver and passengers had sworn at them for blocking the road and driven away, leaving family to send the oldest son running for Doctor Grissom. Two of the horse's legs were broken and he had to be put down, so he had helped the Miller's pull the buggy up to his barn, and then driven them home. They promised to be back that weekend, after the stock sales, where they hoped to find another horse.

I guess they'll find their buggy gone now, too. Damn it, I hate that!

Shane Grissom flicked the reins, urging the plodding horse to move just a little faster. He knew the buggy was worth a lot less than his son's life, and he'd make it up to its owners...if he survived, that is, which wasn't very likely.

Fortunately, he had a horse of his own: an ancient sway-backed chestnut mare that had already been buggy-trained when he had acquired it. The former owner, who had moved to the country from Charlotte in search of peace and quiet, had bought it from an Amish horse trader and used it to pull a wagon occasionally for recreation. He had ended up losing his employment and, with foreclosure looming, had given the aging mare – Bonnie – to the animal doctor, as he had feared she was so old she might be destroyed if she was seized along with the farm.

Now she's pulling an ambulance in the middle of a war zone.

The buggy rocked sharply as they went over a four-inch diameter log lying at an angle across their path so the wheels hit it, not both at once, but one at a time so it doubled the impact. *Thump-rock. Thump-rock.* The frame creaked, one of the unconscious men groaned, and there was a grunt from one of the others as the abrupt motion caused him to bump a freshly stitched wound, but otherwise everyone remained silent, as if their lives depended on it, because they did.

As the buggy continued its necessarily slow path down the long-abandoned dirt road, Hodges, clinging to the back while standing precariously on a rudimentary bumper, blinked the freezing rain out of his eyes. He assumed that Casey Graham, lying up on the roof and being regularly thrashed by wet, low hanging branches, was doing the same thing. Biscoe, in the front seat with the veterinarian, was probably faring no better; the only ones keeping dry were Doug Long and Dee Grissom. They were inside, caring for the wounded and doing their best to keep them warm while keeping their own rifles at the ready.

Mr. Bauer wasn't with them; he had left in his truck, promising to meet them later at the Tarheel base. He said he had something to pick up first, but he assured them that, between his reluctant son-in-law, Corporal Biscoe, and his grandson Dee, they would find their way just fine.

Hodges shivered in the cold and wondered if he was making a mistake in trusting the deserter, and yet his instinct said the man was what he claimed. Besides, Drucci had verified his story, and, in Hodges view of things, anyone who willing to shoot his own people to save one of the Skinhead sergeant's comrades could be safely included in his list of friends.

The buggy hit another bump, and Hodges almost broke his teeth off when he snapped them together to stifle the involuntary yell that threatened to come when his chest wounds slammed against the back of the buggy. He suddenly had a whole new respect for what his Confederate ancestors had gone through in the 1860's.

Son of a bitch! Welcome back to the 19th Century!

Up in front, Johnny Biscoe had pulled his head all the way inside his poncho, leaving the empty hood of stiff, rubberized cloth sticking up like the Grim Reaper. He hated being blind, but he would hate being shot by an enemy seeing the glow from his cell phone even worse, and allowing their only secure form of communication to get wet and stop working would be almost as bad.

"What?" he asked in a desperate whisper. "Come again; you're breaking up. It's this damned storm...Okay, just a second."

Shane Grissom felt Biscoe squirming beside him in his makeshift tent, and he glanced at the unnerving sight of the empty hood and shivered despite himself.

"Hey, Doc? Where does this come out?"

"Carver Road, about five miles north of here, near the Spivey farm. We're about an hour from there at this rate." That was a very rough guess; he had hunted this road, and rode Bonnie on it for recreation a few times, but never at night, especially not in the middle of a storm. Things looked so different under these conditions that there had been a couple of times he wasn't sure he was still on the road at all.

"Thanks." Biscoe went back to whispering, and the veterinarian turned back to the front just in time to catch a low hanging branch that raked across his left eye, leaving it blurred, blinking, and stinging. He wiped at it with one hand, swearing to himself before he caught the faint sound of someone else doing the same thing in the distance ahead of them.

"Damn it to hell!" PFC Osborne exclaimed in a loud voice as he tripped over a fallen branch and went facedown in a freezing puddle. The extra seventy pounds of body armor and pack made breaking his fall impossible, and he bloodied his nose and drove his lower lip back against his teeth. Spitting out a mouthful of blood and muddy water, he wiped at his night vision goggles and added, "Shit!" with great feeling.

Suddenly someone had him by the back of the pack and yanked him to his feet. The six foot-five sergeant shoved his ebony face as close against that of his subordinate as their vision equipment would allow.

"What the hell's wrong with you, Osborne? You tryin' to let ever' freakin' rebel in the state know we're here?"

"Sorry, I...I fell."

"No shit, dickhead!"

"Knock it off! Why don't you two just send up a freaking flair while you're at it?"

Both of them turned towards their company commander, 2nd Lieutenant Peterson. Hailing from Maine, he had that state's almost stereotypical aversion to foolishness. "Now shut up and get moving."

Glowering at his back, the two men, along with the rest of the patrol, proceeded up the old road towards the buggy, less than three hundred yards away.

Deep in the brush, the guerrillas lay hugging the frozen ground and watching as the Federal patrol's point man passed only a hundred feet from their position. The freezing precipitation beat down on them, soaking their clothes and painting them with a thin layer of ice, but beyond involuntary shaking, they never moved. As soon as he passed, Doctor Grissom shifted infinitesimally, and Casey Graham's hand instantly clamped down on the back of his neck like a vice. In contrast to his painful grip, the guerrilla's soft, almost inaudible voice was no more than a breath, like a communication from a ghost.

"Be still; he's only the first. The main body will be coming behind him, and then another one walking drag. Wait."

He obeyed, hoping against hope that neither of the wounded men would make a sound at the wrong time. Long was in the buggy with them, deeper in the trees a few yards to the rear, ready to press a hand over their mouths at the first sign of a disturbance. The veterinarian knew he was there for another purpose as well; as he had turned away, he had seen him set a pair of grenades within easy reach and mechanically check the 9mm pistol he already knew was loaded. It was obviously he didn't intend for either the wounded men or himself to be taken alive.

What the hell kind of fanatics are these people? Do they really believe their own propaganda about American troops torturing prisoners?

Sobering at the sound of a soldier sniffing through a clogged nose on the road just ahead of them, he looked at his son lying on the opposite side of him from Graham. Even in the pitch darkness, the young man's profile was so familiar...Shane Grissom squeezed out an involuntary tear at the thought of his son's likely all-too-brief future. He knew that, fanatics or not, Dee was one of the guerrillas now, and if his father wanted him to live, he would be one too. His hand clenched tighter on his rifle stock, at war with himself.

The second point man passed, walking more at a trudge than a stalk, and paying only the vaguest attention to movement discipline. The miserable weather and cold darkness were taking their toll on morale, and he gave no more than the merest glance of his night vision goggles in the direction where they lay. He never slowed.

A hundred yards behind him, the main body of the patrol began passing in exactly the same fashion...until the horse, as disgusted with the weather as the humans, snorted. Instantly every rifle swiveled in their direction, men ducking behind trees and throwing themselves to the ground and aiming from the prone. A panicked soldier's voice cut through the night.

"What was that?"

This time, it was their officer, still standing on the path, who did the snorting, in his case, in disgust. "It was a horse, you dumbass! You are in farm country, after all. Now get the hell up!"

"Oh," one of them muttered as they got to their feet shamefacedly. Amid murmured curses, they got on their way once more, never knowing of the hidden fingers already putting pressure on triggers only to let off again with silent sighs of relief.

To the guerrillas, their passing took an eternity, and the waiting for the rear guard to come and go took another one. Finally, once the last sound of the patrol had faded away, Hodges' whispered voice reached their ears.

"Alright; let's get this show on the road."

Dr. Grissom's estimated hour took half again as much before Biscoe's cell phone vibrated in his pocket.

"Yeah?"

"We hear something; is it you?"

"How the hell would I know what you hear?" He paused, then said, "I'm going to hoot twice."

The others watched curiously as the man put his hands to either side of his mouth and made the sound of a horned owl calling before putting the phone back to his ear.

"Well?"

"We gotcha. We're about a hundred yards ahead, and we've got transport and a clear route waiting; come on."

Turning his head, the Tarheel looked at the veterinarian; "Let's pick it up; they're waiting on us."

Mrs. Grissom heard the dogs in the kennel barking, and knew what it meant. She flipped on the porch light and opened the door.

"Is someone out there?"

Instantly shouts seemed to come from everywhere, and it wasn't hard at all for Dee's mother to do what she knew they expected: scream, "Please don't hurt me!" The soldiers rushed her and waved guns in her face while their comrades poured around her and into her home while others covered them from behind vehicles and outbuildings.

"Who's in the house?"

"Nobody...just me. What's going on?"

"We'll ask the questions here! Where's your son?"

"Why, Dee's in the Army. He's a sergeant, you know, and he's not going to like it when he hears how you're treating me!"

The man's eyes narrowed in anger. "Have you heard from him?"

"Yes, of course; he calls me at least once a week without fail. He called two days ago, as a matter of fact..."

The exasperated soldier cut her off. "I mean have you heard from him today?"

"No, and I'll tell you something; they ought to let a boy call home more often than they do. You can just tell whoever's in charge that I said that, too. We miss him – "

A voice shouting "All clear!" came from inside, even though she could still hear the sounds of boots, shifting furniture, and the occasional crash of something being knocked over or broken.

"Where's your husband?"

"Shane went out on a call a couple of hours ago to look at a sick cow. He should be back soon if you want to wait."

"Where was this call?"

She shrugged. "I don't know. I didn't answer the door, but he said something about an Amish boy who had come to get him, and he'd be back as soon as he could."

"Where does this boy live?"

"I don't know; I don't know which one he was, since I didn't see him. Most of the Amish families live over that way," she said, motioning in the opposite direction from the one taken by her husband. "That's the way he was headed. Is something wrong?"

There was some back and forth communication on the radio, and the soldiers handcuffed Mrs. Grissom, loaded her into a Humvee, and drove away.

CHAPTER 23

"Samantha," Kerrie said, standing and extending the headset with shaking trepidation, "It's Mike; he says...he needs to talk to you."

Mike hadn't told her anything, but Kerrie had already begun to weep at what she suspected. Cynthia came to her friend and slipped an arm around her, seeking as much as giving comfort, since her own eyes were welling full of tears.

Samantha felt her head begin shaking in denial even as she reached for the headset, and it was only by the greatest physical effort she had ever exerted that she could make her hand obey; every torture the Feds had subjected her to paled to *nothing* next to this. She knew what he was going to tell her, and it was the last thing in this world or any other she wanted to hear. Her vision was already tunneling and she felt like she was going to pass out, so she sat down to keep from falling down even as she put the earphones in place and adjusted the microphone.

"Yes?" Her own voice sounded strange to her ears; she didn't recognize it at all.

"Frank's alive!"

Somewhere in a distant part of her mind she was dimly aware that tears and snot were suddenly running unheeded down her face and even over her lips, but right at the moment, she didn't care.

"Alive? Are...are you sure?"

Kerrie and Cynthia both gasped and instinctively gripped one another's tightly.

"I just got word from some of Suggs' people. He's been wounded – *badly* – and they've already done surgery. He's in critical condition, but they've evacuated him and they think he'll pull through. He's – "

Samantha was suddenly on her feet with no recollection of how she got there, her movement so fast the swivel chair rolled away at the impact of the backs of her straightening legs and slammed into the wall with a loud bang.

"Where is he?"

Mike abruptly realized just why she was asking.

"No, Sammie; it's too dangerous – "

"Where is he?"

Outside Mike's house in Columbia, Captain Tango grinned in triumph as he spoke into his radio.

"We have confirmed the presence of the suspected hostiles at this address." He paused, then nodded at the unseen voice on the other end. "Yes sir, we'll be here."

Turning to his XO, he said, "Make sure everybody's locked and loaded, but don't make a move yet. They've got a snatch team on its way, and they should be here in about fifteen minutes. We'll sit tight and provide backup. They want this bunch alive."

Even as he relayed the order to the sergeants, the Executive Officer, First Lieutenant Van Hauser, shuddered. The CAP guerrillas might be the enemy, but he had been inside one of the interrogation centers once, and he wouldn't wish what he saw there on anybody.

CHAPTER 24

It was early morning, dawn's early light: the killing hour. The three story brick building on the corner with the boarded-up store below and cheap apartments above was non-descript, looking no different than dozens of others in Columbia. There was nothing about it that would indicate it was the lair of a predator.

Confederate Sergeant Ralph Steiner sat at his sniper post on the third floor where he had spent the last twenty-four hours waking and sleeping, watching and waiting.

He was in the apartment's kitchen, one room away from the cracked-open window overlooking the oncoming street. The stretch of traffic and concrete he could see was his killing field. A pair of holes had been cut through the interior wall and into the living room; one for the spotting scope, and the other for the .308 M24 sniper rifle and its 3.5-10X 40mm MK4 Leopold scope. On the living room side, they opened up behind a shelf full of odds and ends – mostly decorative glass, ceramics, and nick-nacks – that camouflaged the military hardware from the eyes of enemy snipers, of which there were several. There were two less than before, though, because Steiner had spotted two of them first last week – one Army and one Marine – and had killed them both, along with their spotters. Still, there were plenty more where they came from, not to mention regular troops, and one had to be careful if he hoped to survive the deadly game of hide and seek played out daily in the war zone that was the South Carolina Capital.

At the moment, Steiner was waiting for a patrol. Despite trying their best to make their travels random, there were only so many streets in Columbia, and eventually, the occupation troops would take this one. When they did, Steiner would be waiting. The target might not be fixed, but the plan was; he would engage the most valuable target – an officer, or better yet, another enemy sniper – at around four hundred yards with one shot and one shot only; any more would make their position too easy to ascertain. Then he, and Private Archie Baker, who was acting as his spotter, along with

213

Lieutenant Harrison and the rest of the backup squad in a downstairs apartment, would leave via the back door of the building.

I wonder if it will mean anything.

Good news travels fast, but bad news has wings to fly. They had heard about the Irregulars, and about Frank Gore. On an intellectual level, the sniper knew the Movement was much more than the General, but it felt as though something had gone out of it, and left with their leader. They still hadn't found his body, which meant there was still a thread of hope, but...

Still, no matter who died and no matter who won, this war wouldn't be over as long as there was one man on the Southern side left standing. The sniper decided that the best he could do in memory of the fallen General – *his* fallen General – was to collect some serious payback, and now was as good a time to start as any.

If I can't see an officer or a sniper, I'll take a grunt, but some son of a bitch is going to die today!

His spotter saw movement on the street, and recognized the camouflage paint jobs and vehicle patterns. He tapped the sniper on the shoulder; it was time.

"Archie," Steiner said calmly as he began taking his steadying breaths, saturating his lungs with the oxygen that would keep his hands and aim from shaking at the critical time, "Notify Harrison; it's a go."

Archie Baker nodded and was already reaching for his cell phone when it rang before he could get his hand on it, the tone an MP3 that sent the mellow tones of the old Robert Lloyd tune, *Sail On, Alabama,* lofting through the kitchen. Steiner frowned at the unexpected interruption as his spotter quickly opened the phone and put it to his ear. He listened for a minute, then nodded while waving his free hand back and forth at the sniper, indicating that the hit had been called off.

Steiner was fuming; any time this happened, he lost all the effort he had put into setting up for the ambush, and the letdown was literally like a weight crushing him, leaving an unrelieved adrenaline hangover that would last for hours...especially now. Squeezing the trigger was the easy part; it was the research, the planning, the stress, and just the plain work that came beforehand that was so taxing, and now it was just so much wasted time. Not to mention the delayed payback.

Archie closed his phone and immediately began detaching his spotting scope from its tripod. As he did so, he spoke out of the side of his mouth to his companion.

"Pack it up quick. We've got another mission."

"We haven't finished this one yet!"

"This is more important. We've got to stop and pick up Tommy; Samantha needs us." He looked over at Steiner with the biggest, broadest grin he had ever seen, and the sniper was shocked to see pure joy glittering in his eyes. "Frank's alive!"

Sergeant Steiner couldn't have packed up any faster if the building had been on fire and his clothes were catching. He was grinning like an idiot himself, and figured it was just as well he wasn't going to attempt the shot now. He was shaking from excitement, and his own eyes seemed to have gone a little blurry.

Facedown on the bed, Donna softly purred, luxuriating under Tommy's caressing hands, and the knowledge that at least some of her friends in the Irregulars were still alive.

And Frank; especially Frank!

Mike woke them to tell them the good news immediately after he notified Samantha, and that had put them both in a good mood, despite the fact that Tommy would have to be leaving within the hour to command his squad during the trip. Someone had to provide an escort to get Sammie to her husband's side, where she belonged.

During the last few hours, Donna had come to an epiphany. She wouldn't stop loving Frank – she couldn't – but she would make the most of what she had. She had no doubt that she loved Tommy as well, and he, at least, was ready, willing and able to love her back. He had proven that many times, and was proving it again right now as she lay facedown on the bed. As he brushed her long brown hair aside, she felt his lips moving across her bare shoulders, kissing first one spot and then another.

"Mmm...what are you doing?"

"Kissing every freckle." Other than a light peppering across the bridge of her nose, Donna wasn't naturally freckled, but her tanned shoulders were spotted with them, from the sun exposure of a typical country girl with a love for spaghetti straps and halter tops. She didn't care for her freckles at all, but it was obvious her boyfriend was of a different mind.

He's silly sometimes, but he can be so damned romantic when he wants to.

As she felt his lips keep working, she sobered and swallowed hard. There was something she had to say. What had happened in North Carolina told her loud and clear that, in their position, chances for happiness were not something to put off until tomorrow. That wasn't a good idea in a time when simply living until tomorrow couldn't be taken for granted.

"Tommy? Tommy! Hey! Quit for a minute."

He pulled back, resting on one elbow and frowning. "What's wrong?"

Reaching out her hand, she laid it on his.

"Nothing's wrong, honey. I just want to talk."

As far as Tommy was concerned, it was a hell of a time to pick to talk, but...

"So, what's on your mind?"

"It's kind of hard to say."

"Try." He was getting concerned, and his voice was carefully neutral; it was the best he could do because he had no idea what was coming, and it frankly scared him a little. He'd had his share of broken hearts before, and it always hurt.

Donna paused, taking in a deep breath. "How do you feel about me? I mean, really, *really* feel?"

"I love you."

She nodded. "Do you mean that?"

"You know I do."

"You know I love you too. You remember when Uncle Sam caught us together that time, and you offered to marry me?"

"Oh yeah." He remembered it indeed; he and Donna's outraged Godfather had nearly killed each other. They probably would have if Frank hadn't been there to break up the fight and talk some sense into them.

"Did you mean it?"

"Hell yes, I meant it."

She took another deep breath, and when it came, her voice sounded very small and frightened. "Does the offer still stand?"

His mouth dropped open in shock before turning up in a smile of pure pleasure. "Yes. Absolutely."

"Then yes," she said, returning his grin with one of her own, "absolutely. Now, where were we?"

Much to her delight, he remembered exactly where they were, right down to the freckle.

The soldiers easing around the outside of the house never spoke, but used hand signals to indicate their desires and intentions. In their black fatigues and ski masks, they looked more like shadows than men. Weapons at the ready, four went to the front of the house, slipping onto the porch; four more to the back, and a pair to either side of the house. Their sensitive listening devices allowed them to hear through the walls, and pinpoint everyone in the upstairs.

"Everybody in place?"

The electronic voice in their earpieces was answered by a series of clicks as mikes were keyed in affirmative response.

"Just like we rehearsed it; entry teams move in conjunction with the breaking glass. On the count of three...one...two...three!"

The pair below the bedroom window bobbed up and the first shattered the pane of the bedroom window with a stroke of his submachine butt. Shards of glass were still falling when the second one dropped the grenade through the hole.

"Now!"

At the sound of the glass shattering almost beside his head, Tommy went from the middle of making love to on his feet in a split second, stark naked but reaching for his pistol and ready to fight.

Unfortunately, being upright, he caught the full force of the stun grenade's blast. Both his eardrums instantly ruptured, and, stunned by the concussion, he lost his footing and fell backwards, slamming his head on the wooden bedpost, splitting his scalp, and knocking himself the rest of the way out.

Donna's ears were damaged as well; she could hear nothing or see it, since the flash had temporarily blinded her. Dazed and confused, she was unable to hear the front and rear entrances splintering, the pounding of boots on the floor, or the shouted commands. Her first clue that something was wrong was when someone fired the Taser needles into the center of her chest, right between her breasts, and held the trigger down, incapacitating her with the charge.

"Upstairs clear!"

Hearing the crashing and yelling in the house above, as well as the pounding as they tried to force the armored basement door, Mike knew what was happening, and knew there would be no escape for him. Suddenly, the initial split-second burst of instinctive fear was gone and everything was crystal clear. He was going to die; that was a given at this point so there was no sense in worrying about it, and no time; he still had a job to do. The only thing that concerned him now, even as he typed in the code that would notify the others that he was done for and a second that would detonate the thermite inside the freezer shell that housed his homemade super-computer, was whether to trigger the mission first. Edge was overseas, Sam was somewhere incommunicado out west, MacFie was underground, and Frank was in North Carolina, barely alive and unable to give the order. It was all down to him now, and that really pissed him off.

Mike had never wanted anything to do with command; he was a craftsman and an artist in the world of cyberspace, and that was all he had ever wanted. Now the decision was left to him as to whether to launch the mission that could change the face of the war. It was a one-shot deal; once it was fired, there would be no reloading. His fingers hovered over the keyboard, hesitating.

Then he heard Donna scream upstairs, and he knew, once the enemy had them, they would almost certainly get the information that would spike their cannon once and for all. Quickly he typed in the word *COCKADE* to get the ball rolling, followed by COMPROMISED, the code word for what was happening to him right now. He hit *SEND* and then set his lips as he pressed *ENTER* to activate the charges.

The thermite hissed like a giant snake as the burning aluminum poured downward in a hellish rain inside the freezer housing, devouring both the plastic and metal of the hard drives of the homemade super computer with equal indifference. The basement rapidly filled with choking smoke that stank of burning electronics, and the enamel paint on the freezer shell that held the assembly charred and curled as the shell itself began glowing. Where it sat near the wall, the wooden paneling behind it caught fire, still more smoke rolling from it as it ignited. He was already choking from the fumes, but at least he knew nobody would get anything out of that computer.

That duty done, he had one more to go. As the Intelligence Officer for the Confederate Army Provisional, he was too valuable to be taken alive. With all the information that was in his head, if they managed to break him, the war would be lost and thousands would die; he couldn't allow that to happen. He's always heard what he was about to do was the ultimate sin, but he also knew what Christ had said: *"Greater love hath no man than that he lay down his life for a friend."* He had no choice; he had to die in order for hundreds, maybe thousands to live, for his people to have their own country, and he reckoned he would just have to take his chances. Swallowing hard and praying that God would understand, he reached in his desk drawer and his hand closed around the checkered rubber grips of his father's old Colt Python .357 magnum. He paused for just a second before lifting it, at thought of Kerrie; for an instant he could feel the touch of her soft, freckled skin, the sweet smell of her hair, and the taste of her mouth. At least he'd had the chance to have her for a while, and he hoped she'd understand. He put the muzzle in his mouth, angled toward the back of his skull, and his finger began taking up the slack on the trigger.

I love you, baby. I'm so sorry, and I'll miss you so much! See you in Heaven, I reckon.

Squeezing his eyes tightly against the coming impact, he said a quick prayer:

Lord Jesus Christ, into thy arms I commend my spirit; have mercy on my soul!

His finger was tightening the final thousandth of an inch when the floor directly above his head exploded in a huge hole as the shaped charge blew through it to provide access to those above, and the concussion left him unconscious.

CHAPTER 25

"Sammie! Sammie, come quick!"

Samantha's head jerked at the sound of Kerrie's voice, or rather, at the urgency of her tone, and she dropped the small bag she was packing and hurried towards the communications center as fast as she could move, cradling her belly in one hand. Cynthia sprinted ahead, and the exhibition of the younger girl's speed and agility unjustifiably irritated her in her current condition. Samantha's aggravation was instantly forgotten, however, when she heard Kerrie scream, "No! Oh God, no!" in a voice like overstressed glass that shattered into tears.

She arrived to find the auburn haired girl with her face buried against Cynthia's shoulder as her body shook, wracked with sobs. Cynthia was pale as she held her friend, her lips set so tightly they nearly disappeared. She nodded wordlessly toward the computer screen in the communications desk, not trusting herself to speak. Samantha leaned over the desk, trying to ignore Kerrie's anguished wails as she stared at the screen. Clicking on the first open email, bearing a bogus address she recognized as one used by Mike. It bore a single word

COCKADE

Samantha was stunned; Mike had begun the operation without Frank's input. Granted, her husband was temporarily out of action and had been intending to start it within a day or two anyway, but...

I know Mike; if he did this, he had a good reason.

She found it in the second message, and fully understood why Kerrie was crying.

COMPROMISED

"Oh...my...God!"

All over the South, in hidden spots, the message was received. Some of the recipients immediately began packing up to bug out, either knowing or suspecting that the sender knew their locations or real identities. Others began putting projects of their own in motion: projects that were to be carried out starting in exactly twenty-four hours. Deep inside the northern states, Confederate agents looked at one another and nodded grimly, noting the exact time of the message.

"Well," as one Missourian from that state's contingent in Michigan put it succinctly, "Here goes."

People began to move, heading toward their carefully planned and prepared-for targets. Throughout the day, they would be walking into power plants with fake ID, wandering along railroad tracks, paddling canoes and pulling the oars of rowboats toward the spots where natural gas lines crossed rivers, and moving into other sensitive areas. Most of them carried disguised devices with timers on them that were already ticking away. They would plant them, and then they would leave, trying their best to get back to their Southern homeland before all hell broke loose.

"Hey Jack!"

Turning at Darrel Putney's booming shout that echoed through their makeshift headquarters in the abandoned coal mine, Jack Boggess saw his big XO coming on the run, boots pounding on the floor and shadows flickering as he passed the bare light bulbs strung along a wire like Christmas lights to illuminate the rock-walled hole. He knew something was wrong; Putney carried a lot of extra weight, and generally didn't run unless someone was behind him shooting at him.

He rose from the battered steel desk.

Whatever it is must be important.

"What 'cha got?"

"Here!" Putney offered a memory stick. "The man on com duty just brought this; he downloaded it from the email a few minutes ago. It's from headquarters, marked priority."

By direct order of both Frank Gore and Jonathon Edge, things didn't get sent priority unless they actually were, which simplified matters quite a bit. By Jack's own sense of caution, he kept the powerful laptop he referred to as his 'planning computer,' the repository for their most important records and notes, unconnected, separate from the Internet, the base network, and even his own personnel due to the security concerns. Grabbing the stick, he plugged it into the USB port.

Throwing himself into his seat, he went through the process: *My Computer > Removable Disk (E:) > nasty_sisters.bmp,* and his screen was instantly filled with a joke: a pornographic image downloaded from the Internet of two naked, nubile young women who were obviously more than a little fond of each other, along with the words: *"Men's Lesbian fantasy."* Scrolling down past it, he came to a second picture of a pair of ugly, very masculine, 'butch' types doing the same thing, with the caption, *"The REAL thing!"* It looked like what it was meant to look like: one of the ubiquitous crude jokes forwarded around all over by people with a warped sense of humor and too much time on their hands. In fact, this one had been forwarded several times, through quietly enslaved computers courtesy of an electronic Trojan Horse developed and used for exactly that purpose. Forwarding to several places tended to allay suspicion as well as making it difficult to pinpoint its actual intended target.

Putney chuckled over the joke, but Boggess had bigger fish to fry; instinctively, he knew this was what they had been waiting for. Ignoring the content, he moved the cursor over the image, right-clicked the mouse, and chose *"Scan With Rover"* from the drop-down menu. Rover was a program hacked and redesigned by Mike Dayton – although only a handful of people actually knew that – for a specific purpose: searching for particular patterns in digital images that fit the code model.

The code used by the Confederates was a cipher, one of the oldest and, in theory, easiest to break of all code systems...or at least it had been, until Mike Dayton got hold of it. He operated according to the paradigm that he held to almost like a religion: *any* code is unbreakable if no one knows it's there. Accordingly, he hid it in plain sight.

223

In any image, in order to display it properly, the computer assigns a code to the color of each individual pixel: white is *#FFFFFF*, black is *#000000*, and everything else is something in between. Rover searched for several particular combinations of color codes, using the last three digits that, found in those combinations, would indicate a code was present; if not, it would simply say, *"Item Not Found."* If it found the markers, however, it would then search the entire image, and give the operator the correct sequence as indicated by particular combination of markers in specified locations. Then it was just a matter of converting the combinations to their assigned letters, whose values rotated on a regular basis. Boggess did so, and looked at the text file on *Notepad* on the monitor screen in front of him.

Put your project into direct execution exactly twenty-four hours after the time of this message: absolutely no earlier, and no later than you can help. The competition will be otherwise occupied at that time, which will maximize your chances of success. Do not depend on standard lines of communication.

Good luck and God bless you all.

F.

"What the hell is he planning on doing?" Putney muttered.

"I don't know and I don't care. This is it! Get everybody together; *Lightening Strike* is a go!"

"You mean..."

"Yeah, I mean! Now get your big ass in gear; we're going to Point Pleasant!"

"Oh shit!"

Tommy had given his squad the address, and they were almost to their turn off when Harrison glanced up to see what Steiner was nodding at over the steering wheel. A block away from the location they had been given to pick up Tommy, they saw a military roadblock across the very side street they intended to turn onto, in the form of a Bradley fighting vehicle parked directly across the road, and infantry deployed on and around it and a nearby Humvee. A couple of the soldiers were flagging traffic past the turnoff. Glancing down the sidewalk past them, they could see more soldiers milling about, and dragging restrained people between them while smoke billowed out of the windows of the nearest house. At the other end of the street was yet another Bradley, an APC, and more Humvees and they could hear the distant siren of a fire truck.

"Go straight on," Harrison instructed, his voice tightly controlled. "Just keep going."

"But..." one of the men began, but Harrison cut him off.

"Shut up!" he barked. "Unless you've got a whole company of infantry in your pocket, just shut the hell up! There's not a damned thing we can do." Shaking his head in anger, he couldn't help but feel vaguely ashamed even though he knew was right. Abandoning a man wasn't something he, or any of the rest of them, had ever pictured themselves doing.

Still, he reflected as the drove past the soldiers motioning them by, trying to keep traffic flowing lest someone park an improvised explosive device in front of them, they had a mission. They were going to Samantha and Frank, Tommy or not. The mission was what was important.

As soon as they got by the armored personnel carrier, Harrison, back in control of his emotions, quietly told one of the men, "Handley, call one of our auxiliaries and have them do a walk-by; see what you can find out."

CHAPTER 26

Email Message

From: President, Cygotron Financial Corporation
Date: 2/22
To: Undisclosed Recipient
Subject: Fwd: Fwd: Fwd: Urgent!

DO NOT FORWARD, COPY OR PRINT!

We have reliable information that, with the opening of the markets this morning, the governments of China, Japan, and Russia will order the immediate sell-off of all United States currency. All Cygotron executives are to report to their department heads immediately...

Email Message

This was forwarded to me from a friend of mine who works in DC, who swears it originated with the White House:

"We must mobilize immediately to prevent financial panic, or a run on the market. All government agencies are hereby ordered to dismiss the information of the currency sell-off as fraudulent. When it happens, we will close the markets, but not until that time..."

"I...I've got it," Kerrie whispered. Samantha had immediately put her back to work in finding where the Feds were taking prisoners from Columbia; it would help take her mind off what had happened, and give her something to do that might – just *might* – actually do something to alleviate the situation.

"They're taking all of them to an old grade school west of Walhalla. It's been closed for years, and the Oconee County school board was using it for storage. The Army took it over for a temporary facility for holding and primary...interrogation."

Samantha laid a hand on her shoulder and felt the vibrations. She didn't know which of them was shaking; she knew far better than most what the word *interrogation* meant in the present context.

"Good people have to know how to do bad things in order to do good," she had heard one of the Federal talking heads say on the news once, trying to justify the torture. Hearing a strange sound, she realized it was her, grinding her teeth, and forced herself to stop it, seeking the calm that had always carried the man she loved through.

If they've hurt them, those bastards will learn what bad things good people can do before I'm through! she thought to herself even as a plan began to form.

Turning, she bellowed "Captain Carnes!" loud enough to be heard throughout the entire barn and set a startled hen to flight, and Lucky Charlie immediately came in with his strange, mechanical bounce that served him as a run.

"Ma'am?" He knew from her tone this was going to be a military matter, not a social one, and adjusted his attitude accordingly.

"Come to my office; we need to talk."

Once away from Kerrie and Cynthia, she turned to him.

"I'm going to my husband; you are now in charge of the South Carolina Theater of Operations until further notice. Our Columbia headquarters has just been raided, and at this moment, we are unsure if the Chief of Intelligence for CAP has been killed or captured, or what the status is of the data he possesses."

Charlie swore under his breath with much more violence and feeling than usual even as she continued.

"I believe he *probably* managed to destroy his data; my husband told me he had a series of thermite charges directly over his hard drives that a single line of code would detonate."

"If he had the chance to activate it, that would do it; it's unlikely that anything would be recovered from that. That stuff can melt steel."

228

"Good. For now, I've got my people on trying to find out if they're dead or alive – "

"How many were there?" he asked, as willing to interrupt professionally when time was of the essence as she was to accept it.

"Three."

Nodding, he said, "We have to assume the worst, that the enemy used a trained snatch team; if so, then at least one or two of them are almost certainly alive, unless they blew themselves up along with their house to keep from being captured."

"I don't think so; the house was on fire, but neither the local media nor our own forces in the area have mentioned any explosions. Lieutenant Harrison tells me they caught a glimpse of the soldiers taking at least two people out. We'll have to assume they've all been taken alive, then, and act accordingly."

She looked thoughtfully at Charlie, wondering how much to tell him, and then decided he needed to know it all.

"Before he was captured, Mike sent the order that put the largest operation of the war into action. Twenty-four hours from now, the entire power grid, along with air and rail transportation, will be abruptly shut down throughout the Continental United States."

Charlie's twisted mouth gaped, and for once he was so surprised he was even at a loss for profanity.

"How?" he finally managed.

"How doesn't matter; besides, I don't know, and neither does anyone else besides Frank and Mike...and General Edge, of course. All three of them believe it will work."

"Then it'll work," he said simply, accepting it as fact.

"Can we take advantage of the chaos to rescue these prisoners?"

He thought about that for a few seconds, then shrugged fatalistically. "It still won't be easy – in fact, the confusion may well present its own set of difficulties – but we'll still have a better chance of success then than otherwise." He thought for a moment, then added, "You know the IO and possibly the other two could compromise the plan, and blunt at least some of it if they break. Do you think they can hold out for twenty-four hours?"

Samantha thought of the horrors she had endured for twice as long, and then thought about her friends.

"Yes, if for no other reason than they know they'll have to." She thought she was speaking from intellect, not mere hope, but she had no way to tell. The pain of her own captivity swept over her like a wave, and she almost staggered.

"Alright; we'll consider it a given then, and formulate our plan accordingly." Actually, Charlie considered it not a given at all, but a toss-up at best. Still like at a drag race, 'you run what you brung.' This was what he'd been handed, and, as a professional soldier, he would go with it.

"Good. Use the time we still have before communications drop to get any and all available resources in this state assembled at a location of your choice near the North Carolina border without being discovered; I'll try to pick up some more personnel from up there." She looked around. "Since the prisoners know about this location, it will have to be abandoned immediately anyway. Kerrie's the communications specialist, so I'm leaving her with you." Considering the potential danger of what she was about to do, she would have liked to leave Cynthia too, but there was no point in giving an order she knew wouldn't be obeyed. The only way to get her petite bodyguard to remain behind would be to handcuff her to a solidly fixed object. "She has the information you'll need." She paused. "Please be careful with her. She's very upset."

Charlie's scarred brows tightened. "The IO – Mike, the guy in the wheelchair – he was her boyfriend, wasn't he?"

"Yes, but please don't speak of him in past tense...at least not yet."

"Of course...sorry."

Both of them couldn't help reflecting that, if her three friends were *already* past tense, they were lucky.

CHAPTER 27

US News Conference

"There is no need to panic. The President himself has assured me that they have been in contact with the Asian Markets, and there is no planned sell-off of United States currency."

"But what about the reports coming directly from the major financial institutions that say just the opposite?"

"The FBI has discovered those messages to be forgeries..."

"But they have the correct ISPs, and virtually every large bank in the country has called in its executives for special meetings..."

"The messages are hoaxes, and the meetings are to try to get to the bottom of it."

"Do you really expect the American people to believe that? Especially after the leaked memo from the State Department that the situation was to be kept secret."

"That message was faked as well."

"Look, we're here because we want to know the truth!"

"You know, you're playing right into the hands of the terrorists!"

Ten minutes after Tommy's squad arrived without their leader, they were ready to pull out again.

"Here's the way it's going to work," Harrison told her, gesturing at the four vehicles: an older model white Lincoln, a beat-up blue Chevy pickup, a green Toyota Landcruiser, and a burley black Dodge Ramcharger. Both the Dodge and the Toyota were beefed up four-wheel drives, capable of serious off-road use. "Mr. and Mrs. McAllister will be in the Lincoln, on point."

The couple, both well dressed and in their eighties, nodded. They might be too old to fight, but they were proud and eager to have a part to play nonetheless. With their bifocals and white hair, they also looked completely innocuous, which was the whole point.

"They'll travel a couple of miles ahead, and relay back to us concerning what's in front that we need to know about."

"You can count on us, Mrs. Gore!" Mrs. McAllister said, but before Samantha could thank her, Harrison went on, nodding at the gangly sixteen year-old boy by the pickup.

"This is Wally Mack; he's the second point, our failsafe. He'll be half a mile behind the McAllister's, and if he sees them get stopped before they have a chance to call back, he will."

The sixteen year-old boy, his eyes wide with hero-worship, swallowed hard and his pimpled cheeks blushed deeply when Samantha looked at him. She was so touched she would have smiled if the situation had been different.

"Jim and Billy will be riding with you and Cynthia in the Toyota." He looked down at the big bulldog at Samantha's feet. "And Thumper, of course." The animal opened his huge jaws at the sound of his name, in what looked for all the world like a tongue-lolling grin. He seemed to have attached himself as permanent part of the Information Officer's entourage. "They'll be armed, and ready to either turn around or go off-road at any word from our point men. We've got multiple alternative routes mapped out if necessary."

She knew there was no more chance of Billy and Jim leaving her than Cynthia, and maybe even less, if that were possible. Not only were they her friends, but Frank was responsible for saving both their lives at the risk of his own, and he had asked them to guard her. There was no doubt they would do so, regardless of the cost.

"Our squad will bring up the rear in the Ramcharger, and will precede you if we have to go off-road. We're armed to the teeth with assault rifles, grenade launchers, and two RPGs, and if something happens, we will engage any hostiles in order to allow you to get away."

Sergeant Steiner and the other four men nodded calmly, their eyes hard and steady. Samantha knew they were ready to lay down their lives if necessary in order for her to live. She felt horrible about making them take that risk in order for her to be with her husband, but she was going there anyway, with or without them. Besides, she rationalized, they were going to have to immediately evacuate their current headquarters anyway, and Captain Carnes could move everyone to the staging area near the northern border just as easily as he could move them anywhere else. He had already put out the call, and other Palmetto auxiliary forces were making their way to join him even now. She had to go somewhere, so she might as well go to Frank.

"Thank you all," was all she could think of to say.

"No," said Mr. McAllister, "thank you, for all you've done and all you've suffered for Dixie." He straightened as much as his stooped, elderly bones would allow and saluted her. "It's a privilege, ma'am; by God, it's truly a privilege!"

CHAPTER 28

European Union Newscast

The American financial markets are in a full-blown panic at this moment, over the rumors of a massive overseas-currency sell-off of the US dollar. The Plants Administration denies this, but even if it is not true, it may become a self-fulfilling prophecy, as some panicked international investors have begun doing exactly that...

Executive Order, the White House

Any person or persons, or any group spreading false or malicious rumors designed to damage or destroy the financial system of the United States shall be considered an enemy combatant, and arrested under the charge of terrorism...

"The prisoners should be here within a couple of hours, sirs, and we've got ID on all three."

United States Army Major Clifford Wills and his Mossad advisor, Captain Israel Rosenberg looked expectantly at Master Sergeant Cussler, who had just entered the room. All three were interrogations specialists, the modern equivalent of a Medieval Inquisitor.

Reading from the papers, the hard-faced NCO with the Special Forces insignia and the mouth like a razor slash continued. "The first male is Thomas Lee Richardson, formerly an E-5 in the Army Special Forces – medical and small arms specialties. Civilian occupation: paramedic."

Slipping that sheet beneath the next, he continued. "The female is Donna Lynn Waddell: no known military experience or occupation. However, she's the Goddaughter of the wanted terrorist, Samuel Alvin Wirtz."

"Wirtz!" Wills exclaimed, sitting up straighter at the sound of the Councilman's name. The one-time pig farmer was just below Edge and Gore on their wanted list, and anyone related to him was a valuable catch indeed.

"The third one – the one we caught in the computer room – is Michael Wayne Dayton. He's in a wheelchair – paraplegic."

Rosenberg looked at him thoughtfully. "Is the woman intimate with either of the men?"

Sergeant Cussler answered in his deadpan voice. "Yes sir, with Richardson. As a matter of fact, the snatch team reported that they were getting it on when they were captured."

"Excellent," the advisor replied in his thick Hebrew accent, absently tapping the tip of his large, hooked nose. "That will make it much easier, give us more leverage."

Major Wills asked Rosenberg if he had a plan as the Sergeant looked on without emotion.

"I think so. I believe we should deal with this Dayton separately from the others. In fact, I think we need to separate all of them at first for softening up; that alone may break the woman, at least. Failing that, we can bring the two lovebirds together again, and see just how far they'll go to save each other."

"Sirs," Cussler broke in, "if I may make a suggestion?" He waited until the Major motioned him to go ahead. "I'd like a to take a crack at Richardson." He gestured towards his own shoulder patch. "He was a Green Beret, same as me, and has gone through the same training as I have. I know exactly what he expects, and as quick as they get his SERE school records faxed down here, I'll also know exactly where his weak points are."

"Makes sense." Turning to the Israeli, Major Wills asked, "Which one to you want; Dayton or Waddell?"

Licking his thick lips, Rosenberg said, "I'll take the woman, I think."

Wills laughed out loud.

"How did I know you were going to say that?"

CHAPTER 29

Homeland Security Phone Conversation

"I'm telling you, he was there!"

"If he was – if – he got out first. That means you lied to me."

"Damn it, I didn't lie! He was – wait a minute...I just got word; we found him, and he's still in North Carolina!"

"Bullshit!"

"One of my men just brought me a message. Gore is wounded – badly, he said – and he's currently being taken care of by one of the Tarheel units."

"Which one and where?"

"I don't know yet, but I'll find out; I'll go check it out myself."

"You do that. Now. He's not, you owe me ten million."

That was one hell of a trip.

Samantha sighed audibly with relief, and felt her shoulders slump, the tension leaving as soon as she saw the man on the four-wheeler. He was sitting at the entrance to a driveway that was no more than a pair of muddy tire tracks with a livestock gate across it. Cynthia had made the call when they were less than five miles away, and the Tarheels had sent an escort out to meet them.

Armored cavalry regularly patrolled the roads, but, due to the guerrillas' dual point vehicles and a fair amount of traffic despite the weather and gas rationing, they were able to get through. They weren't quite halfway to their destination when the McAllister's came upon an unexpected roadblock, but Mrs. McAllister had her cell phone already in her hand, ready for just such an emergency, and called back to tell them there was "a delay."

Both they and Wally Mack had enough advance notice to turn around and seek an alternate route. The soldiers gave the McAllister vehicle a cursory search before letting them go on. Their part was finished.

Only ten miles from their goal, Wally called, his young voice high-pitched with tension, to tell them there was another roadblock. Steiner, who had been navigating their journey, immediately sent them up a side road. The big Dodge pulled around the Landcruiser, taking the lead, and, after two off-road detours that involved cutting through six fences and crossing terrain that pounded Samantha's rear end black and blue despite the seat's upholstery, they finally made it to yet another modified barn, not much different from the one they had left.

She didn't recognize the man lying on the bed at first, despite being told it was Frank. She stepped forward until she was beside him and hesitantly reached out to touch him. She knew the feel of her husband's skin, but she couldn't reconcile that familiarity with the swollen, bandaged features, the IV snaking into his arm on one side, and the catheter tube leading out to the bag of yellow fluid on the other. She tightly closed her lips and eyes, and swallowed hard before asking what she had to.

"How is he?"

"Serious," Doctor Grissom told her, "but I think he'll live. It's a good thing he's so strong and fit, or he'd never have made it this far."

He proceeded to read off his injuries calmly, like someone reading a grocery list that never seemed to end, and each one felt like a blow.

"He had eight shrapnel wounds in the backs of both legs and his right buttock, and the force of the blast caused massive bruising to the entire area. One fragment passed through the man he was carrying and penetrated his middle back, lodging in the outer portion of his right lung. He has a cracked sternum, three fractured ribs, and three fingers on his left hand were dislocated. His nose was broken, with the fracture continuing into both orbital sockets, accompanied by some leakage of cerebral fluid. He also has multiple concussions, although at least there appears to be no bleeding into his brain. There is also a spider web fracture of his frontal sinuses, and assorted contusions, avulsions, and abrasions of varying severity. I didn't bother to count the stitches."

Samantha leaned against the wall at the head of the bed to keep from falling down.

Get control of yourself! What would Frank do?

She knew; he'd get control of himself by taking control of the situation.

"What about the lasting effects?"

"In all likelihood, barring infection or other complications, he'll eventually recover more-or-less totally from his physical injuries, although he may need plastic surgery for his face; it's too early to tell yet, and that's out of my league anyway. My main concern is his concussion, combined with the large amount of blood he's lost. With the equipment we have available, I can't tell as much as I'd like about the state of his brain."

Hearing that made her feel nauseous, like someone had just kicked her in the guts.

"What's your opinion?"

"I don't have one; I don't form opinions until I have the facts, and the facts aren't here yet." He turned to go, then paused and turned back. "Can I ask you something, just for my own peace of mind?"

"Yes, of course," she answered, still looking at her husband.

"That tape you played, the one that started this whole thing: was it real? And the one afterwards, when you described being...tortured?"

"Oh yes," she said, caressing Frank's hand as she glanced up at the veterinarian. "They were as real as it gets. I can show you the scars if you want."

He shook his head and swallowed hard. He sensed that she was telling him the truth, and, while it flew in the face of everything he had ever believed, when he looked into her eyes, he couldn't bring himself to deny it.

"Let me ask you this, then; was it worth it?"

Looking at Frank's battered, bandaged figure, she didn't know how to answer at first. Finally, she said, "He thought so." Then she realized, if not for that, she would never have met this wonderful man, and would never have had this new life of his squirming in her belly. Turning her gaze back to Shane Grissom, she locked eyes with him and answered in all truthfulness.

"And so do I."

Donna was disoriented, which she knew on an intellectual level was their purpose. After they had taken off the blindfold, she found herself standing under lights that seemed as bright as the sun, and she squinted against the glare. There were several men in the room, one of them, their apparent leader, spoke with a thick Yiddish accent.

"Take off your clothes," Rosenberg told her.

They had clothed her in a coverall for transport, just as Samantha had described in her training on resisting interrogation.

"They try to make a woman take off her own clothes. It's a psychological ploy; it's like you're subconsciously offering yourself to them, giving them permission to use you as they will."

Donna wasn't about to give them her permission for anything. Blinking involuntarily at him through the glare, she told him to go to Hell. In less than a second, her body arched backwards when one of the men jammed a stun gun against the small of her back and held the trigger down, sending a hundred thousand volts through her. Then she was on the floor with no recollection of how she got there.

"You'll find that cooperation will be rewarded, and that defiance will be punished – *always*. Take off your clothes."

The pain was impossibly intense, and very disorienting, but she remembered what Sammie had told her; even when you obey, it doesn't stop, and it gives them a foot in the door of your mind.

"No!"

Still on the floor, the shock, this time from two of them at once, sent her sprawling and flailing. They held the electrodes on her longer, and she could hear herself screaming, as if her voice was disconnected from her mind. She still screamed for several seconds, after they had stopped. She could only lie there quivering and gasping, and was humiliated to realize her bladder had let go and soaked the crotch of her coveralls. She couldn't stand any more, she would strip for them, do anything for them, if they just wouldn't shock her again...

"Take off your clothes."

She heard the foreign voice once more, saying the same damned thing, perfectly calmly, but in the back of her mind she heard Sammie.

If you're ever captured, they may very well break you, but make the bastards work for it! Don't think about what they're going to do; block it out of your mind. Every minute you can hold out, is one more minute for your people to make arrangements to minimize the impact of what they manage to squeeze out of you, and one more life you might be saving. Don't worry about the next hour, or even the next second; just worry about holding on through this second you're in. Above all else, remember this; we'll come for you. One way or another, no matter how long it takes, someone will come, and then, there will be a payback!

Still shaking from the shocks, Donna was unable to stop her voice from stammering when she said, "R-r-rot in H-hell, you s-s-son of a b-bitch!"

Then she was screaming as the shocks came again. Her teeth slammed together so hard under the stimulation of the electricity that three of them snapped off under the pressure from the powerful spasming of her jaw muscles.

Tommy was in a world of hurt, but he'd had worse...maybe. He wasn't too sure about that, despite having been through Special Forces training and more fights than he could count.

He knew the head shaving, the beating, and the electric shocks were just a softening-up process, designed to terrify a prisoner, and to put him in a more cooperative mood. What was coming next, though, he was afraid might do just that.

Tommy had been through it during his training, and had lasted about three minutes before breaking, and that was the longest of anyone in his class. He was about to be waterboarded; not the towel over the face with water dumped on it he had experienced in the Army POW school; no, this was the real McCoy, not that it mattered too much. Either one played on one of every man's most atavistic fears; that of drowning.

Stripped naked and strapped facedown on the long plank lying atop a pair of sawhorses, he watched the soldiers taking turns urinating and spitting in the cut off fifty-five gallon drum full of water as the stone-faced Sergeant Cussler looked on. That was just part of the head game of course; he could already see and smell the raw sewage it was filled with.

"Last chance, Richardson. You couldn't take the sanitary treatment in SERE School, so you know damned well you're not going to hold up through this. You can save yourself a lot of grief if you cooperate.

From the corner of his eye, he saw the sergeant watching him intently, looking for a reaction, but he'd rather be damned than give him one.

The biker turned Confederate officer sought the detached place of inner calm as he began readying himself for something they wouldn't expect. It would take every ounce of determination and control he had learned in his years of martial arts training, and at Fort Bragg to override the most basic instinct for survival. He knew too much, and anyway, he reasoned, it wouldn't take over a few minutes; not so bad, all told. He knew he had seen more than one person die a hell of a lot harder, and had caused a few of them to. He was going to kill himself in a horribly painful way, and they were going to provide him with the means to do it.

When life gives you lemons, make lemonade.

As they dragged the barrel bottom beneath his head and the disgusting odor grew stronger, he thought, *I just wish I didn't have to make it with shit!*

His inhibitions down and much of the fear leaving at the thought he would soon be dead, he found his own joke so inexplicably funny he laughed out loud at it, even as the blood ran from his crushed nose and split lips, and fell into the slimy water in a steady drip.

"What the hell's so funny?" one of the men, a PFC, demanded, and when Tommy twisted his head to look at him, he laughed even harder. The interrogator had broad hips, tapering upward to a narrow, shallow chest, topped by a long neck, chinless face, and prominent, beak-like nose. He looked like the kind of guy everybody in school picked on, which was probably why he gravitated towards this position of power. He had no self-esteem of his own, and he could only be on top when he could force other people's pride even lower than his own.

Perfect! This will make him mad, and he won't think.

"I was just wondering. I went to juvenile hall about twenty years ago for screwing a chicken, and I thought maybe you were my son, you ugly, bird-beaked son of a bitch!"

Even Cussler chuckled at that one, and the other interrogator began howling with laughter at the expense of his comrade, who flushed bright red and shouted, "Laugh at this, you prick!" as he grabbed the back end of the board and tilted it upwards. The head end slid forward and down, landing with a splash and then a thump when it hit the bottom of the barrel, plunging Tommy upside down below the surface past his shoulders.

The words of one of his many martial arts instructors spoke to him once more.

The warrior does not fear death; it is his best friend, his constant companion, waking or sleeping. It is the culmination of his life; it is what he was born to do! Do not flee from death; embrace it!

God, have mercy on my soul!

Not giving himself time to think about the filth he was in, Tommy immediately did what he had been psyching himself up to do; through sheer force of will, he overcame every instinct in his being, blew out all his remaining air, opened his mouth, and then took the deepest breath he could, violently sucking the vile, stinking fluid into his lungs. The combination of agony and atavistic terror was so great it took on a life of its own; it became a palpable thing that he seemed to be able to dispassionately analyze with what was left of his rapidly fading consciousness.

As Tommy began to die, his body moved of its own accord, fighting against what he had done, straining and writhing of its own violation against his bonds.

"How do you like that, Big Mouth?" the homely soldier shouted. "How do you like that? Huh? Does it taste good?"

While he taunted the man who couldn't hear him with his head beneath the surface, Cussler frowned, studying the twitching, clenching movements of their captive's bound hands and feet. Yes, that was normal, but not this quickly...He thoughtfully rubbed his chin with his rubber-gloved hand. As he watched the frantic motion of the fingers slow until they became no more than a snail's pace opening and closing, he became concerned.

Something's wrong here...

The movement stopped, and then suddenly he knew. When he found his voice, it was a panicked shout.

"Damn it! Get him out of there!"

"To Hell with him!" the target of Tommy's barb responded. "He hasn't been in there nearly long enough to – "

His words were cut off when the sergeant shoved him hard, sending him staggering out of the way as he grabbed the back end of the board.

"Help me!" he yelled and a third soldier joined him in levering Tommy out of the water. His body was limp, his eyes were closed, and the fluid poured from his nose and half-open mouth. Pulling the plank back to rest across the sawhorses once more, Cussler put his hand to Tommy's carotid.

"Get him off the board! Hurry up, damn it! He's still got a pulse, but he's turning blue!"

He wasn't lying; their captive's lips and fingernails were turning a distinctively unhealthy shade as his fading body used up the very last of the oxygen in his bloodstream.

Rapidly untying him and lowering him to the floor, they rolled him onto his back and one of the soldiers began driving the heel of his gloved hand under Tommy's solar plexus. Each time he pushed, more water gushed out, and suddenly the man jumped back, cursing as a the body convulsed, gagged, and began spewing a flood of vomit in between gasps as the air pumped in to refill the damaged lungs. Quickly they rolled him onto his side as the puke kept coming, and along with it, Tommy's consciousness.

Damn it! I'm still alive! Son of a bitch!

Mike sprayed vomit on the floor and noticed through the haze of his swollen, watering eyes that a couple of his teeth had come out with it this time. The beating was more intense than he had expected; at first, he had thought – and hoped – they would accidentally kill him, but they were far too experienced for that. Instead, it just hurt like hell, just like it was meant to.

Not as bad as the one that paralyzed me though. I've been through worse before; just hang on awhile longer!

Mike had developed a plan on his way in, but he would have to wait a little longer to make it believable; besides, every second meant more time for the CAP to minimize any damage he might inadvertently cause. Still, as the fists and boots and saps and prods kept coming, it was getting harder and harder to delay, especially when he felt a rib snap after one of his tormentors put in the boot a little harder than before. With his hands cuffed behind him he couldn't block or evade, and with his paralyzed legs, he not only couldn't kick out, but couldn't even hold himself up, and was left squirming on the floor like a naked slug. The sheer humiliation was even worse than the pain.

"Tell us what we want to know, and you can end this."

Mike looked up at Major Wills, drooling blood and slobbers, and repeated the words that had brought him an increase in the beating in the first place.

"I want my lawyer!"

"You stupid son of a bitch!" one of the soldiers yelled, grabbing him by the hair and lifting him halfway off the floor by it. "You're not entitled to a lawyer! You're not entitled to anything! Now answer the damned question!"

"I've got rights!"

"There's your rights!" a second man yelled, leaning over to punch him in the face with a lead-filled sap glove, "and here are a couple of lefts to go along with them!"

By the time he finished, the crippled programmer was unconscious, but they revived him with a bucket of cold water. Through his grogginess, he heard Wills say, "Bring in the dog."

Mike had never had a dog, and even though he liked Thumper, he was more than a little uneasy about them, and...

Yes! This just might be my opportunity!

He shuddered, trying his best to steel himself for what he was going to have to do while confining his plan in another compartment of his mind, separate from the fear and pain.

DAY 332

CHAPTER 30

"I'm not wasting my men on a wild goose chase!"

Even though she had never dealt with him directly, Samantha knew enough about the North Carolina political leader's reputation to expect him to be a pain in the butt, but she didn't expect this – not now, of all times. She had laid out the mission and its importance, and, even though he had no authority to do so, he had refused.

LC Tarbox looked and acted like what he was: an arrogant ass. The tall, forty-five year-old lawyer had arrived just as she ordered all the available personnel to assemble, and had demanded a meeting with her first. His purpose, she quickly realized, already fuming at the loss of precious organizational time, was to tell her 'no.' He seemed to think his law degree, his influence in the movement, his glib tongue, and probably his thick dark hair, handsome features, and carefully cultivated tan were enough to win any argument. When he found that none of it cut any ice with Samantha, however, he switched to simple refusal. After all, he was in his home state; what could she do?

For one thing, she was made of sterner stuff, and was unwilling to accept his refusal; for another, she had also been awake for more than twenty-four hours, was stressed out over her husband and her friends, and to top it off, she was nine months pregnant. She wasn't in the mood to put up with much crap from anybody.

Struggling to keep her voice calm, Samantha said, "Mr. Tarbox, the future of this war is at stake; these people are our headquarters company, including the chief intelligence officer for the entire Confederate Army Provisional. Do you realize what he has in his head? We cannot leave them in custody to have the information tortured out of them. I'm either going to rescue them, or I'm...going to kill them." The slight hesitation in her voice was the only indication of the agonized scream erupting from her very soul at the thought. "The North Carolina forces are the only ones available in the timeframe we have to work with, and they're the ones I'm going to use."

"You are not using this state's forces! I don't know who the hell you think you are –"

Samantha had finally reached the end of her patience, and it showed clearly in her voice; when it came, her tone was as hard, sharp and merciless as the razor edge of a fighting knife. "I'll tell you who the hell I think I am, *Mr.* Tarbox!" She leaned forward across his desk, pushing her face towards his, invading his space and forcing him to lean back in retreat. "I am a commissioned colonel in the Confederate Army Provisional under the direct command of Generals Jonathon Edge and Franklin Gore, and these North Carolina forces are part of that Army! As such, my authority over the military trumps that of any civilian *politician* hiding behind the lines and afraid to fight! Now I am going to go out there and *take* the men and I need and get this show on the road, and I suggest you stay the hell out of my way!"

L.C. Tarbox gaped like a stranded carp for a second, and then lost his own temper, and promptly made a very serious mistake. His hand shot out across the desk, grabbing Samantha's right arm just below the shoulder as she turned to go.

"Damn you, you little bitch! You don't talk to me that way!"

At the very beginning of the war, Samantha had been rescued from a brutal beating, administered by an angry man who used similar words, but that had been a lifetime ago, and she was not the same woman. This time, she reacted instinctively, just as Frank had taught her. Her left hand grabbed his, pinning it in place where it gripped her bicep, and at the same time, she swung her right arm beneath his and back over top of his elbow. Twisting her body hard and rotating his arm in the process, she dropped her weight as she yanked the off-balance attorney forward, slamming his chest down on the desk and locking his elbow out to its fullest extension and then beyond. The dull but startlingly loud *pop* of the dislocating joint was eclipsed by his agonized scream. Unfortunately for him, she was just getting started. All the stress, all the grief, all the rage she had bottled up inside her had just found a target, and she couldn't have stopped then, even if she had wanted to...and she didn't.

Keeping hold of his wrist with her left hand, she jerked her revolver out with her right even as she shouted.

"Never put your filthy hands on me, you – damned – dirty – rotten – cowardly – son of a – bitch!" Each word was delivered at the top of her lungs, along with a brutal downward chop for emphasis as she slammed the pistol against his skull again and again.

"Excuse me, ma'am."

Instantly she snapped the revolver up and pointed it at the source of the voice, and Watis Suggs, along with the shocked North Carolina private who was pushing him in his wheelchair, found themselves looking straight into the unwavering muzzle. The effect was made even more disturbing by the hair clinging to the weapon, and the blood dripping from it, as well as the gore spattering her clothes, right hand and face. Worse yet was the look in her eyes, accompanied by the fact that her finger had already taken up most of the slack in the double action trigger, leaving the hammer slightly back, waiting for the merest nudge to complete its movement. Watis only grinned, apparently unruffled. Not that he could go anywhere; the legs of his jeans were split to the hips, one leg was in a cast almost that high, and the calf of the other was heavily bandaged.

He nodded toward the unconscious Tarbox, still lying stretched across the desk with most of his scalp hanging down in tattered, bloody flaps to expose the bone as his head dangled limply over the edge and bled onto the carpet.

"Daddy always told me never to get rough with a lady; I reckon that must be why. Congratulations, ma'am; that was just about the best ass-whuppin' I've ever seen." He struggled with what he was about to say next. Nothing would have made Suggs as happy as to let his rival bleed to death, unless maybe having the opportunity to hasten the process along himself, but this was the wrong place, and the wrong time. The SN faction would blame both him and the Confederate Army Provisional leadership, and strengthen their hold using the propaganda of Tarbox as a martyr; he would be far more valuable to them dead than alive, and Suggs didn't need any more complications right now. Heaving a sigh of disappointment, he told her, "I reckon you'd best not kill him if you ain't already. He ain't worth a fart in a windstorm, but he's got a following anyway." Glancing over his shoulder, he said casually, "Carson, take LJ to the infirmary and get his head sewn up before the stupid son of a bitch bleeds to death."

"Yessir!" the guerrilla said hastily, moving to obey as fast as he could, nervously eying Samantha the whole time. Her muzzle never moved as he hauled her victim off the desk and over his shoulder like a sack of bleeding potatoes. Once he closed the door behind him Watis nodded again.

"I reckon you must be Colonel Gore, ma'am. I'm Watis Suggs; it's a real pleasure to meet you."

Samantha relaxed; even though she had never met him in the flesh, she had spoken to him a few times, was familiar with his reputation, and liked what she had heard. More importantly, Frank both liked and trusted him, and that was good enough for her.

"Colonel Suggs, it's good to finally meet you in the flesh." She transferred the weapon to her left hand and started to stick out her right when she realized it, like her revolver, was covered with blood studded with clumps of hair. Seeing her hesitation, Suggs grabbed it anyway, making a slightly squishy sound when he squeezed their palms together.

"Don't worry about it, ma'am. This ain't the first time I've had blood on my hands. Here." He produced a red bandanna from his back pocket and handed it to her. "Clean your pistol before it starts to rust. Blood's hard on 'em."

"Thank you," she said, wiping down the Smith & Wesson as Watis wiped his own hand casually on the leg of his jeans. "Colonel Suggs..."

"Watis, please, ma'am."

She managed a smile that looked like anything but. "Samantha, then. Watis, I need your help."

"I know; I was rolling down the hall when I heard you having your little discussion with LC, and I got to the door just in time to see what happened." He treated her to a grim smile of his own. "You don't know how many times I've wanted to do that myself. Anyway, like I was saying, I know what you need. I don't think it's going to work, but I don't see that we got a hell of a lot of choice either." Pausing, he glared maliciously at his injured legs as if contemplating shooting them again for letting him down. "You're probably all going to kill yourselves, but still I wish like hell I could go with you."

Samantha was sincere when she said, "I wish you could too."

"Sammie? You wanted to see me?"

She sighed with relief. Charlie had finally made it.

"Yeah, I do. Are our people in the staging area?"

"Everybody that we could get."

"How many do we have?"

Captain Carnes hesitated for a split second, then laid their cards on the table.

"We don't have a real unit, just something pieced together with half-a-dozen veterans and the twelve students from our school, plus whatever North Carolina has available. We've got a grand total of one BATF Humvee and one armored car with a battering ram on the front and a homemade flamethrower mounted on top, plus some assorted civilian vehicles. I understand the Tarheels have another Humvee and a bus, and that's good, because we'll need 'em. It's not much, but still, everybody's armed and motivated, and ready to go at your order.

Samantha looked down, thinking.

Plus Tommy's squad and the three mobile Irregulars. And with that, we need to go approximately one hundred miles through territory crawling with enemy forces, and attack and destroy a military police company guarding a makeshift prison housed in an old grade school.

"Will that be enough to secure the release of the prisoners..." she swallowed hard before saying what she had to, "...or kill them if that's not possible?" At the thought of Donna, Tommy and Mike, her tears began to reach for her eyes, but they never reached her voice.

251

Lucky Charlie knew these people were much more to Samantha than just prisoners, but he didn't let on that he noticed.

"Not a problem," he lied. "Get me all the intel you have, and I'll get our people ready; I'll pull out as soon as everything collapses."

"No; *we'll* pull out." Straightening up, she looked at the widow, her view obscured by water droplets. "The forecast says this storm system is stalled over us. Good; we need to take advantage of every minute of the cover this weather will provide, for as long as it lasts."

Lucky Charlie's good eye blinked in surprise when he realized what she meant by *we*. "Sammie, you can't do this!"

"I have to. I know how dangerous this mission is, which is why I have to go. Most of the students have no combat experience, and most of our available veterans are from North Carolina. It's a mess up here; the leadership's divided, and half the men are at each other's throats; we can't depend on them to get with the program and take orders on their own, especially not from an officer out of another state. They'll need someone from the overall leadership, a figurehead, a rallying point to follow. My husband's wounded and nobody else from CAP command is here, so that just leaves me. Maybe having a pregnant woman in front of them will make them too ashamed to turn and run when it really hits the fan. I've got the feeling this is going to be bad."

Captain Carnes nodded his understanding. He didn't want her to risk herself by going, but he also couldn't deny that she made good sense.

"It's *always* bad; sometimes it's just worse than others." He didn't voice the rest of his thoughts.

I've got the feeling this one is going to be the worst of all...but by God, I still wouldn't miss it for the world! It's good to be a soldier again...

As for Samantha, she was already thinking about her next conversation; it was the last one she wanted to have.

"Damn it, Sammie, Frank told me to protect you!"

252

She looked steadily at Billy, turning her head upward so she could see the giant's eyes. She was about to do the hardest thing she had ever done, and on the very verge of it, she still didn't know if she could do it. She just knew she had to.

"I know, and now I need you to protect him." She glanced at the bed where her husband lay, still unconscious and swathed in bandages.

"You're goin' off to rescue Tommy and the others; you need me with you. I need to be with you; he's my best friend, and he helped rescue me!"

"Billy, I need someone I can trust to look after Frank."

"I'm not a nurse! Besides, these are still good people up here; they'll take care of him."

She shook her head. "This unit is in turmoil, and there are elements here that I can't trust any farther than I can throw them. Even the ones I'm sure of, I can't trust them to do what might need to be done. I can trust you."

The big biker's eyes widened with a dawning look of horrified realization.

"What are you gettin' at?"

"I need you to do more than just protect him from the North Carolina SN faction. If the Feds raid you, and there is a danger of Frank being captured, I need somebody here I can trust to see to it that doesn't happen." She suddenly sobbed, and clamped her hand over her mouth as the tears let go and began flowing. "I've fought beside you, and I love you like a brother. If that happens...I want you to kill my husband."

Billy recoiled, unable to help drawing back at what she was asking.

"Sammie! I can't –"

"You can!" she shouted, punctuating it with a hard, frustrated shove against Billy's chest that didn't move the biker's body in the slightest, although it sent his soul reeling. "It's what he wanted! He told me, the first night we went on the run together, that he wasn't willing to be taken alive because of what would happen to a White ex-cop in the prison system. Well I can tell you from experience that what will happen to him if the Feds get their hands on him now is much, much worse. I know, Billy; I know what they did to me, and I won't have Frank go through that! I won't have them torture him, and then drug him up and give him a show trial before they execute him. Do you understand? I will not have them break his spirit! If he has to die, I want him to die like a man!"

Billy thought about that, looking back and forth between her and the figure of his friend and commander lying on the cold white sheets, and finally nodded, the tears flowing from his own eyes now.

His voice was breaking when he said, "Alright, Sammie...alright."

"Promise me, Billy!"

"I promise. God help me, but I promise!"

They embraced for a moment, and when she finally let go, she went to her husband, kissed the part of his cheek that was unbandaged, and left without looking back.

She knew that she might have just sentenced the man she loved to death, but she tried her best to put it out of her mind; she had troops to round up and a job to do.

"This is a suicide mission!"

Samantha was standing in front with Lucky Charlie on one side, Cynthia on the other, and Jim Reynolds, the remaining trio of strung out Irregulars, and Tommy's squad spread out beside and behind them. Thumper lay at her feet, watching. Looking across the crowded barn, she furrowed her brow slightly at the man who had spoken.

I should have known this BS wouldn't end with Tarbox!

Fatigue was beginning to tell on her, but through an effort of will, she forced herself to remain calm. She began to understand firsthand why Frank often seemed to stay so frustrated with command in general, and why he was so concerned about this one in particular.

"No, Captain McEvoy, this is not a suicide mission. It is a dangerous mission that has to be done, and we're the ones who are going to do it."

"What's this 'we' stuff?" he bristled before waving his arm at the other Tarheels. "We'll be the ones who do the dying!"

"I said we and I meant we. I'm not Tarbox. I'm going with you in overall command of the force; Captain Carnes will be in direct command of the mission itself, and Sergeant Dee Grissom will be guiding."

"A pregnant woman, a cripple, and an enemy deserter," the Captain sneered, "just beautiful!"

Lucky Charlie took half a step forward, fully intent on killing McEvoy, but was halted by Samantha's hand on his forearm and by movement in the crowd of guerrillas.

"And me," a lone voice said quietly, and Johnny Biscoe stepped forward, his eyes red and glassy and his body twitching from speed and fatigue.

"What the hell do you think you're doing?" McEvoy demanded, and Biscoe fixed him with an empty stare that seemed to be looking through him, at something far, far away.

"I'm fighting, sir." His eyes flicked to the Irregulars and back again. "I've come this far with these boys, and I'm going to see it through to the end. I'm in it all the way."

"In case you forgot, you're fighting for North Carolina!"

Biscoe shook his head with a jerky motion, like he was flinging water out of his hair. His voice was flat, but it had a weird, up and down cadence from the combined stress, and was all the more poignant for it.

"No sir. I'm fighting for the Cause, and that's bigger than North Carolina, South Carolina, or any other state." He pointed an arm in the general direction of the door. "They get the information those people have, this war's over, and we've lost. All this killing, all this dying, none of it will mean shit. It'll mean even less than that damned political 'me-me-me' shit you and Tarbox keep spouting. This is *war*, and all the fine-sounding philosophy in the world don't mean nothing if we don't win it."

"I'm ordering you – "

Without raising his voice, Biscoe said two words to his captain: two words that started with 'F' and ended with 'you,' followed belatedly by a tacked-on 'sir.'

"And all God's children said 'amen,'" Watis Suggs growled as he wheeled himself into the room, and every eye turned toward him. "Shut the hell up, McEvoy, and form up your men; you're moving out!"

McEvoy was visibly startled and somewhat intimidated by his Colonel's abrupt appearance, but he still showed no inclination to obey.

"What does Mr. Tarbox have to say about this?"

The Colonel smiled evilly through his beard.

"Number one, Mr. Tarbox is not in the military chain of command; I am. Number two, Mr. Tarbox is temporarily indisposed," he said with satisfaction plain in his voice. He nodded at Samantha. "He tried to manhandle this lady here, and she *indisposed* his sorry ass up along side the head about half a dozen times with her pistol butt." He grinned without humor. "I figure he'll wake up in the next day or two. Regardless, he's not the one in charge of the North Carolina military forces – *I* am – and I'm telling you to get your ass in gear – *Now!* That's an order!"

"Until it goes through Tarbox, it's not a lawful – "

"To hell with lawful!" Watis shouted even as his hand came to rest on the butt of his revolver. "We ain't got time to worry about lawful! We stand or fall on the decision we make right now, and I've made it! Lieutenant Preston!"

McEvoy's XO, a short, deceptively plump-looking Tarheel with a blonde bur haircut straightened up.

"Sir?"

"Captain McEvoy is relieved of command; you're in charge now. Disarm him and detail a squad to shackle him to something somewhere out of the way until he can be court-martialed for disobedience to orders and insubordination."

McEvoy gasped, his face first going white, then red.

"You're a traitor to your state!" he shouted as his hand closed around the sling and he yanked his rifle from his shoulder, apparently with an intent to do something besides surrender.

The members of his former company were stunned into momentarily immobility by the rapid escalation of events, and they hesitated for a fraction of a second. Suggs was lifting his pistol even as Sammie drew hers. Charlie, Jim and Cynthia raised their weapons even as they stepped in front of Samantha, and the three Irregulars and Dojo Squad lunged forward, aiming and getting ready to unleash a barrage of small arms fire that would doubtless have killed McEvoy and probably everyone standing close to him. If that wasn't enough, even Thumper was on his feet as well, sensing if not understanding the threat posed by the Tarheel Captain, and a deep warning growl echoed from his throat and oozed out between his huge teeth. The recognition of certain death preempting his fit of anger, the McEvoy released his sling as if it had suddenly become hot. However, even as his rifle slid to the floor with a clatter, he couldn't help but issue one final parting remark.

"Fine, but this isn't over yet, you – "

Whatever else he was about to say ended abruptly with a loud *crack* when the steel butt plate of an old Model 97 Winchester trench gun slammed against the side of his head, splitting his ear almost in two and fracturing his skull before sending him sprawling on the floor, unconscious. The gun's owner, Stanley Bauer, stepped over him, pausing only to spit a brown stream of tobacco juice in the fallen man's face as his body jerked and twitched on the plywood.

"Mouthy sumbitch!" the old man muttered before walking up and taking his place beside Samantha and Lucky Charlie. Facing the crowd, he said, "You can add one fat, very pissed-off old man to the list! I was from North Carolina when your all's grandmothers were still wiping your daddies' butts, and I'm going!" He glared at the officers, daring them to tell him no, but Samantha only smiled and nodded her appreciation and Captain Carnes offered his right hand along with his twisted grin.

"Welcome aboard, sir; glad to have you!"

"Same here," Suggs said, extending his own hand.

257

Bauer looked as if he had suddenly grown about six inches, and another voice cut through the murmuring.

"Make that two old men."

Everyone stared in shocked amazement as Dr. Andrew MacFie appeared seemingly from nowhere and made his way through the crowd that parted respectfully before him. His small stature, pot belly, bald head and gray beard made him instantly recognizable as the Southern Nationalist icon he was, but also made him look like anything but a warrior, despite the M16 slung over his shoulder and an old Colt single-action .45 on his hip. Taking his place beside the surprised Samantha, he nodded to her and whispered, "I heard what happened, and I thought you might need some help."

Turning towards the crowd, he saw every eye upon him.

"I've been sampling Mr. Bauer's hospitality for the past few weeks, but it looks like the fun's over." He paused for effect, looking around and making brief but telling eye contact with each man in the room before continuing. "This is the day, boys; *this is the day!*" He emphasized the second part of the sentence by clinching his fist, as if seizing the object under discussion. "The future of Southern independence rides on what we do today."

Waving his arm southward, he said, "Our people being held captive are from the Confederate Army Provisional's intelligence headquarters, and they know everything about us, book chapter and verse. If the enemy gets that information, it's over. We're through, and all of us, along with our families, will be arrested, tortured, and executed. If we fail, we condemn not only our Cause and not only ourselves, but our families to death. The dream of a free Dixie will be over, dead and buried, and our own families along with it. There'll never be another chance; the South will never rise again."

He deliberately tweaked his sling, causing the gun barrel poking up over his shoulder to wave for emphasis. "I've never been a soldier, but I'm a soldier today. On this day of decision, every man, woman or child who can carry a rifle and pull a trigger must be a soldier. The time has come to test the courage of our convictions, and just how far we're willing to go for them.

"Win or lose, this is the fight they'll talk about for generations. In the future, every man who fights this battle will get down on his knees and thank God that he can say, 'I saved my country!' The ones who shirk will go to their graves wishing they had stood with their people, and will hang their heads in shame as cowards forever, who hid while pregnant women, wounded men, little girls barely out of their pigtails, and decrepit old men did their fighting for them." Pausing to look at Samantha and the small crowd with her, he added, "I'm going even if nobody else does, and if I die, at least I won't have to live in a South full of cowards."

One man stepped forward, and once he had broken ranks, others followed, first in ones and twos, then en masse.

CHAPTER 31

"Get him off! Get him off!"

It wasn't hard for Mike to scream realistically, since the Malinois – a large breed of dog better known as a Belgian Shepherd – had his left forearm in its jaws and was mauling the hell out of it while its handler urged the animal on to greater efforts. Besides the agony of his ripping flesh and tendons, and the tips of the fangs grating against the bone, the dog was shaking him so hard it felt like his arm was being pulled out of joint.

Mike hated the thought of being crippled still further, but logically, he knew it didn't matter in the long run; he was going to die here. That was a fact, and he accepted it, and, by now, actually looked forward to it. He didn't know what they were doing to Tommy and Donna; he was confident Tommy could take it, but he wasn't so sure about her. If he could allow them to believe they had broken him first, then maybe he could stave off any more pain to them, and shift the interrogators' attention solely in his direction, allowing him to send them off on a false trail.

Well, here goes!

"I'll talk! Just get him off!"

Wills barked a command, and the handler backed the dog away, still snarling and showing its teeth through its blood-covered muzzle.

"Spit it out!" someone shouted, and Mike nodded, gasping for air.

"My a-arm," he whined intentionally, although the pain was so great that wasn't really too hard to do.

"We'll fix your arm. Now who do you work for?"

"I-I work for the Confederate Army...Provisional."

Major Wills turned to one of the others. "Get him a chair and some water, and get a medic in here." Turning his gaze back until he was looking down at Mike once more, he nodded pleasantly. "You'll find that cooperation will always be rewarded."

One of them placed a folding metal chair in the center of the floor, and then two of them lifted him and sat him on it. The one to

261

his left moved behind him, steadying him with a surgically gloved hand on his shoulder to keep him from falling out in the floor, while the other unscrewed the top of a plastic water bottle and handed it to him.

"What do you do for the CAP?"

"I steal," Mike told him, swallowing a mouthful of water and wincing as the medic worked on his arm as he stretched it out over the back of the student's desk they had dragged over the purpose of propping it up. "I'm a cracker; I raise money for them."

The man eyed him coldly.

"Do you want me to get the dog back in here?"

"I'm not bull-shitting you, man!" Mike said in a panicked voice that wasn't entirely faked.

"Convince me."

"What the hell do you want me to say?"

"How long have you worked for them?"

"Years; they hired me back before the war started to raise money for the Cause. They've been stocking weapons and ammo for a long time, ready for when the revolution finally happened."

"Who hired you? Those two we caught upstairs?"

Mike shook his head, giving the interrogator a look like he thought the Major was stupid without making it so obvious about it that it would earn him another beating. With his face battered and swelling, he really had no idea what kind of expression he was showing, but he had to try to make it as real as he could, for the sake of his friends. With Donna being Sam Wirtz's Goddaughter, there was no way in Hell he could fool his questioners into believing they had nothing to do with the CAP, so he decided to minimize their role.

"You've got to be kidding! Tommy's been my friend since school, but he's too hotheaded to be anything but a minor player. It's the same thing with the girl; she's just a stupid redneck. I was the one who recruited them, mainly because they needed a place to stay, and I needed some security, somebody to cook and run errands, that kind of thing."

The interrogator looked at him skeptically. "Are you trying to tell me they don't know anything?"

"They know I work for CAP, and I suppose they know I do it with a computer, but they never asked and I wouldn't tell them if they did. It's none of their business, and anyway," he added, looking around pointedly, "You can't be too careful, or you'll end up some place like this."

Wills snorted with laughter, but the sound came out like a tap on the trigger of an electric saw.

"So they never went on any missions?"

"Not that I know of; not for me, anyway, other than to the grocery store, running errands, and stuff like that."

"So, what do the Confederates provide you?"

"Protection, plus I get a percentage of the take."

"Protection from who?"

"The police, who the hell do you think?"

The interrogators exchanged a hopeful glance.

"And how," the voice continued, "do they protect you from the police? Do they have someone on the department?"

Mike looked down, swallowed hard and sighed, doing his best to give the appearance of being reluctant.

"Yeah."

"Are you talking about Frank Gore?"

Mike shook his head, which he quickly discovered to be a bad move. His concussion from the beating suddenly kicked into overdrive and he abruptly threw up the water he'd just drank into his lap, sending the medic staggering back, cursing. The soldier's grip on his shoulder tightened to insure he didn't fall out of his chair.

"Give him a towel," the interrogator said. As Mike's head slowed down its spinning, he clumsily mopped the puke off himself, someone took his blood pressure, and the man handed him another water bottle before repeating, "Are you talking about Frank Gore?"

"No. Oh, I've met him a few times, but that's about it. I hear he's just what that film – you know, that video they released – said he was. Just an innocent bystander caught up in this until the Feds pissed him off."

263

The voice became sharper, more insistent. "Then who in the department do you work for?"

"Willie Duckett; he's CAP's inside man on the Columbia PD."

The interrogator turned his head and nodded towards one of his assistants, who immediately left the room. Mike watched him go, no doubt to verify his information.

"Who exactly is Willie Duckett?"

"He's a cop and a Captain in the Confederate Army Provisional. He's their primary recruiter in South Carolina, and acts as CAP's source of inside information."

In fact, Willie Duckett was little more than a child molester hiding behind a badge, who, on frequent occasions, had used his position to force young teenaged girls in trouble to submit to his lusts. He was also an unknowing asset of CAP, but an expendable one; he believed he was working undercover for the FBI as part of a deal to keep him out of prison, as long as he left the girls alone. So he kept his nose clean, delivered messages and planted bugs in the Columbia Police Department, completely unaware that he was working for the Confederates. Besides the role of oblivious gopher for the guerrilla forces, he served an additional purpose. He took the risks for the Columbia PD's real CAP operative, and he was the designated "lamb" to be thrown to the Federal wolves if that particular intelligence operation was ever compromised. This situation didn't exactly fit that description, Mike knew, but sacrificing an amoral pervert with a badge in order to hopefully save Tommy and Donna, as well as keep the Feds from uncovering real intelligence, was a choice he was willing to make.

"As I said, cooperation will be rewarded. Private! Get this man some clothes and..."

His voice trailed off as the room plunged into darkness, and the hum of the furnaces and computers abruptly shut off.

"Damn it! Corporal Hancock! Get those generators on line!"

Fortunately that took a few minutes, long enough for Mike to get himself under control and stop grinning at what he had done.

It worked! It freaking worked!

Over a hundred miles to the north, the barn where Samantha stood was plunged into darkness and confusion. Cries of, "What the hell happened?" were muttered back and forth, and Samantha's voice cut through them all.

"That was our signal, people; do what you have to do. We pull out in exactly one hour!"

CHAPTER 32

Russian Newscast

Russian and Chinese satellites have independently confirmed reports that nearly the entire continental United States has lost electric power in what appears to be a massive attack on its infrastructure. Communications from the region are difficult at the moment, but there are reportedly fires from multiple natural gas lines, several train derailments, and ships on fire in numerous inland and coastal ports. Field Marshal Jonathon Edge, Commander in Chief of the Confederate Army Provisional, has claimed responsibility.

In related news, rioting has already broken out in several blacked-out American cities, with fires set by looters burning completely out of control due to the water systems being powered by electricity that is no longer available. With the cold weather, many shelters are already overwhelmed by people seeking warmth, food and water...

"Willie Duckett?" Chief Carter exclaimed in shock, certain he hadn't heard the man right. That wouldn't surprise him, really; things in Columbia had turned into utter chaos in the hour since the power failed, and, as the man everybody looked to as the city's symbol of order, he'd hardly had time to take a breath since, let alone think.

He supposed he should be grateful. The Internet and phones were still screwed up, so everybody with a problem had to take it seriously enough to brave the cold rain to come in person, but at least the Columbia Police Department had its own generator, so they had light and heat. He suspected half the people were there simply for that.

"Willie Duckett," Captain Tango said firmly, looking like a cyborg in his helmet and thick body armor as he stood in the head office of the Columbia Police Department. "Where is he?"

Carter pursed his lips thoughtfully for a moment, but a moment only. He was a cop, and cops stood up for each other. Then again, dirty little perverts like Duckett were what gave the profession a bad name. Besides, to the Chief's way of thinking, the worthless bastard wouldn't be any great loss.

Turning to the monitor on his desk, he quickly tapped his fingertips on the keyboard; they had rebooted the department network once they got the generator online, and he managed to get the internal network, at least.

"Let me bring up the schedule for today...There; he's on patrol right now. You want his twenty, or you want me to have dispatch get him back here?"

"When's his shift end?"

"About an hour, but he'll probably be in a few minutes early to do his paperwork." Actually, the Chief knew the cheesy little goldbrick would be in as early as he thought he could get by with, assuming he wasn't shacked up with some teenaged girl. Sexually preying on adolescent hookers and runaways was Duckett's personal obsession, and as Carter thought about that, his eyes hardened.

Even if I had a choice, I'd still cooperate on this one! He's a disgrace to the Columbia's finest, and if this is what it takes to get rid of him, I can live with that.

"We'll wait."

Carter gestured towards his personal coffee maker. "Grab a cup of coffee and have a seat, then. You'll know when he gets here, since he has to call in when he leaves the car in the garage." Taking a sip out of his own half-empty cup as he watched officer comply, he idly asked, "What did the asshole do this time?"

Captain Tango looked at him carefully, then decided to favor him with an answer.

"He may be a Confederate spy."

"Duckett?!" Carter exclaimed again, then suddenly became poker-faced as the thought hit him. He knew there had to be at least one or two CAP sympathizers in the department, and maybe a hell of a lot more. He was also positive that Willie Duckett wasn't one of them. The Confederate Army Provisional had proven on several occasions that it was always willing to take a moment out of its busy schedule of assassinations and bombings to kill a child predator, and the cop in question wouldn't have lasted five minutes with them...if he was lucky.

In much less time than it would have taken to tell about it, the thoughts slammed into place one right after the other, in logical progression. If they took Duckett, that would leave the real CAP resource or resources still in place in his department. He didn't owe the Confederate Army Provisional anything...except his position as Chief. Frank Gore himself had told him that he would be getting that position, and damned if he didn't find himself in the catbird's seat in less than a month. All he had asked for in return was Carter's neutrality in this war. So far, he had given it, and as a result, the guerrillas steered scrupulously clear of confrontations with the Columbia PD, occasionally provided covert assistance to them, and not infrequently took out their trash, in the form of the violent, habitual criminals they killed when the opportunity presented itself.

He couldn't say the same about the Army, however. The fate of Patrolman Howard Smith still galled him; having to stand before a brother officer crippled on duty by a bunch of thugs in military uniforms, and tell him he was fired had gone against the grain. He, and half the other cops in the department who wanted to kick a few dollars in his direction were directly forbidden to do so by Homeland Security, lest they be funding terrorism. Someone – Carter assumed it was the Confederate Army Provisional – had been slipping him a few dollars anyway, at least allowing him and his family to eat.

Giving them Duckett would protect Confederate resources and be a covert slap against the occupation forces.

And give me immense personal satisfaction!

"You know," he said carefully, rubbing his chin, "you might just be onto something. He's been acting pretty strange lately."

Tango leaned forward, his steaming cup momentarily forgotten in his hand. "Tell me more."

At that very moment, in the locker room below the Chief's office, a patrolman was frantically rummaging in the locker belonging to Willie Duckett. He had been one of those who had received the word, COMPROMISED in his email, and he already had a contingency plan in place that would definitely shift the blame onto the intended fall guy...and maybe do more than that.

He just needed time to plant the irrefutable evidence. Heedless of the risks, he made more speed and used more material than was probably necessary or even wise, but, since his ass was on the line, he wanted to be sure.

"Alright, listen up." The soldiers looked on attentively as Tango spoke. Chief Carter stood beside him, ostensibly as an observer, but actually because the Captain wasn't about to take the chance that he might relay word of their interest to Duckett.

"The target will be allowed to come into the department and complete his after-shift paperwork. Following that, he will head for the locker room, where First Squad will be waiting, along with Chief Carter, who will positively identify the target for you. Wait until he takes his weapon off before moving. There's no point in taking any unnecessary risks; besides which, Intel wants him taken alive. In the meantime, First will also turn away anyone else entering the locker room. They will be escorted out of the emergency exit and taken to the first floor conference room by Second Squad, and Third Squad will see to it they don't leave or communicate with anyone else until the operation is over. Fourth Squad will remain with the Humvees in reserve. Dundee!"

A small, dark laconic man with three sergeant's stripes, flat, emotionless eyes and a scoped sniper rifle over his shoulder simply said, "Sir," with no inflection whatsoever to his voice.

"I want you and your spotter on the roof where you can cover the emergency exit. If the target exits that way, take him down."

The sniper nodded before silently jerking his head to his spotter, and both of them headed for the stairs without a word even as the rest of the soldiers began moving to their assigned positions.

Willie Duckett descended the stairs with a bit more spring in his step than usual. Falsely convinced he had been working for the FBI for months now, he was sure his official promotion to the Bureau would be coming at anytime. Surely all the bugs he had planted and intelligence he had passed to the anonymous callers requesting it would soon amount to something big. Besides, he just had a good feeling about today; some instinct hinted to him that there were big changes in the air.

Grinning to himself, he thought, all things considered, it had already been good. Not two hours ago, he had coerced a fourteen year-old runaway into giving him a freebie in the back seat of his patrol car in order to keep from being hauled down to Juvenile Hall. He had even roughed her up a little, something that he vastly enjoyed, so all in all, he was feeling pretty pleased with himself. His "FBI" handlers had warned him to cease that kind of behavior or the deal would be off, and he actually had quit for several months now. This opportunity was too good to miss, however, and he was careful, so he saw no way they could ever find out he had returned to his old habits. As far as he was concerned, today, life was good.

Stepping off the last metal-edged cement step, he turned left and opened the door marked, MEN'S LOCKER ROOM. As soon as he entered, he frowned at the silent ranks of lockers and empty wooden benches. No showers running, no snapping of equipment being removed, no chatter or grab-assing; the only sound was the echo of his own breathing.

That's odd; I wonder where everybody is?

Lifting his left hand and tilting his wrist, he glanced at his watch for a second, then shrugged. If the others wanted to work past quitting time, more power to them. As far as he was concerned, though, he was out of here just as soon as he changed.

271

Willie was already loosening his tie and unbuttoning his shirt by the time he reached his locker, about halfway down the first row. Dropping the tie on the bench, he paused to work the combination lock, then pull up the latch with his thumb and forefinger. Instead of swinging wide open as it usually did, the sheet metal door only opened a couple of inches, as if something was holding it, but he didn't notice; his mind was occupied with the relief divesting himself of the binding weight of his Sam Brown equipment belt would bring. After popping the snaps on the leather belt keepers that attached it to his pants belt to keep it in place, he then proceeded to unbuckle the broad strip of black leather, with its accompanying cuffs, pepper spray, telescoping baton, and holstered Glock with its pair of extra clips. Clipping the buckle back together to form a loop, he reached for the locker again, only to see motion out of the corner of his eye. Turning his head, he was startled to see Chief Carter stepping around the corner of a bank of lockers.

"Oh, hi Chief. What brings you down here to the 'dungeon'?"

"Put your stuff down and come here for a second; I need you to help me with something."

Willie shrugged and set the belt on the bench. He had only taken a single step away from it when someone hollered, "Now!" and half a dozen uniformed and armored soldiers rushed him from around each end of the lockers, guns pointed. Before he could move, he was thrown facedown on tiles. Someone knocked his gun belt off in the floor and kicked it out of reach even as others pinned his arms and jammed rifle muzzles against his head.

Duckett was so frightened he was screaming. "What the hell's going on? What are you doing?"

"Homeland Security wants to talk to you, Officer Duckett," Carter explained calmly. "I suggest you cooperate fully."

"Secure that locker!" Tango barked, and a black PFC from Detroit named Lucien moved to obey. Taking hold of the latch, he pulled it the rest of the way open.

As the sheet metal pivoted on its riveted hinges, the stiff, insulated copper wire that had been secured to it on the inside, holding it partially closed, moved with it. The plastic insulation had

272

been stripped off the other end before it was bent into a loop. Inside that loop was another, identically bent piece of wire, and as the door opened, the bare loops slid along the wire's insulated surface until they made contact with one another, closing the circuit and allowing the 9 volt battery connected to the other end to send its electricity to the detonator.

The bomb itself, affixed to the locker's top shelf at head level, wasn't particularly large, as bombs go, no bigger than a drugstore paperback novel and weighing not even a pound. Still, since it was made with C4 plastic explosive, it was more than big enough. After all, the real Confederate inside operative had been in a hurry, wasn't experienced in working with high explosives, and figured it was better safe than sorry.

Even though the locker shattered – blowing the top into the concrete ceiling overhead and the the sides outwards into and through their neighboring receptacles, shredding or crushing three more lockers on one side and four on the other, the brief confinement of the thin sheet metal was still sufficient to direct most of the blast through the path of least resistance: the open front, right where Private Lucien was standing instead of the expected Willie Duckett. The arm he had extended to open the locker, along with just about everything he owned north of his navel, instantly painted the lockers behind him, themselves crushed and torn by the force of the high explosive he had barely slowed down. In the process, his flesh and bone, along with the contents of Duckett's locker and most of the locker itself, were instantly converted to shrapnel.

Most of the soldiers were knocked flat by the concussion, and the remainder standing farthest away, along with Chief Carter, hit the tiles voluntarily. The room immediately filled with smoke, the frightened curses of the healthy and the agonized screams of the wounded. There was still some residual pressure in the waterlines, and sprinkler system went off automatically, drenching everything and everyone with cold rusty water as it added to the confusion before petering out to a steady drip.

Duckett found everyone else on the floor with him, but, as he was already down, the main force of the blast had passed him by, doing no damage beyond rupturing his eardrums and quite literally scaring the shit out of him. Violently released from his captors' grips and dazed and confused, Willie panicked and followed his gut instinct; he got to his feet and ran like hell.

Captain Tango struggled upright, blinking eyes that felt as if they were filled with sand from the ruptured capillaries as his ears rang so loudly he could hear nothing more than the faintest echoes of his men's yells. It took him a moment to realize Duckett wasn't there, and the emergency exit door was closing.

Fumbling for his radio, he yelled into the mike for his sniper. He heard no reply, but then, he could barely hear his own voice.

On the roof, Sergeant Dundee and his partner felt the vibrations as clearly as they heard the sound of the explosion in the basement. The exchange of a brief look was all the communication they needed. The spotter turned back to his tripod mounted scope, and the sniper to the one that rode atop his rifle.

Compartmentalizing their officer's rasping, almost incoherent shouts over the radio into the back of his mind in a communications triage, the spotter picked out the words he needed to hear, and calmly repeated them back to his partner.

"Target moving. Prepare to engage."

Dundee was already regulating his breathing even as Duckett came into his crosshairs. Calculating his speed and the amount of lead in less than a second from the instinct that came with long practice, the sniper's finger began tightening on the trigger.

His uniform shirt hanging open and his pants full of his own waste, Willie Duckett was moving at full speed, running in a blind panic. He didn't know what had happened, and, frankly, didn't need to; right now, he just knew he had to get away. Pounding across the parking lot as fast as his legs could carry him, he raced for the most familiar thing nearby: his car.

He was only three steps from it when something punched him hard between the shoulder blades. The full metal jacketed bullet severed his spine, punctured his heart, and blew apart his sternum, snapping it across the middle into splintered halves. His bullet-resistant vest belatedly caught the slug in front of his chest as it left his body.

The momentum was all that kept him going until he was brought up short by slamming into the side of the car. Body bending forward unnaturally at the break in his spine, Willie's head snapped downward and his face bounced hard off the roof before his body recoiled from the sudden impact with an immovable object, and he fell to the wet asphalt on his back, spread-eagled in the rain.

He died four seconds later, still trying his best to answer the question he had screamed inside the locker room, but he never managed to figure out what the hell was going on.

Dundee watched carefully through his scope for several seconds, looking for signs of life, then nodded without looking at his spotter, who promptly keyed his mike.

"Target down."

Ignoring the others as he lay on the tiles awash with bloody water, Chief Carter gingerly gave himself what the cops referred to as a "Cross check" because its hand motion was similar to the sign of a Catholic benediction, with the questing hand moving up and down, then side to side. As the hoary old joke went, "Spectacles, testicles, wallet, watch – yep, everything's still there." Other than being spattered with dirt, water, and with blood not his own – apart from some bleeding from his ears – and having the hell frightened out of him, he seemed to have no injuries besides minor bruises and itching, burning eyes. To his inexpressible delight, even though it throbbed with pain, his damaged hip and femur hadn't re-broken themselves either; the pins and plates had held, thank God. The deliberate shot that had made that crippling injury was just one more thing he had to thank the Feds for, and he hoped and prayed never to have to go through it again.

Once he ascertained that everything was still more or less where God originally intended it to be, he slowly rose to his feet to find the soldiers ignoring him.

In fairness, Carter reflected, they had other problems. What was left of PFC Lucien was very obviously dead, as was a second man had been decapitated by a piece of flying sheet metal. They upper arm of a third was hanging from the bone in rags, and a fourth lay on the floor screaming, both hands pressed over the red ruin where his eyes and the flesh of his face used to be. The Chief was lucky to have been the furthest away, as he appeared to be the only one not wounded to some degree. The distance and the intervening armored bodies of Captain Tango's men had evidently absorbed the brunt of the blast and shrapnel from the locker.

Staggering as he moved to one side, the Chief sat down on the far end of the bench, out of the way of the rush he was certain was coming when the rest of the platoon belatedly came to the aid of their comrades. He needed to think, and he was still too shaken up to do that and stand at the same time.

His first thought was the obvious one: that Willie Duckett *had* actually been the Confederate spy the Army had accused him of being. After all, the last man anyone would think capable of doing something would be the first one you'd want to do it, if you didn't want him suspected. Mulling it over in his clearing head, he tentatively rejected that argument, if for no other reason than that his former underling, Frank Gore, was one of the leaders of the guerrilla movement. He knew Frank very well, and there was no way in hell he could see him tolerating a...a *child molester* like Duckett, no matter how valuable he was. Gore's dislike for him was so strong when he was on the department that no supervisor would have dared to ever let the two work together.

Suddenly, he pursed his lips to prevent a grim smile as the thought came to him. It was so obvious to him because he knew more about how the Confederate Army Provisional operated than he had ever wanted to. That bomb had never been meant for the Feds; it was meant for Willie Duckett. Either the sneaking bastard had known something, or...

CAP needed an expendable patsy to throw the scent off of their real assets in the Department.

In his eyes – and he was sure it was the same in Frank Gore's – nobody was more expendable than Duckett. A CAP guerrilla secretly operating inside the Columbia PD, accidentally blowing himself up with his own booby trapped locker...He had the gut feeling that was how it was meant to be seen. Now, after all this carnage, the Homeland Security troops would see it as their target not having the chance to disarm the trap that ensured the security of his locker, that doubtless contained all sorts of interesting things, if they could ever sort out the pieces.

As he watched the other soldiers pouring in through the water still dripping from the overhead pipes and soaking him along with the rest, Carter decided he would keep that particular thought to himself. After all, he was neutral in this conflict.

"The prisoner Dayton says they don't know anything."

"I think he's lying."

"Could be."

"I think it's time we up the pressure."

Major Wills looked at Rosenberg. "What have you got in mind?"

"Sergeant Cussler reports that Richardson shows no signs of breaking." He paused, toying with a pen by rolling it back and forth between his fingers. "He believes he may not break at all."

"Um. What about the girl?"

"She'll give in...eventually. However, I think we can speed up the process if we bring them together, and we might break him as well."

"What do you suggest?"

"Give both of them to me."

Wills regarded him thoughtfully.

"I don't care about him, but I want that girl alive. She's Samuel Wirtz's Goddaughter, and, besides what she must know, she could be a valuable bargaining chip."

"Don't worry about her; I've done this in Palestine for more than ten years, and I know what I'm about. I may have to kill him during the process of making her talk, but she'll still be alive...more or less."

The American Major blew out his breath in resignation.

"Do what you have to. I want regular reports on your progress."

"You're not going to observe?"

When it came, his answer was so definite as to leave no question about his feelings.

"No."

CHAPTER 33

Chinese Newscast (English)

Rioting continues in the blacked-out United States, particularly in the West Coast cities of Los Angeles and San Francisco, areas with large Chinese populations, whose homes, businesses and lives may be endangered by racist marauding looters from other ethnic groups . Beijing has issued a stern demand to the Government of the United States that the lives of Chinese citizens must be protected...

Mexican Newscast (English)

Stepped-up Confederate Army Provisional attacks are occurring all across the Southern US, according to our sources there...

"Here's the plan," Lucky Charlie told the assembled officers and squad leaders as they gathered around their staging area, just over the South Carolina border. Samantha, Lieutenants Harrison and Preston, Sergeants Steiner and Hodges, and Dr. MacFie stood in what was virtually a huddle due the small size of the only private room they could find at the time.

Dee Grissom was with them; he had drawn the map of the school from memory, having been there once while part of his duties. It wasn't hard for him to remember, because some of what he'd heard and seen during a brief walk through the place still gave him nightmares.

"We'll be posing as mercenary contractors from Sythian," the one-eyed Captain continued, "and all of our regular troops are to be in fatigues, with all the body armor they can find. We'll try to bluff our way inside the gates. We'll knock them down if we have to, but the closer we get to the school before we're discovered, the better our chances for getting our people out alive.

"The armored car will be Alpha Squad; we will be the lead vehicle. Colonel Gore and her bodyguards will be assigned to it, along with myself and two of whichever South Carolina auxiliaries who have any experience with it and the flamethrower. It's so tight in there with the fuel tank, that's about all it will hold. Once inside the gates, we will engage any visible enemy via the vehicle's firing ports. That will be the signal to begin.

"Following that, everyone in the vehicle except for the driver, gunner, and yours truly will immediately dismount, secure the gate area, take cover, and then take the left front guard tower and the front of the building under suppressing fire. You'll have to keep their heads down. If you can't see anything else to shoot at, concentrate your efforts on the window immediately to the left of the front door; that's the arms room, where the weapons belonging to those inside working with the prisoners are stored. Just be careful of the friendlies in front of you.

"The rest of us will swing to the right and engage the guard tower on that side with the flamethrower. Then we'll haul ass around to the rear of the school and attack the barracks – the blue metal building at the left rear.

"The black BATF Humvee will be Bravo Squad, with Sergeant Hodges commanding, and the one belonging to North Carolina will be Charlie, under Lieutenant Preston. You'll both go to the left, circling to the rear of the building. Bravo will engage the barracks and both towers with suppressing fire, and Charlie will assault the school's rear door.

"The bus will contain the primary frontal assault force, under the command of Lieutenant Harrison. When it stops, everybody out ASAP. You've got those RPGs; use one of 'em to blow off the front door. Then charge inside and shoot everything that's not ours and doesn't surrender immediately. Alpha Squad will remain behind to neutralize the remaining guard tower, and provide covering fire and outside security in front. Bravo will do the same thing in the rear."

And, as Samantha will be part of Alpha, she'll be at the gate, out of the main bulk of the fighting. I don't intend to have to tell her husband that she died, along with their unborn child!

280

"Once inside, the main assault force will join Charlie in securing the ground floor; be careful not to shoot each other, as you'll be entering at opposite ends. Half the assault force will take the ground floor, and the rest the second. Charlie will take to basement."

He paused, looking at each one in turn in order to make certain he had their attention.

"There is only one way this assault will work; once we start, we can't stop. We can't dig in; that will give them a chance to recover, and possibly use their prisoners as hostages. We have to keep the initiative, and keep moving forward, no matter what happens. There will be casualties amongst the prisoners during this operation; accept that and get it clear in your heads right now, that we don't stop, regardless! If you have to shoot through a hostage to kill the enemy, do it and move on. If this fight lasts more than five minutes, we're royally and totally screwed. They'll have time to call for help, and then we'll be the ones running. That happens, we won't survive. That's just the way it is.

"Just so you know, if we can't take this building, we'll have to blow it up or burn it, along with everyone, friend and foe alike, inside it. There's a prisoner in there with too much knowledge inside his head to allow the enemy to get at it. So unless you want *everybody* in there to die, you're going to have to do your jobs, no matter how hard it gets. And I'm telling you right now, it's going to get damned hard!

"Now, in case we run into trouble on the way, here is our contingency plan..."

The more she listened, the more afraid Samantha became, but she refused to let it show.

CHAPTER 34

Even though he was handcuffed, it still took two large soldiers to hold Tommy down while four more – two Negroes, one Mexican, and one White – took turns raping Donna in front of him. He cursed them, cursed their mothers and their wives and their children and their dogs, and they laughed in his face.

Donna tried not to scream, for Tommy's sake more than her own, and actually managed it until they sodomized her; then she couldn't help it. Her cries echoed through the halls, even louder than the jeers and cheers of the soldiers. Prisoners in the other cells clamped their hands over their ears, knowing full well what was happening, because it had already happened to many of them.

"Just tell us what we want to know, and we'll stop," Rosenberg said casually. Rosenberg's voice was calm and relaxed, but then, of course, he'd taken the first turn, before he let the *goys* and *schwartzers* at her. His interrogator's job had its perks, after all, and one of them was that he didn't have to take sloppy seconds.

Actually, he was surprised that neither of them had broken by now. They were Southerners, and he would have thought, especially when the Negroes started, that one of them would have talked, from the social implications if nothing else.

Even if the social implications are a moot point as far as these two are concerned. It's not like they'll ever see society again!

"This is your fault," he tried once more, speaking to Tommy. "You're the one putting her through this. You can stop it any time you want to; just answer our questions."

It was tempting; God only knew how tempting it was, but Tommy only spat at him, called him a hook-nosed sheeny kike bastard, and called on God to damn his soul to Hell.

"I think he likes watchin' her git it!" one of the Blacks called out. "Take a look at this, Rebel!"

Suddenly Tommy seized a thread of thought in passing, the same one that had given him the power to inhale with his head under the tub-full of sewage. The red rage was not lost, but eclipsed by a cold, white anger, as hard and unyielding as a glacier grinding across an Arctic stone. That they were both going to die was a given at this point, and he realized his captors were too careful to allow him a chance to overpower and kill one of them, but eventually, one of them might make a mistake and come close enough to hurt. It wasn't much, but he would take what he could get. Someone, anyone, would have cause to regret what they had done. That they would probably kill him for what he was about to do was a bonus, if for no other reason, they might stop hurting her in an attempt to make him talk.

Despite the soldiers' taunts and Rosenberg's imprecations, Tommy refused to speak again. He stopped struggling, but even though his muscles relaxed, his spirit lay like a coiled rattlesnake, waiting its chance. He divorced himself from reality, compartmentalized it into another part of his mind, even when they finished with Donna, and one of the Negroes showed him the condom before stepping behind him while the others kept him pinned. Through sheer force of will, Tommy held himself from any reaction even when he felt the tearing pain as the unthinkable happened, even when he saw the horror in Donna's eyes as they held her head up by a fist-full of hair and made her watch. Worse, and even more horrible, he saw her pity, and saw her lips begin to part, ready in a moment of weakness to give the enemy what they wanted in order to spare him.

"Shut up!" he barked at her, the agony making his voice a rasp. *"Not-a-word!"*

Rosenberg slapped him into silence before turning to Donna.

"You can stop this anytime; just say the word."

Donna was tempted, but then the thought slammed down on her. *If he can stand this, I reckon I can!*

Donna said the word then; in fact, she said several of them, any one of which, in other circumstances, would have gotten her mouth washed out with soap by her horrified Godfather, Sam, if he had even imagined that kind of obscenity passing her lips. She cursed the interrogator and the government he represented with such fervor and fury that even the foul-mouthed soldiers were startled by her vehemence, as well as the mouthfuls of bloody spit she defiantly propelled in their direction.

Teeth clenched, Tommy nodded his approval, launched his own cussing towards the Mossad agent just to make sure he had his attention, then intentionally turned his head, making it obvious he was looking away from Donna. He had been trained in interrogation himself, he understood the principles, and he counted on provoking a reaction. Just as he'd hoped, Rosenberg grabbed for his face to jerk his head around, and make him see her.

"Look at her!" the Israeli shouted, reaching for the prisoner's jaw with his left hand, and the torturer's shout abruptly turned into a scream as Tommy's head snapped around and his teeth locked onto the advisor's thumb at the first joint. The biker bit down hard, there was a loud 'pop' as the joint exploded, and more screams as he shook his head like a dog, severing the flesh and ripping the appendage away before the startled soldiers could stop him. He swallowed it with a hard gulp, and, lubricated with his enemy's blood, it went down his throat in a painful lump instead of lodging in his windpipe as he had halfway hoped.

Belatedly, the surprised soldiers reacted, and the nightsticks and blackjacks came down on him for a long time, driving him into darkness. The last thing he heard was Donna screaming his name, and Rosenberg simply screaming.

CHAPTER 35

"Damn it!"

The confusion caused by the infrastructure collapse had largely cleared the roads, and the Confederate force had been rolling uneventfully for an hour and a half, and were now just over thirty minutes from their target. Sitting in a small padded seat in back, leaning against the flamethrower's fuel tank while Thumper lay at her feet, Samantha jumped when Lucky Charlie's curse snapped her out of her reverie. Their vehicle, and the convoy behind it, began slowing.

"What is it?" The words no sooner left her lips when she looked between Lucky Charlie and the driver and out through the windshield to see the answer right in front of her. A Bradley fighting vehicle, one of the rubber-tired variants, was parked directly in the middle of the road, blocking it with its gun aimed at them. She heard the hiss as the men in the compartment behind them opened the compressed air valve to the flame thrower, the only weapon that had a chance of stopping the killing machine...maybe. Of course, the idea of getting in a firefight at point blank range with a Bradley armed with a 25mm armor piercing automatic cannon while sitting in a truck with a hundred gallons of gelled gasoline wasn't very comforting either. Meanwhile, an electronically amplified voice ripped from the Bradley's speaker.

"Attention convoy! Stop where you are. Identify yourselves."

Charlie's eyes lit up with recognition and he snapped, "Perfect! I know this guy!" before looking at Samantha. "Go with the contingency plan." He whispered briefly to Samantha and the other personnel, and told them to pass the word on the radio so no one did anything stupid. Then he opened the truck door and jumped to the asphalt, splashing in the shallow covering of water and bouncing up and down briefly on his spring feet. Bracing his hands on his hips, he threw his head back and yelled out through the falling rain.

"Hey Jack Spalding! You still got that stupid-looking dragon tattooed on your ass?"

"Son of a bitch!" the amplified voice returned, and an instant the commander's hatch popped open to reveal a short, sandy-haired Army captain. "Lucky Charlie! What the hell are you doing here?"

Spalding clambered down, and the pair closed on one another and clapped each other on the back. "Damn!" the newcomer exclaimed. "I didn't expect to see you here! I didn't know they had you back in uniform!" Actually, the sight of it and what it meant disturbed Spalding more than a little. If they were recalling one-eyed triple amputees, things must be going much worse than he thought.

"I've been called up on limited duty: military liaison to these Sythian Contractors." Gesturing over his shoulder with at the vehicles behind him with the thumb of his good hand, he said, "We've got a bus load of prisoners heading up to Pleasant View."

"You're nuts to be doing it in unarmored vehicles. We're taking sniper fire damned near every day. The dumb bastards gotta know they can't penetrate this armor, but they keep on trying." He smiled tightly. "And we keep on blowing the hell out of them when they do."

Charlie laughed, causing the scar tissue on his face to twist so disturbingly that Spalding had to look away for a moment. "They won't shoot at us; we've got their kinfolk inside, along with one *very* special prisoner this time."

"Oh yeah?" he asked, clearly skeptical of just how special their captive could be. "What did you do; catch Frank Gore?"

Charlie's good eye winked.

"Nope; we caught his wife: none other than Samantha Norris-Gore."

Spalding's jaw dropped, and it took him several seconds to recover his power of speech. "You're shitting me!"

Charlie slapped him on the upper arm with his organic hand.

"I wouldn't shit you, Jack; you're my favorite turd! She's riding in the seat of honor, right there with me in the armored car." Leaning in closer, he whispered, "If they *do* decide to shoot at us, I don't want to take the chance of losing this one."

Grabbing Charlie by his right shoulder, Spalding told him, "I've got to see this!"

"Sure thing..." Suddenly he stopped, snapping the fingers of his remaining hand. "I've got an idea; how'd you like the Army to get part of the credit for capturing her?"

"I'd like that one hell of a lot," Spalding replied, visions of promotions dancing in his head. He well remembered all the hoopla concerning the capture of Saddam Hussein, and how the posed pictures were circulated everywhere.

"Tell you what we'll do; I'll get her out of the car while you get some of your men out, and you and the contractors can all line up together next to your Bradley and we'll take the pictures. These mercs don't care; they'll get the reward money while the Army gets the glory. The Pentagon will freaking love it! They'll have it on the front page of every paper in the country!"

Spalding whistled. "I owe you, man; I owe you big-time for this one." He hesitated, suddenly fearing it was too good to be true. "Are you...sure that's Frank Gore's wife you've got?"

"Take a look for yourself." Turning back to the convoy, he bawled, "Hodges, have your people get the prisoner out of there so Captain Spalding can have a peek at her!"

Hodges, Graham and Long jumped out of their Humvee, and, in less than a minute, the pair reached the armored car handed down a handcuffed and very frightened-looking Samantha.

The fear wasn't feigned. She knew the contingency plan, and had agreed to it in case they ran into trouble, but she also knew things could go wrong and that she and all the rest of them could easily die here. Still, she was used to living in fear of her life; that wasn't the problem. The application of the cuffs, the shouted orders and the manhandling of the fake soldiers brought the trauma of her previous capture crashing back down on her full-force. Despite the fact that she knew it wasn't real, the memories of terror and pain from her captivity and torture just over nine months ago hammered her like an avalanche, she began to shake uncontrollably, and unbidden tears were streaming down her face.

Spalding stepped closer to her, then grabbed her long blonde pony tail and brutally wrenched her head back as he thrust his face almost against hers.

"You're not so brave now, are you, you terrorist whore!"

Abruptly, Charlie Carnes forced his way between them. The glare from his single eye on top of the cold steel in his voice did as much to make the captain instantly let go as did the painful pressure of the articulated hook clamping down on the officer's wrist.

"Back off, Jack; I said you could see her, not touch her!"

Spalding was so angry his words came out in a burst that sprayed Charlie with miniscule droplets of saliva like liquid machinegun fire.

"Do you know how many of my men have died because of her? The Charlie Carnes I know never defended terrorists!"

"This isn't about her, numb-nuts, and it's not about you or your men. It's about orders; she's not to be touched...not by *us*." He grinned evilly, something not at all hard for him to do. "They're going to pick her up at Pleasant View and fly her off to DC. They want to squeeze all the propaganda value out of her they can. They'll show her unmarked on the TV before they give her to the spooks over at Langley for interrogation. They're the ones who'll be doing the dirty work."

"That's not very satisfying!"

"You know better than that; if you wanted satisfaction, you shouldn't have joined the Army. Now, do you want you and your men in on this or not? I don't have time to fart around here all day; I've got to get her up the road!"

"Alright, already. I'll get a perimeter set up."

"I'll do that; we need to get this photo-op done and get the hell out of here." Turning, he took the prisoner's arm spoke to Hodges, who was visibly seething over the interloper's treatment of Samantha.

"Sergeant, give me a perimeter."

"Yes sir!" Turning his bald head, he bellowed, "Alright, un-ass that Humvee! Harrison, get off that bus and get a perimeter set up! Graham! Put 'em where we need 'em. Dover, stay with the truck. Reynolds, Long, you're with me; let's get this prisoner over to the Bradley. Move it people! Assholes and elbows!" Casey Graham began quietly giving clipped orders to the men while Hodges and Long then each linked an arm through Samantha's elbows and half escorted, half carried her to the side of the APC. Refusing to be far from his charge, Jim Reynolds followed close behind.

"It's alright, ma'am," Hodges whispered, barely moving his lips. "We've got you. When the shit hits the fan, just be ready to drop."

Samantha couldn't see how she could drop in her condition, and Doug Long sensed the reason for her fear. "When it comes, just let yourself go limp. I'll fall with you and take you down on top of me to save you from hitting the asphalt. Trust me."

Traumatized by the flashbacks more than she could have imagined, she could only nod jerkily as they dragged her stumbling into position just as there was a loud clanging when the rear door of the Bradley opened. Abruptly she was surrounded by a sea of faces with expressions that ranged from simple curiosity to outright hatred to one or two of naked lust. One of the latter, a dark-skinned Mexican PFC with TORRES on his uniform's nametag, grabbed at her breast only to find his wrist encased in a grip that threatened to grind his radius and ulna together.

"Hands off, Pancho!" Hodges growled menacingly as he twisted the offending arm aside before releasing it. "This is a photo-op, not a titty bar."

"Hey, watch it, *pendejo*..." the soldier blustered, but the disguised skinhead didn't let him finish. When Hodges grabbed the edge of his body armor, jerked him close, lifted him up on his toes, and spoke, his voice was a hiss, meant only for the soldier's ears.

"This is my prisoner, you little shit-skin! Now keep your greasy meat hooks to yourself, or I'll twist your spic head off and take a dump right down your scrawny brown neck! Do you *habla* that, or would you like a demonstration?"

Torres started to say something else, then, taking in Hodges' size and the eager gleam in his crazy, bloodshot eyes, along with the muzzle of Jim Reynold's rifle that had casually shifted to point at his face, wisely thought better of it, and, once Hodges shoved him back, he turned away grumbling in Spanish under his breath as the bruises began forming on his wrist.

Captains Carnes and Spalding were busy giving orders and the Bradley's sergeant was bellowing for everybody to fall the hell in.

291

Meanwhile, the Dojo Squad moved closer, apparently setting up their perimeter, while Casey Graham moseyed casually towards the rear of the fighting vehicle.

"Hey," Spalding demanded, "who's got the camera?"

Lucky Charlie responded with, "Private Long – *now!*" and several things happened at once.

Samantha's world turned topsy-turvy as she was abruptly yanked off her feet. True to his word, Doug Long held her back tightly against his chest as he fell on his back, letting his body armor take the impact that still drove the air from his own lungs in order to save her. Immediately rolling Samantha over onto the road on her side, he rolled over her himself, placing his armored body as a shield overtop of hers, keeping his weight off her by bracing himself on his hands and knees, pressing against her and sheltering her beneath him even as he gasped for breath. Jim Reynolds threw a long leg over them, stepping astraddle of the pair in the same motion of knocking a soldier aside with a butt stroke of his rifle stock in order to make room to bring the weapon into action. The roar of gunfire sounded like a freight train as Tommy's Squad opened up, carefully choosing the targets that were farthest away from their comrades.

Charlie Carnes whipped his steel prosthetic hook across his body and into Spalding's face just below the lip of his helmet. The hook went through the captain's eyeball, caught on the edge of the bony socket, and slammed him back against the Bradley's armor. With no hesitation, Lucky Charlie jerked out his pistol, jammed it between the rear lip of the helmet and the collar of the body armor the soldier standing in front with his back to him, and pulled the trigger. Most of the spray was either contained by the helmet or exited through the front, below the rim. Turning back, his next round blew through the falling Spalding's hands that were clenched in agony over his ruined face. The enemy officer slammed back against the side of the fighting vehicle once more before sliding down and falling to the side, dead before he hit the ground. A millisecond later, Charlie himself jerked forward and grunted under an impact from behind, but managed to stay on his feet.

Steiner and the rest of the squad began blasting hasty but carefully aimed single shots at the soldiers on the periphery not standing too close to their own. They were few, however, and they didn't want to risk shooting their own men. Cynthia Dover leaned out, using the armored car's open door for cover. She rested the barrel of her MP5 against it and began firing short, controlled bursts at the heads of anyone close to Samantha who wasn't one of their own.

Straddling Samantha and Doug Long, Jim Reynolds jerked his rifle to his shoulder and fired a single shot through the neck of the soldier standing quartered toward him. He flinched and ducked involuntarily when a bullet fired by one of their own screamed past his ear and ricocheted from the vehicle armor at his back. He remembered yelling a curse at the unknown rifleman even as he looked for another target, but he himself had no idea of what his own words were.

Hodges was packed in too closely to bring his M4 to bear, so he used his hands. Torres was in front of him, back to him and trying to raise his own assault rifle, and the big man reached over the Mexican PFC's helmet with his left hand, catching the bill and yanking it backwards while at the same time slamming his massive right forearm against the back of the soldier's neck. With the helmet acting as the lever and the arm as a fulcrum, the man's neck snapped like a rotten branch. Dropping his victim, the Skinhead finally found room to use his weapon and, shooting from the hip, sent a four-round burst into the side of another enemy's neck and head.

Two soldiers broke for the Bradley just as Casey Graham's rifle jammed. He let it fall and pulled his pistol even as he darted through the rear door after them, figuring it would be handier in the confined space anyway. One of the two soldiers inside was trying to bring up his M16, and was only a few degrees from lining up on the Rebel interloper when Graham began squeezing the trigger. The first two rounds punched ineffectively against the Class 3 body armor, but the recoil of the rapid fire walked the impacts up his body until the third one hit his throat, and the fourth entered his brain by way of his cheek.

Before he could switch his aim to the final soldier kneeling on the floor, the man brought his own weapon to bear, jerked the trigger, and held it down in a panic. Three rounds hammered a marching line across the chest of Graham's body armor; they failed to penetrate, but the shocks were like being punched by a heavyweight slugger. Stunned, the staggering Rebel bounced from the inside wall of the vehicle and screamed in fury even as he returned fire just as wildly, blasting off shots as fast as he could work the trigger. Some hit the soldier's body armor and some missed completely, and ricochets produced by both men flew like angry hornets around the inside of the Bradley. Another round grazed the length of Graham's right jaw line, leaving a shallow cut that he didn't immediately notice. One of his own 9mm projectiles hit the soldier's right hand, going through one side and out the other, clanging against the grip of his rifle and knocking it from his grasp. The round was ejected and the Berretta's slide locked open, empty.

Refusing to give his enemy the opportunity to recover, Graham jumped forward and front-kicked him under the chin as hard as he could. Even as the man's head rocked back at the impact of the combat boot and he tumbled backwards, slamming his Kevlar helmet against the steel, the guerrilla closed on him. In the heavy body armor, the half-conscious soldier was like a turtle turned on his back, and he screamed, *"No!"* and threw both hands out as Graham dropped on top of him. Pinning the enemy's unwounded arm with one knee, the berserk Irregular pounded his face with his empty pistol over and over again, until he finally broke through to his braincase.

"Alright," Lucky Charlie yelled, his voice slightly more strained than usual. "It's over! Strip the bodies and drag 'em off in the brush out of sight! Was anyone hit? Graham! Shit! What happened to you?"

Casey Graham staggered around the open door of the Bradley, so smeared with blood from the bludgeoned soldier that he looked like he's stuck his head in a bucket of it. His teeth were bared in pain, and the hand not holding his pistol was clenched tight against his torso.

"I've been hit in the armor, but I don't think it went through. It feels like it may have busted some ribs though."

"Can you still function?"

Casey Graham was so numb with fatigue and, at the same time, wound up on speed and adrenaline that he really had no idea. Still, he wasn't about to admit it. Besides, he was angry more than anything else, and the mission wasn't over yet, so there's be more of the enemy to take it out on. "Hell yes, sir!"

"Good. Have the medic look at it while we're rolling. Okay, people, let's get this show on the road! Anyone here ever drive a Bradley?"

"I've qualified on them," Steiner offered.

"Great; get your ass in the seat. This is my command car and you're my new driver; bring your squad. Colonel Gore, you and your people, take over the armored car. We've got some real whup-ass now, and we're going to have a little change of plan.

"The armored car's job will be the same as before; secure that gate and put suppressing fire on the school. The Irregulars and Tarheels in the Humvees will be our spearhead for the frontal assault; with this Bradley, we can handle anything in the back. The bus will still be the bulk assault force, but Dr. MacFie will be in command. Lieutenant Harrison and his people will be with me. Doc, as quick as that bus comes to a stop, get those people the hell out and moving, got it?"

Andrew MacFie nodded curtly, but inside, he knew he didn't have it at all. He knew he was in way over his head and sinking fast, and he felt weak in the knees, but he couldn't bring himself to refuse. He had always considered himself a leader, but...

Now I guess I'll find out! God help us all!

As Charlie explained, Jim Reynolds knelt as Doug Long rolled off of Samantha, and the two men carefully began easing her to her feet. That came much to her relief, since her only view from the ground had been that of quickly moving boots and the fallen, bloody dead. The gore had pooled and ran beneath her while she was pinned down, and she could feel it's sickly warmth seeping through her uniform. Laboriously getting her knees under her while each of her protectors supported an arm and Hodges reached to help, her eyes abruptly widened as they reached the level of Charlie Carnes' waist.

"Charlie! You're hit!"

"What?" He yelled, trying to look behind him and noticing the blood running down the back of his right thigh and dripping out over the cup of his artificial leg. Putting a hand cautiously behind him, he suddenly exclaimed, "Damn it, somebody shot me in the ass!"

Jim snipped the flex cuffs holding her wrists just in time for Samantha to clamp her hands over her mouth, unable to stop the crazy giggle that broke forth like water over a dam.

Fortunately, the wound in the captain's right buttock was, literally, a flesh wound. It was a fragment from the copper jacket from a ricocheting bullet, probably one of their own, that had broken apart when it bounced off the Humvee, and the stray chunk had hit him. The squad medic, John Sergeant, dug it out while they were rolling in the new lead vehicle, while Charlie stood with his pants down, bracing himself against a grab handle inside the Bradley. At any other time, the situation would have been hilarious, but right now, no one thought to laugh. Finally Sergeant finished, applied a bandage and the officer pulled up his pants with little time to spare.

"Alright," his voice came over the radio, "We're within one mile of the objective. Lock and load, and remember the plan changes."

Throughout the convoy, hands began checking chambers, and making certain for the hundredth time that holsters, spare magazines, grenades, and knives were accessible. Lips were licked, deep breaths taken, and fingers caressed rifle stocks like prayer beads as the motley group of Rebels prepared to go to war. Samantha knew what they must be going through, just by looking at those in the armored truck with her: Cynthia, Kerrie, Jim, and two Palmetto auxiliaries – one driving and the other operating the flame thrower.

"Remember what you've been taught," Samantha said quietly into the radio. "Just do your job; don't worry about anything else, and we'll all come out of this alright."

What the hell do I know about it? she wondered to herself. Still, her words were what they expected, what they needed, and thus she gave them. She could hear whispers invoking good luck, the murmuring of quiet prayers, and saw the two auxiliaries crossing themselves, one finishing by bringing the crucifix hanging around his neck to his lips and kissing it. If the Protestant majority around them minded, none said anything; they were all busy with their own hasty devotions, and besides, at times like this, you took whatever you could get. Suddenly Samantha heard her own prayers inside her mind:

Yea, though I walk through the valley of the shadow of death...
And then they were slowing down for the gate.

CHAPTER 36

Frank awoke suddenly, feeling disoriented. His ears were ringing, and everything was black. For the life of him, he couldn't remember where he was, only that something wasn't right. He stirred slightly, and a big hand immediately grasped his.

"Hey, bro, it's good to have you back."

He frowned beneath the bandages at the sound of the voice.

That doesn't make sense.

"Billy?" he croaked, barely understandably before swallowing, or attempting to, because his mouth was too dry to work up any saliva.

"Here, man, I got a drink for you. Just go slow so you don't choke yourself."

The big man put the straw between his cracked lips and held the cup, and Frank gratefully sipped the ice water, swirling each mouthful around before swallowing to re-hydrate the tissues.

"Thanks."

"Don't mention it."

He lay there quietly for a moment, collecting his thoughts, and as they came back, his body grew more and more rigid with tension.

"Billy, why can't I see?" His voice was deathly calm, but it was obvious he was fighting to keep it that way. "Am I...blind?"

Inside him, another voice was not so calm; in fact, it was screaming in terror at one of his worst secret fears, a terror that he would never let show on the outside, even if what he feared was true.

"No, not permanent anyway; you're face is all puffed up and your eyes are swollen shut. I don't know if you'll be winnin' anymore shootin' championships anytime soon, but you'll be able to see Sammie's pretty face just fine in a couple of days. Right now you're in a Tarheel CAP hospital; kinda makeshift, but it's all they've got. Do you remember anything?"

Frank thought hard.

"I remember...the helicopter! Yes, there was a fight in North Carolina! I...I was carrying Caffary; he was shot in the leg. That's the last thing I remember."

"It was damned near the last thing you'd ever remember. That chopper opened up on you with rockets. You're lucky to be alive."

"What about Caffary?"

"Sorry; he didn't make it. They said the thing hit right behind you, and with him on your back, he took the main force of the blast. You tryin' to save him was the only thing that saved you."

"Damn it! He was a good man."

"He was that," Billy agreed, even though he had barely known him. Still, the fact that Frank thought so was good enough for him. Suddenly he realized the General was speaking again.

"What about Rob and the rest of the Irregulars."

"Look, you need to rest now and get your strength back, instead of worryin' about all this stuff. There'll be plenty of time for that later."

"I've been resting; now I want to know what happened to my men."

Billy sighed.

"Four of them are still alive that we know of: Hodges, Graham, Long, and that little smart-assed Yankee – Drucci, that's his name. He's shot up pretty bad, but they think he'll make it. Suggs is wounded, and about a dozen or so of his Tarheels that were with you all got away. There may still be a few more of ours out there on the run an' hidin' out yet, but so far that's it."

"So many...how?"

Feeling miserable for what he was putting his friend through, Billy told him the truth as it had been relayed to him, beginning with Rob giving his life to bring down the chopper, continuing with Buchanan, Kowalski and the rest sacrificing themselves to cover the survivors as they spirited their wounded commander away in a brutal cross-country run.

The General made a horrible, choking sound in the back of his throat that Billy had never heard come from him before, and his body shook with grief for the men – for *his* men, for the men he had trained and commanded, who had stood at his back through it all. They were the people maligned by society as violent thugs – Klansmen, rednecks, Skinheads, militiamen, conspiracy theorists – but every time it really counted, they had stood their ground for the Cause...and for Frank Gore. In the end, they had willingly laid down their lives so he could live. Inside he shouted at God.

Why didn't you take me instead?

"It's alright, Frank," Billy told him, laying his hand on his shoulder. "They were good men, and they did a man's duty and then some, I reckon. Everybody dies, but they died in a way folks'll talk about for a long time. They made the choice; don't begrudge 'em the glory."

"My life wasn't worth that!"

"They thought so. For that matter, so do I."

Frank gasped for breath, fighting for calm, and Billy tried to change the subject in order to get his mind on something else.

"So, do you wanna know what your score is now?"

"Yeah, I guess."

"You took shrapnel in both legs, your back, and your right lung, as well as havin' the hell beat out of you by the blast; you're like one big bruise. The worst part was when the explosion threw you forward into a ditch. You came right down on your face, smashed your nose and a bunch of the bones around it, and busted a few of your ribs."

"Ouch."

Billy started to nod, then realized Frank couldn't see him. "Got that right. You're guardian angel must have gray hair, bro. He's probably sittin' there on his cloud, chain smokin' and shootin' tequila right now, trying to get rid of the shakes."

"I suppose so. Has anyone gotten word to Sammie yet? She'll be worried."

"Yeah, she knows; we came up together, along with Jim Reynolds and Tommy's Squad."

"Where is she now?"

Billy mentally crossed his fingers.

"She's...okay. She had to go somewhere for a couple of hours, but she'll be back."

Something in his voice sent up a red flag in the wounded man's fogged mind, and despite the fact that he couldn't see, Frank turned his head in the big biker's direction.

"Give me your hand again, Billy."

"Sure," he said, reaching out again, only to have Frank grasp it far more tightly than the big man would have thought him capable of, especially in his condition.

"You're one of the few people I trust completely, inside this movement or out of it. I consider you to be my friend. Now on our friendship, don't lie to me; tell me the truth! *Where is my wife?*"

Writhing under the imagined glare from the bandaged eyes, Billy told him. When he finished, Frank simply lay there, still clasping his hand until the giant biker couldn't stand it any longer.

"Man, I tried to get her not to go..."

"No," Frank said, the difficulty in his voice evident as if the words were being torn out of him, "she was right. She had to go; she was the only one they would follow, and she couldn't leave our people behind, not with that kind of information in their possession. If they aren't gotten out, the war is over, and the other side wins. She was also right in what she told you to do in the event of something happening. She did the right thing, God help her." He paused thoughtfully at the sound of thunder rumbling from outside, and the rain and sleet on the metal roof. "It's storming. Good; that'll give her some cover at least, keep down their air support."

"Yeah," he said, unconvinced, "I reckon so. If it helps, Mike put your plan into action before he got caught; the phones, lights, everything's down."

"Yeah, it does; the chaos will give her a real chance. Still...Billy, would you help me pray for her?"

"*Me* help *you?*"

"Yeah; I don't know what they've got me on −"

"Some kind of veterinary tranquilizer I reckon; they had an animal doctor patching you up."

"Yeah, that stands to reason, then. Anyway, I'm having trouble keeping my thoughts ordered in the way they need to be; they're swirling around like leaves in a whirlwind."

"Frank, I don't think God's gonna listen to me; me an' Him ain't talked much over the years."

"You ought to; you're fighting on His side now. Look, I need somebody to pray with me. The Bible says that the heathen man can be justified by his believing wife, or the heathen wife by her husband. Maybe you can be justified by your friend, or maybe just the side you're fighting on. I don't know, but I'm willing to take that chance."

"Alright, then, if you really want me to."

Hell, I reckon somebody really needs to!

"Sir? You...wanted to see me?"

Frank's face twisted in what was meant to be a welcoming expression, but it was so painful he quickly gave up the effort.

"I don't think I'll be able to see you just now, Private Drucci, but I wanted to talk to you. Please come in."

Danny obeyed, limping slowly and painfully, half-doubled over with one arm braced across his wounded gut. Billy got up and crossed the room, closing the door before turning to put a hand on the Italian's shoulder.

"I want to thank you for what you did." He whispered as he nodded at the bed. "He's more than a friend, and if you need anything, anything at all, you just ask me and you'll have it. You hear? I owe you."

"I owe you too," Frank told him, having caught the exchange, and Danny nodded numbly as Billy took Danny's arm with surprising gentleness and helped ease him into the chair at Frank's bedside. Afterwards, Billy retreated to the other side of the room to give them as much privacy as he could without failing in his duty to stay with his friend and commander.

"This is a debriefing," Frank said. "Tell me everything that happened, starting with the chopper attack." Gesturing towards his bandaged face, he added, "It's a little hazy from my end."

Danny began calmly, but was choking as he finished the tale, and when Frank blindly groped for his hand, he grabbed onto it like a lifeline.

"Why?" Drucci was yelling. "Why did I have to live? I belong with my unit! Oh God, sir, I'm so ashamed!"

Frank winced. *I know just how he feels!*

"There's nothing to be ashamed of. You did your duty and then you went way above and beyond. You willingly laid down your life just like the rest of them, but God gave yours back to you. He isn't through with you yet; He saved you for a purpose."

"What purpose, sir? What the hell could He want with me that was worth this?"

Frank squeezed his hand. "Two things I can think of right offhand. One is that you brought that defector with you, and in turn he's giving my wife and her unit a better chance of success in rescuing our people, winning the war, and...even in keeping Sammie and our unborn child alive." Frank paused, swallowing hard to painfully clear his throat of the huge lump that had suddenly appeared there before continuing. "Second, someone to bring the story back so the Irregulars' glory could live on. That was you, Danny; you were spared to tell the people, so they'd know what happened, and remember the 1st Columbia forever. If you hadn't lived, that might not have happened, and they might have lost their place in history." He paused, remembering his history. "That was our Thermopile, and someone had to go tell the Spartans."

CHAPTER 37

Steiner drove the Bradley right up to the entrance, and a private stirred in the outhouse-sized plywood and glass guard shack beside it. Swearing under his breath, he pulled the poncho's hood up over his helmet and stepped out into the freezing drizzle; the mud splashed on his boots as he walked to the gate. Cold, bored and miserable as he had been in the unheated shack, he could now add being wet to his ever-growing list of woes. Recognizing Captain Spalding's vehicle, he said the hell with passwords and procedure, and simply unlocked the gate, threw it open, and stepped back out of the way.

What the hell are they gonna do about it: send me to the South?

The Fighting Vehicle rolled through the gate, the rest of the convoy close behind. When the soldier saw them, he frowned slightly at the sight of the black Humvee and the armored truck with what looked like...a *flamethrower?* mounted on its roof.

I expect there's a story there, but right now I don't give a damn what it is. I just wish they would hurry up and get through so I can shut this gate and get back inside.

As the last vehicle – the weird looking armored truck – passed, the soldier began turning to drag the gate closed. He was so wrapped up in his own miseries and getting out of the weather that he didn't see the small firing port on the side slide open, or the thick muzzle of the suppressed MP5 that sent a three round burst into him. The bullets pounded him, and he hit the ground.

Lucky Charlie gave the command to go ahead by the expedient of giving the order to Harrison, who promptly blew the front door off the school-cum-prison with a burst from their main weapon, the 25mm chain gun. Since the rear door was in line with it, it was smashed to pieces as well by a double handful of slugs that continued straight down the hall and out the rear of the building, in one side and out the other and off somewhere into the distance. Another quick burst and the air was filled with flying brick fragments as most of the wall in front of the arms room

305

disintegrated. Swinging the aim upward, they blew off the rooftop antenna, and a good bit of the front edge of the rooftop along with it, sending a shower of shattered bricks and mortar bouncing off the wet sidewalk in front.

Steiner jerked the vehicle to the left, Harrison hit the triggers once more, and the front guard tower on their side, along with the sandbags and the guard crouching behind them, abruptly ceased to exist except as a hail of steaming pieces falling to earth. Long before the last one hit, the motor gunned, the churning tires bit into the mud, and they were roaring for the back of the building.

"Go-go-go-go!" their driver yelled, and Samantha, Kerrie, Cynthia, and Jim went, straight out of the back of the armored car, closest to the gate. Unfortunately, as soon as he saw Samantha and Kerrie exiting, the fast reacting tower guard on the right sent a burst of 5.56mm full metal jackets that kicked up mud and rattled against the truck's armored side. Fearing Samantha would be hit, the driver punched the gas and swerved the truck, trying to get the vehicle between her and the guard tower. His plan worked, but the sudden swerving acceleration threw Cynthia into Jim just as they were setting their feet to jump down, and both of them were slung out of the open back. They went down hard in the frigid muck, with her on top.

Having no more time to waste, the driver ran directly at the tower and slid to a stop just within range of the flamethrower. The gunner was on the ball, the air compressor that powered the weapon running, and the tongue of fire was already reaching out, questing for its target. At first, it hit the structure's legs, but with the operator's rapid adjustment, its arc went higher and licked its way onto the platform itself, splattering over and inside the vain protection of the sandbag ring.

Leaving the conflagration to the screams, he spun the truck, making its wheels throw brown rooster tails of grass and mud as they raced across the schoolyard for the rear and their second objective, leaving their passengers to sort out their own end of things.

Both of Murphy's laws were in full force: anything that can go wrong will, and when it does, it will be at the worst possible time. It's considered something akin to military gospel that no plan ever survives contact with the enemy: something true in well-planned operations involving even the most highly trained special operations troops, and much more so with a motley, loose-knit group of sporadically trained volunteer guerrillas. Even as he hit the brakes, a bullet fired from one of the soldiers in the school hit the bus driver in the hollow of the throat and cartwheeled into his spine, severing it fatally, before slamming into the metal frame of his seat. Flopping like a rag doll, he tumbled sideways and fell down the short stairs, coming to rest upside down against the folding doors, jamming them closed. The bus rolled another twenty feet before one of the men on board managed to get into the seat, apply the brakes, and kill the engine. More were manhandling the limp corpse from the stairs even as Dr. MacFie was repeatedly shouting for them to use the back door, but it wasted precious seconds they didn't have. Bullets began shattering the bus windows and puncturing its thin sheet metal sides even as the others on board frantically jammed together, trying to get out the rear exit, and still others climbed through the emergency exit windows. A few of those trapped onboard waiting their turn to leave had the presence of mind to return fire through the nearest windows, but they were wildly inaccurate, due in large part to the jostling going on inside. Shouts and screams echoed through the falling rain as several people were hit before they could get free.

Dr. MacFie finally resorted to shoving and kicking what had become a disorganized mob in the direction they needed to go. He kept repeating, "Off the bus and charge! Off the bus and charge!" over and over again, and couldn't seem to make his normally glib mouth form any other words.

Dr. Grissom, along because the Confederates rightly suspected they would need his services before this mission was over, was the only one not attempting to get out of the bus. As flying droplets of blood spattered his face and the screams filled his ears, he realized his work had come to him.

Samantha saw movement inside the shattered front of the building, jerked her submachine gun to her shoulder, and opened fire. Kerrie engaged the target an instant afterwards, and they saw a camouflage uniform sprout red flowers and collapse out of sight behind the sill.

The last bullet fired from the now burning right guard tower had found another mark besides the armored truck; it struck the forehead of the black Humvee's driver, one of her South Carolina students. The round hit from the side, from such a shallow angle that the bullet actually glanced off the bone and went sailing off into the distance instead of burrowing into his brain, but the impact cranked his head to the left, stunned him, and instantly filled both eyes with blood from his torn flesh. Involuntarily jerking, his foot, already on the accelerator, jammed the pedal to the floorboard, and his vehicle plowed into the rear of the second Humvee, throwing everyone in the back of his into a cursing tangle of arms, legs and guns. The Tarheel guerrillas in the second machine were just beginning to jump out, and instead of a fast, controlled dismount, their truck slewed sideways, catapulting people in all directions, one of them breaking a leg in the process. He rolled in the mud shouting and holding his injured limb, and his loud, chanting cries and curses could be heard above the gunfire.

Samantha saw the bulk of their forces in the bus had panicked and lost all cohesion, and it would be a moment they didn't have to spare before the mixed veterans of Irregular and Tarheel veterans could extricate themselves from the wrecked vehicles. The volume of gunfire from the building was increasing, and unless an attack was carried out on it *now*, the whole thing was going straight to Hell. She knew her job was to stay where she was, and protect the gate; she also knew it would take at least a minute or more to get the bulk of the guerrillas together, and that would be far, far too long! Something inside took hold of her.

I didn't bring these people here to die!

"Let's go! Charge" she heard herself shout, and then she was running as fast as her swollen, bobbing belly would let her, only vaguely aware that the command that filled her ears had come from her own lips, along with the shrill, screaming Rebel yell that came spilling out after it. All she knew was that she had to get everybody moving, and, firing as she made her clumsy charge, it never occurred to her to see if anyone besides Kerrie, still at her side, had come with her.

Behind Samantha, where she couldn't see, only a handful noticed and followed, but too few and too far behind. The rest were milling around, trying to find cover or figure out what was going on despite MacFie's increasingly shrill shouted orders to the contrary. Her self-appointed guardian angel, Cynthia, had a clear view as she scrambled to her feet from her tangled position on top of Jim. Two of the people she loved most in the world were making what was virtually a lone charge on the enemy positions.

"No! Sammie, stop!"

Samantha couldn't hear her, and Cynthia charged forward with such single-minded determination that she didn't notice when Thumper passed her any more than when she set the sole of her boot on the back of Jim's head and drove his face deep into the mud as he was struggling to rise.

Two more rapid strides brought her past the fallen gate guard. Cynthia had no way of knowing the rounds that knocked him over had expended themselves on his body armor with bruising, rib-cracking force but no real damage. She assumed he was dead until his arms whipped round her passing ankles and tumbled her to the ground. Managing to keep her face from slamming into the mud, she immediately scrambled onto her side as the soldier lunged forward on his belly and grabbed her submachine gun, wrapping his hand around the barrel just ahead of the receiver. Knowing with the instinct of hard training that the weapon would be useless in a clench, instead of pulling away, she simply held on and went with it. Using the impetuous of his jerk she rolled in the same direction, all the way on top of it and him, landing a savage knee in his groin as

309

she grabbed the Randal dagger on her belt. Holding the blade point downward in her left hand, she screamed in fury and punched it from left to right, slashing him across the right hand where it held onto her weapon, completely severing one finger and ruining three more. Without pausing she reversed direction and stabbed it backhanded into the left side of his neck like an ice pick, and, torquing her entire body, ripped it all the way across and out the other side, halfway decapitating him. She shook her head to clear her vision as his arterial blood sprayed into her eyes.

When they were finally clear, she blanched at what she saw.

Doctor MacFie was horrified as he jumped, fell or was knocked out the back door of the bus and onto the body of a gut-shot guerrilla who screamed at the impact, but he was in sheer terror when he saw Samantha pass him, accompanied by Kerrie, as they charged the building.

"Up!" he screamed as he scrambled to his feet. "Get up, damn it! Get the hell up and charge! Charge!" Grabbing a frightened, half-trained guerrilla, he jerked him to his feet with more strength than he ever though he'd be able to muster, and shoved him in the direction he needed to go.

If I can just get them moving...

Glancing up again, he saw Sammie rapidly moving ahead towards the building, with only a scattering of Confederates following behind, and something inside him took over. He couldn't wait any more. He was frightened, and some detached part of him wasn't sure that he hadn't pissed himself, but the duty he had preached all his life drove him on. He's also decided he'd be damned if he let Samantha die for him.

Andrew MacFie was a sophisticated college professor, an articulate spokesman for the Cause; maybe that's why the ear-splitting Rebel yell that burst its way out of his mouth got everyone's attention. Stanley Bauer took it up next, and then both old men launched their own charge, firing as they went and never looking back.

310

They were the catalyst that finally got the rest moving forward, first as a trickle, and then, once inertia took over, as an unstoppable flood as the veterans finally got free of their crashed Humvees.

With her head start, Samantha was still in front of the charge, with Kerrie to her left. Dimly some part of her heard people screaming for her to stop, to go back, to get down, to wait for the rest, but for the first time in her life she found herself in the killing zone, and responding to or even acknowledging anything extraneous like their frantic pleas was more than she was capable of. Every fiber of her being was wrapped up in moving forward, and controlling the bursts of the MP5 bucking against her shoulder.

A head and a gun muzzle appeared in one of the first floor windows, and it seemed as if she had all the time in the world to aim on the run and knock it down with yet another three round burst while bullets buzzed past her like angry bees.

There was a loud *whack!* like someone slapping a side of meat, and suddenly Kerrie O'Brien was no longer beside her; she was alone, but she was so caught up in the moment, she barely noticed. Instead of looking to see what had happened, she continued firing, joined by the other guerrillas and the increasingly desperate Cynthia gaining ground behind her, they riddled a rifleman in another window.

When the slide on her MP5 locked open, and Samantha slowed slightly as she thumbed the clip release while reaching for another magazine with her free hand. She caught a flash of brown from the corner of her left eye, and turned to see one of the prison guard dogs, a Belgian Shepherd, charging her. The animal was only feet away, and sprang for her throat as she tried to get the empty gun between them. Looking at the mouthful of teeth that seemed to fill her entire field of vision, she realized she wasn't going to make it. She instinctively hunched her shoulder and ducking her chin to protect her throat. The fangs were no more than a foot from her face when something slammed into her in passing, knocking her aside like a glancing blow from a truck fender. Stumbling and falling to her hands and one knee in the mud, she glimpsed a streak of white, and the Shepherd crashed to the ground, driven there by a furious Thumper, whose enormous jaws had already closed on its neck. In his element now, the huge bulldog roared his own battle cry as he shook her attacker like a rag, and the guard dog yelped once before she heard the dull popping of canine vertebrae snapping even as she slammed home a new clip while rising. Just as the slide racked forward, a screaming and cursing Hodges caught up, threw both arms around her chest in a bear hug, lifted her from the ground, and turned her, putting his own armored body between her and the building.

"Get her out of the way, until it's over, damn it!"

As the bulk of the assault force finally caught up and ran past, she immediately felt two pairs of hands – Cynthia's and Jim's – grab her and hustle her back towards the vehicles. Fighting against them and digging in her heels, her struggles finally forced them to drag her into cover behind the generator, still chugging away beneath its wall-less tin roofed shelter.

Her troops, now led by Irregulars, Tarheels, and accompanied by an excited Thumper, who had dropped the limp body of his latest prize for the chance at bigger game, poured through the ruins of the front door, the men tossing concussion grenades ahead of them. Meanwhile, those still outside kept a steady rain of fire against anything that showed in the shattered windows, almost drowning out the sounds of battle from within.

Lucky Charlie's Bradley never slowed as it made mincemeat out of the rear tower on the left, and spun on its tracks to engage the off-duty troops just beginning to spill out of their makeshift barracks. Thinking at first the war machine was one of theirs, they failed to take cover until it was too late. The big 25mm began blowing them apart, forcing the survivors to seek what cover they could. Instinctively, they fled back for what little the sheet metal classroom offered. It was a fatal mistake, but they were so far out of options by then that any other choice would have had the same end result.

Coming around the other side of the school, the driver of the armored car screamed, "Hold on!" and barely slowed as he punched the vehicle's bumper into the door. The portal crumpled and flew off its hinges, sailing into the room beyond and killing one man who had been sheltered behind it. He was the lucky one; the driver reversed a few feet and backed out, far enough to be able to depress the nozzle of the flamethrower, and its operator triggered a five second tongue of fire in through the open door, swiveling the flame back and forth. The gelled gasoline licked over furniture, books, and men, and turned the whole place into an instant inferno. The huge holes blown by the Bradley's automatic cannon only served as ventilation to fan the flames. No one escaped, and, almost as an afterthought, the Bradley's gunner raised the 25mm far enough for the next burst to disintegrate the final tower platform, along with its occupant, who was torn apart in the air as he desperately jumped from his post.

Leaving Charlie, his gunner and his driver behind, Harrison and the remaining three men from the Dojo Squad charged the shattered ruins of the back door. They entered tactically just as they had been taught, and fortunately, both they and ones coming in through the front, recognized one another before opening fire.

Crouched in one of the second floor cells, holding his pistol in his good hand and cradling his mutilated one against his chest, the Mossad advisor Jacob Rosenberg knew he was in deep, deep trouble. He cursed the Army that had refused to send the helicopter to med-evac him due to the confusion resulting from the infrastructure collapse, cursed his own government that had sent him here in the first place, and especially cursed that savage *goy* who had bitten his thumb off and eaten it. That he had paid him back for that action in spades was little comfort now; even an idiot could see they were being overrun, and the Confederate guerrillas would undoubtedly kill him out of hand for what he had done. Or even worse, they might sell him to the Muslims like they had done the previous Israeli agents who had come against them. He licked his thick lips and swallowed hard in fear as he looked around, hopelessly seeking an escaped he knew wasn't there. Then his eyes fell on the naked twelve year-old girl crouched in terror, wedged back the corner of her makeshift cell as far as she could go. She had been the lone prisoner in this room when he entered to take cover, but now, he quickly realized, she was his ticket out.

Rosenberg grabbed her and pulled her close, and she screamed and struggled until he slapped her twice in the face with the automatic's barrel. Despite his adrenaline, he was careful to hit her only hard enough to bloody and lightly stun her; he needed her alive and conscious. She was his only chance for survival, and he had no intention of screwing that up.

Hearing their boots on the steps, he took a deep breath and stepped into the hall, clutching the girl against his chest in a chokehold, his forearm across her throat.

"Stop or I'll kill her!" Rosenberg shouted, pressing the barrel of his 9mm Berretta against her neck just below her ear.

The hard eyed guerrillas – auxiliaries from the bus – looked at the hostage, scrawny and naked with fresh blood on her face and the dried blood of previous rapes still caked between her legs, and hesitated even as the fury emanated from them like a wave. They knew their orders, but no one was willing to be the one to sacrifice the wide-eyed kid.

Rosenberg couldn't help but grin at their hesitation, their utter softness.

The grin faded a little when Stanley Bauer stepped forward and pulled the hunting knife from his belt; the keen six-inch blade glittered even in the poor light, but its razor edge was no harder or sharper than the glint in the old man's eyes, or the truth in his words.

"As God is my witness, you hurt that little girl and I'll hang you up and skin you alive, you sumbitch!"

To his horror, Rosenberg realized the old man meant every word.

"Get back!" the interrogator shouted once more in a voice tight with fear, jamming the pistol tighter against his captive. As the muzzle was forced hard against the nerve center in her neck, the intense pain and fear caused her to scream.

Before anyone could decide what to do, there was an outraged roar and a slavering Thumper broke through the crowd at an all-out charge, knocking the guerrillas aside, sending several of them stumbling and two actually sprawling.

Thumper was a natural protector, and back on the hog farm, he had grown up playing with and protecting Donna and her older sister, Linda, whenever they came to visit. The sight of a girl in the grip of a stranger, and her scream, was all the stimulus the huge dog needed to kick his protective instinct into full overdrive. True to his nature, he was doing what he was born and bred to do.

The big animal charging him with an open, gaping mouth full of teeth and eyes full of death unnerved Rosenberg for just an instant, leaving him uncertain as to what his next course of action should be. It didn't take long to realize that, whether he shot his hostage or not, the dog wouldn't stop unless he stopped it. His hesitation proved fatal; by the time he began to take the pistol from the girl's neck, it was already too late. Thumper had gathered his powerful hindquarters under him without breaking stride and launched himself through the air, his massive shoulder brushing the girl aside to fall on her hands and knees, and his jaws clamped down on the wrist and hand holding the pistol with a force that splintered bones and sent the automatic clattering to the floor tiles. As the leap carried him past Rosenberg to his right, the impetuous of the weight swinging from the interrogator's hand spun him into the wall face-first. Rebounding from the cinderblock, he fell to the floor on his back. Thumper released his grip on the broken arm to take a better one, and the last thing Rosenberg saw was the massive set of jaws converging on his face.

As Dr. MacFie quickly grabbed the hysterically screaming girl and pulled her out of danger, even the most hardened guerrillas winced and swore at both the sight and sound as the bulldog took everything between Rosenberg's chin and eye sockets in his mouth and bit down for all he was worth. Thumper shook his prey violently for an instant, his teeth audibly grating against bone, and came away with a huge mouthful of flesh, ripping Rosenberg's face off and leaving behind little more than a bare, bloody skull on the front of the torturer's head. That the Israeli could still scream was more than a little surprising.

Stanley Bauer nodded his approval, muttered, "Good boy!" at Thumper, and spit a stream of tobacco juice on Rosenberg as he passed, leaving him to his fate.

The bulldog was getting ready to go in for yet another bite when one of the Confederates, unable to deal with the screaming anymore, mercifully put a bullet in the dying man's head. Robbed of his fun, Thumper looked accusingly at him before snorting in disgust and turning his back. Stopping abruptly, the white bulldog caught a faint, familiar scent, and barreled back through the crowd, heading back down the steps the way he had come. This time, everyone quickly got out of his way.

"Damn it, Sammie, don't you ever do something like that again!" Jim shouted, his face white in the few tiny patches where it could be seen through its coating of mud. His eyes wide with fear. "You could have been killed!"

"It's war," she told him flatly, angry at being stopped, even though she understood their reasons for stopping her, at least on an intellectual level if not in her gut, "and my friends are in there."

"Yes, and your child is in *here*," Cynthia snapped, poking at her commanding officer's swollen belly, "and your husband is still in North Carolina waiting for both of you to come home, and as long as I have anything to say about it, you *will*!" Jerking an electrical tie out of her pocket, she waved it at her superior officer. "So help me, we'll handcuff you right now if that's what it takes! The others can take care of the rest."

"I'm the leader; they followed me here!"

"Yes they did," Jim told her harshly. "Now stay the hell out of the way and let them do their jobs without having to worry about you!" He rose far enough for his eyes to barely protrude above the piece of equipment. "I think they've about got them pacified anyway."

Samantha had already heard the change of sound from inside, with the firing and occasional grenade explosions gradually giving way to shouted demands for surrender and panicked cries of those begging to be allowed to exactly that. She also heard screams and growling as Thumper enthusiastically mauled somebody who evidently did something he shouldn't have. She joined Jim at his observation post, and in less than a handful of minutes, she recognized old Stanley Bauer standing on the building's roof with a bloody scalp wound from a piece of flying glass and a big tobacco stained grin. Amid the cheers from those still on the ground outside, he waved a Battle Flag for a moment before hanging it from the stump of an antenna, then danced a little jig of glee. Samantha smiled, but her enthusiasm was dampened by the thought that this was only the first round.

We've got a long way to go before we're home free.
Wait a minute; where's Kerrie?

As she stood and looked around, she saw Kerrie's slender body lying where it had fallen. She was still on her back in the mud, arms and legs spread-eagled, and her red hair turned even redder by the blood oozing from the bullet hole above her left eye at the hairline. Raindrops were spattering the scarlet puddle that surrounded her head like a martyred saint's halo, draining from the enlarged exit wound in the back of her skull. Cynthia saw her and clamped a hand over her mouth, and quickly slid her sunglasses on to hide her silent tears for her best friend. With her bodyguards trailing behind, Samantha rose and walked to the fallen girl, pausing to kneel down and gently close her wide, staring eyes with her fingertips. Her vision was tunneling, and it was only through sheer willpower that she kept herself from fainting at the emotions roaring through her head like a hurricane made of broken shards of glass. Even though she knew Kerrie was long past caring now, she took a moment to brush the soaked auburn hair back out of her face and turn down a corner of her shirt collar that had folded upwards as she fell. She was reminded of the way she had worked the tangles out of that same hair, and how she cleaned her up the night Frank and Sam had brought her home from off the streets of Columbia. She how had wondered if they had just found a daughter.

God be with you, honey. I'm so, so sorry I got you into this! If it's any consolation, I'll be paying for this one for a long time. The price of this dream just keeps climbing and...God help me, I don't know how much more I can pay!

Refusing to let her emotions go and struggling to be strong for the sake of the rest, despite the involuntary tears flowing down her cheeks to join the falling rain, she bit down on the inside of her mouth until she tasted blood of her own, rose again and headed for the building, Jim in front and Cynthia right behind her.

It was obviously over. As Samantha approached, the hard eyed Confederates, shouting, swearing and red-faced, were driving the bloodied enemy prisoners, male and female alike, outside with a remarkably savage flurry of kicks and rifle butts. She was utterly shocked at their brutality. An unusually large, grim-faced woman auxiliary dragged female soldier out onto the porch by the expedient of both fists clenched in her captive's hair, and she used it to throw her prisoner so hard that she landed on the ground several feet in front of the steps. The last enemy prisoner, a wounded Negro, fell to his knees at the top of the steps, only to be kicked all the way to the bottom by Casey Graham, and receive a several more full-force combat boots in the ribs, groin and face once he got there. The Irregular obviously wasn't intent on making the prisoner move anymore; he was intent of killing him.

"Stop that!" she shouted. "That's not the way we do things!"

Graham glared at her with his already wild eyes red and crazy from anger, fatigue and drugs, and his voice was a screaming rasp.

"You take a look inside that shit hole, and then you tell me how we do things!" Turning quickly, he bent down, grabbed the fallen man by the collar and jerked his head back before driving it forward again with a loud martial arts *kiai*, slamming the prisoner's forehead against the edge of the cement step with bone-crushing force, sending a fan-shaped spray of blood across the concrete. Obviously the blow did far more than superficial damage; the body began shaking and quivering in a ghastly manner. Then, as a finishing

318

touch, Graham raised his knee to his chest and stomped down, driving his heel into the back of the man's neck at the juncture of the skull, and Samantha actually jumped at the sound this time. That the man was dead was not open to question. Graham turned his back and unslung his rifle as he walked towards the other prisoners. There were eight of them still alive, three women and five men. Samantha noticed they had been shoved against the nearest wall of the bullet-pocked building, and she realized what it meant when she saw the line of hard-eyed guerrilla veterans from both states forming in front of them as they inserted fresh magazines into their rifles.

"Stop it!" she shouted, but suddenly no one was paying any attention to her.

They paid attention when a burst of 9mm slugs peppered the ground in front of them.

"Listen up!" Lucky Charlie shouted, bouncing like a grasshopper on his steel spring feet as he stepped around the building, a thin tendril smoke curling from his submachine gun's muzzle. "Colonel Gore is in command here, and she will decide what to do with them!" He glared at them, muzzle still pointing in their direction, until they finally dropped their eyes. "Graham! Put a guard on the enemy prisoners, and get the rest of these people busy! I want this perimeter secured, and I want our people the hell out of here and loaded up ASAP! Let's go! Do it now!"

"Yes, sir," Casey responded, before shouting at the rest, "You heard him! Move it!" Turning back to face her, he nodded towards the door, his eyes as red as before if a bit less insane, and his body shaking from the two-way war between anger and the exhaustion that had stretched his nervous system quite literally to the breaking point. A continuous, repetitive twitch that had developed on the left side of his face within the past few minutes only added to the disturbing effect.

"You go in there, you'll understand."

Something in his voice sent chills down her spine, and Jim put his hand protectively on her arm.

"Don't put yourself through this, Sammie."

319

Cynthia shook her head, her young eyes hard despite the tears that still ran from their corners. "No, she has to. It's the only way she'll understand."

"You don't know what's gone on in there," he said, glaring at her.

"Oh yes," she said grimly as she eyed the first of the rescued prisoners now being helped out, followed by a thoroughly satisfied Thumper, his head, shoulders and chest covered with blood that was not his own, "yes, *I* do!"

The bloody dog stopped on the top step, obviously impatiently waiting for them to follow. Samantha instinctively knew he had found someone familiar inside, but from the actions of the angry guerrillas, she was so deathly afraid of what it might be she had to force herself to move forward.

Whatever happened, they're my friends, and, dead or alive, I won't leave them here!

More of the Confederates were coming out with the freed captives now, and she stepped aside at the bottom of the steps to let them pass. Every one of the freed prisoners – young and old, men and women and even a few children – had wide, frightened eyes. Several of them were crying openly while others gibbered nonsense, talking mostly to themselves. Suddenly, a woman her own age recognized her, broke away from her escort, and threw herself down on her knees in front of Samantha before anyone could stop her. She almost lost her balance as the freed prisoner clutched her tightly around the hips, and only Jim's quick grasp prevented her from falling. The woman's voice was a scream.

"Thank you! Oh thank you so much! Oh, God, how I prayed that you or your husband would come for us! They took my baby! Please find her! Please!"

"Shh," Samantha shushed her as Cynthia carefully disentangled her imprisoning arms. Reaching down, she brushed the woman's wet face with her fingers. "If your baby is here, we'll find her. You go on with the rest now, okay?"

She turned and shouted at Casey Graham to question the prisoners and find the whereabouts of the woman's child as, gently but firmly, one of the Confederates lifted the distraught mother to her feet and half-led, half-carried her away. More and more detainees were being brought out, and she was startled to notice that, despite the freezing temperatures, many of the guerrillas were suddenly shirtless. She saw the reason why coming behind them; they had given them to women with shattered looks to cover their nakedness. A couple of them were little girls, who couldn't have been over ten or twelve.

Oh my God!

"Lieutenant!" It was Hodges' voice, and she looked to see the former skinhead frantically gesturing towards the basement steps, using his M4 as a pointer, while the increasingly impatient Thumper bounded in circles around his feet. "Down here!"

Dr. Grissom knew that, if this wasn't Hell, it didn't miss it by much. Kneeling on the floor of the bus and bloody to the elbows, he quickly slapped a plastic bandage cover over the sucking chest wound in a guerrilla's ribcage. The screams and moans of other wounded filled his ears as the First Responder he had chosen for his aide frantically tried his best to perform first aide and some sort of triage in the midst of the insanity. Now they were bringing in the freed prisoners, and many of them were wounded too, or so completely traumatized that they were out of their heads. Their cries added to the pandemonium.

"Dad!" he heard his son call out to him, shouting over the noise. "I've got someone – "

"Triage him, damn it!" he replied without looking up, even as he slapped on some tape and turned to his aide. "Bring me that abdominal wound next! Hurry!"

"Shane?"

The veterinarian froze at the familiar sound of the woman's voice, the one he had known for twenty-five years. Twisting his head to look, he saw his wife, Jennie, standing in orange prison clothes and staring back at him.

Rising slowly to his feet, the wounded forgotten for the moment, his mouth worked several times before he could actually get the words out.

"What are you doing here?"

"They arrested me."

"Oh my God...Are you...alright?"

"No, Shane, I'm not alright, but at least I'm in better shape than most of the poor women in there. They manhandled me, stripped me naked, and put their filthy hands up inside of me – looking for *contraband*, they said – but at least they hadn't gotten around to raping me *yet*, like they did most of the others."

"I-I didn't know they would arrest you!" he blurted. "If I had even thought that, I would have taken you with me!"

Looking at him with surprising calmness, she said, "Everything the Confederates said about those monsters is true...no, it's not true. It doesn't even begin to cover the things I saw and heard in there!" She swallowed hard. "I chosen my side in this thing; I hope you choose the same one, but, I know where I stand, regardless."

He nodded. "You and I have stood together for half a lifetime; I'm not about to change that now. My place is with my family, with my wife and my son."

She nodded in satisfaction, and went to him, embracing him despite the blood he was covered with.

"Thank you. I love you, Shane."

"You know I love you too."

"I know..." her voice trailed off as the tears began to fall, and then he heard the background screams once more.

Turning, he looked down at the waiting wounded. "Can you help me here?"

"If you're going to stay by my side," she sniffed, wiping at her nose with the back of her hand, "then I'll stay by yours. Tell me what to do."

Donna lay naked on the concrete floor of the first cell they came to, curled in a fetal position. Even from the back, it was obvious she was severely battered, but she showed no reaction, even though she had to have heard them entering, or felt Thumper's tongue as he licked her.

"She won't answer, ma'am," Hodges told her, his lips set tight. "Since you're a woman and her friend, I thought maybe you should be the one to get her moving; I don't want to traumatize her anymore." Overcome with anger, he suddenly turned his head and roared violently before driving the toe of his boot through the plaster wall. He left the room trailing white dust from the shattered wallboard behind, along with a steady, repetitive stream of curses. Donna had trained with him, with the Irregulars; she was practically one of them...one of the few that were left. To see this feisty girl, always so full of piss and vinegar reduced to this, was more than he could take.

If Sergeant Hodges had his way, some son of a bitch – preferably a whole big bunch of sons of bitches – was going to die for this!

Samantha motioned the others to stay back, and grunted with the effort as she knelt beside her.

"Donna?"

"Now I lay me down to sleep." Donna's voice was singsong, and tiny, almost like a child's. "I pray the Lord my soul to keep."

Samantha laid a hand on her bare shoulder, and the girl cringed, hugging herself tighter, trying her best to squeeze into herself and disappear. Thumper sat back and whined in distress, instinctively knowing that something was terribly wrong here.

"Donna, it's me; it's Sammie."

"If I die before I wake..."

"Please, Donna, it's alright now. We're here."

If the girl heard her, she gave no sign.

"I pray the Lord my soul to take. Now I lay me down to sleep..."

Samantha felt like screaming with the horror of it.

Be strong! For just a while longer, be strong!

"Help me, Cynthia," She called back over her shoulder, and together they turned her over and gently lifted her to her feet, despite her obviously desperate desire to keep her body stiff, with her arms folded over her bruised breasts and her legs drawn up and held tightly together.

"Here," Jim said, stripping off his own shirt and extending it, "put this on her; maybe she'll feel better if she's covered." As soon as Cynthia took it, he went to the door of the makeshift cell and turned his back to give them privacy, showing the puckered skin from the old bullet scars. As an old friend of Sam's, he had known the girl since she was a child, long before Samantha had ever met her, and as she noticed his tensed shoulders, she suspected that Donna's privacy wasn't the only reason he had turned away where they couldn't see his face.

"Come on, Donna, put your arms in here. Let's get you dressed."

Finally she loosened up enough for them to get the shirt on her, and Samantha saw her glance quickly at her out of the corner of her blackened, swollen eyes and quickly look away again, only to cautiously repeat the process a second time for just an instant longer. The third time, she held her gaze on her rescuer.

"S-S-Sammie? I-is it r-really...you?"

Samantha forced herself to smile, although it was one of the hardest things she had ever done.

"It's me, little sister, and I'm taking you out of here."

It took them almost a solid minute to get the sobbing girl off her.

"I'll be there in a few minutes, honey," Samantha told her. "I promise. You go with Jim now."

She didn't want to leave, but Jim scooped her up in his arms and carried her. Samantha was idly surprised at the slender man having that much strength left, but he managed the girl with never a wince. As they left the room, over Donna's sobs, she heard him whispering what seemed to be the guerrilla mantra:

"Shh. It'll be alright."

No it won't! Nothing's going to be alright, ever again!

For the first time in months, the rage she kept ruthlessly suppressed inside her began to build, the monster she knew had crouched in the shadows of the back of her mind since she had been brutalized began to awaken, and she fought to keep it in check.

Abruptly she heard Hodges calling for her.

Tommy was in a cell halfway down the building, and his naked body was only recognizable by his tattoos. He was hanging limply from shackles attached to the ceiling. His features were as swollen and bruised as Frank's had been, but his face was not nearly in as bad a shape as his legs. They were both a mass of bruises and at least one of them – the right – was obviously broken, the jagged end of a shattered tibia pushing through a bloody hole in his skin. They had manacled him by the wrists, and suspended him from an eyebolt screwed into the ceiling, high enough that he had to support himself on the balls of his feet. Then they had gone to work on his legs with nightsticks, and left him there when they finished. Unable to support his weight with his injured legs, his arms had to take the strain, forcing the cuffs to cut deeply into his wrists, shutting off the circulation and causing his hands to bloat until his fingers looked like purple sausages. The position also put pressure on his lungs, making it difficult to breathe. In fact, there was something very wrong with his respiration; it was a hideous bubbling wheeze the likes of which she had never heard. Hodges had called for a set of bolt cutters, and while he waited, the big man had dropped his armor in order to remove his shirt, and was in the process of wrapping the garment around the prisoner's waist. He didn't get finished in time, and Samantha saw that Tommy's testicles were blackened and swollen as big as her fists from being kicked, and then she blanched at the dried blood caking her friend's rear and the inside of his thighs. In that instant, she *knew*.

Merciful Christ, why?

The monster inside grew more and more powerful, screaming at her to be loosed. She wasn't sure how much longer she could hold it.

"Sergeant Hodges, can you get him around the waist and pick him up so it will take the weight off his arms, please?"

Hodges bit his lip in consternation even as he moved to obey.

"You'll need to steady him while I do; from those marks, his ribs are probably broken too, and God only knows what else. *Son of a bitch!*"

She silently nodded her understanding and he complied, and when, as gently as he could, he hoisted the smaller man's body up a

325

few inches, the prisoner moaned with a horrible, gargling noise. Instantly, Samantha was beside him, her hand on his chest, trying futilely to find a spot that wasn't bruised.

"It's me, Tommy; you're safe now. We're going to take you home."

The former biker and Green Beret moaned again, head lolling in semi-consciousness as he wheezed, and she put her arms around him and offered him what comfort she could until they came with the bolt cutters and a stretcher and the Confederates carried him outside with the rest.

Seeing the prisoners, and the abandoned stun guns, clubs, and water boards, and the cells with bloody floors, Samantha felt the thing still rising inside her, waxing stronger and stronger. Another part of her – her conscience, perhaps, or maybe just her sanity, tried to deny what she had seen, but she refused to let it. Taking a deep breath through her flaring nostrils, she drank in the smell of shit and piss and powder smoke, of blood and fear and death. Like oxygen to a fire, it fanned the monster's flames.

The final horror, and the last straw came when they began hauling the bodies out of the school's walk-in freezer that had been pressed into service as the prison's morgue. As a half-dozen stiff rubber bags were being carried by, she caught a glimpse of a familiar name marked on one of the tags wired to a zipper. Samantha stopped the ones carrying it – a man and a woman from her class – and unzipped it, revealing the smashed but still recognizable features of eighty year-old Reverend John Gibson. Despite having only met him once, she recognized him immediately; he was the marker of the happiest day of her life. He was the preacher who had married her and Frank, and had exposed the Feds for what they were by allowing the showing of the journalism club's film in his church hall.

The monster rose up inside her and roared through her veins; it felt as if thick steel doors weighing tons apiece began slamming in her mind with great, echoing bangs, and her features began to change as she unzipped the bag further and looked over the carnage on the old man's body; his gray chest hair failed to conceal either the welts, bruises, electrical burns, or the fact that his chest had been crushed so badly his ribs were actually sunk in.

Suddenly the fire was gone and replaced with something far worse. It was as if someone had doused her soul with ice water, and she felt as cold as the refrigerated corpse before her. Her blue eyes seemed to freeze, and turned as frigid and hard, and everything became as clear as crystal. Her conscience fled squealing in terror as she gave up all control to the cold-blooded stranger that had taken her over – not that she had any choice now, even if she would have cared to resist.

With remarkable calmness, she pulled the zipper up, and when she raised her head, everyone watching blanched at the look on her face; several took an involuntary step back. She was not the same woman who had walked into the building.

"Sergeant Hodges." Her voice was cold and sharp, like a straight razor, and the big skinhead automatically straightened to attention at the sound.

"Ma'am?"

"Find some rope."

He bared his teeth with satisfaction.

"Yes, ma'am!"

Less than ten minutes later, the caravan pulled out, almost two hundred people, two Humvees and one bus stronger than when they came in. Samantha chose to ride in the bus with the wounded and the dead. As the driver put it in gear and it began to roll forward, there were cries and pleas for mercy and a scrambling of booted feet on the roof: a sliding, thumping sound that rapidly lessened as the bus continued to move. Finally it ceased all together as the last soldier ran out of roof and hung by his neck from the spreading limbs of the big oak in the schoolyard, kicking and thrashing alongside his seven comrades.

Samantha looked back until they were out of sight, burning the image of their deaths into her memory in order to make the other, much worse memories of this day a little more bearable.

Justice is done; I just wish there were other things that could be undone!

Finally the thing inside her subsided, and she turned back to the front and ordered the driver to let her know if there were any problems. Her conscience was just beginning to chance a quick peep over her shoulder, but she'd deal with that later; there would always time for the dead. For now, she had some things to do for the living that wouldn't be easy.

It was hard for her to get through the bus, not just because of her bloated belly or the blood-slick floor, but because of the wounded filling that floor and seats, and Doctor Grissom and the hastily-appointed medics scrambling every direction, running first to one, then to another. The dead themselves were out of the way for the most part; they had had no choice but to jam the bodies the five guerrillas and three prisoners killed in the attack, along with six more corpses from the school, beneath the seats like so much luggage. It seemed that every rescued prisoner they passed recognized her and reached for her, grabbing her hands and pawing at her clothes, murmuring "Thank you," and "God bless you." She absently returned their touches, but her smile was distant and fragile. Part of it was what was in their eyes; they had all seen what she had done, and they looked at her with a mixture of adoration and fear, as if she were a dangerous supernatural being. She even heard the whispered words, "Valkyrie" and "Fury" behind her, comparing her with the savage and supernatural women warriors.

Supernatural – I wish! Then it wouldn't hurt so bad!

Suddenly a hand gripped hers and wouldn't let go, and Samantha looked into the face of the mother who had accosted her outside the prison.

"Did you find...my baby?" she asked in a hesitant, very tiny voice, and Samantha felt like her own heart was going to shatter into a million pieces. Gripping the woman's hands in hers, she forced herself to look into her eyes.

"No," and she hurried on as the woman's composure began to come apart, "but I think we can find her. Corporal Graham questioned the prisoners..."

Samantha didn't know how Graham had extracted the information so quickly; considering that, when he reported back, he was splashed with fresh blood that hadn't been there before, she didn't care to imagine it despite knowing she had been responsible for it. And, after all she had seen in that man-made hell, she didn't really care.

"...and they told him that your child had been sent to the State Child Protective Services for adoption. I'll get my people on it as quickly as we get back."

"Please...find her! Please!"

Samantha nodded. "I'll do my best. I promise."

"Thank you," the woman whimpered, and pressed her lips to the back of Samantha's bloodstained hand over and over again before she could gently work herself loose and move on.

Dr. MacFie didn't look up from his seat as she passed. He held the little girl they had rescued from Rosenberg on his lap, while Thumper sat on the floor at their feet, his bloody jaw propped up on her leg. Even though the girl was stroking the big dog's head, Samantha could tell it was a mechanical reflex rather than a conscious decision. Both she and her comforter who held her had fixed eyes that seemed to be looking at something far away.

She found Mike Dayton half-sitting, half-lying in the floor about halfway down the bus. He held Kerrie's blanket-wrapped body in his arms, whimpering and rocking her like a baby. Forcing herself to hold her own emotions in check, she stopped beside him and put a hand on his shoulder.

"Did you tell them anything, Mike? Tell me now if you did; there's no shame, but I need to get the information to what's left of our people right now, so we can minimize any damage."

His voice was slurred through his split lips and broken teeth as he told her the story, his eyes continuously jerking back towards the body. When he finished, Samantha squeezed his arm in sympathy.

"Okay, that's all I need to know for now. I know you loved her, and I know for a fact she loved you. Go ahead and grieve for her, and get it all out; we're going to need you soon." She paused and swallowed hard before putting her mouth to his ear and whispering,

"Please, Mike, grieve for me too! I loved her too, but I can't...not yet, not until we're out of danger."

He put his hand on hers and squeezed painfully tight. "I know, Sammie, and believe me, I can grieve enough for the both of us." As if to prove his point, he dropped his face to the corpse of the only woman he had ever loved and wept bitterly.

It was Donna's turn next. The bus turned onto a secondary road; now it was bumping along so hard Samantha had to fight to keep her balance, and to keep from stepping on the wounded that littered the aisles or on the frantic people working on them until she reached the girl's side. Donna heard her grunt as she clumsily knelt down.

"S-Sammie?"

She forced herself to smile for Donna once again as she took her hand. "Hey, how are you feeling?"

"I-I'm okay now. I just...you know." She burst into tears and Samantha gathered her into her arms.

"I know, Donna. I know."

"It's not just me! Tommy...they..."

"Yeah," Samantha told her softly, "I know that too."

Donna swallowed hard, afraid to ask but desperately needing to know.

"How is he?"

Sammie wondered how much to tell her, and decided to settle for the truth. If nothing else, giving Donna someone else to think about might help take a little piece of her mind off what had been done to her. "He's hurt badly; one of his legs has a compound fracture, and his ribs and some of his facial bones are broken. I'm worried about his hands; they hung him in cuffs for a long time, and the circulation was cut off."

Donna had been through their first aide classes, and knew what that meant.

"Oh, God! I-is he going to lose them?"

"I don't know, Donna; I just don't know yet." She sighed. "He's also got pneumonia, and the doctor pumped him full of antibiotics for that after drawing some fluid off his lungs. He hopes the medicine will help retard any possible gangrene as well."

330

Swallowing hard, she finally told her what she needed to know. "It's bad, honey; right now he's fighting for his life."

Donna tried to rise even as she gasped at her own pains. "He needs me! I have to go to him!"

Samantha nodded and began helping her into a sitting position just as Cynthia made her way to them and knelt down, the muzzle of the MP5 slung over her shoulder bumping against the rubber matt that covered the floor. Samantha had noticed her stopping beside several of the freed women prisoners and questioning them briefly, then handing most of them something.

"I've got something for you, Donna. You're not pregnant or allergic to any medicine, are you?"

"No."

"Here you go then." She offered the injured girl a pill. "This will help you feel better."

"What is it?"

"It helps the body fight off any infections that might be in it so you'll heal faster. My mother gave them to me. Open wide."

Looking like a helpless baby bird, Donna obeyed, and the hard eyed younger girl quickly popped the pill into her mouth and held a plastic bottle of water to her lips to allow her to wash it down. All the while, Cynthia ignored Samantha's increasingly suspicious look, and helped assist the girl to her feet. Between the two of them, they maneuvered her to where Tommy lay wheezing on his stretcher, heavily bandaged and staring blankly through his slitted left eye – the one that wasn't completely swollen shut – in the direction of the vehicle's ceiling, gurgling while he breathed and looking at nothing. He never moved or acknowledged their presence when they lowered Donna beside him.

"Tommy? Baby, are you alright?"

When he didn't answer, she simply lay down beside him and held him, offering what comfort she could. Samantha had to turn away to keep from completely losing it.

As soon as she stepped away from the pair and got Cynthia off to one side, she demanded to know what she had given her.

Cynthia looked at her commanding officer, and her voice was flat. "Don't ask a question unless you're really sure you want to hear the answer."

"I'm sure; now what did you just give her?"

"A morning-after pill."

"An *abortion pill*?"

"Yeah; my mother got one for me the day after I was raped, and I've carried a stock of them with me ever since, just in case of emergency, which this obviously is."

"Damn it, Cynthia, you know – "

"Yeah, I know, just like you know it's legal by CAP's own law to abort in case of rape! Donna's broken now, and she doesn't need her condition aggravated by carrying some son of a bitch rapist's bastard around inside her for nine months!"

"You lied to her!"

"I didn't lie to her; that's an infection! It's not a baby; it's a freaking disease, an involuntary STD, just like I have!" Cynthia finally let out the rage of her own she'd been hiding, and it rolled from her like a powerful wave, a flood that was impossible to hold back any more. Her voice never rose above a hissed whisper, but it was all the more powerful for all that. "How about it, Sammie? You want her to be reminded of what happened for the rest of her life, every time she looks at that little bastard – probably half-nigger – that one of those pieces of shit probably planted inside her?"

"That's not the point! That's Donna's call, not yours!"

"No, damn it! It's my call because I understand! I've been there!" She punctuated her sentence by slamming her thumb against her own chest with force enough to bruise. "And I'll tell you something else: I hate a rapist! I'd kill him, I'd kill his shit kid, I'd kill his parents, and if I could go back in time, I'd kill every one of his freaking ancestors, and it wouldn't bother me *one-damned-bit*!" She realized she was literally slobbering in her fury as she recalled her own pain, and calmed only slightly, wiping the strings of spit from her chin with the back of her left hand. "That's a sacrifice I'm willing to make for her, or any woman who's a victim; she didn't ask for this! She doesn't owe it to those sons of bitches to pass on their genes! To Hell with them! Besides, do you think she's capable of choosing *anything* right now? Look at her!" She paused a moment, then gestured at the first aid kit sitting nearby. "Tell you what; you're her friend. Do you want to go and tell her? There's probably a bottle of ipecac in the first aid box; go ahead and give it to her, and she'll throw that pill right back up, and then she and Tommy can have a little reminder of all the hell she went through following her around for the rest of her life. You're in command, so it's your call; what do you want to do? What's best for her?"

Samantha thought about it for just a moment, then simply went back to Donna, patted her again, and told her to rest quietly, call out if she needed anything, and everything would be all right

Mike had finally laid Kerrie's stiffening body down. He had cried himself dry, but he hadn't gotten her out of his system. He supposed that would never happen, even if he lived to be a hundred. For that matter, he never wanted to.

"Are you all right?"

He turned his red eyes to Cynthia, who had come and squatted beside him, and he tried to manage a smile, but it didn't work very well.

"No. You?"

"No," she said, shaking her head. "She was my best friend. She was the last one of my friends from school I had left."

"I know. Here; sit." He scooted more tightly towards the body and patted the floor space beside him. She looked at him with something almost like fear in her eyes and then obeyed.

"I already miss her," she finally admitted in a barely audible quivering voice.

"Yeah," he said, taking her hand and gripping it reassuringly, squeezing Kerrie's sticky, drying blood between their palms. "Me too."

"I know. She loved you; you know that, don't you? She really did." Cynthia shook her head. "You were her first real love. She told me that."

"And she was mine. Being a nerd in school wasn't conducive to much of a social life, and after I was crippled...well..." He sighed, and then admitted his secret. "Where I had the nerve damage from the broken back, I'm not always sexually...functional."

The girl's eyes widened at his painful confession. "But...Kerrie never told me that! She talked like you were the greatest lover in the world. Oh, she never got real specific, I mean, but listening to her talk about it was like reading one of those bodice-ripper romance novels."

He blushed. "I appreciate her lying for me."

"I've got news for you; she wasn't lying. Anytime she was alone with you, she'd come back looking so smug, like the cat that ate the canary. Whatever parts of you did function, evidently did it pretty well." Looking at the corpse lying there, she added, "She looked so satisfied and so happy, I was a little jealous."

Mike closed his eyes and swallowed hard as he felt yet another tear he wouldn't have thought he had left slide down his cheek. "I'm jealous of her now. I'd gladly trade my life if she could just be alive again. I know it's stupid, but I prayed for that a while ago, you know? I prayed so damned *hard* that God would take me instead, that if He had to have a life, He would take mine and give it to her. And when I looked over and she wasn't sitting up and smiling, I felt...lost, like a kid that finally realizes that Santa Claus isn't coming anymore. I'd trade places with her in a heartbeat."

"No you wouldn't, not really. She's finally free from this whole damned mess, away from all this fear and pain. I would have given my life for her too, but then she would be sitting here suffering over us like we are over her. Oh God!" She finally broke down, put both hands to her face and began sobbing while her body shook violently. "I wouldn't wish that on anybody!"

Unable to console his lover anymore, Mike put his arm around her friend, pulled her close, and offered what comfort he could. Drawing her knees up tightly to her chest, Cynthia sat beside him and bawled as she rocked back and forth.

As she had done before, Samantha turned her back and refused to look at them lest she be caught up in the emotion too. There wasn't time, not yet. Later she would let it out; of that she had no doubt.

For now, they still had a long dangerous road ahead.

Suddenly, for some reason, she thought of Colonel Boggess up in the Mountain State, and wondered how his prison break was going. Closing her eyes but unable to close her ears to the moans of the wounded or her nose to the stench of spilled blood, she spent a moment in prayer that it would go a lot better than hers had.

CHAPTER 38

The Depot had been through half a dozen different agencies and names, but the people of Point Pleasant, West Virginia called it what they always had: the Navy Yard. Sandwiched between the Ohio River and the railroad on the edge of town, the government facility had been a local landmark since its construction in 1940, when the United States was already gearing up for a war its president insisted it would never be involved in. Serving only two years as a shipyard, it had been converted into a storage facility, primarily for the metallic ores and other raw materials necessary for defense. Since this latest war, however, it had stored a different product.

Squatting with his back against a bare sycamore tree in the freezing darkness, Walter Bennett lowered his night vision binoculars, and squirmed painfully, his joints stiff with cold. Hidden in the thick brush just outside the fence, he had watched the facility long enough this evening to insure that things were going as usual, at least beyond the dull roar of the emergency generators now powering the lights. He should know; he'd been watching the place for months now.

Grinning through his bristling white beard, showing his nicotine stained false teeth, the grizzled old septuagenarian trapper was, for the first time in his life, part of something much bigger than he was.

A native of the little river town, he had joined the Confederate effort early on. Over the years, he had watched everything he had valued and believed in go straight to hell, and he was thankful to finally have the chance to do something about it.

The Confederates thought he was too old to fight, so they made him their scout for that part of the state. Since he was a fixture in town, and had hunted, trapped and fished both Old Town Creek and the Ohio River that bordered the facility all his life, people were used to seeing him coming and going, to the point that the guards waved at him and often spoke to him through the fence when they saw him passing along the bank with his fishing pole or carrying a bundle of steel traps. He always waved back and smiled, often even doing a little black market trading with them, never letting them know what he really felt inside.

Small towns have few secrets. Most of the people in Point Pleasant knew there were prisoners being kept at the old Navy Yard now. Civilian internees, they called them; they weren't guerrillas – those went to the hard core interrogation facilities – but rather their families and friends, labor union activists who failed to toe the line, or anyone else that wasn't a fighter, but just suspicious. For the most part, the town's people didn't like it, but nobody talked about it; to do so could be damned unhealthy.

Walter knew just how unhealthy; he had watched and listened for long enough to know what went on in there, beyond the chain link topped with barbed wire. With the aid of the powerful binoculars, night vision gear, and parabolic microphones issued to him, he knew more about the place than anyone who hadn't been inside it, and more than most of the local civilian contractors who were occasionally brought in to do maintenance.

For instance, he knew which three of the twenty-nine buildings – ranging from giant Quonset huts to assorted wood and metal pole buildings to small shacks – held the approximately one hundred inmates. He knew where the punishment cage was, in the center of the compound where it couldn't be seen from outside the fence, where they locked prisoners naked for hours or, occasionally, days, exposing them to the elements in the name of discipline. He also knew where the little wooden building was, behind an ore pile near the creek bank, where groups of soldiers frequently took their female charges for a little forced 'R&R.'

In fact, five of them – including the guard assigned this section of the fence – were in there right now. He'd seen them enter with a shackled teenaged girl and a woman who looked to be about thirty. Over the laughter and grunts, he could hear the girl crying, and the woman's pained voice telling her to try not to think about it, but just give them what they wanted so they don't hurt her anymore.

The old man's blue eyes blazed in the darkness as he motioned behind him.

I got a surprise for you sons of bitches!

338

Seeing the trapper's gesture through the greenish glow of his night vision, Jake Boggess nodded at the other eleven men in the pair of big johnboats moored against the bank under a drift pile, covered with sticks and dead weeds like a duck blind. The boats had been concealed the best part of a mile up the creek days before, and had been brought down again to ferry them across after they made their way through the uninhabited farm land on the creek's far side. Quickly but carefully, so as not to make any noise or fall into the freezing water, they crept up the bank, weapons in hand. The incline was steep and slick, so they went up by keeping their free hands on the ground or grasping at the bare hardwood saplings that grew thick on the slope.

Lowering himself all the way to the ground as he neared the top, Jake crawled up beside the old man.

"Where're the guards?"

"Bastards are having a party with a couple of girls in that shack yonder," he whispered, jerking his head in the direction of the once-white building with the peeling paint. "This would be a good time to take 'em."

"Not yet; we haven't heard from Putney, and the Sergeant of the Guard may come along, checking on them."

"Not likely; he's in there with 'em."

"Shit." As he did out of habit whenever he was frustrated, Jake scratched furiously at his scalp. With most of the guards together in one place, there would never be a better time than the present to begin securing the facility, but Putney hadn't given the word yet...

Damn it to hell, Putney will either be here or he won't!

"Alright, no more waiting. Let's take them, but remember – *quietly!*"

In the darkness, his team silently nodded, and began sliding under the fence. It wasn't hard; due to the burrowing activity of a particularly energetic groundhog, the bank had begun eroding there. The old man had discovered it weeks ago, trapped and ate the groundhog, and, since then, had gradually been hollowing its hole out more with each visit, so much so that now, even with the frozen ground, it took less than two minutes' work with an entrenching tool, and they were slipping under the wire, crawling on their bellies like snakes. In their dark clothes, they were no more than passing shadows.

Assembling around the shack, they looked at Jake for their orders.

"Well?" Walter whispered.

"Well nothing. You said there were five men and two women in there; how many more guards are on duty?"

"There're two more outside, but they're down towards the other end."

"Alright, then; we'll wait."

"Wait? Those women – "

"I know about those women, damn it!" In fact, he could clearly hear the younger one sobbing hysterically over the masculine jeers, shouts of encouragement, and the occasional sound of a blow, and it grated on his very soul. "There's no way we can take that room full of people quietly, without someone yelling or shooting or something; there're no windows, and that door's only big enough for one of us to get through at a time. We're going to have to wait until they start leaving, and then we'll take them out, one at a time."

"I can't stand listening to – " one of his men began, but Jake rounded on him, grabbed him by the collar, and pulled him close, shoving his face almost against that of his subordinate.

"If those women can stand to have it done to them, I reckon you can stand to listen to it! We've got almost a hundred more people to worry about too; now take your positions and shut the hell up!"

They did so, splitting up to cover all the routes the soldiers might conceivably take as they departed, but they couldn't block their ears from the sounds coming from inside. Their wait was only a few minutes, but it seemed like a very long time.

The Sergeant of the Guard was first out; silhouetted in the light of the door, they could see he was tall and skinny, with a satisfied grin that seemed to shine in the darkness. He carried an M4 on a sling over his shoulder, and he was heavily bundled against the cold.

Pulling his jacket tighter around his neck, he had taken half a dozen steps directly away from the door, and was just passing the corner of another building when they were on him. One hit him high, clamping a hand over his mouth, and the other right afterwards hit him low, wrapping his legs in a bear hug and taking him off his feet. Before he fully realized what was happening, he felt something sharp and cold slide under his chin and a sharp pain in his throat.

Both men lay on top of him, holding him still under their weight to keep him from making too much noise. The knife man kept his mouth covered while he continued sawing the blade back and forth, and the one pinning the sergeant's legs reached up and grabbed their victim's wrist, feeling until the pulse stopped. Slapping his partner to signal it was over, they dragged the body out of sight behind the nearest ore pile.

One down, four to go.

Five minutes later, the second one left: a private with a slung M16, heading the opposite direction. He was walking through a patch of shadow when a guerrilla, lying flat and concealed in it, pushed himself to his knees with one hand. His other hand held a replica of World War I trench knife with a set of brass knuckles for a grip, and, using a technique he had learned in the Marine Corps, he drove the six-inch double-edged blade upward into his target's groin, below the body armor with all the force he could muster. The man gasped and doubled over, and the guerrilla grabbed his collar and yanked him down, ripping out the knife and punching him hard between the eyes with the knucks as he bent forward. Shoving his face in the ground by jamming the back of his helmet forward, the Mountaineer finished by driving the blade into the juncture of the base of his target's skull and his spine, and the body went limp.

Number three came out only a few seconds later, before they were ready for him, but a burley rebel and former mercenary soldier who went by the moniker of "Popeye" leapt on him from behind and caught him around the neck in a figure-four chokehold: the right arm around the throat, right hand gripping the left forearm, and left hand against the back of the enemy's head at its juncture with the neck. A Jujutsu black belt, the guerrilla could have choked him unconscious

341

in less than a handful of seconds, but didn't want to wait that long. Instead, he jerked the man backwards while throwing his own feet out behind him, resulting in his target landing hard on his back while Popeye landed on his stomach, still firmly attached. The lock gave the neck nowhere to go, and the dull crack of it breaking was almost as loud as their mutual impact with the ground.

A few minutes later, when the last two exited with the shackled, stumbling, softly crying women, the guerrillas were waiting on either side of the building. The first the soldiers knew of something wrong was when the one in the rear was hit across the throat with the sharpened edge of an entrenching tool swung in two strong hands. Even as a second blow finished the decapitation while he lay on the ground, his partner was already staring wide-eyed at the gun muzzles aimed at his face.

"If you want to live, do exactly what we say!"

The women had dropped when the action started; rather, the older one had, and had pulled the younger one down with her. The skinny teenager still crouched and hid her face and shook, but the somewhat heavier-built woman rose to her knees and met their eyes with trepidation, but the beginnings of hope. Despite her obvious fear and the disheveled condition of her dark hair, Jake could tell she was quite a looker, or would be once she had a chance to clean herself up.

"Don't worry, ma'am," he told her. "We're with the Confederate Army Provisional, and we're going to get you out of here."

Swallowing hard, she fought back the tears and whispered, "Thank you." Turning to the girl, she patted her on the shoulder. "It's alright, now."

Jake knelt down beside them and laid a comforting hand on the teen's back, then quickly removed it when she jumped as if she had been burned.

"Sorry..."

"She can't help it," the woman told him, protectively pulling the girl close and holding her head against her shoulder. "They've...*used* her hard...a lot."

Jake's eyes narrowed, but he kept his voice calm.

"Nobody's going to use you anymore, honey, either one of you." Looking at the woman, he asked, "Are you all kin?"

"No, not really, but don't have any family, and I try to look out for her." Caressing the girl's back, she added, "She's only fifteen."

He heard the nearest guerrilla, who had a daughter of his own that age, swearing violently under his breath and nodded his own agreement with the sentiments. Still, after all she'd been through, the older of the pair was obviously a strong one.

"I'm Jake Boggess, ma'am. It's a pleasure to meet you."

The younger one raised her head and fearfully glanced at him. "I've heard of you, s-sir," she managed before looking away again.

"I have too," the woman told him. "This is Tiffany Johnson, and I'm Philindy Storm. Thanks for coming."

Jake raised his eyebrows as he took the hand she offered.

Philindy? I never heard that one before; I take reckon her dad must've wanted a boy.

"You're more than welcome. Are you both able to walk?"

After glancing at the girl, the woman answered in the affirmative.

"Alright then. Now this is going to be hard on you, but we're going to have to leave you shackled for just a little while. I need you two to help us get everybody else out."

"I just want to go home!" the girl wailed, or started to, but Jake instantly clapped one hand over her mouth to stifle her cry. Meeting her eyes, he put his the index finger of his other hand to his lips. As soon as he felt her relax, he uncovered the lower half of her face again.

"I know you do, honey," he told her, "and so does everybody else locked up in here. Everybody here wants to go home just like you do, and we're going to take them, but I need you to help me do that."

"We'll help," Philindy told him, answering for both of them. "Just tell us what you want us to do."

Even as he opened his mouth to speak, Jake felt the radio on his belt vibrating against his thigh. Checking the number without answering, he saw that Putney, finally, was on his way.

"What in the hell?"

Darrel Putney looked at the civilian security guard in the shack at the front gate, who was alternately glancing from him to the railroad company truck parked on the tracks that ran not twenty feet away. The vehicle had a set of hydraulically operated steel wheels on the front that were made to fit the rails, allowing it to run on the tracks exactly like a train. A trailer was hitched behind it, bearing a small front-end loader.

"Here," the disguised guerrilla told him, pointing a thick finger at the words on the official-looking work order. The reason it looked official was that it was a creation of the Mountaineer's own intelligence officer in Richwood, made some months before in preparation for this raid. "We've been ordered to sever the spur going into your depot."

"Why?"

"It's a vulnerability. My supervisor told me Homeland Security had contacted him in person just this evening; with everything gone to crazy like it has, they're afraid the terrorists will steal a train and drive it right into your facility here. That chain-link gate you've got across there won't even slow it down, so we've been ordered to take out fifty feet of track from the spur, starting at the main line. About twenty feet of that is on your side of the fence, and we need to access it. It won't take long; once we get started, we'll be out of here in three or four hours."

"I've got to call this in," he said, picking up the phone only to hear silence on the other end. "Damn it, they're still down!"

Putney knew the Depot's lines, at least, were down, because the guerrillas had severed the ones on either side of it an hour before.

"Look, I ain't trying to rush you or nothing, but I'd like to get home sometime. The sooner we get started, the sooner we can get the hell out of here."

"I'm sorry, but I can't open that gate without authorization. I'd call the commander, but he's in bed. Maybe I can get hold of the Sergeant of the Guard..."

As the guard picked up his radio, Putney turned to look behind him at the men in the truck. One of them, a radio to his ear, gave him the thumbs-up.

"Well, alright," Putney said as he slipped the silenced Ruger .22 automatic out of his coveralls and put three quick rounds through the guard's skull; the trio of dull coughs was largely absorbed by the walls of the guard shack and the sound of the truck engine outside.

Before the body could bleed all over the floor, he grabbed it by the collar, dragged it to the steps that led downward to the tiny bathroom beneath the shack, and gave it a shove, sending it flopping limply down the concrete passage until it came to rest in a heap at the bottom.

Already two more men were out of the truck. While Putney fished the correct key off the board hanging behind the desk and flicked the alarm system to OFF, one of them stripped off his coveralls to reveal a security uniform identical to that of the dead guard, while the other wore a set of US Army fatigues and carried a rifle.

"Get that cleaned up," Putney growled as he left, gesturing toward the steps. Even as he spoke, the guerrilla in fatigues was already working, dragging the corpse into the privy and out of sight from anyone of might come in.

In a moment, the truck had reversed and was rolling backwards down the track towards the spur. They made another call on the way, and two more identical trucks with similarly loaded trailers, parked on the tracks a mile away, just past the outskirts of town, came rolling down to meet them.

Corporal Fong looked up from the porno magazine he was reading at the annoying sound of the buzzer. Leaning forward, he pressed the speaker button on his desk.

"Yes, sir?"

"It's Gillespie and Galer returning the prisoners. Open up."

"Hang on." Fong gave the monitor a brief glance and saw Gillespie with the two women and another soldier he took to be

Galer on the security camera, so he saw no reason not to press the button that popped the electronic lock on the door.

The two women entered first, their shackles clinking, followed by the soldiers, who left the door open behind them as they stepped to the left.

"Hey, man! It's cold out there! Shut the freaking – "

A third soldier stepped around the door, and Fong just had time to realize he didn't recognize him when his voice was cut off by a pair of silenced .22 rounds that entered his skull. Even before his body could decide which was to fall, the shooter had darted into the room past the others, jumped at the dying man and kicked him out of his chair on the fly, away from the control board that held the alarm button, and into the floor. Just to make sure, he shoved the muzzle almost against the back of Fong's head and pulled the trigger once more.

"Alright," Jack barked from his position behind Gillespie, the 18" barrel of his Ithaca Model 37 12 gauge shotgun pressing tightly against the back of the soldier's neck, held there by the piece of wire looped around his throat and tied the barrel just behind the muzzle. An M16 or M4 would have been easier to attach due to the perforated flash hider, but the shotgun had a greater psychological effect; a brave man might accept being shot, but few people would find the thought of being literally decapitated quite so acceptable. Just as he had suspected, it had insured the soldier's full cooperation so far. "Where are the keys to those cells?"

He punctuated his request by shoving the muzzle tighter, and Gillespie frantically yelled, "Above the desk! The pegboard!"

"Possum – "

"I'm already there!" the guerrilla who had shot Fong returned and snatched up the indicated ring. So far, despite the slight change in plan, everything had gone like clockwork, but that didn't mean there was time to poke around. They still had two other buildings to enter.

The entry into the two other prisoner barracks went off without a hitch, other than the teenaged girl, Tiffany, having an emotional meltdown that left her so hysterical that all she could do was curl into a ball and cry, so they modified their plan slightly. Still using the same soldier, along with the lone Philindy Storm playing the part of a prisoner being transferred, they talked their way inside. Three more guards were dead, and they had one more prisoner...more specifically, *one* prisoner, since Jack summarily shot the original one that had participated in the rapes of Philindy and Tiffany once he had outlived his usefulness. Other than the identity of one particular liberated inmate, which surprised the hell out of Jack and made him think about what a small world this war actually was, there were really no surprises beyond the startling fact that the mission had worked pretty much as he had planned.

Putney hadn't been idle either. Two of his men, in stolen US uniforms and night vision gear, took out the other two perimeter guards by the simple expedient of strolling up to them and shooting them in the head with silenced pistols before they realized that the approaching soldiers weren't part of their unit. Meanwhile, the rest of his team began setting the charges.

Boggess had determined to close this camp once and for all, and to do it with a bang: a controlled bang, granted, because he didn't want to damage the civilian homes just across the narrow blacktop road opposite the tracks from the facility, but a bang nonetheless. Each building containing cells got its own charge: a five gallon gas can sitting on top of a block of TNT with an electronic detonator inside.

The personnel barracks got special treatment; instead of attempting an entry into a building full of sleeping soldiers with rifles by their bunks, the Confederates set a jerry can of gas a couple of feet in front of the entry door on either end of the Quonset hut with a claymore mine behind each one to push the fire in the direction they wanted it to go.

The heavy equipment on the trailers was simply dumped where it was at; they needed the space.

They waited until they were ready to go before physically releasing the prisoners, as fearful, traumatized people are unpredictable. The guerrillas unlocked only two cells at a time, and waited until those occupants had been escorted out of the building before opening the next pair. Still, the loading took less than five minutes, and with everyone accounted for, the jam-packed trucks pulled, beds and trailers full, out onto the tracks, rolled down the spur and out the open gate onto the main line. They barely made it to the end of the fence when Jack put his radio to his lips.

"Blow it."

Putney nodded to one of his men, who had won the poker hand they had earlier played for the privilege. He flipped a switch on the remote detonator, the night was shattered by the noise, and fire lit up the sky.

Each of the three prisoner barracks with the charges inside split open like shaken-up soda cans dropped on a sharp rock, spewing flames outward and upwards.

In the guard barracks, the spray of steel ball bearings from the Claymores tore through each end of the building, carrying walls of fire with them that rushed towards each other down the center, turning the interior into an inferno of flames and flying steel. Most of the soldiers inside were killed in the initial blast or died soon afterwards in the conflagration that followed, but three managed to escape via the windows, although one was badly burned.

The trucks rolled on through the night, through the blacked-out town, with nothing but the their own headlights glimmering off the endless double row of rails to show the way. They crossed the track's intersection with the Viand Street, the city's main drag, and heard the sirens and saw the flickering red lights of the fire trucks rolling out of the station just a few blocks down the street; evidently one of the survivors or someone living nearby had called 911. Not that it mattered; they were clear of the intersection and around the bend before anyone saw them.

Meanwhile, the guerrillas were passing out blankets to the former prisoners, with 'blanket' being a loose term in this case, as the covering was just as likely to be a rug or roughly cut piece of old carpet. Still it was what they had, and it worked.

The trailers were full, and it was still a tight fit in the trucks; Jack was standing in the bed of the first one, leaning on the cab and facing forward despite the cold wind that stung his face and made his eyes water, when he suddenly found the female prisoner he had first met beside him. She had seen him there and worked her way forward.

"You doing okay, Philindy?"

"I am now, thanks to you." She paused, swallowing hard. "I know this must sound awful, but I wanted to thank you for killing that raping son of a bitch."

Jack had seen the mixed look of shock and gratitude on her face when he squeezed the trigger of the shotgun still wired to the soldier's neck, and, like a gory magic trick, instantly made most his head disappear. The only reason their other prisoner was still alive was because the released inmates swore that the Rhode Island native had not only never mistreated them, but was sympathetic and even kind to them, as much as he was allowed to be, anyway.

Jack had nodded, and said, "As you sow, so shall you reap," and then bound the greatly relieved man and brought him along.

Looking at Philindy now, he shrugged.

"Wasn't anything awful about that; I can truthfully say it was my pleasure. I'm just sorry we couldn't have done it sooner."

"Yeah, me too...like months ago."

He noticed she had one of the blankets wrapped around her shoulders, but was still shivering violently. Jack expected it was as much from stress as from cold. Unfastening his coat, he held the right side open in invitation.

"If I'm not being too forward, you're welcome to snuggle up in here if you're cold."

She did so, and slipped in facing him. He wrapped the edges of his coat as far as he could around her shoulders as she clung tightly to him.

"Thank you," she whispered. She had been brave as long as she had to be, but now she could feel again, and it really hurt.

"It's dark, and nobody can see," he whispered back. "Go ahead and let it out, if you want to."

She wanted to and she did, sobbing and clinging to him with her face buried against his chest as their little convoy rolled on.

CHAPTER 39

What have I done? What have I become? Have they finally made me what they are?

We're here.

After winding through a maze of pitch dark back roads and hours of fear, it was almost eleven o'clock that night by the time the remainder of Samantha's convoy came to a halt at its point of origin in North Carolina. Still, under Suggs' direction, they were ready for them, and men and women – mostly elderly, barely pubescent, or handicapped – came pouring out to help. A lot of them couldn't even handle one end of a stretcher by themselves, but they could pat shoulders, hold hands and give comfort. That meant a lot.

"Leave all cameras with Private Dover," she heard herself calling out. Most of the guerrillas had carried them, and the pictures and video they had taken of the interrogation facility would make for invaluable propaganda...and to justify to others the thing she knew she could never justify to herself. She hadn't forgotten her job, but she would review the photos and footage later, much, much later. Not now; she'd had enough for one day.

Looking at the bodies stuffed beneath the seats, and the floor almost awash in blood, she would have grimaced if she hadn't been afraid she would shatter with the effort.

I've had enough for ten lifetimes, a hundred! Oh God, Frank, I need you so badly right now...

Doctor Grissom brushed by her without a word and stepped out the door of the bus like an automaton, mechanically giving orders and organizing the triage nurses and medics. He was a man whose faith in the country he once believed in with all his heart had just been brutally ripped away, leaving a hole in his soul he refused to think about. Actually, he was so tired he couldn't think about much of anything at all, but he kept moving by sheer force of will because he was needed. Jennie Grissom walked by his side, helping where she could but somehow afraid to be separated from him again.

Biscoe and the three Irregulars were literally staggering, and Lucky Charlie requisitioned a couple of bottles of clear homemade whiskey from somewhere, handed it to them, and ordered them to go find some quarters and not stop until it was gone. He knew from hard experience that, barring medical sedation, it was the only way they would unwind enough to get the sleep they desperately needed. With them taken care of, he went back to giving orders in a much quieter and less profane fashion than usual. He had proven that what was left of him was still a soldier, and he was immensely satisfied, but very, very tired.

Doctor MacFie painstakingly climbed down off the bus, carrying the skinny twelve year-old girl Thumper had rescued in his arms, and she clung to him like she never intended to let go. She was wearing his shirt, and his grizzled chest hair fluffed as his skin goose-pimpled unnoticed in the cold. His face was pale, his lips set, and his eyes stared at something far away that no one else could see. He finally understood the cost of freedom in reality, rather than academically. More importantly, he finally understood what it really meant to lead.

A bloody bandage around his head, a proudly grinning Stanley Bauer and his grandson carried the stretcher with Tommy on it. Donna limped along beside him, telling her lover it would be alright, but the bruised, swollen slits of his eyes refused to look at anything but the empty, black, night sky. They passed two of the Tarheels heading towards the bus with a wheelchair, and Samantha saw them coming. She turned to the intelligence officer.

"It's time, Mike. They're coming to take you inside." She nodded at Kerrie's body. "Somebody will be back to take care of her in a few minutes."

"I'll stay with her until then," Cynthia added, her voice breaking ever so slightly, having cried herself out. "I promise."

Mike looked one last time at the silent, blanket wrapped form beside him, and nodded before turning his eyes back to Samantha.

"I reckon they can take care of it all, Sammie. Go to Frank...right now. Please."

It was her turn to nod in weary agreement. She briefly hugged him, then Cynthia, and turned to go. As she stepped off the bus and in the direction of the building, her legs were already wobbling, and her body shaking. Wide-eyed people nodded respectfully at her and most of those in her way quickly stepped aside, but thank God nobody said a word.

Slipping in the door between two stretchers, she headed straight down the hall, her boots sticking to the floor and pulling away with every squelching step, leaving tracks of blood behind her. Finally at her husband's door, she paused to take a single deep breath in a futile attempt to pull herself together, and opened it.

There was Frank in his bed, his eyes bandaged but wide awake and waiting, and his old .45 lying un-holstered on the sheets covering his stomach, a cold steel security blanket ready for action despite his blindness. Billy was standing on one side with his shotgun at port arms, and a heavily bandaged Danny Drucci was in a wheelchair on the other, an M16 lying across the armrests. She saw that both men were hung with pistols and grenades as well, ready, willing and able to protect their leader at any cost. She wearily nodded her approval, and mouthed a silent but heartfelt 'thank you.'

Although sightless, her husband somehow sensed who it was, and swiveled his head in her direction.

"Sammie?" he croaked.

"I'm here, Frank." Her voice was already starting to break, and Frank turned his swollen face towards their friends.

"Billy, Danny, would you all mind going outside and watching the door, and make sure we're not disturbed?"

The giant grinned through his beard and patted Frank's shoulder. "Count on it, bro," he said, and paused only to hug Sammie tightly before helping Danny up and closing the door behind them as they left.

As soon as he heard it shut, Frank blindly held out both arms, and Sammie went to him, sitting in the chair beside his bed and leaning over him, laying her head on his tightly-bandaged chest as he held her. It hurt, but it felt too good having her there after fearing he might lose her for him to ever complain.

"Frank...Kerrie's..."

She couldn't finish, but she didn't have to; from the tone of her voice, he knew.

"Tell me."

She told him the story of the raid, of the charge she led and why, of the people who died, of what she found and what she did. It all came pouring out, and he said nothing but the occasional word of encouragement to go on.

"Kerrie..." she whimpered through her tears that wouldn't seem to stop.

"I'm sorry, Sammie; I'm so sorry."

She knew that; even if she didn't know him, the catch in his voice was a dead giveaway.

"I'm the one that's s-sorry," she suddenly wailed. "She died because I...I screwed up! I was assigned the gate and...I didn't stay!"

She felt him shaking his head.

"No; things just happen, sometimes. It was just her time." He had to pause for just a moment before going on. "You did good, Sammie; you did real good. You did everything right; if you hadn't led that charge to get our people moving, the whole thing would have turned into a slaughter. I'd like to think I'd have had the presence of mind to have done the same, but I'm not sure I could have done half as well as you did."

"But...what I did at the end...I murdered those..."

"No!" he said so sharply she jumped. "You didn't murder anyone; you executed monsters who had forfeited their right to live!"

"But I had no right..."

"Let me ask you something, Sammie; why did you do it?"

"Why? Why, after what they did to those prisoners, to Tommy and Donna and Reverend Gibson and – "

"You didn't do it for Kerrie?"

"No, she was killed in the fight, but – "

He interrupted her again. "And you didn't do it for you?"

She stopped, her voice locking up. Mouth gaping, she pondered what he had just said, searching her soul for the honest answer as to whether it had been in revenge for her own torture, and it surprised her when it came.

"No...I didn't. I-I really didn't!" That was true, she realized, but she was still determined to punish herself, because she couldn't bring herself to believe the hanging had been right. "But I was able to do it *because* of me!"

"Could you have done it before you were abused?"

"No, of course not, but – "

"Then who gave you the ability to do that?"

She struggled over the words before they came of their own accord. "They did."

"That's right; they did. They created this damned bloody world we're stuck in, and we adapted to it in order to live. That's their fault, Sammie; not yours."

"You don't understand! I don't want to be this way!"

"Do you think I do?" he asked quietly, and she stared for a moment.

"What do you mean, you? You wouldn't have hung them, and don't tell me you would've!"

"No, I wouldn't have; after what they did to Tommy, to Donna, to all those men and women and little kids in that place, I would have probably brought around the damned flame thrower and burned the sons of bitches alive: every last one of them!"

She had never heard so much savagery in her husband's voice, and she was frightened by what was suddenly so obviously hiding inside under his cool, un-rippled surface.

"You wouldn't have..."

"Yes, I would! I can deal with people dying in combat; at least that's an honest death. But what they did to you – when they did it to you – they did it to me too in the process, just like they did it to Cynthia, just like they've done it to every Southerner who's seen the things they've done to our people. They were the ones who raised the black flag, and we're the ones who have to fight under it. If they wanted mercy, then they should have given it!

"As for what you did – for everything you did – that was *right*!" His voice mellowed, and his swollen lips twisted in a semblance of a smile. "I'm proud of you."

She cried for a long time, both at his harsh words of comfort...

And for the part of us we've both lost!

DAY 333

CHAPTER 40

Later that night – actually early the next morning – still unable to sleep despite the crushing fatigue, Samantha debriefed him while lying beside him, clutching his hand for comfort, sobbing while she relayed everything in greater detail, including Cynthia's passing out the pills.

He was quiet for a few moments, thinking about it.

"She didn't make the *right* decision, but she made the only decision she could've made, just like you did by not saying anything about it. When you can't do what's right, I reckon you do what you have to and let the chips fall where they may. God knows I've done enough of that, way too much to criticize her for it, anyway. I'll talk to her tomorrow, and make sure she's alright."

"Frank?" She swallowed hard, frightened to ask the question that had been burning inside her for months now: a question whose answer she wasn't at all sure she was prepared to hear. "How come you never asked me if I had been...raped when I was a prisoner?"

"I told you whenever you wanted to talk about it, I was ready to listen, and that still goes."

"I wasn't," she told him quickly. "They were threatening to, and they came close, but it didn't happen. I promise, Frank! I swear to God, they didn't..."

Her voice choked off with emotion, desperately wanting him to believe her, and he stroked her hair.

"It's okay, honey; it's okay. It's also a relief; at least that's one thing you didn't have to go through."

"But you couldn't know that!"

"True. Actually, I thought maybe they had – hell, to be honest, I was pretty sure they had – but you didn't want to tell me. I can understand why, but I want you to know it wouldn't have made me love you any less. It wouldn't have been something *you* did, but something done to you. It wasn't like you had any say in the matter. I don't believe in blaming the victim of anything."

"So...how did you know this baby was yours? You've never seemed to have any doubts."

"Sammie...well, it's my turn to ask a question. Do you want me to tell you what I know you want to hear, or the unvarnished truth?"

"The truth," she whispered.

"Alright. I was tempted to tell you that I just knew, but I'm afraid I was like Thomas in the Bible. I got to verify it for myself."

"I don't understand."

"You started your period the day after we rescued you. You probably don't remember because of all the painkillers we had you on; besides, you had other things on your mind." He grinned through his scabbed lips. "I don't claim to understand women, but I do know what 'that time of the month' means. I had to send Donna to buy the maxi-pads."

"I...I don't remember that." *Good Lord, I feel so stupid for even bringing it up now!*

"Like I said, I'm not surprised, the condition you were in."

"And you let me worry all this time?"

"No, *you* let you worry all this time. You could have told me when it first bothered you, just like you did tonight."

She tried to frown but couldn't quite pull it off. Besides, it wouldn't do any good; after all, he couldn't see it.

"That's typical male logic."

"Am I wrong?"

"No," she said, snuggling closer and carefully putting an arm protectively across his abdomen, "but it *is* typical. So there!"

"And I love you – so there!" he playfully mocked her and held her as best she could, and despite everything that had happened, she was content.

And then, a moment later, she was also asleep. As Frank watched the lines on her face smoothing out as she relaxed, he thanked God with all his heart that she was alive and with him once more.

358

Tommy refused to even look at Billy when he came into the room with the first light of dawn. If the big man was offended, he never showed it, but came over, pulled out a chair and set it beside the cot. The straining metal groaned in protest when he plunked his bulk down into it.

Seeing all the tubes and bandages and casts going every which way, Billy fought to keep his feelings from his face just in case Tommy did look. The makeshift medical staff had managed to get him stabilized, but just barely; worse than all the trauma, the pneumonia from inhaling the filthy water and exacerbated by the constriction on his chest from hanging in the shackles had nearly killed him; another hour and he would have been a dead man. Doctor Grissom had told Billy that his friend still showed no response to stimulation in his hands, and he wasn't certain if they could be saved. Looking at his tough little buddy lying there, looking so damned small, made the big man want to bawl out loud, but he wasn't about to let it show. That wouldn't do either of them any good.

"You've been hangin' around me too long; you're gettin' lazy, layin' around and eatin' all day. You're gonna end up as fat as I am."

Tommy still didn't respond, and his friend frowned and leaned in closer. "Look, twerp," he said, matter-of-factly, "I ain't one of the damned nurses who's come in here to mollycoddle your skinny ass. This is Billy, and so help me, if you don't look at me when I talk to you, I'm gonna grab you and shake the shit out of you 'til you do."

Knowing Billy was not only capable of it, but dumb enough to actually do it despite his condition, the little biker's eyes flicked at him involuntarily, panicked at the thought of the pain that would bring.

"I thought that'd get your attention. Now listen up, man. Donna's over there in the other room squallin' her eyes out, worried sick about you. She needs your help to pull herself outta this; she needs you to be strong for her. Every minute she waits all by her lonesome, what was done to her is gonna dig in deeper like a chigger. If somethin' don't happen pretty soon, she'll never be rid of it. She don't deserve that, and the Tommy I know wouldn't let her go

359

through it either. Even if he is a little popcorn fart, he's still too much of a man for that."

Billy recognized the pain in his friend's single visible slit of a swollen eye and felt like hell for having to cause it, but it needed to be done; this was one boil that had to be lanced. "Yeah, I know what they did to you. Them nurses around here get real cooperative when you threaten to hold them upside down and stuff their heads in the toilet. The thing is, bro, that doesn't change who you are...or what you are."

"What the hell would you know about it?" The voice was no more than a nasal mutter as it had to pass through wired jaws and split lips, reverberating through a broken nose along the way, but it was intelligible just the same.

Billy nodded inwardly with satisfaction. Even though the voice was unrecognizable, the words made it clear it was the real Tommy speaking, and that simple act had opened the door just far enough for the big man to wedge his size 14 boot into it.

"The same thing happened to me, back when I was twelve or thirteen. Not the beatin', just the bad part. It was a cousin; he talked me into comin' over to his house, and...well."

Tommy's face wore an expression of pure shock, at least as far as was possible for the battered features, as he forgot his own pain for an instant. "Billy...I didn't know; you never told me."

"No reason to," he said with a shrug, "and not somethin' I particularly wanted to go around talkin' about, you know what I mean? Still, it don't mean nothin'. I've always been a man, haven't I?"

"Yeah, but...how do you deal with it?"

"What's to deal with? Either I controlled my life, or I let what he did to me control it for me. I got bigger, lured the son of a bitch out in the middle of nowhere, out in the swamps, and beat him to death; broke every damned bone in his body. I kicked some leaves over him and they never did find him. The thing is, partner, there're two ways to go through life. Shit happens, man; that's just the way this screwed up life is. Now, you can either let that shit bury you underneath it like it wants to, or you can dig your way out of it and walk off and leave it behind you where it belongs. You're in a septic tank full of self-pity right now, clear up to your eyeballs. It's up to you if you want to climb out and get cleaned off, or if you want to keep backstrokin' around, spittin' little streams of water up in the air. None of the ones who hurt either one of us are still alive to keep us in there; ain't nothin' holding you back except yourself. A pussy might keep wallowin' in it 'cause he's afraid to do anything else, but man will climb out and go on. Are you ready to be the man or not?"

His friend lay there so long Billy was about ready to try again when he finally spoke.

"Yeah," Tommy muttered with a sigh. "Yeah, I reckon I am. I'm sorry, man, it's just...you know?"

With remarkable gentleness for one so large, Billy patted him on the shoulder as he rose to his big feet. "Hell yeah, I know, and I never told you it'd be easy; I just said it had to be." He grinned, showing his big, gap-toothed smile. "I'm gonna send her in now, and I'm gonna tell her you're askin' for her. You be ready; she's dyin' to take care of you, so let her. I mean it! Let her baby you around all she wants; it's the best thing you can do for her. By helpin' you, she'll be helpin' herself at the same time by givin' her something else to think about besides what they did to her. Hell, lay back an' enjoy it while it lasts. An' try to make yourself halfway presentable before she comes in, will ya? You look like hell."

Tommy's lips parted in as close to a grin as he could manage. "Thanks. You're a pretty good philosopher for a big dumb-ass."

"Huh!" Billy snorted, looking offended. "Some people!" He laughed as he went to get Donna.

For the first time, he had lied to his best friend; there had never been any molesting cousin, or any revenge killing. Still, it was what Tommy needed, so Billy gave it to him. He reckoned things like that were what friends are for.

DAY 334

CHAPTER 41

Russian News Service (English)

The United States Government is reeling as the images of their prison camps and torture chambers overrun by the Confederate Forces reached the Internet and the international media. Only hours before President Plants' press conference condemning the Confederate execution of several government soldiers for crimes against humanity, apparently by forces under the direct command of Colonel Samantha Gore, pictures and taped interviews with the tortured and raped Southern survivors hit the news.

Rioting has broken out in several American cities in protest of the inhumanity, and the savage military putdown of these demonstrations has only added to the damage of the US Government's reputation both at home and abroad. The President's attempt at damage control seems to be a lost cause; before his government can answer one charge, another one is brought as a seemingly endless stream of revealed brutality floods the airwaves and cyberspace...

International News Wire

In a surprise move, Russia has joined the Vatican by officially giving full diplomatic recognition to the Confederate States of America, as represented by the Confederate Army Provisional. Argentina, Chile, China, Cuba, Iran, Ireland, Italy, Libya, Macedonia, Nicaragua, North Korea, Pakistan, Serbia, Switzerland, Syria, Vietnam, and Venezuela have all indicated that they intend to follow suit. The governments of several other countries are discussing taking the action as well.

The US is still considering its response...

"Jim?"

The other man nodded.

"Fred, how are you?"

"Fine. How are the wife and kids?"

"Great, just great. Sally's in pharmacy school and Johnny is due to graduate from VMI this fall." He paused to grin. "Top of his class!"

"Outstanding! You must be proud."

"You'd better believe it, buddy."

"Lets take a walk."

The two men strolled casually along the paved pathways that crisscrossed the very expensive and exclusive West Virginia resort that had catered to the recreational needs of the Washington crowd since the nineteenth century, and whose guest books read like a who's who of American politics. Even among the other movers and shakers they passed through, however, these two men stood out. Both well into their fifties with hair beginning to gray, there was nothing outstanding about their clothing; expensive, heavy overcoats topping shirts and slacks. Rather it was in their bearing; both of their lives had revolved around the military for so long it showed in the way they walked and carried themselves. They wore their still-fit bodies like a uniform.

Looks were not deceiving; James Lannigan was a Lieutenant General, and Fredrick Hardy, who had invited him to this meeting, was a Rear Admiral, both still on active duty, and veterans of many conflicts of many kinds. They were also good friends, although due to their careers, they only saw each other on occasion. More importantly, they were both professionals, and respected one another.

They continued the small talk about families and friends as the crowd began to thin, until finally they were alone on a secluded walking path that wound through one of the manicured lawns of a less frequented part of the complex. With studied casualness,

Admiral Hardy remarked, "Things are in a hell of a shape, aren't they?"

General Lannigan snorted.

"You've got that right! Everything's going straight to hell in a hand basket, and all the while we pretend it's all hunky-dory." He smiled without humor. "I think the light at the end of this tunnel the President mentioned is a train coming, and God help us all when it gets here."

"That's what I wanted to talk to you about. I know about your involvement with Red 4."

Red 4 was the code name for a secret organization within an already secretive organization: a much-feared faction within the Special Forces community, centered around Fort Bragg. Dating back to the 80s, there had been a sort of loose-knit brotherhood of those members who were dissatisfied with the direction the country was heading – dangerously dissatisfied, and particularly so considering the training they had received and the types of information and technology they were privy to. Efforts had been made to find and root them out through several administrations, but they had only gone deeper; after all, that's what they were trained to do.

Even the most acute observer would have had trouble seeing the General's reaction: perhaps a momentary flickering of the eyes, a tiny jerk, or a sudden break in his step. Seeing it, they still wouldn't have had any idea the impact that simple statement made.

"I'm not certain I know what you mean." He enunciated each word carefully.

"I understand." Hardy took a deep breath. With what he was about to say next, not only his career and reputation hinged on how accurate his information was and how well he had judged Lannigan; his very life depended on it. "I'm part of the Secret Team, Jim."

The Secret Team was a smaller Naval counterpart to Red 4.

They walked on in silence for a few minutes. The General suddenly stopped and turned to face Hardy.

"Why bring it up?"

"I've been contacted by our counterparts in the intelligence community; you know, the dissident elements in the CIA, FBI and

NSA. The time is coming when we're going to have to make a choice, and it's coming fast."

Lannigan was still wary.

"What makes you so certain?"

"Due to my intelligence contacts, I've been privy to some data that's not commonly known. I've analyzed it inside and out, from every imaginable angle, and there's only one acceptable conclusion. We can't save all of America – it's far too late for that – but we might at least have a chance to save a piece of it – *might*."

"Good Lord, I knew it was bad, but – "

"Let's sit down."

Once they were side by side on the decorative iron bench under the bare limbs of a big white oak, Admiral Hardy continued, "You already know the economy's in the toilet and we're making no headway at all against the CAP forces; on the contrary, in fact."

"Yeah, I know. They're some smart, tough bastards, the smartest and toughest I've ever seen. That raid they did on the infrastructure, that was a master-stroke." He grinned in professional admiration. "If I had a brigade of them, I'd invade Hell, kick the Devil in the ass, and take over."

"What do you expect? They're our people after all."

Lannigan nodded. Both he and Hardy were natives of the South, from Arkansas and Virginia, respectively.

"The thing is," Hardy said, "there are some other factors that are coming into play even as we speak. I heard from a friend in Europe yesterday who owed me a favor. The EU is getting ready to launch total trade sanctions against us, probably this week."

"The hell with them! Everybody else is sanctioning us, so why not them?" After a moment, he calmed and asked, "What was the reason given?"

"War crimes, crimes against humanity, lack of freedom – the same thing we used to sanction people for. Once they saw the footage the guerrillas released from the internment centers, they went ape shit. Looks like the shoe's on the other foot now, and they intend to use the second Bush Administration's precedent for unilateral action against us, bypassing the UN Security Council, where we still have a veto."

Lannigan blew out his breath in disgust.

"This whole damned war has been a crime. It never had to happen; it should never have been *allowed* to happen."

"Well, it's about to get worse. You see, most of those electrical transformers, turbines, and other big equipment the CAP boys nailed are manufactured in Europe – *on demand* – and the EU knows it. There is a very limited stock of extras – not nearly enough – and there will be no more where they came from. What do you think the President's reaction will be?"

"We'll be ordered to take them from somewhere else to route the power back to the major cities. If they take them from the Midwest and Northwest, though, they'll start their own war and may very well join the Confederates once they start freezing their asses off; there's a distinct lack of sympathy in that region for New York and DC right now as it is.

"Because of that, we'll be ordered to take them from the Southern States, and have to fight roadside ambushes and surface to air missiles all the way through with them. It'll be ten times worse than it was for the National Guard when they first went in there: just like the second Iraq War all over again. Even worse, when we do that, every Southerner sitting there cold and in the dark is going to jump in on the side of the guerrillas if he hasn't already. We'll have everything from little kids to old men lining the highways plinking at us the whole trip with their deer rifles and shotguns for stealing their power, and everyone of them we have to kill will drive that many more into the Southern camp. Either way, we'll be left holding on to our asses with both hands; it's a no win situation. They slicked us pretty good on that one."

"That's not the worst part; China is getting ready to make a move. When the South explodes following the removal of its generation equipment, it is going to tie up literally everything we've got and then some to deal with it. We've crunched the numbers and figured the odds, and my people believe that the most likely possibility is that China will look for or even create a situation to use as an excuse to 'protect their citizens' concentrated on our West Coast, and will dispatch carrier groups to do just that, giving them the foothold they've been looking for in the Eastern Pacific."

Lannigan swore softly but with as great feeling as his friend continued.

"We're going to lose Hawaii; that's a given at this point. China has been funneling arms and assistance to the various Island independence movements for some time, and they're going to waltz right in there soon – *very* soon – and pick the island chain up. We don't have the resources to resist credibly, so we won't fight; we'll pull back to the mainland. The withdrawal is already being planned."

"So we'll meet them at the Golden Gate?"

Hardy nodded grimly.

"There or in the Alaskan oil fields, which is expected to be another primary target...that is, if the Russians don't decide to make a play for it first. We won't have any other choice then; we'll have to stop them there. The thing is, our analysts believe we'll have to use tactical nuclear weapons to accomplish that, and I think you can guess what they predict the Chinese response to be."

"Yeah, I can pretty well guess; millions dead, and that's just on our side."

"Try tens of millions, and if the rest of the Shanghai Cooperation Association allies with China, the brainiacs are not at all certain we would win such a confrontation, and almost certainly not with the troops tied up fighting the Southerners. With the Chinese Army to the west and the CAP guerrillas to the South, we wouldn't have a snowball's chance in Hell."

With the calm demeanor that had served him so well on battlefields across the world, Lannigan drew out a pair of outrageously expensive and highly illegal Cuban cigars. Handing one to Hardy, he lit up and savored the smoke before speaking.

"Is there any evidence that CAP has allied itself with the Chinese?"

"No. Oh, China gives them arms as a matter of principle and to weaken the US, though not nearly as many as they get from the Russians, the Muslims, and at least some factions within the EU and

Latin America. Hell, rumor has it that they've even cut some kind of economic deal with Japan! If Rebels actually formally ally with anybody, though, at this point the Russians are the most likely candidates. No doubt most of the CAP would prefer the EU, but the hard-right nationalists running things over there haven't yet fully secured their own positions well enough to openly support a 'racist' faction just yet. Of course, the Russians are desperate and don't give a shit about political correctness; they'll back whoever it is to their advantage to support. Still, I think the hard-line nationalists in the Kremlin genuinely admire the Southerners courage and ability, and no doubt the bulk of the Confederate Army Provisional prefers to do business with other Whites whenever possible."

"If this goes on much longer, and CAP makes significant gains, this move by the Chinese against the West Coast is pretty much a given, isn't it?"

"Yeah, pretty much."

"Well, it's obvious we're not going to defeat the Confederates, at least anytime soon, so unless we want about two hundred million highly pissed-off Chinese troops showing up on our doorstep, we'd better try something else. Has anyone tried to open up negotiations with the Rebels?"

"Yeah, but what can we offer them? Independence? When they confronted him with the cold, hard facts of the situation, the President said, and I quote, *"I will not be the one to lose Lincoln's union!"* I hate to say it, but I'm starting to miss the damned Democrats."

"Would CAP accept something less? Some sort of autonomous home rule maybe, that would put an end to this thing and at the same time allow both sides to save face."

The admiral shook his head.

"Not a chance; for some reason, they don't trust us." Both men smiled without humor at the very thought. "Oh, there are a few moderate elements that would accept it in a heartbeat, but the rank and file never would, and Jonathon Edge has sworn to shoot anyone who even suggests it. In fact, the way the members of the moderate faction seem to keep disappearing, I suspect that he or some of the other hard core believers may be doing just that every time they pop their heads up."

Lannigan peered at him through a cloud of smoke.

"Jonathon Edge – friend of yours, wasn't he?"

"You might say that," Hardy said, nodding his agreement. "He saved my life once during Desert Storm, when we were both with the SEAL Teams; won the Bronze Star for it in fact. He and I were pretty close at one time."

"What happened?"

"He was a better man than I was and refused to be a hypocrite. The day he resigned his commission, he walked down to the end of the dock and threw his medals out into the bay. I still remember him walking by me and saying, 'We need to be fighting for our own people's freedom, not to take someone else's away.' I never forgot that, or how low I felt when he shook his head and just kept walking, leaving me standing there. I still feel it."

"He seems like a capable man."

"He's damned capable, and utterly ruthless when the need arises. Even for the Teams, he was considered a tough one. There's no back-up in him, and there's no chance of him being removed since he and Frank Gore patched up their differences."

"Gore's his second in command now, I hear."

"Yeah, and I wish I could say he wasn't. Edge is at least a borderline military genius, but with Gore beside him, he's literally hell on wheels. Edge has a couple of problems; he's ambitious as hell and paranoid to a fault. Sometimes he's a little too pragmatic, if you get my drift: the shoot first and ask questions later mentality.

"Gore, though, seems a perfect foil. He's a natural leader but not ambitious at all, and he's a bit more concerned about right and wrong than Edge. Oh, he'll kill alright – after all, we firmly believe he's the one who set up that blood bath in Columbia – but he does it out of necessity or maybe because he's pissed, not simply as a precaution. Do you know much about him?"

"Only what I read in his file; College grad, BA in Criminal Justice with minors in History and English Lit, and served a single hitch as an MP in the Army Reserves to pay for it while working as a

Columbia Police officer. Military rank at discharge was Captain. Qualified as expert with every weapon he ever picked up, participated in boxing, wrestling, karate, and judo, and won several trophies in each. Went through sniper training, qualified close combat and shooting instructor. He's a natural warrior and a natural general; a lot of people on both sides have compared him to Nathan Bedford Forrest and Stonewall Jackson, and they're not far off.

"He's next in line to the leadership of the CAP military. If something happens to Edge, can he be bargained with?"

"Not hardly; you'd stand a better chance with Edge. Gore is an idealist: a patriot who also happens to have a very personal score to settle after what those sadistic dick-heads in Homeland Security did to his wife, and he won't settle it for anything less than full independence." He paused, taking a drag off the cigar and expelling a stream of blue smoke. "Under the circumstances, I can't say I blame him.

"So, what do we do?"

"I said we need to save at least a piece of America; now we need to figure out which piece is most worth saving, and how far we're willing to go to save it."

Lannigan blew a smoke ring, and thoughtfully watched it rise. It went without saying that, once he committed himself to this, there would be no going back.

"I reckon we both know the answer to the first question, or we wouldn't be talking about it. As for the other, we'll go as far as we have to; there's too much at stake for anything less. So, what's your plan?"

"I want to approach Edge and Gore directly. I have an intelligence lieutenant on my staff I can trust to open the negotiations with them, but I have limited ability to reach the rebels."

"You get him to Fort Bragg, and I'll get him to someone who can set up the meeting." He paused for a moment, then grinned. "The Red 4 boys are trained to sneak and peek, after all, and I know one or two of them that I suspect have been doing it for the Confederates already."

"I was counting on that. In the meantime, we need to do some serious planning. It's past time to end this thing."

DAY 335

CHAPTER 42

"We are gathered here today," Doctor MacFie intoned, his voice echoing across the barn where everyone not on guard duty and able to stand stood at parade rest, and the ones not able sat, fighting back their emotions with varying degrees of success, "to pay our respects to our comrades who fell in battle. I don't say last respects, because I have no doubt they'll remain in our hearts and minds every day, and in the hearts of those who hear the story of their valor, their sacrifice, and their glory."

He paused, and cast a look at the line of homemade plywood coffins that contained the remains of Kerrie and the other guerrillas who died during the raid.

"Here within these boxes, lie the earthly remains of those who made the ultimate sacrifice for their country, for their people, and for their friends." He went on for a while, naming names and telling stories about the fallen, ending with, "We will miss them all, and we will never forget.

"Still, I'd like to talk a bit more about one of them who was special to many of us here." He looked pointedly at Frank, Samantha, Cynthia, and Mike. "To one of us, she was a best friend, to others, almost an adopted daughter, and to another, the woman he loved more than life itself. She was one of the bravest, and she was little more than a girl; her name was Kerrie O'Brien. She went against all odds, in order to rescue her Southern brothers and sisters, and laid down her life in making that attempt successful. We do honor to the broken vessel that once held that brave soul, which has gone on to the loving arms of our God. We shall not see her again until the resurrection, but rest assured that she will see us. Her eyes will be upon us from above; let us always try to be worthy in her sight."

Standing beside her husband's wheel chair Dr. Grissom insisted he use, Samantha clenched Frank's hand tightly, and he returned her grasp. Looking down, she saw he had managed to get at least one eye open to the merest slit.

Thank God he can see this, at least!

She saw Cynthia standing by Mike, one hand gripping his shoulder, although which one of them the gesture was intended to comfort was open to question. Looking at Mike's face, she shuddered involuntarily; the battered features were set like a stone, and she knew that she and her husband were not the only ones who had lost some of what made them human.

Turning to the other side, McFie nodded at the twenty-five pairs of empty boots sitting in precise ranks beneath the banner of the 1st Columbia Irregulars, hanging forlornly at half-staff.

"And here is the symbolic presence of the fallen men of the 1st Columbia Irregulars, who willingly and intentionally gave their lives for their leader, and for their Cause. They walked to the altar of liberty, stretched themselves across it, and bared their breasts for the tyrant's knife. They could have saved their lives, but they chose surrender them willingly for the greater good. Theirs is the rare glory of the sort that belongs to the lone Viking at Stamford Bridge, to the Spartans at Thermopile, to the Texans at the Alamo. And, like those illustrious predecessors, it shall never be forgotten as long as one Southerner remains! It deserves to be recognized with the greatest honor we can pay it."

Reaching into his pocket, he drew out an iron cross and laurel medal, the Medal of Honor of the Confederate States of America. Holding it aloft, he began reading the names, and at the sound of each one, one of the Tarheel ladies rang an iron bell they had borrowed from a nearby farm.

"Lieutenant Robert Johnson.

"First Sergeant Basil Caffary.

"Sergeant Andy Buchanan.

Every time the lonely bell rang at the sound of each name, Samantha could feel the vibrations coursing through Frank's body through his hand that she unobtrusively held.

"Sergeant James Kowalski.

"Sergeant Marion Stock.

"Sergeant John Thompson.

"Corporal Wayland Fowler.

"Corporal Jack Lewis.

"Corporal Mitchell Stanley.

"Corporal William Wilson.

"Corporal Jay Knott.

Each name was like a knife-gash through Frank, Tommy, Danny, Hodges, Long, and Graham. These were their comrades in arms...their brothers, and each tolling of the bell carved another name into their souls.

"Private George Cox.

"Private Jack Davidson.

"Private Frank Godwin.

"Private Arnold Kessler.

"Private Tim Matthews.

"Private Bill McGuire.

"Private Hubert Moore.

Donna, standing by beside the battered Tommy's wheelchair, shook her head back and forth in denial, not able to fully grasp the reality. *So many! So many!*

"Private Jerry Smith.

"Private David Snipes

"Private Henry Toland.

"Private Daniel Worley.

"Private David Worley."

The twins, Samantha thought. *Their poor mother!*

"Private Dean Yates.

"We, the Provisional Government of the Confederate States of America, salute you!"

Frank turned to Sammie. "Help me up."

"What? Frank, you can't – "

"I said, help me stand!" It was not a request.

Even though it hurt her to hear his teeth grinding through the pain, she took his arm, and with her assistance, he managed to painfully pull himself erect. His battered legs were determined to wobble, but he was more determined not to let them.

"Here," Tommy said, and Donna got on one side and Billy on the other, pulling him upright despite the agony.

"Hodges?" Danny asked, and the big skinhead Sergeant gently helped the Italian to his feet, supporting most of his weight with an arm around his bandaged waist. Bringing their right hands to their brows, the Irregulars saluted their fallen.

In the back of the barn, Casey Graham, the remains of his ear still swathed in bandages, put his lips to the mouthpiece of the borrowed bagpipes, and, after a few pumps to inflate the bag, the strains of a slow, sad version of *Dixie* filled the air, and, unlike in the song, no one looked away.

Stepping to the banner, Doctor MacFie reverently hung the medal from the pole's brass end piece.

"Such is the stuff of heroes."

As MacFie stepped back, for the first time in days the cloud cover outside abruptly parted, and a shaft of sunlight poured through the window, falling on the coffins, boots and banner like a spotlight, making the floating dust motes glitter like stars. A latch slipped and a door banged open on its own, and the wind found its way into the building. Swirling through the crowd and raising cold chills on everyone it touched, it reached the place of honor. The 1st Columbia Irregulars' white banner suddenly unfurled. It waved so hard its fluttering was clearly audible, and the figure of Linda Waddell emblazoned on its front seemed alive for a moment. The movement loosened the knot that held it in the position of mourning, and it began slipping as the flag climbed on its own, all the way to the top of the staff where it finally caught, held, and continued to wave, snapping and cracking. All over the crowd, mouths gaped in wonder, and Doctor MacFie bowed his head.

"It's a sign," he said needlessly.

Over the years to come, many people would ascribe accounts of the occurrence to coincidence or mere legend, but not any of those present. None of them doubted that they had just witnessed something very special.

The miracles weren't quite through for the day. Later that evening, just as the sun was setting behind the pines, Samantha appeared at the bedside of the woman from the school whose child had been taken away.

Laura Bowen lay on the cot on her side, face to the wall. Her tears had been cried out, and she was left with nothing but an empty red-eyed stare into space. She didn't move or look back when Samantha sat down on the edge of the mattress beside her.

"Hey, how are you doing?"

There was no reply, and Samantha put her hand on the woman's shoulder.

"How are you?" she repeated.

"How do you think?" she murmured.

"What I think is that you've lain around here long enough. Now get up; I need you to help me with something."

As she turned over, Laura managed an indifferent "What?" before her eyes widened and her jaw dropped.

"I need you to hold this for me," the smiling Samantha said as she extended the sleeping baby towards her.

Laura had thought she had cried all her tears out, but she was wrong; they were coming fast and furious as she tentatively reached out, not quite daring to believe it, and took her child in her arms.

Samantha patted her cheek. "I told you I'd get my people on it."

She had more than put them on it; in her husband's name, with his approval, she had given not only the order, but also given a rare *carte blanche* to do whatever was necessary to find and recover the child, and despite their fatigue, she sent Tommy's old squad as the most reliable. As with Graham questioning the prisoners as to the baby's whereabouts, she never asked about the methods they used to extract the information that enabled them to locate and take custody of the baby. Samantha was soon to be a mother herself, and once the enemy made children their prey, the conflict had reached the stage that such niceties no longer mattered, at least as far as she was concerned... especially after what had Harrison told her upon their return.

"Once we found out where she was, it was no trouble at all, because we knew the layout of the place. They had given her to the O'Brien's: poor Kerrie's parents. They were going to let them adopt her."

Samantha had blanched. That two people who had already turned one daughter's all-too-short life into a living hell of scarring abuse would be given a chance to do it again to someone else was something she had trouble imagining even the enemy doing...for just a second, until she thought of all the terrible things they had already done. After all, the O'Brien's were staunch political supporters of the current State and Federal Administrations, and the missing little girl was evidently to be their reward.

She looked away and swore violently at the thought, and then turned back to Harrison.

"Whenever you get the chance – "

He interrupted her with a smile that had no humor in it whatsoever.

"Don't worry about that; it's taken care of. Those two will never hurt another little girl again, unless they do it in Hell, because that's where we sent them, along with the social worker who approved it and gave her to them."

Harrison hadn't asked before doing it; he had simply made the decision and gone ahead with it when he had the chance. Outside the chain of command? Definitely. Against all standard procedure and standing orders? Certainly. What she or her husband would have done in the same situation themselves? Absolutely! She had thanked him for it, and she meant it from the very bottom of her heart.

Now, Samantha watched as Laura held the child, and how its tiny face wrinkled in irritation as she dripped tears of joy all over it.

"They said they fed and changed her about an hour ago while they were on the way in, so she probably won't need anything for a little while yet."

Raising her head to look into Samantha's eyes, Laura grabbed her hand and said, "I'll do anything for you; all you have to do is ask. I'll die for you!"

Samantha swallowed hard and shook her head as she laboriously rose, the picture of auburn haired Kerrie lying spread-eagled in the mud branded forever behind her eyes.

"No, Laura, I never want anyone else to die for me. It hurts too damned much!"

"Ma'am?"

Samantha lifted her gaze to see one of the Tarheels standing in the doorway. After a moment, she recognized him as Lieutenant Preston, the one who had replaced McEvoy.

"Yes, Lieutenant?"

"It's Captain now, ma'am," he said with a proud smile. "Colonel Tarbox promoted me."

"He should have," she told him sincerely as she rose. Preston had been one of the first to recover during the confusion at the school, and had been right there with Hodges and the rest of the Irregulars when they followed her in the charge. "You did a great job."

He blushed and hung his head, reminding her of a shy little boy.

"Thank you, ma'am. Coming from you, that makes it really special."

Slightly embarrassed by the worship in his voice, she blushed a little and smiled.

"Thanks. Is there something I can do for you?"

"Oh, yes ma'am. We just brought in some guy and a lady; they say they were sent from the West Virginia commander, Colonel Boggess. He's looking for someone from your state by the name of Cynthia Dover. Do you know where I might find her?"

"That's me, sir," Cynthia said, stepping forward from her position against the wall as her eyes narrowed with suspicious curiosity. "What's this all about?"

He shrugged, and gestured towards the door with his thumb. "I don't have any idea. They're in there; you'll have to ask them."

Samantha rose to her feet. "I'll come with you, if you don't mind. I've been expecting Jack to send some stuff to me, but I didn't know when."

A moment later, they were standing before a dark-haired man with a long, pointy nose and a broad, toothy grin. Recognition flared in his eyes and he flipped Samantha a relaxed salute.

"Howdy, ma'am. You must be Colonel Gore; I've seen your picture. It's an honor to meet you."

Samantha returned the gesture.

"Thank you, uhm..."

"Sergeant Larry Hall, Ma'am, but everybody calls me 'Possum.'"

The two women glanced at each other, fighting smiles. After one look at his instantly likeable and friendly, but homely features, it was obvious how he had picked up that particular nickname. Samantha shook his hand.

"Alright, Possum; what can I do for you?"

His smile grew broader with pride that she had used his nickname, and he nodded his appreciation.

"I'm looking for Cynthia Dover, Ma'am."

"Well," she said, turning her head in the direction of her bodyguard, "here she is."

Possum's already impossibly wide grin grew even wider.

"Miss Dover, I've got a present for you, compliments of Colonel Jack Boggess."

Cynthia frowned. "For...me? But...why?" She hadn't even met the Mountaineer commander, and had only spoken to him by encoded phone a few times when taking her turn on com duty.

"He said he thought it would do you good." Turning his head, he said, "Ma'am, you can come out now."

A middle-aged lady with short brown hair on her head and tears in her eyes stepped around the corner and into the room. Although small in stature, she was a handsome woman who looked as if she had once weighed several pounds more than she did now. Seeing Cynthia, she smiled broadly, and extended her arms in invitation. Cynthia blinked hard with disbelief, paled, and began shaking.

"M-m-m-mommy?" she stammered in a tiny voice.

"I'm here, honey."

In an instant the submachine gun clattered unnoticed to the floor as the hardened fighter was reduced once more to a little girl, who could only hold onto the mother she had thought dead for over half a year and cry for all she was worth. Samantha, more than a little choked up herself, looked at Possum with a smile and shook her head in wonder.

"How in the world did you manage this?"

"Damnedest thing; when we were liberating the prisoners from the camp at Point Pleasant, all of a sudden this lady jumps up, grabs me by the arm, and hollers, 'Are you all Confederates?'" He chuckled. "I don't know who else she thought we'd be, but anyway, once I said yes, she asked if we knew her daughter. I took her to Jack, and he sent her to you with his compliments, along with this."

She reached out her hand reflexively to take what he offered before realizing it was a 'stink stick,' and quickly pulled back, making the irrepressible Possum laugh out loud.

"It's alright, ma'am; this one wasn't carried anywhere nastier than my front pocket."

Samantha took it then, as he added, "It's a big, multi-gig storage model with all the current info from the raid on the detainee camp, including pictures and video. Jack figured you'd want it for propaganda, and he told me to wait around to see if there's anything you want carried back."

Eyes lighting up at the thought of the data, then going to Cynthia and her mother crying all over each other, Samantha shook his hand yet again.

"I can't tell you how grateful I am for this. For everything."

"Hell, ma'am" he said with a shrug, "Seeing a mama and her little girl back together is all the thanks I need."

"Well, that's not all the thanks you're going to get. Would you please do me the honor of having supper with my husband and me? That girl means a lot to him, and I've got the feeling he'd like to thank you himself."

"Why thank you very much, ma'am. I am a little hungry."

DAY 338

CHAPTER 43

"Frank?"

Instantly awake in the pre-dawn darkness, he turned his head toward the sound of his wife's voice, pleasantly surprised to find the swelling had finally gone down far enough that he could now see almost normally out of both eyes.

"Yeah, Sammie?"

Slowly, she lowered the covers, exposing her swollen belly. Pointing towards her outie navel, she said, "If you want to touch it again, I don't mind."

Wondering what had gotten into her but not about to question it, Frank did touch it, followed by kissing it gently but thoroughly, despite the rather severe pain of gingerly bending down to do it.

Raising his head, he smiled and asked, "And to what do I owe this honor?"

There was a touch of fear in her eyes, but her smile was evident even in the darkness. "I didn't want to deny you one last chance at your private obsession."

"One last chance? What do you mean?"

"I mean the contractions have started, and I think it's about that time."

If she hadn't caught him by the arm and restrained him, under the power of panicked instinct, he would have leapt out of bed, wounds and all.

"Doctor Grissom, I guess it's too late to change my mind, huh?"

Shane Grissom looked up at the sweating Samantha from his position on the stool at the end of the bed between her legs, and actually managed a grin at her little joke. Cynthia's mother, who was a registered nurse, laughed out loud.

"Yes, it's a little late for that."

Frank had graduated to crutches, but still couldn't stand for long, so he had kicked a chair as close against her bed as he could get. Now he sat in it and held her left hand, occasionally stretching painfully to mop her forehead with a damp cloth.

"It'll be alright, Sammie."

Sensing another contraction coming, she wriggled her fingers between his, taking a better grip on his hand. "As long as you're here with me," she gasped, then clamped down tighter.

"Push," Mrs. Dover encouraged her, and Samantha pushed, but the only result she could tell from her end of things was an increase in the terrible pressure and the veterinarian calling for a towel. Wiping at her crotch, he eyed it critically and motioned his nurse down to get her opinion, since he was much more familiar with four-legged births than two.

Twisting her head back to the patient, Mrs. Dover said, "Alright, Samantha, when the next one starts, I want you to push for all you're worth, okay – "

The contraction came before she could finish the sentence, and Samantha gritted her teeth, squinted her eyes, and went almost purple in the face as she strained. Suddenly her mouth flew open and she yelled, spraying spit all over the front of her gown.

Frank was going, "Push, Sammie! Push!" at the same time Mrs. Dover was saying, "Push. Push."

"I am pushing!" she shouted.

"No yelling, Samantha; just push!" Mrs. Dover told her at the same time her doctor said, "I see the head! Push now! Push! Come on! Push!"

"Oh God, it *huuurrrts!*"

"I know, baby, but you have to push!"

"Keep pushing! Keep Pushing!"

"Push! Push!"

"Aaaaahhhh!"

There was a tearing sensation, a blinding pain, and suddenly the pressure was gone, and relief was so great she felt as if she were melting, sinking into herself and being absorbed into the mattress.

Over Samantha's exhausted gasping, a newborn's protesting cries over being dragged into the world filled the air.

Doctor Grissom lifted a small, red, squirming object into the air for them to see, and announced, "It's a girl."

CHAPTER 44

"Sammie?"

Looking up at the open door, Samantha smiled. It was evening, and she was alone for the moment. Frank was in another room being examined by Dr. Grissom to make certain everything was still healing properly, and there was finally a break in the seemingly endless stream of well-wishers and the just plain curious.

"Hey, Donna. Are you alright?" The girl had been in momentarily to see the baby earlier, but the room was crowded, and she evidently didn't want to talk in front of others. Samantha could understand that very well.

As she closed the door behind her, Donna said, "I was getting ready to ask you the same question."

Laying the sleeping baby on the bed beside her, Samantha swung her own feet off in the floor, and then patted the mattress, indicating for Donna to sit by her side. As her visitor complied, gingerly lowering herself so as not to wake the little one, Samantha couldn't help but reflect that it must look almost like a sleepover, with two friends sitting beside one another to talk. Of course, no teenaged sleepover should have anything like the conversation she suspected was coming.

"I'm okay, just a little sore. You?"

"As well as can be expected, I guess. I...I..." She suddenly began sobbing. "It's so damned hard, Sammie!"

Reaching out to her younger friend, taking her in her arms and embracing her, Samantha said, "I have no doubt. Still, you're a strong woman, and I believe in you. I'll help you make it through this, whatever it takes. I promise."

"I don't know why you're so nice to me."

Samantha smiled and held her at arm's length so she could look in her eyes.

"Oh, I don't know. Let's see; maybe because I love you like the sister I never had. Do you think that might be it?"

The tears were coming faster now, and Donna's next words came out in a stammer.

"D-do you m-m-mean that?"

Ruffling the back of her hair with her fingers, Samantha said, "Hey, I came to get you, didn't I? Big roly-poly belly and all."

"You should never have taken that risk! Especially not with the baby!"

"I'd take it again, if I had to."

"I didn't deserve it!"

Samantha looked at her like she'd gone insane. "Why in the world not?"

When she was finally spoke again, her voice had grown very small muffled, almost drowned out by guilt. "I...I have a confession to make."

Samantha sighed. She'd come to know Donna very well in the past few months, sometimes, she suspected, a lot better than the tender but headstrong teenager knew herself. She had been afraid this was coming for awhile now, and she still hadn't figured out exactly how to handle it when it happened. Finally, now that the moment had arrived, she decided to approach it exactly like her husband would have: directly and head on. First though, she pulled her friend close once more and held her tightly.

"If it's about you – " she paused for the slightest instant, unable to say 'being in love with' even though they both knew what she meant, "having a *thing* for Frank, I already knew that."

She felt Donna's body jerk.

"H-h-how long h-have you...known?"

"Since the first day you met us."

"It was that obvious?"

"Yeah, I'm afraid so." She smiled trying to soften the mood and show she wasn't angry, and her voice turned teasing. "You get these big puppy dog eyes whenever he's in the room."

Donna whimpered before pulling back just far enough to look up at her. She was suddenly irrationally afraid that if she let go, her friend would never hold her again.

"But weren't you mad?"

"What for, Honey?" She grinned. "Personally, I don't see how any woman could help but be in love with him. Look, you never made a play for him..."

"I would *never* do that to you!"

"I know," Samantha reassured her as she stroked her shoulder, "just like I know he would never have accepted the offer if you had. I knew how you felt, but I knew you and I knew my husband; I trusted you both enough to know that neither of you would betray me, so I never really gave it much thought."

That's not entirely true, her conscience chimed in; *you've wondered about it quite a few times,* to which her heart replied, *but it's close enough.* After a split-second's consideration, her conscience shrugged and responded with, *I can't argue with that.*

Donna shook her head. "I don't know how to thank you for understanding."

"Do you really want to thank me? I mean, really?"

"Yes – anything. I mean it; I'll do anything."

"Alright then. I want you to take care of Tommy. If you're my sister, he's my brother. Both of you need each other, and after..." *Oh, Lord, how do I put this?* "what happened, I think he needs you more now than he'll ever admit."

Donna nodded through her tears.

"I know, and I'm trying...oh, God, Sammie, I'm trying so hard, but it's like he wants to push me away!"

"Then you have to hold on even tighter. I know what they did to him, Donna, and it even was worse than what they did to me. If it hadn't been for Frank in those days that followed, I couldn't have made it. I pushed him away too; I yelled at him, screamed at him – I was a world-class bitch – but he held on through it all because he knew it wasn't me talking, but just the pain coming out. The pain has to come out, honey, or it'll rot you from the inside.

"The problem with you two, as I see it, is that you're both hurting too badly to take much of each other's pain. If you want to thank me, you'll take Tommy's pain, and then you can come in here anytime, day or night, and I'll take yours. Fair enough little sister?"

389

"Fair enough!" Donna cried over and over as she clung to her. "Fair enough!"

DAY 342

CHAPTER 45

"I'm sorry, sir, but General Gore ordered – "

"I don't give a rat's ass what *General* Gore ordered! I want to see Sammie and her baby, and I want to see them right now!"

Samantha heard the commotion outside the door and smiled as she looked at Frank, who grinned back.

"It's alright," he called out to Doug Long, who was standing sentry duty. "You'd better let him in before he has a stroke."

Instantly, the door flew open, and Sam Wirtz came barging into the room.

The Indians had brought him most of the way back, in a limo, no less, complete with Federal Government Bureau of Indian Affairs plates. The plates were real, as was the Apache driver; a BIA officer who was Indian first, government employee second. He supplied Sam with ID as well, and it greased their way through roadblock after roadblock. To the Federal Government's knowledge, the Native Americans were about the only ones they hadn't pissed off recently, and they had put the word out to the soldiers not to do anything that would add them to the list. That situation – along with the Councilman's naturally deep, weathered tan, some black hair dye, and a pair of sunglasses – allowed him to pass as one of the many mixed blood members of the various nations, and gave him a greater freedom of movement than he had ever expected, which turned out to be a bigger pain in the ass than he had ever imagined. Among other things, it meant that his driver/guide got to introduce him to influential elders of half-a-dozen different tribes; great for the movement, but, with no news of Frank, and Samantha's time drawing near, Sam had been chafing to get back. His hosts refused to be hurried, however and even seemed to find his sense of urgency mildly amusing. Finally, after what seemed like forever, he made it to the Cherokee Reservation in the Smokies, and Suggs' people brought him on from there.

By the time he convinced the close-mouthed, security conscious Tarheel driver to even surrender the bare-bones news that Frank was alive and a father, they were already pulling up outside their headquarters. In fact, when they arrived, Sam had left the car on the run, leaving the door open in his hurry to get inside.

"Sammie, are you..." he tentatively began, approaching her bed where she sat with a pillow behind her back while she held her daughter.

"Yes, I'm fine, Sam."

"Are you sure?"

"Yes, I'm sure. Women have been doing this for a long time."

Frank laughed. "How are you, Frank?" he teased, taking Sam's part of the conversation as well as his own. "Oh, hey Sam, I'm just fine, thanks for asking."

"You didn't have a baby, you..." His voice trailed off as he turned to look at Frank, and took in the damage. Both the General's eyes were as black as a raccoon's mask, and his face was still swollen. "Good Lord! What happened to you?"

He shrugged. "Oh, you know how rough women get when they're in labor, blaming their husband and all."

"I did no such thing!" Samantha informed him primly, and Sam sat on the edge of her bed and reached out to gently brush a strand of hair out of her eyes.

"Well, I wouldn't blame you if you did! You poor little thing, are you sure you're okay?"

"I told you, I'm fine, and so is little Linda here."

His eyes widened. "Linda? Like...my Goddaughter?"

"Not like your Goddaughter," Frank told him, "*after* your Goddaughter. After all, you might say she's the one who brought us together, so we thought it was appropriate."

"Her middle name is Mary, after another mutual friend."

Sam suddenly seemed to have something in his eye, and brushed at it for a moment before looking at the lump in her arms, half-buried in the blankets, he smiled longingly.

"Can I hold her?"

"In a few minutes; she's eating right now."

"Doggone it," he complained, obviously offended, "I haven't forgotten how to feed a baby!"

Frank began laughing, which promptly doubled him over in his chair from the pain of his still-healing ribs, but despite gasping and cursing under his breath between chortles, he still couldn't seem to stop.

"What? What's so damned funny?"

Samantha giggled. "I'm sure you know how, Sam, but I don't think you're really equipped for it."

He glared at her for a moment, and then came to an abrupt understanding when he realized just what the baby was feeding on below the fold of cloth.

"Oh hell!" he exclaimed, turning bright red and quickly jumping to his feet and spinning his back towards her. "Why didn't you tell me you were breast feeding?"

Over Frank's howls of pained laughter, she said, "I was trying to."

"You should have seen your face!" Frank told him as soon as he got enough breath to speak. "Oh, that was precious!"

"Yeah, very funny!"

Samantha was delighted to hear Frank laugh; it had been so long. Still, she decided the fun had gone far enough.

"Oh, turn around, Sam; I don't like talking to your back. She's got the main part covered up, and anyway, you were one of those who rescued me, so you know darned good and well what's there. Besides, I couldn't be embarrassed around you; you're like my father."

Turning back slowly, he asked, "Do you mean that?"

"Of course I mean it, or I wouldn't have said it! You stood up for me and gave me away at my wedding wearing your wife's dress. You risked your life to come with my husband to rescue me. You've been a father to me, and to every other stray little girl that's come into this thing since the start.

"Now, sit down, and just as soon as she's finished, you can meet your newest Goddaughter."

Frank pointedly ignored the joyful tears of his friend so as not to embarrass him any further. He also wanted to allow him a few moments of joy, because, while he had heard about the birth, he obviously hadn't been informed of what had happened to Donna, Tommy, Mike...and Kerrie.

Suddenly something got in Frank's eye as well, although for the opposite reason. He was the one who was going to have to break the news to his friend about all of it. He also knew he'd rather be blown up all over again than do it, but he had no choice; it was his responsibility.

Sam's back was to him, but Samantha looked at him over the shorter man's shoulder, and when she saw his expression, she knew what he was thinking, and her own happiness fell away with his, making him feel even worse.

Wait a bit, she silently mouthed, and Frank nodded his agreement.

I'll give him a few minutes before I tell him...Damn it!

DAY 348

CHAPTER 46

US Naval Intelligence Lieutenant Jacob Lewis took off the blindfold, only to be somewhat startled by the sight before him. Samantha Norris, with her blonde hair and her crisply creased fatigues he recognized right away, of course – her picture was everywhere – but he would never have guessed who the seated figure with the swollen, battered features was if she hadn't been present as well.

"General Gore?"

"That's me, Lieutenant. I understand my appearance has changed a little, so if you'd like to see my fingerprints to verify it, there's an ink pad on the table here."

Lewis refrained from nervously licking his lips. The guerrilla leader hadn't offered to shake hands; in fact, his right hand had yet to show itself, remaining concealed beneath the desk, and he knew there was almost certainly a pistol in it, pointed right at him. "It's not a lack of trust on my part, sir; it's just that we have to know..."

Frank waved the apology away with his left hand before pulling a sheet of paper to him and pressing his thumb onto the pad before casually rolling it onto the white surface. "Don't worry about it; you'd be a fool if you took it on face value." He chuckled at his own unintentional pun, then waved the ink-stained hand in the general direction of his battered head. "Such as it is, I mean."

The three were alone; the officer had insisted he had authority to speak with no one other than Frank or Jonathon Edge, so even the two Councilmen present at the Tarheel base, Sam and Dr. MacFie, were excluded, and were reduced to babysitting little Linda in the next room. Samantha was there because she had set her foot down and declared that, orders or no orders, there was no way she was leaving her husband alone with an enemy in his disabled condition, and it didn't matter what he or anyone else had to say about it.

Lieutenant Lewis wisely decided that was an acceptable compromise, so now, under her watchful eye, he took the paper from Frank and compared the print it held to the one on the wanted poster in his briefcase. It verified the identity, and he nodded in confirmation.

"If you're satisfied, Lieutenant, please sit down." He looked at Sammie and added. "If you don't, my wife won't, and I don't want her standing too long in her condition."

Samantha couldn't decide to smile or frown at her husband's babying her, so she decided to keep her expression neutral and concentrate of the affair at hand, namely the man in the room with them.

"Of course, sir," he said as he parked himself in the comfortably upholstered chair, sitting his briefcase on his lap. Once he was seated, Samantha sat down across from him, beside her husband. That she kept her purse on her lap was not missed by Lieutenant Lewis, nor was the type of purse it was. He recognized the Coronado Hobo bag, made of fine leather and especially designed to conceal a handgun in a discreet side pocket. Knowing that, it didn't take a rocket scientist to figure out where her right hand that he couldn't see from this angle was, and he gave himself a mental note to keep his own hands in sight and not to make any unexpected moves.

"I had heard you were pregnant, Colonel; I take it congratulations are in order?"

"Thank you, Lieutenant," she said, never moving her concealed hand. He knew the pistol in it was pointing right at his center of mass. That was a disconcerting thought, but then again, it was no more dangerous than this assignment...in some ways, probably less so.

"Yes, thank you," Frank said, and then his voice turned cold. "Now, tell me who in the Confederate Army Provisional approved sending you here."

Lewis gulped, fighting the urge to tug at his collar. "Sir, I'm sure you'll understand the...delicacy of the intermediary's position..."

"I want to make equally sure you understand your own position, Lieutenant. I make myself difficult to find for a reason; the last time you all caught up with me, you nearly killed me. I value the secrecy of my location, and yet here you are. I want to know who authorized this, and who set it up. Whether you leave here or not depends on your answer."

Their visitor looked back and forth from the battered general to his hard-eyed wife with her hand inside her bag, and made the only decision he could.

"I was sent by Admiral Fred Hardy, via certain Red 4 elements at Fort Bragg. My contact there said that, if it was absolutely necessary to disclose that information ..."

Looking him straight in the eye, Frank said, "It is."

"He said to tell you G412 sent me."

Frank mashed the intercom button on his desk. "Mike?"

"Sir?" the voice came back through the speaker. Frank would have smiled under other circumstances at the thought of his friend calling him that.

"Are you alone?"

"Hold one. Okay, go ahead."

"First a name: Admiral Fred Hardy. Is he associated with us?"

There was a moment of silence as he ran the data on the borrowed Tarheel computer, then, "Not currently, but he once served with the Field Marshal on the SEAL Teams."

"What about the code G412? Do we know him?"

"Yes," Mike told him with no hesitation this time, recognizing the name from memory. "He's okay."

"Thanks." Letting off the button, he turned back to Lieutenant Lewis.

"Alright. Now, what can we do for you?"

"Sir, I have a message for you and Field Marshal Edge from Admiral Hardy."

"Give it to me in a nutshell."

"A portion of the United States military is willing to come over to your side, and, if an agreement can be reached, the Admiral has a plan insure your victory."

Frank's teeth bared and his eyes glinted disturbingly as he leaned forward with obvious interest.

"Tell me more."

EPILOGUE

It was snowing when Edge stepped out of the car and onto the tarmac of the airport. No boats this time, at least not yet. Instead, he would be returning part of the way in style, in the private jet owned by one of the Russian President's political cronies, on loan for the occasion. It would take him to Cuba, and from there, he would be picked up by a fishing boat to later rendezvous with another craft out of Florida. He was almost giddy, having accomplished everything he had set out to do, and much, much more.

He smiled, thinking back on the Russian reaction when the US infrastructure had collapsed. The first he had known of it was when the loud pounding at his bedroom door awakened him, along with Vika, who was with him. A humorless bureaucrat backed by an equally unfunny squad of Spetsnaz commandos had demanded that he come with them at once.

Four hours later, one military jet and an armored convoy later, both of them were in Moscow, at the Kremlin. Vika was cooling her heels under guard, and Jonathon Edge was face to face with both the President and the Prime Minister of Russia this time, along with several high-ranking military officers. The United States power grid had failed, and damned near everything else along with it, and they wanted to know how in the hell he had done it. It didn't take long for Edge to see a new depth of respect in their eyes, along with just a touch of fear for the vulnerabilities in their own infrastructure. Six hours later, the promised help – intelligence, equipment, and advisors – was no longer vague; it was guaranteed. In fact, some of it would begin arriving in Dixie even before he did.

With international help and, perhaps just as importantly, recognition, the South finally had a real chance of victory and independence, as well as a promise of assistance in getting itself back on its feet. Yes, it would come at a cost, but did everything else in life. This, at least, would be worth it. He knew beyond a doubt that this was the turning point in the war.

So why am I so damned sad?

400

The cold steppe wind blowing in his face ruffled his gray hair as he nodded his thanks to the driver and removed his single bag. Pulling his collar tighter against the chill, he crossed the concrete parking lot to where the jet waited, its polished fuselage gleaming white on white against the falling snow...as white as Vika's ivory skin.

Saying goodbye to her had hurt; there were no two ways about it. For the first time in a very long time, Edge felt as if his heart was being ripped out of him, despite having only known her for a short time. He suddenly felt a little guilty when he realized that he missed her soft, dark hair, wise blue eyes, and gentle laugh almost as much as he missed the other woman he had loved and tragically lost so many years before, but he was too honest to deny it, at least to himself.

I never thought I'd be able to love anybody else, and when it happens, it turns out to be someone I'll never see again...

Maybe someday, after this thing is over...

No. That's fantasy, nothing more, and I don't have time for it. I've got a war to fight and a country to build!

Swearing at himself for going soft, he turned his attention back towards the plane and had just started to pick up his pace in an unconscious effort to leave the pieces of his broken heart behind when he came to such a sudden halt that the soles of his shoes scraped on the frozen, snow-dusted concrete as they fought the abrupt arrest of his forward momentum.

Vika stood there in front of him.

She was dressed in a dark fur coat and hat, and the fur rippled in waves in the wind like a field of grass. A few strands of black hair escaped from beneath her headgear, and accentuated her beautiful face perfectly. Her self-confidence was gone now, and he saw her throat move as she swallowed hard, unsure, even afraid for the first time since he had met her. Looking down at her high, fashionable boots, he saw the backpack at her feet, bulging from the quantity of stuff crammed into it, and realized what it meant. He shook his head.

"No."

Her small nostrils flared as she took in a breath of the icy air before answering.

"Yes."

"You can't!"

"Are you saying you don't want me?"

Edge knew if he said that, she would stay. He knew it would be a clean break, the best thing to do, for both of them. Suddenly, he also knew that was something he could never let pass his lips.

"No," he sighed with defeat, "I didn't say that."

"Well then; I'm glad that's over. Let's go."

"It's too dangerous, Vika."

"I understand; I was an intelligence officer, remember? I'm going with you." Her lips set in a stubborn pout, even as she bit the right corner of the lower one in fear...not of the danger, but of him leaving without her. It came to him then that she was just as in love with him as he with her.

If that's the case, she must have it bad!

As the wind picked up and howled mournfully, swirling the snow in patterns around them like ghosts, Edge's arms seemed to move of their own accord, and his hands closed gently around hers.

"It's not only the war and the Feds. A lot of my own people won't like you either. They won't trust you; they'll think you're a spy."

"I may be, but if I am, at least you'll know who the spy is." A single tear trickled down her cheek. "I...I love you, Jonathon. I've loved you since before I knew you."

Reaching out a thumb, he wiped the moisture away even as he thought about all the problems her presence would cause, all the danger to her and distractions to himself, and then he looked into her eyes once more, searching and, ultimately, finding.

I've given up everything for this movement; by God, I'm entitled to something for me!

He said nothing, just scooped up her backpack in his free hand. Vika smiled then, crinkling the corners of her eyes for joy, and slipped her arm through his as they walked towards the plane that would take them home.

His decision made, Edge turned his thoughts back towards the direction they were heading.

I wonder what all's changed since I've been gone.

Coming soon: the final volume in THE THIRD REVOLUTION Saga

While still celebrating its independence, Dixie is devastated by a cowardly attack that leaves unfathomable tragedy in its wake, and the Confederates find that winning their country may have been much easier than keeping it. As events spiral out of control until the entire world teeters on the brink of nuclear war, only one man has a chance of stopping Armageddon while saving his country...if he will. When Frank Gore is forced to step up once more, this time with an implacable, avenging fury that shakes the Earth to its very foundations, all bets are off, and there will be Hell to pay!

No matter who wins, nothing will ever be the same again.

It's a time of terror unspeakable, war unimaginable, and vengeance unrestrained. It's the time of

THE WARLORD

AUTHOR'S NOTES

Congratulations; unless you're one of those impatient ne'er-do-wells who read the *last* page before the rest, you've just finished the third installment in THE THIRD REVOLUTION series. Since there will be a total of four, you've only got one left to go, and I'll do my best to make it a grand finale.

I'm pleased to note that this series has been very well received (especially considering its *slightly* controversial subject matter), so much so that I get letters and emails, and even the occasional gift from fans, which is a novel experience for me. I like it – to be honest, I love it – but I didn't expect it. Still, your input is a valuable tool, because it lets me know what kind of job I'm doing.

One or two of those who have seen excerpts or advance copies of this work have expressed some surprise at the tragic death of Kerrie O'Brien. Rest assured, it was as difficult for me to write as it was for you to read, but that is the nature of war. People die on both sides, and not everyone who starts a battle will finish it alive and in one piece. Death doesn't care if you're good or bad; you might say he's the ultimate equal opportunity employer. That's hard, but it's just the way it is.

Others have indicated strong concern over the depiction of the mistreatment of Donna and Tommy while in captivity. Sadly enough, even though the story is fiction, their experience is all too real. It's occurred at places like the notorious Abu Grahaib prison at the hands of United States troops and military interrogators, most likely at the urging of their Mossad advisors; interrogation via heterosexual and homosexual rape as depicted here is commonly used against Palestinian prisoners by the Israelis as a way to break the captives' will by degrading their sense of self-worth. Hell of a world, isn't it?

Brutality is the face of war – any war, but guerrilla conflicts in particular – and is far more common than that elusive thing called glory. That might be something worth keeping in mind...

3223155

Made in the USA